THE SUDDEN SILENCE

a tale of suspense & found treasure

All roads lead to Thailand—where the lovers of ancient treasure tangle with international black markets. In this complex landscape of protectors and predators, we meet Martin Moon and Delia Rivera. Both have been defeated by the dark powers of the art-trade netherworld.

Together, they seek to rise again—to escape the sudden silence of lives extinguished and loves lost.

But the savage forces that nearly destroyed them before are still at large. Their quest turns deadly.

Is there any such thing as a fresh start in this wicked world? Or is there only the wisdom of failure?

Other books by Susan Barrett Price:
Passion and Peril on the Silk Road
Tribe of the Breakaway Beads

THE SUDDEN SILENCE

a tale of suspense & found treasure

Susan Barrett Price

Susan Barrett Price

MAD IN PURSUIT, ROCHESTER NY

Author's Note

to Jim
always my inspiration

It is by going down into the abyss that we recover the treasures of life. Where you stumble, there lies your treasure.

—Joseph Campbell

ONE

Rochester, New York

Delia watched Martin's face as he opened the door. First, a puzzled blank. *He was expecting someone else.* Then, a rush of grinning affection. *He still loved her.* Next, a deliberate hardening of the lip and jaw. *He didn't want to deal with her.* Finally, as he stepped aside to let her in, a false-friendly smile. *His professional graciousness won out.*

"Delia! My God, come in!"

With a deep breath, Delia Rivera broadened her own false-friendly smile. "I was in the neighborhood." *Joke.* In a hundred years she would never have occasion to visit a tacky townhouse complex in a suburb of Rochester, New York. She strode through the living room toward the back, noting the cheesy realtor carpeting, the dead-white walls, then the pebbled linoleum and fake-wood kitchen cabinets. He followed.

She parked her rolling suitcase and her purse on the white kitchen floor, which did, to his credit, look spotless. "So…are you in some kind of a witness protection program?"

Another joke. She was trying to sound merry, but the effort only annoyed him. His effort to smile faded.

"What are you talking about?" he asked.

"I thought you might like to see me." She grinned.

He blinked.

"Okay, I thought *I* might like to see *you*."

Her eyes flitted away from his, and she turned to look out the back window at a tight maze of mown grass and treated-lumber fences. She n't help a small puff of exasperation. *Mistake.*

.is hands landed on her shoulders. "What's up? Look at me."

Slowly, focusing on her breathing… in… out, she let him turn her around. He was squinting at her. But, then, as he studied her face, the crease in his brow softened.

"Trouble. You're in trouble, aren't you?" he murmured. "Big. Trouble." His fingers tightened on her shoulders.

She squeezed her eyes into a well-practiced glare. "Wrong," she said. "You don't know what you're talking about. I'm fine." *But just hang on to me,* she cried inside, *and that will make me fine. Pull me closer. Hug me.*

But he let her go, with a barely perceptible little shove. *Message sent and received.*

M artin Moon was torn: should he run her out of his house or wrap her in his arms with gales of laughter and buckets of tears? His dear old Delia, magically appearing out of nowhere. But magic Delia always had something up her sleeve and this visit was no exception. He needed to know what kind of rabbit was in her hat.

"I know your eyes, Delia. I know the set of your jaw and the language of your shoulders." Her eyes only hardened. *Hopeless.* He nodded toward a kitchen chair. "Sit down. I'll get you something to drink."

She sat down and crossed her legs, letting her shoe drop to the floor… pretending to relax, no doubt, and calculated to disarm him.

He pulled a bottle of iced tea from the refrigerator and asked, "How did you find me?"

"The taxi driver had to call his dispatcher to find this little cul-de-sac." She glanced at the small TV on the counter. "What are you watching? A soap opera? Seriously?"

"I was—it just—" He snapped it off and finished pouring the tea. "Come on, how did you find me?"

She took a sip, then popped out of the chair. Leaving both shoes behind, she headed toward the kitchen cabinets. "This could use a splash of some-thing. Where do you keep it?"

"Nothing here. If you're staying, I'll run across the street for a bottle. Are you staying? Are you going to calm down and talk to me or should I call you a cab?"

"Okay, okay. I'd like to stay, yes." She turned toward the living room. She walked through with hardly a glance at what she used to refer to as his *tesoro*—the array of treasured knick-knacks, now displayed on a hodge-podge of second-hand tables and bookcases. She moved a stack of art reference books from the seat of the armchair and sank into it.

He followed and settled onto the couch across from her, elbows on his knees.

She toyed with the buttons on her dress. "Well, of course, I've had my eye out for you all along—ever since I heard Lana was killed. You have to know that, don't you? I was in China when it happened. I tried to call, left a dozen messages but you…"

He refused to give her the satisfaction of a nod and she sped on.

"Anyway, I happened to be in New York this week and had a feeling you might have moved back to the States, so I thought maybe I'd try to look you up, thought I'd like to talk to my old buddy, see how you're doing." She was talking too fast. "But, of course, I still didn't know where you were. But then I found a number for your parents on the west side and called them up. Winston said you were in Rochester but was none too pleased about how long it took you to get in touch—weeks, he said. They were worried sick. Everyone was, you must know that. Not that I blame you for running off—it must have been horrible finding her like that—seeing the kind of... ordeal she went through..."

His turn to squirm. "So here I am. Found. Delia Rivera, girl detective, always gets her man."

He crossed his legs and shifted his gaze out the window. It was a gorgeous June afternoon and a breeze was blowing petals from a crabapple tree.

"I'd just as soon not talk about Lana," he said. He let the silence go on and outside he heard a cardinal calling for his mate.

Delia cleared her throat.

He looked back at her. Delia's eyes were hazel, so smoky compared to Lana's sunny blues. "I know I didn't act rationally but to tell the truth once she was dead I didn't give a damn about anything. I never wanted to talk to anyone in the antiquities trade ever again and all the heritage theft and idol-running in the world couldn't add up to what was stolen from me. I stayed stone drunk for days, weeks. It's complicated how I wound up in Rochester, but it turns out I like it. The past six months here have been a tonic. I'm a new man."

Choosing to ignore her raised eyebrow, he surveyed the collection of artifacts that crowded his small townhouse. They were his oldest possessions—Buddhist, Hindu, and Jain votive figures. Sacred art.

"Obviously, I still love my old 'knick-knacks,' but I don't miss being a dealer and I certainly don't miss the undercover work, all that shady pretense. That kind of a double life was for the young Martin Moon, for Martin Moon the hunter."

"Don't you mean *fisherman*?"

He had to turn his head away to prevent her from seeing the hint of a smile that surely brushed his lips. Yes, in their earliest, most enthusiastic days together, they agreed that they didn't like the hunting metaphor. They didn't want to *stalk prey* or *set traps*. They preferred to *cast their nets*, and to experiment with the most tantalizing *lures* and *baits*. It was only wordplay and yet that fishing image helped them decide how they would inhabit their world, together. And Delia, daughter of a deep sea fisherman, loved her corny *fishing by Moon-light*.

"Right—the fisherman who fouled his line and lost his hook on the rocky shoals of madness."

"Oh, spare me the self-pity."

"What?"

"Self-pity! Since when did you become afraid to cut loose your line and start over? Time to get back to work, Marty. You need to work. And you certainly can't think you're doing Lana's memory any good by holing up in this fucking..." Her eyes swept the apartment. "This fucking *nowhere*."

"Why are you here?" he growled.

"I'm here... because Edwin wants you to come back to the agency. They need someone with your experience, your—"

Martin sprang from his seat. "No way, forget it, out of the question. Isn't it clear, Delia, that I disappeared for a good reason? That I don't want to do—*can't* do that kind of work anymore?" He headed for the kitchen and ran water into the sink for no reason. His pulse raced. Edwin Jones-White was a manipulative bastard to send Delia after him this way. And something else bothered Martin, something not quite logical in Delia's story, something just below the surface, but he was too irritated to think it out.

She followed him to the sink. "Not even one more case? We'd be going to Thailand."

"We?"

"It's my case. One I can't do alone. I'm in a little over my head. *Puh-leeze*, Martin."

"Thought you said you weren't in trouble."

"I didn't say anything about being *in trouble*. I said—"

"Look, it doesn't matter. Don't even bother to tell me about it because there's no way in hell I'll ever go back to Thailand. In fact, Thailand *is* hell—a steamy, wet, thug-infested hell."

He rinsed a clean dish and propped it in the drainer, then rinsed another waiting for her retort. When she finally spoke, her voice was soft.

"I'm on the trail of Jeremy Bellingham."

As Martin turned to Delia, water sloshed from the sink and soaked into his clean white socks. His knees went soft.

"Yeah, Martin, Lana's murderer."

BANGKOK, THAILAND

Mr. Bellingham here to see you. I bring extra glass."

"Here? Oh, he must have come straight from the auction—terrific." Tony Savani slipped the papers he was reading into a manila folder. "Oh, Chen, any word from Ms. Rivera?"

"No, sir," the young man said. He set a tray on the desk. It contained a plate piled with deep-fried banana slices and a pitcher of frozen pineapple-coconut drink. "But we get word that shipment to Vancouver make it through customs."

"Outstanding!" Tony turned to the computer screen at his elbow and punched at the keys for the status report. He used a finger to find the line he wanted—*Vancouver, Assorted Thai Handicrafts*. "Outstanding, yes."

Chen mopped his forehead and neck with a handkerchief. "I wonder about the heat, sir, and humidity. Don't you think we should talk again about air conditioning for offices? Really steamy season just beginning and equipment so sensitive."

"Nonsense. All the units have a customized power supply. Haven't lost a digit in years."

Even though the polluted Bangkok air was becoming less breathable by the day, Tony loved the sensation of his bones being baked in the sauna-like teak house and delighted in the sights, sounds, and smells of the busy canal that flowed by his window.

"Go now, get Bellingham in here," Tony said, more cheerful than he'd felt in days. "And, say, I'm famished. Tell cook to make plenty of noodles with lunch."

"Oh, yes, another thing. Mr. Clearwater call to ask if his team might come by this afternoon. Give me impression they want more money. Some kind of new survey equipment. Sound like *radar*?" Chen looked puzzled. He didn't usually have much to do with the archaeologists supported by Tony's foundation.

"Subsurface radar, very high tech. Tell them to come on over and I'll listen to their proposal, though I can't imagine what they're up to. Now show Jeremy in, will you?"

Tony was pulling the auction catalog from a drawer when Bellingham walked in. "Jeremy! I've been on the edge of my seat waiting for you to call. When will my statue arrive? You're having it shipped directly to Chiang Mai, right?"

The auction had been at Christie's in Hong Kong and the statue was a Cambodian Buddha, Angkor period, Baphuon style. Its superior condition and its powerful aesthetic made the corresponding piece in Tony's current collection look insipid by comparison. Tony had had no choice but to buy it, whatever the price.

"It's about the statue, actually, that I came. There's been a bit of a dustup, you see." Jeremy was drenched in sweat, his face London pale, the whites of his eyes alarmingly bloodshot. He paused. Tony only glared in response, so he plunged ahead. "You see, I awoke yesterday with the most hellish GI upset. Really, I couldn't get more than a few feet from the loo before I'd have to—"

Tony felt his teeth clench. "The auction wasn't till four in the afternoon."

"But you see I didn't actually get to bed till about 6 a.m., so when I got up—"

"You knew, damn you, how critical that piece was to me. If you're going to tell me that a little diarrhea made you miss the auction—"

"But it wasn't a little diarrhea. I may have broken blood vessels in my eyes from vomiting so hard and—"

"Spare me." Tony covered his eyes, infinitely less interested in Jeremy's nausea than in the tragedy of the missed auction.

"But see here, I did know how critical it was. I sent a mate of mine over to Alexandra House with specific instructions, very specific instructions. It's just that he's a little inexperienced about how those big auctions go and, when the price broke a hundred thousand pounds, he felt a little dazed, had to think a minute about whether he was authorized to spend that much—even though I specifically said I had no limit, very specifically said that I must have the piece at any cost—but he panicked, and—and the Heldt-Luther snagged it for a mere hundred ten." Jeremy sank into a chair. "I'm so sorry," he whispered.

Tony steadied his hands along the edge of his desk. The sacrilege of it. *His* statue, going to a museum in damnable Houston, Texas.

"I tried to fix it," Jeremy went on, staring at his hands, picking at his nails. "I made several calls to Jason Nugent last night, even went over to his hotel about midnight, once my belly settled a bit, but when I offered a hundred fifty for it he merely laughed, said he'd made the buy of a lifetime. I spent the morning on the phone with Texas but no one would deal."

Tony didn't blame them. The statue was unique in its class. His stomach soured at the thought of his own Baphuon-style Buddha, second-rate by comparison. It had already been shipped to New Cathay for sale, to make room for what turned out to be the Heldt-Luther Buddha. How in the world would he get his hands on the prize now?

"If there's anything I can do, Mr. Savani... Tony..." Jeremy drew a long breath and lit a cigarette.

This screw-up was unusual for Bellingham. New Cathay Galleries had assigned their star agent to Savani and Jeremy had been breaking his back to close as many deals for Tony as possible, hoping eventually to become Tony's sole agent. Tony's best collections were his very private business and he needed a discreet and reliable agent to do his buying and selling. Jeremy should have been perfect. Aside from being Michelangelo handsome, Jeremy was a brilliant scholar, with a sharp eye for fakes and clever restorations. He was an engaging and successful seller—no doubt why the team at Cathay loved him—and his skill as a buyer was improving. Beneath the charm, he also had a nasty predatory streak that kicked in at the right challenge. Tony like that.

But the man was flawed. Oversexed. Promiscuous. Too often missing in action because a torrid whatever had waylaid him. Observing Bellingham's sexual adventurism might intrigue Tony under the right circumstances, but never if it ruined business.

"You know Delia Rivera?" Tony asked.

Jeremy was pouting, arm over the back of the chair, staring out the window at the boat traffic, running his fingers through his damp, curly hair. "Of course. What about her?"

"She's coming to Bangkok."

Jeremy straightened up. His eyes narrowed. "What the hell for? I thought she was—this doesn't have anything to do with me, does it? I mean, she's been after me because—"

Tony leaned forward and slapped his hand on the auction catalog. "This has *everything* to do with you, you cocksucker. I can't trust you to show up at an auction anymore. You've got your fly unzipped for every little—"

Jeremy stood. "I told you I was deathly ill. It was a bad lot of raw fish—"

"Where you managed to fall asleep at 6 a.m. and with whom is none of my business—except when it screws you up for the most important purchase of your short professional life."

"I told you I'm sorry—I'll keep nagging the Heldt-Luther about the blasted statue till—what does this have to do with Rivera?"

Tony took a calming breath. "She did some buying for me in Europe this spring. We are... negotiating some terms. It's very likely that she'll become my sole agent in the future."

Jeremy's face turned as pink as his eyeballs. "Rivera! But, but she—that's preposterous! She's not—she can't—you said—"

"Get out of my sight."

"You can't cut me off—we have a string of commitments—I've made arrangements—and what about the deal up north? You simply can't—"

"Stick around Bangkok. Stay at a hotel that takes credit cards and has phones in its rooms. And spend time there. Be there when I call and maybe we can work something out."

Jeremy reached over to the ashtray on Tony's desk and put out his cigarette. His lip curled away from his small, perfect teeth. "Yes. I will. I will do as you wish. I will redeem myself, you'll see."

Rochester, New York

At the mention of Jeremy Bellingham, Delia watched Martin's face turn from anger to disbelief. As he gripped the edge of the sink, he stared hard into her eyes, fishing for some unspoken truth. *Please don't turn me away*, she tried to beam back to him. But she could see rejection in the twitch of his jaw.

The front door slammed and Delia and Martin were startled from their face off.

"Hey, Martin!" A very tall man entered the kitchen. When he saw Delia, his smile turned into a magnificent grin, even as his chin tucked down in shyness. "Oh, you have company."

"Jack Scanlan," Martin said softly, "meet Delia Rivera, my first wife."

Jack hadn't taken his eyes off her face, studying it with flattering attentiveness, as he shook her hand. He was a giant kid, dressed in workout shorts and t-shirt, his dark blond hair pulled into a short ponytail. He moved with the grace of a young athlete, but his face bore the kind of weathered landscape that said forty.

Scanlan finally looked at Martin. Delia observed him pick up on Martin's distress. His eyes flickered a question—*you okay?*—and Martin, almost imperceptibly, nodded. Then Martin's frozen face broke into a genuine smile and Delia felt a huge wave of gratitude toward the man who was clearly Martin's friend.

"Jack here lives across the driveway. We do some running together."

"I had to show you this." Jack handed his pal the July 1990 issue of a magazine called *Teen Sass*, open to a page full of tutus and swirling blonde hair. "Arrived on the newsstands today."

Delia and Martin studied the multipage layout—a profile of a young ballerina, who was also making a splash in ads for Cappezio and Danskin.

Jack beamed at Delia. "My daughter. Theresa. Lives in Manhattan with her mother—well, actually on a scholarship in London till the end of the year. Just turned sixteen."

"And you!" Martin pointed to a small photo with a *Sports Illustrated* logo across the top. A young man in Cornell colors was catching a football, frozen for all time in a leap worthy of Barishnikov.

"Oh, yeah—Theresa's favorite picture of me. More a tribute to the photographer than to my actual skill. Funny thing, though, on the very next drive, I dislocated my shoulder. By the time that photo was published I was a has-been."

The text gave Jack credit for Theresa's start in ballet, as well as for her athleticism.

"And her beauty," Delia said. "Look at those eyes. That's what makes her a star. Those big green eyes. They make love to the camera." She looked up at him. "Your eyes."

A blush flooded his face. "The bigger news is, well, I talked to Monica this afternoon and, between the scholarships, the ad work Theresa did over Christmas, and what's already lined up for fall, I don't have to pay any more child support. The kid's rolling in dough."

Martin teased him about Theresa having to pay parent support, but Delia watched Jack's eyes widen with distress.

"Isn't that good news?" she asked.

"Of course it is. It's just that, all of a sudden, she..." He shrugged, then let out a big breath. "All of a sudden, my summer's opened up. I don't have to teach the horrible summer school courses I do every year. And I can ease off the weekend house-painting gigs."

Martin bumped Jack on the shoulder. "Empty nest, old buddy. Time to retool. Treat yourself to a vacation. Visit her in London, why don't you?"

"She'd die." With a wry smile, he explained to Delia. "I've become an embarrassment to her. It's this compulsion I have to screen all her friends, grill all her teachers, and lecture her about the world's dangers. I made a promise to Monica that I'd use Theresa's year in London to break the habit." He turned to Martin with a gesture to Delia. "Anyway, I guess you want to cancel our run...?"

"Our run, yeah..." Martin hesitated, his eyes clouded with thought. "Yeah, I probably should trot over to the liquor store... and there are a couple other things... Look, I bet Delia would love to take my place. Last I knew, she was a pretty keen runner."

Jack waited for Delia to change and saw her transform from a weary businesswoman to a long-legged athlete, her hair pulled back in a bushy ponytail. With hardly a word, she launched herself out the door and down the lane. He loped after her and caught up.

"So you're a school teacher?" she asked.

"Yep. Middle school. Sixth-grade social studies and a smattering of this and that. So many years I can do it in my sleep. You an art dealer like he was?"

"Roughly. We started out as partners but wound up on different paths. I'm more of a buyer's agent, helping institutions put together collections that meet specific criteria. Martin deals—dealt—with more of a private clientele. With Lana's dough, they had working capital, could buy collections or high-priced blockbusters outright. They'd exhibit at the big shows. Lana even had a shop for a while in London, but Martin hated it and she let it go."

"Are you—is he—are the two of you going away—going back to work?"

A pause, then, "Yesss." The air rushed from her lungs. "We'll be going to Thailand." He caught her giving him a glance. "From time to time, the two of us—Lana too—we've done research for an agency in London—a firm that researches market trends, new sources of high-value art objects, that kind of thing. I have a contract to look at some new stuff coming out of Thailand. Kind of thing Martin's an expert on, so it's a good chance to get him back to work."

He felt himself squinting at her half-truth. "Not that its any of my business, but are you referring to the work that got Lana killed?"

"He told you—?" She slowed her pace.

"We jog, we talk." From their start, as neighbors who both happened to do their running in the late afternoons, the two had begun to exchange stories. Jack had watched Martin emerge from a kind of numb despair to become an affable companion. But he was a hermit. He needed someone like Delia to pull him back into the world. On the other hand, Jack had seen the tension between them. Was she going to help or only push him back into the darkness?

Suddenly, Delia stumbled over a bump in the pavement. She recovered her balance without falling, but stopped and clutched her chest.

"What's wrong?" he asked.

"I'm—" She gulped a breath. "Okay."

But she was trembling and wild-eyed.

"You're not okay. Can you tell me—" She seemed disoriented. Jack grabbed her shoulders. She took his arms. What was it: asthma, epilepsy, a goddamn heart attack? But it was clear from the way she clutched him that, whatever it was, she was terrified. "Tell me where it hurts."

"Where it *hurts*?" She made a gasping little giggle. Then she wept.

The tears lasted for all of ten seconds before she let go of him.

With one hand on her hip and the other screening her mascara-streaked eyes, she turned away, still sniffling. "I can't believe it. I just can't believe it." *Sniff.* She started walking. "This is terrible. I can't believe I'm this screwed up."

When he caught up with her, Jack was still touching his arms where she'd held on. "What exactly—?"

"It was a stupid, goddamned panic attack. It's a sudden feeling like you're going to die, like the world is caving in. It's not so bad now that I know what they are, but I can't believe I had one in the middle of a goddamn run." Angry tears brimmed in her eyes and she swiped at them with the back of her hand.

Weary, vibrant, terrified, angry—such volatility frightened Jack. "Want to stop? Go back?"

"No, I can't let Martin see me like this. Let's keep running."

But instead, they walked. Against the rhythm of their footsteps and the rumble of traffic, silence hung between them.

Cool it, Scanlan, he scolded himself. *You can't do anything about this one.* But fear and worry were in his nature. Since the age of ten, the year his mother died and for years after, whenever his dad was at the firehouse, he lay awake nights, monitoring the police band, listening for sirens, praying he wouldn't be left alone to care for his sister. He had worried Monica through medical school and surgical residencies, worried Theresa through adolescence, and worried nearly a thousand 12-year-olds into seventh grade.

"What are you thinking?" Delia asked.

He tried to smile. "I worry... I've gotten to know Martin over the past few months and..." He shook his head. "I'm not very good at saying what all I worry over..."

"Then why don't you just come with us? I'll pay you to worry. Bet you got a passport, in case Theresa needs you in London this year, right? Am I right?"

"What?"

She stopped and grabbed his arms. She was beaming now. "I'm telling you. Come with us, expenses paid. Fantastic idea! Perfect!" Then she let him go and jogged away down the street.

He followed.

So was this the Delia Rivera Martin told him about? Impetuously befriending strangers? Throwing money their way? Reading their minds?

He caught up. "You know, he told me you were impulsive, that—"

"Blah-blah. I've heard it a thousand times from him. But I'm not impulsive. I'm quick. I see, I decide, I act. He's more methodical. And, if you want my opinion, it's too much *thinking* that drove him to drink, that finally fried him."

She stopped again to look at him. "I desperately need Martin to come with me, to finish some pretty serious unfinished business. But I'm also scared we'll screw it up somehow, stumbling over the petty stuff—the unfinished personal shit between the two of us. A third person would force us to be civil with one another, would put us on our best behavior, you know? I can already tell you're a steady kind of a guy and that you really care about Martin. Am I right?" Her deep-set eyes bored into his. They caught the light in a golden kind of way and made him think of all the places in the world he'd never seen.

Today brought change. His daughter was nearly independent and he had money in the bank. Suddenly, he was free to take time off. Suddenly, a curly-haired woman with a graceful stride and terrifying panic attacks was offering him a place to go. It was crazy, but... she was irresistible.

"What the heck," he said.

That evening, Delia kept the conversation light while she and Martin sat across from each other at the kitchen table, sipping wine and dining on his butternut squash stew. Her plan was to ease back into the Thailand business after they were more relaxed.

Once the dishes had been stacked in the dishwasher, they began picking through Martin's *tesoro*, the treasures that crowded his small living-dining room—from small bronze figurines to taller wood carvings to a few faded paintings mounted on silk scrolls.

Martin's collection was really more orphanage than *tesoro*. His most important purchases, in the finest condition, went for top dollar to his circle of wealthy and discerning buyers. For himself, he put aside the worn-out pieces, usually from the Buddhist tradition, the sacred artifacts that had been handled by a thousand hands, dented, chipped, and scratched. Or paintings darkened from decades of illumination by smoky butter lamps and incense. He claimed they had more spirit—*qi* he called it, using the Chinese word for *steam* or *breath*. Or sometimes he used the Polynesian word *mana*, for a life-force of great power and magic. Their voices were louder, he claimed. They told him a richer story, he said, than the pieces stashed away for centuries in palace vaults.

It reminded her...

"Almost forgot! I brought you something," she said, as she dug a small pouch from the bottom of her handbag and tossed it to him.

Martin opened it and widened his eyes at the small stone object. "A fish!"

"An Egyptian amulet," she explained. "Maybe New Kingdom, say 1500 B.C.E." Years ago, she had plucked the red jasper fish from a pile of small antiquities, while she was helping a museum in Alexandria clean out its back rooms to raise money for restorations. She knew it would be a gift for Martin, if she ever saw him again—if she ever needed a favor from him. Today was the day.

Martin rubbed the charm between his fingers, pressed it to his cheek, and closed his eyes as he passed it across his lips. His appreciation tickled her.

"Lots of *mana*," he said, grinning, as he replaced it in its pouch, slipped it into his shirt pocket, and pressed his hand briefly over his heart. "Thank you."

"It reminded me of our early days, when you were a 'stone fisher,' and when you impressed me nightly with your 'catch of the day.' So... an amulet, a tiny treasure, but also a memento..."

He nodded and for a moment they were quiet.

Then they went on with their survey of his ancient and well-loved enchantments.

"I remember lots of these from way back, Martin. Where are your larger pieces?"

He nodded. "This is all stuff I had in storage. They date from before I married Lana, before my tastes got grander."

Lana Tuthill had been rich—a child of old medical and scientific elites. She'd been on track to join the family business as a leader in large-primate field biology but when she met Martin during the autumn auction season in Hong Kong, human behavior became much more interesting to her than orangutans.

"Those larger pieces?" he continued, his face shadowed now. "Sore subject."

She gave him a quizzical look.

"Come on, Delia," he continued, "surely Edwin let you in on the cosmic joke. Look around you. What you see in these rooms is the sum total of my fortune."

Delia was confused. "Didn't her will—?"

"The will contained some ambiguous language and Lana's mother decided to contest the whole thing, casting me as some kind of shallow fortune hunter. Everything's snarled in red tape—American courts, British courts. It's a mess. It's why I grudgingly relocated to Rochester, Lana's home town. The old lady and all her lawyers are here, where I can at least try to deal with them face-to-face. She blames me for Lana's death, so the upshot is that I may have lost it all."

"Wow." Delia took a breath. "So to blazes with her money. You made plenty on your own. The house alone must have been worth—"

He shook his head. "We played a lot of games over the years with our personal versus business assets, to minimize our taxes. The house and personal collection wound up in Lana's name—including my Shinto temple guardians—the huge ones—you saw them, didn't you? As damaged as they were, they were still the best pieces I ever owned. When I left London, they were on exhibit at the British Museum."

"I can't believe it," Delia murmured. "Do you need money? I can lend you whatever—"

Waving away the offer, he laughed again. "No need, babe, really. You know we kept our business inventory pretty small, tried to buy only what we could turn over fast. What we had, I shipped to Patsy Greenberg in

Manhattan. Consignment. She and Evelyn are selling enough to pay the rent here and keep me in white socks for a while." His smile was looking more like a wince. "Meanwhile, I jump through hoops for a battalion of lawyers. The reconstruction of my life through bank records, sales slips, and affidavits from dealers and museum directors all over the world has been a three-ring circus. Luckily, our business had partner insurance, so that pays the lawyers."

"Oh, Martin…"

"I'll make out fine, don't worry. The trick's winning over Emmaline Tuthill. She can end the whole business with a single phone call and I think she was weakening last time I paid a visit."

Martin poured more wine, while Delia drew the curtains against the prying eyes of darkness. She took measure of the situation. Martin was stressed—lingering grief, financial woes, legal battles. But he looked healthy. Sipping wine had replaced martinis. No evidence of smoking. Still in his mid-forties, he was young to have a head of silver hair, but it softened his sharp features. His stomach was flat and his eyes were bright. He had benefitted from his friendship with Jack. Good.

He handed her a topped-off glass of wine. He stood too close. It made her anxious. She was vulnerable and slightly drunk. She had intended this visit to be like all the other times, the times after he and Lana had married. Friend to old friend. Colleague to colleague. He'd ask what the trouble was. She'd deny any trouble. He'd pry it out of her over the course of lunch, then scold her for being too impulsive or for mismanaging her cash or for not understanding the market. Then he'd agree to help out. And he'd ask her about her love life. She'd blab about someone she'd been seeing. He'd look relieved and blab about something wonderful Lana was up to. Then, with a brush of cheeks, they'd part.

She stupidly didn't foresee how drastically Lana's death had changed his life. And she didn't foresee how disturbed she'd be, standing so close to him. She meant to explain her infatuation with Tony Savani, her plans to move her things to his house in Thailand, her toying with the idea of making a life with him, but the mood was all wrong. Her plot to get him to help with the Bellingham case seemed equally out of place.

Martin pulled her close and, with a purring sigh, nuzzled his head against her hair till his lips grazed her ear. "It's been a long time, Delia. I'm so glad to see you."

Suddenly, she couldn't catch her breath. Her heart thumped wildly. It was exploding. *No. No, it was the panic again. Damn it, Martin mustn't see her fall apart. Too much was at stake.* But she blurted out, "Oh God!" and pushed away, spilling her red wine all over the beige carpet. "Oh, shit!" Then the glass dropped on the floor.

"It's nothing. Really." He rushed to the kitchen for paper towels and a bottle of club soda. "This carpet is crap anyway. Tell me what's wrong, Delia. I came on too strong, didn't I? Got carried away—"

She was pacing back and forth to keep her heart from exploding out of her chest.

"You were coming on?" she said too loudly. She swooped the wine glass off the floor and took it to the kitchen sink. Her pulse was returning to normal, but, as usual, the attack left her feeling out of control and defensive—a bitter reminder of the whole purpose of the visit.

Martin followed her and dropped the wet paper towels in the trash. "Delia, what's the matter?" He stood too close again. She focused on his shirt buttons.

"I didn't come here to—look, I came here with a job offer and from the sound of things you could use one."

"A job?" He stepped back. "I can get a job any day of the week—Patsy and Evelyn are already begging me to work with them."

The thought pained him—she could see it in his eyes.

"Whatever I do, Delia, I'm sure as hell not going to run off after murderers. I'm an art guy. I understand the greed, the lust, and the pride that infect the human heart. Violence—above my pay grade, kiddo. If the police, Scotland Yard, and Interpol haven't pinned Lana's murder on Bellingham by this time, we're not about to."

"The contract isn't about murder. It's about smuggling. It's about getting Bellingham off the streets."

"Well, who the hell is paying Jones-White for this job anyway? The stuff Bellingham was trying to sell us was twelfth-century Khmer. Anything of value that could be hauled out of the jungle was looted the minute the French colonized Indo-China. It's been dispersed all over the globe for decades. I can't imagine smuggling being much of an issue at this stage of the game. Even if it is, I'm just not sure I care enough about it anymore."

"But you'll waste away up here. How long before you wind up selling the things you love most in order to pay your rent? Can you really afford to sit around for as long as it takes to pry loose the Tuthill millions?"

"I don't give a shit about the Tuthill precious millions. I want what's mine. What I spent a lifetime building. I want my damn Shinto guardians."

He marched back to the living room and settled into a corner of the couch. She followed, back to her armchair.

For a moment he was silent, gathering thoughts.

"It's more than that," he said. "For years, playing spy, passing little secrets, was a lark. But when the market boomed in the eighties, the work changed. The bigger the profit, the nastier the criminal. It used me up. I couldn't get through the day without a dozen precautions and a fifth of gin. Didn't you see that happening to me, babe? You tell me I'm wasted up here. Well, that job wasted me. And it killed Lana. I'm not going to throw away the peace I found at last on somebody else's disputed sculpture."

Delia glared at him, who, in spite of his strong words, looked so damned comfortable there on his old leather couch, bathed in yellow light from the table lamp, his limbs stretched out and relaxed. His voice was a lazy growl—a bear resisting the onset of spring.

"Well, let me make myself clear now," she said. "It's not a single piece of sculpture that I'm trying to track back to its origin, but a whole new wave of pieces working their way slowly, discreetly, into the world market. There's a fountainhead of new sculpture—maybe an illegal excavation somewhere—that needs to be found. It's Khmer but not Cambodian. I'm sure it's coming from Thailand. The match isn't perfect, but the big sandstone statues are damn close to the style that grew out of Lopburi. Lopburi, in central Thailand?"

"I know where the hell Lopburi is." His voice was still grouchy, but his fingers betrayed his interest, scraping along the arm of the couch as if it were the rough surface of stone.

"None of it has ever been in museums, never on public display, not part of any historical inventories or well-known collections. What's most disturbing, what tells us this is a sophisticated operation, is that the paperwork is flawless. Each seller has been able to produce decades worth of sales slips and owner authentications. There have been about ten sales that we know of—none at public auction. When you put all that impeccable paper together, the picture is utterly bogus. Am I right? Statues of a similar rare type—showing up on the market at about the same time—none with a public history, yet each with a pedigree a yard long—*tilt!* Now Jones-White

18

has a contract to track down their true origin."

Martin pressed his fingers to his eyes. "Christ, it's a HAWC-I contract, is it?"

Delia was no more a fan of HAWC-I than Martin. She'd had her share of hassles with the militant archaeologists and always dreaded running into them on an assignment—more likely when the HAWC-I Foundation was footing the bill.

The acronym HAWC-I stood for *Heritage Archaeologists Watching Crime—International*. It was formed nearly twenty years ago, in the seventies, as a watchdog group against the growing traffic in third-world antiquities. The members—known informally as *hawkeyes*—liked to take direct action against anyone removing artifacts from their original sites. To hawkeyes, antiquities dealers were the lowest form of life.

Her worst encounter with a hawkeye was in Munich a couple years ago. She'd gotten a lead that a dealer on the Ottostrasse had the head of a priceless second-century statue, recently dug up in Turkey. She knew the dealer. He was a known smuggler whose organization remained beyond the reach of the law. When she informed Jones-White, he got a contract through Interpol for Delia to buy the head and return it to the Turks.

She pumped adrenaline for days, closing the deal and arranging a switch between the ancient head and a reproduction. The real head was transported by an Interpol courier to the Turkish embassy, while she repacked its crate with the fake and prepared to export it to London.

On her way to the customs broker, a tanned young man with pale hair and unresolved acne stopped her in the hotel lobby.

"Delia Rivera?"

"Yes?"

"I am Hans Seidman and I represent HAWC-I." His English was slightly accented. "Do you know—"

"What do you want?"

"You are aware that the Demeter head you carry was stolen from the people of Turkey, no?" Beads of sweat appeared on his upper lip.

"No, I am aware of no such thing. I paid good money and got legitimate export papers. Go talk ideology with your academic cronies. I have a living to earn and a plane to catch."

Right in plain sight of a lobby full of people, he shoved her back against the wall. While Delia was upset about being tracked, this confrontation was strictly amateur night.

"On behalf of the people of Turkey, I liberate this artifact of their cultural heritage." He tried to yank the crate out of her arms, but underestimated her strength. As she struggled to hang on to it, she shifted its weight to her left arm and managed to position her right thumb under the tip of one of his fingers.

"Look, you little shit, if you ever butt into my business again I'll see to it that someone breaks more than your finger." Before he could react, with all the force she could muster, she bent back his finger till she heard it snap. He gasped. As he crumpled in agony, Delia marched out to the taxi stand.

What a spitfire she'd been. Now she couldn't make it through a casual run or an evening's conversation without falling apart.

Martin had to ask again: "The contract's from HAWC-I, isn't it? It's the only organization I know that keeps tabs on sales like that. And I'd hardly call it a job—not at the rates they pay."

Before Martin could make HAWC-I the issue, she rushed on. "Listen, I did find out that a couple months ago a French archaeologist by the name of René Malraux—yes, an active member of HAWC-I—was killed in Bangkok. He was sexually assaulted, then stabbed repeatedly in the chest and abdomen."

Martin crossed his legs and took a sip of wine. "So?"

"Don't play dumb, Martin. That's exactly how Lana was killed."

"Well... don't you think it's a little farfetched? We were in London... halfway around the world... and you said *he...*"

"You think only women can be raped? Anyway, when I found out, Edwin contacted HAWC-I headquarters in Mexico City and they admitted that Malraux had been snooping around and may have found out something about the source of the Khmer statues. That's what you and Lana were working on when she was killed, wasn't it? A Khmer piece that the British Museum was interested in?"

Martin studied the bottom of his glass. Oh, he was bullheaded.

"Maybe it's time you saw this." Delia stood up and unsnapped her jeans. "When Lana was killed I was in Beijing. When I got home..." She pulled up her turtleneck to reveal the jagged scar that snaked down from between her breasts. "When I got home, I got a call from one Jeremy Bellingham of New Cathay Galleries." She pushed down the waistline of her pants so he could see how the scar curled across her belly. "Jeremy Bellingham."

Martin's eyes moved from her torso to her face, then he took her hands. Her knees wobbling, she let him pull her onto the couch beside him. Tenderly, he eased her shirt back over her flesh. Then he hugged her.

"Tell me everything," he whispered.

BANGKOK, THAILAND

Tony Savani checked his watch. "It's morning now in London, Chen. Would you mind calling the Spanish Arms there to see if Ms. Rivera has checked in or not?"

"Already have, sir. She not currently in residence. No return date. No forwarding address. I leave another message with her service that you anxious to hear from her."

Damn. Delia said she'd be in Thailand by the day before yesterday and he hadn't heard a word from her in a week. Tony hated it when she disappeared like this. She was so fragile lately, anything could happen, but she continually refused to be pinned down about her itinerary.

"All right. Show the visitors in, please." Tony scanned the office. It was decorated with works by the best contemporary Thai artists—not to his taste, but politically correct for a man who spent millions to preserve antiquities within their proper cultural contexts. He spotted the Christie's/ Hong Kong catalog for the Southeast Asian sale and slid it into a drawer. His visitors would never approve of Tony's private collections.

The three archaeologists filed into the room, two men and a woman. The young men had made a passing effort to look presentable to their benefactor—long pants and clean shirts—but they still radiated the scruffy aura of boys who liked to play in dirt. The woman, however, was a natural goddess—royally tall, in a flowered voile dress, her long blond hair fluttering in the breeze of the ceiling fan.

He extended a hand to each of them. "Ms. Lundquist. Mr. Clearwater. Mr. Andriotti. Have a seat. Chen will bring in some juice momentarily."

"We won't waste your time, Mr. Savani," said Clearwater, the team leader. He had an Australian twang, barely modified by years of schooling in England, and ugly gaps in his teeth. "I'll get right to the point. We started up our project and right off we discovered a completely unexcavated site up north of Chiang Mai. We want to do this right, see, survey the area in the least destructive way possible because we have every reason to believe it's a major find—one that could rewrite Thai history, in fact. So we wrote up a proposal here to get a Subsurface Interface Radar system. The use of impulse radar will allow us to more or less see underground without disturbing any fragile artifacts till it's time to decide about a regular dig." He handed Tony a manila folder.

Tony flipped through the pages of the proposal while Chen brought in a pitcher of apricot nectar and a plate of locally made chocolates. What with Bellingham's fiasco and not hearing from Delia, the day was not going well. He bit into one of the chocolates. Now these fellows...

Caleb Clearwater and Bruno Andriotti had received generous fellowships from the Savani Foundation to catalog the location and status of sites related to the Khmer empire in Thailand, which, from its center in Cambodia, occupied nearly all of what was now modern Thailand at its peak in the twelfth century. The graduate student Ingrid Lundquist had been hired as their assistant. The project was dog's work and suited their capabilities—assuming the brilliant Ms. Lundquist could keep them organized. But already they'd gone off track. He couldn't imagine an SIR System in their hands.

"Where did you say this undiscovered site is?"

"North of Chiang Mai. It's on the property of the Li family. Who knows how extensive it is. What we can see looks like the portico of a major Khmer temple."

"Can't be, Cal," Tony said. "The Khmers didn't do any building in those hills. Whatever you found is probably Burmese. Anyway, I thought you were starting in the eastern provinces. You're supposed to be adhering to a work plan, not running around willy-nilly—"

"Pardon me, Mr. Savani," Ingrid said, her husky voice and high-toned Oxford inflections a perfect match for the body. "It's my fault, if you will. I know the Li family here in Bangkok. It was Arthur Li who told me what their workmen found. We drove up and I saw statues they'd picked out of the rubble. The site is most definitely Khmer. There is no doubt whatsoever."

Tony stared at her. The nectar had left her lips moist. "Ms. Lundquist, did you know that the Li family runs a heroin refinery on that property?"

She blinked. Twice. "All the more reason for the Thai people to know what national treasures they're at risk of losing."

Bruno chimed in, but spoke to Cal rather than Tony. "If they smuggle heroin, why not statues? Why, the Li property might even be the source of the Khmer statues HAWC-I's been making such a fuss over."

Tony couldn't bear looking at Bruno. He wasn't quite fat, but lumpish, like sunbaked gobs of clay, clothed in what seemed like an inexhaustible supply of rumpled madras shirts, each with at least one button missing. An aesthetic abomination.

"What do you have written up about the site, other than this proposal for equipment?"

"I have extensive notes," Ingrid said, "plus photographs. We're going to take the video camera when we return next week."

"I'd appreciate it, Ms. Lundquist, if you'd write up a preliminary report. If the site is what you say, Mr. Clearwater, I think we should follow protocol and notify the Ministry of Antiquities. They should be the ones to decide what kind of survey work is called for. And who will do it. I'm not sure your team is the best for the job."

Cal stiffened. "What d'you mean by that? We're perfectly capable. Besides, if we discovered it, it wouldn't really be fair now to pull us off the job, not after all we've done for—"

Tony raised his hand. "Calm down." Last thing Tony wanted was to have the boys angry and out of control. "All I want is a report. I'll be happy then to consider your proposal for the SIR System."

As the three were leaving, Tony rose to his feet and called Ingrid back. They stood facing each other across his desk.

"Ms. Lundquist—Ingrid, the committee sent over the report on your foray into Cambodia. The photos of the ruins at Angkor were stunning—and tragic, of course. You have a brilliant career ahead."

She beamed. "Thank you, Mr. Savani. It was an exciting project and I'm grateful for the funding. I had so much material, of course, that it was difficult to decide what to include in the report to the Foundation."

"Yes, I'm sure. That's what I was going to speak to you about. Could you prepare a supplemental report for me? Statuary only. I prefer digital to prints, especially close-ups that might show the surface condition. Know what I mean?"

Her eyes narrowed and her lower lip protruded.

"It's a special interest of mine, dear. I'm thinking about a major gift to the World Monument Fund for a longterm preservation project—you know, once things settle down there."

"Why, of course. Always thinking ahead, aren't you?"

Her back arched slightly. Tony couldn't help noticing how the thin fabric of her dress clung damply to her bosom. He pictured Cal's calloused hands slipping the dress from her shoulders, pressing his full lips and gapped teeth against the small breasts, making her gasp... Tony sat down. Popped a candy into his mouth.

"By next week, then?" He savored the sharp chocolate as it melted around his tongue and teeth, the liquid center a tart burst of raspberry.

"Of course. I shall have both reports for you by Tuesday."

As soon as she left the room, Tony picked up their proposal, flipped through it again, and pitched it into the wastebasket.

ROCHESTER, NEW YORK

Delia twisted around to get comfortable and let her head rest on Martin's shoulder. They both stared ahead at the wall, at a faded Zen painting of a Hotei figure pointing at the moon. As she began her story, she prayed she'd be persuasive enough to get Martin to join her hunt.

LONDON, ENGLAND

When Delia returned to London from Beijing, she was on top of the world. She had worked hard for months to recover a cache of Warring States jades looted from the Imperial Palace during the Revolution. The Beijing government gratefully allowed her to buy and export a more recent trove of jades so special and rare that, with a few phone calls during her Hong Kong layover, she'd sold the lot at immense profit. Her imagination blazed with the kind of merchandise she'd be able to reinvest in. Maybe she could stop being a mere buyer's agent and become a full-fledged private dealer. It wasn't till she stopped by Jones-White Investigations—to say hi to Edwin and drop off her report—that she found out about Lana's murder and Martin's disappearance. Edwin was distraught. Her euphoria evaporated.

For a couple of days, she tried to track Martin down. No one had heard from him in the month since the murder. She discovered that his house was for sale, but the agent had stopped showing it and wouldn't return her calls. She found the executor of Lana's will, but he revealed nothing.

"I daresay Mr. Moon gave me explicit instructions, in most graphic terms. I suspect that when he wishes to resume his acquaintanceships, you will hear from him." He sniffed.

Half respectful of Martin's choices, half peeved at his melodramatic departure, she backed off and got caught up in the rhythm of the trade—a mix of straight business and undercover work. For Jones-White—and a fat insurance commission—she was trying to position herself to be offered an ancient elephant tusk, carved by a master craftsman in China, recently stolen from a gallery in Paris, thought to be in London. Then Jeremy Bellingham called.

"Miss Rivera, I hear you're in the market for tusks. I have something you might find quite a bargain..."

Yes! The profile fit. Bellingham was fresh face, pressing for a quick sale. He worked for New Cathay Galleries—a newcomer to the marketplace, already gaining a reputation among insiders for its fast-paced trade, no questions asked. At that point, she didn't know that Bellingham had been questioned in regard to Lana's death.

"Absolutely," she responded to him. "Can you describe the piece?"

"Really, you'll have to see it for yourself. It's utterly remarkable. Let me check with my client and I'll meet you at his place. Have any time tomorrow?"

That evening her service took a message that the meeting had been arranged for the next day at 7 p.m.

While it was always a thrill to bait her hook for one of these slippery guys, Delia left for the meeting hoping the tusk was legit. She had enough cash in the bank to buy it outright and would be able to turn it over within a week to one of three collectors. The profit from an outright sale would be far more than the insurance recovery fee.

When she arrived at the large home in Hampstead, she was surprised to recognize the name—D.W. Wallace—on the gate. He was a wealthy man and a respected collector. Her hopes soared.

She approached the door, heard footsteps behind her—and everything went black.

She awoke to a pounding headache, her eyes blindfolded. She lay on a mattress. Her hands were bound together, tied to something above her head. One ankle was lashed down. Someone held the other.

"Hey, what the hell!" she yelled and kicked wildly. He cursed when she landed a blow, but caught her leg again, and tied it fast. Her cries of anger turned to screams for help, but she knew immediately that they were useless. The house was set back behind a hedgerow, a hundred yards from the noisy boulevard.

"What do you want?" she demanded.

"You, love," he whispered as he grabbed her silk blouse and ripped it open. A knife. She felt the steel blade against her chest, under her bra, and with a terrifying snap the garment was torn apart. She screamed again. With a groan of pleasure, he pushed up her skirt and tore away her pantyhose. She clenched her teeth as he jammed himself into her.

It went on and on, ugly and painful. The only sounds were his grunts of effort and the sobs she couldn't seem to control. She kept trying to black out, to duck down some quiet side street of her mind, but it wasn't until she felt the point of the knife again, tracing a hot line down her breastbone, then stabbing into her belly, that the sweet darkness closed in.

When she came to, the blindfold was gone but her vision was blurry and beeping noises filled the air. Straps tied her down in a new way. Someone touched her arm and Delia jumped. A pale woman with a halo of blond hair came into focus. She smiled down at her.

"Welcome back, Delia. I'm Karen Fletcher, your doctor. You're at St. Francis Hospital, recovering from emergency surgery."

Delia wanted to ask a million questions but the doctor put her hand on the side of Delia's face.

"Don't try to talk—there's a feeding tube down your throat, but you're okay. You're okay. You're going to be a hundred percent."

Dr. Fletcher explained that a neighbor who knew the Wallaces were on vacation called the police when he saw activity in the house. Delia was in shock from loss of blood by the time the ambulance arrived. Her assailant had vanished.

26

"Your abdomen was a bit of a mess from the stabbing, but luckily no arteries were nicked. Lots of clean-up, but everything essential to a normal life was repaired and tucked back into place. I'll explain what we removed when—"

Delia began to gag.

As soon as she was able to tell her story, Bellingham was picked up. He denied leaving a message, saying that his client with the tusk had been unavailable. The client—an elderly don in Knightsbridge—confirmed Bellingham's story.

But Edwin Jones-White saw the parallels immediately between her assault and Lana's murder: the identical wounds, the lack of biological evidence, the dealings with Bellingham, and perhaps the fact that both women were Jones-White operatives. Despite his pressure on Scotland Yard, the investigation sputtered to a halt.

ROCHESTER, NEW YORK

When Delia finished her story, Martin hugged her again. "It's... incredible," he said. "You look so strong, so healthy—really beautiful. What I saw in your eyes—I assumed it was the usual business trouble—or maybe only jetlag."

"Well, of course it's jetlag. Of course I'm healthy. I'm not the type to waste away out of pity for myself. You know me better than that."

She pressed her face against his chest. *Healthy, yeah, but far from okay.*

LONDON & THE WORLD

Delia needed two more surgeries to finish the repairs. Back on the job, she was fine at first. She began to travel as soon as she could walk. She brokered important collections of antique ivory carvings—medieval French and Byzantine items, as well as some Japanese netsuke. Eventually, in fact, she was offered the stolen Chinese tusk and, on secret behalf of the insurance company, bought it back at a good price.

What she did not tell Martin was that Tony Savani had been a wonderful support throughout her ordeal and beyond her recuperation, caring for her, taking her to specialists, and then advising her on business.

Nor did she tell Martin how her nerves started to fray. As her health improved, her mind found deep reservoirs of fear. She was being walloped with post-traumatic stress. Then a couple months ago, Jones-White offered her the Buddha-smuggling assignment in Thailand. She'd accepted eagerly, hoping that the multilayered challenges of undercover work would snap her out of her anxieties. And Tony was delighted to hear she had "business in Thailand"—that she would finally get to see his beautiful home there.

Still in London, she began nosing around, talking to dealers in Southeast Asian antiquities. In general, they were still abuzz with Lana's murder. Those who knew of Delia's assault sympathized and expressed their alarm about "what the world was coming to." One of them mentioned the similarity between Lana's death and that of the archeologist René Malraux in Bangkok. Edwin managed to confirm Malraux's membership in HAWC-I, which would make him a militant against any trade in ancient Buddhas.

When she began to drop Malraux's name here and there, another dealer mentioned a connection between Malraux and Bellingham. Suddenly, her professional work merged with the obsession she was trying to let go of.

Delia's fears became crippling. But she had to pursue it, had to put an end to it. What she wanted most was an answer. Her assault had not been a random act of violence. She'd been carefully set up to be murdered in the same brutal way that Lana had. Living the rest of her life without knowing why was intolerable. That was what her rational self told her. Her primal self wanted to see Bellingham blotted from the face of the earth.

Yet, after six weeks, she found that she'd done nothing, could do nothing, alone. She couldn't pick up the phone to make her reservation to Bangkok. Tony was her darling friend, but was not privy to her work with Jones-White or to the facts she'd assembled. He'd spent a huge amount of energy helping to get the bloody mess behind her, wanted her to work closely with him as a buying agent, and was pressuring her to join him at his home in Thailand. He'd heard enough of her Bellingham accusations and felt it was a matter between her and her psychiatrist.

But the thought of going to Thailand with Bellingham on the loose there—even if she gave up the case—intensified her terror. So, that's when she crossed the Atlantic to find the one man in all the world she could trust to help her—Martin Moon.

ROCHESTER, NY

They sat quietly on the couch, huddled in a small pool of lamplight, staring at that painting of Hotei pointing at the moon. Her head still lay against his shoulder and he stroked her hair. Rain pattered on the windows.

She needed sleep, but she also needed Martin's commitment. And to get his commitment, she needed to understand why he couldn't bear the thought of going back into the world. She needed to know his story.

"Your turn, Marty. Out with it."

Martin made a noncommittal sound. "Mmm." He would rather focus on the sensation of Delia's curly hair under his fingers. He leaned over to kiss it, then rested his cheek against her head. He didn't like the decision she was pressuring him to make. He didn't want to deal with murder and mayhem. Lana's death was behind him and Delia should put her ordeal behind her as well. Telling his story would make him face the ugliness again, would pull him back into hell. He shook his head.

"We're six months into the nineties, Delia. Can't we just look forward to the quiet collapse of the twentieth century?"

She poked him. "Come on. You owe me that much."

"Okay, but why can't we wait till tomorrow when—?"

"I want to know now."

He closed his eyes and smelled the faint spice of shampoo in her hair.

"Martin?"

He resigned himself to the dreary saga. Maybe if he explained it well enough to Delia, she'd understand and let it drop. He heaved a great sigh and started in.

"It was in Thailand—I started falling apart in Thailand. But I guess I need to begin my tale in London."

London, England

At the London office of Jones-White Investigations, housed discretely within the Jones-White & Abermarle law firm, Edwin explained the project to Martin and Lana.

"HAWC-I is on a tear about these ancient burial sites in Thailand. Official inquiries have failed. Amateur snoops have failed. HAWC-I has finally bullied the Thai Antiquities Ministry into matching a UNESCO grant to see if the operation can be infiltrated and the looters nailed. It's a flat fee, plus a modest per diem."

"Isn't this a little late in the game?" Martin asked.

For a decade, carloads of ceramics had been showing up in Thai antique shops. Rumor had it that they came from sites deep in the mountains along the Burmese border, somewhere between the towns of Tak and Mae Sot. No single piece was very valuable, but archaeologists and art historians were frustrated that massive plundering was taking place at sites they knew nothing about, had never even seen. A team from Chiang Mai University managed to get enough information to theorize that the items came from the cemeteries of a mysterious hill people who had occupied the area sometime between the fourteenth and sixteenth centuries. They were eager to learn more.

But the area was largely inaccessible. Not only was the terrain hostile, but the land was also infested with Communist insurgents, outposts of the Karen nation fighting for independence from Burma, secretive local hill tribes, and bandits. It had been Martin's impression that, after a few years of highly publicized efforts, the government and Chiang Mai University had despaired of ever gaining access before the sites were stripped bare.

"Yes, I should have thought so myself," Edwin said. "But there have been new developments. Past few months a fresh wave of artifacts hit the market—fabulous ceramics—much finer craftsmanship, exquisite aesthetic qualities, the type of stuff that could easily catch on in fashionable Western galleries."

He continued. "And another little complication: HAWC-I has reason to suspect that the new looting is being organized by Burmese Karens to finance their rebellion against the Rangoon government. Karen leaders working out of Bangkok are likely to have enough information to pinpoint the operation geographically—to someone they trust. That alone may give the Thai government the wherewithal to put a stop to it. That, plus a few names."

Martin was reluctant to take the job. Aside from being fatigued from months on the road, he didn't like the political angle. He preferred dealing with outright thieves, who had nothing but their own self-interest in mind—no impacts outside the antiquities world, no moral ambiguities. Lana was also travel-weary and yet it was the very political angle that piqued her interest.

"Sounds fascinating," she said and Martin's hope for a few quiet weeks at home evaporated.

Bangkok was awash in steamy monsoon rains. Lana booked rooms in the upscale antique district, at the Oriental, in the old Authors' Wing once frequented by the likes of Somerset Maugham, Graham Green, and Joseph Conrad. In their suite, against the continuous drumming of rain, she cultivated a house-party atmosphere. Their reputation as big spenders attracted a stream of dealers daily, from noon till midnight. Because Lana and Martin expressed interest in ceramics, the traders brought samples of the best antique celadon from Sawankhalok and Sukhothai.

"These are all lovely," Martin said to one of the dealers after a few days of this. "But to tell you the truth, my customers for this sort of stuff—the serious collectors, at any rate—won't jump at it. Too common now in the West. I hear that more interesting merchandise is coming out of the hills near Tak. Got any of that?"

The dealer did and Martin bought the best of it. As they chatted about its origins, the name of a middleman came up—Taw Hla. It was a Karen name.

Martin traced Taw Hla to an unremarkable antique shop off Sukhumvit Road. It took several excursions and many bottles of Karen moonshine to get Taw Hla to open up. The taxi trips across town, through sheeting rain, skirting accidents in the traffic-clogged streets, wore on Martin's nerves. Sogginess seeped into his joints. And Taw Hla got to him.

Taw Hla's English was broken but he spoke eloquently about his people's struggle. The Karens—noble, honest, hard-working, democratic—had been persecuted by the Rangoon government ever since the British left Burma in 1948. They deserved self-rule. But their villages were being razed, their families massacred.

Martin understood. His mother's family had been Basque separatists, who financed their cause through black-market sales of anything they could get their hands on. The family stories had piqued young Martin's curiosity about both noble causes and underground economies. In so many ways his profession served the vanities of the rich and powerful, yet he still harbored a soft spot for the underdog. When nationalist governments wanted to strut their fabricated unity in big museums, when they needed the support of treasure-loving aristocrats, it was usually the peasants who suffered… the Basques and the Karens.

"What is wrong with you?" Lana asked. It was after midnight and the last of their acquaintances had finally left the suite. Martin had spent the evening in the bedroom conferring with his gin bottle. He had balled up his suit and thrown it into a corner, then turned off the air conditioner, and opened the window. Rain soaked the carpet and the air was sodden.

"I hate this fucking hotel. Did you ever notice how fucking obsequious the staff is?"

Scowling, she shut the window and switched on the air conditioner.

"I told Taw Hla I'd buy a containerload of ceramics if I could have the pick of their digs," he said. "He offered to have his cousin take me there. I can leave tomorrow."

Her face brightened. "That's great, honey. From what I'm learning, they have an incredible organization. It'll be a real feather in our cap to break it up."

"I'm not going."

"You're kidding. If it's the weather, you could wait awhile, till—"

"It isn't the weather."

She said nothing, began to undress.

"It's the Karens," he finally said, picking at the picture of Queen Victoria on the gin bottle. "I believe in their cause, their struggle for independence. If they can do it selling pots, more power to them. Let's go home."

Lana groaned. "You're such a romantic," she said as she lay down next to him. "And the gin makes you a sucker for all the losers in the world. But, Martin, you're also a man who honors his commitments and tomorrow you darn well better be on the road."

He went on the road all right, up to his ankles and occasionally his knees in red clay, as the wicked monsoon rains made him an intimate of the Tak Province landscape. Taw Hla's cousin guided him through the hills, by mule and by pickup truck, through a series of new grave sites being carefully excavated by friendly Karens.

The booty was spectacular. Martin earmarked several lots to be shipped out and, whenever he managed a dry, solitary moment, annotated his findings in a pocket-sized notebook. The lots he bought were not the most commercial but told the best story. The items would be transported to his customs broker in Bangkok, labeled as *Assorted Thai Handicrafts*. But instead of being shipped to London, they'd be sent to the University of Chiang Mai for scholarly analysis. As soon as he hit civilization again, he would mail them his notes. It was lousy archaeology, but better than nothing.

He'd keep the items bought in Bangkok—part of his deal with Jones-White—letting him be a real antiquities dealer and preserving his reputation for being casual about the source of his merchandise. It was the kind of compromise that made HAWC-I furious enough to use Jones-White only as a last resort.

His journey ended in the town of Mae Sot on the Burmese border. He should have immediately boarded one of the buses that left hourly for Tak, but by that time Martin's belly was full of bugs and his heart full of sorrow at the thought of betraying the Karen cause. So instead, he took a room and camped out at the cesspool that passed for the hotel bar, where he sat watching his hands tremble as he tried to figure an honorable way out of his commitments...

"You Martin Moon?" A big guy with an attitude stood behind his barstool.

"Used to know a guy went by that name."

From out of nowhere, a second gorilla grabbed his arms and yanked him off the stool. "The one we know is a bloody grave robber," he said.

Shit—hawkeyes. How the hell...? "Look, fellas, tell you what..." He groped for a line of bull, but they were already shoving him out the door. The bartender had disappeared.

Martin threw a couple of punches but they didn't connect. Dragged into a dark side street, Martin was shoved against a fence—rusted iron, from the scrape of it against his cheek. He slid to the ground, where he tasted blood and dirt.

"HAWC-I's been tracking you. Headquarters gave us the okay to teach you a lesson."

"That's a lie!"

He struggled to his hands and knees, but they fell on him, pinning his arms and legs. He bucked and tried to roll away but they were massively strong. He was beat. A horrible cramp seized his left leg.

Then gunshots. Female voices barked shrilly in Pwo Karen. The hawkeyes took off. Martin propped himself up on his elbows and was pushed back down by the long barrel of a rifle. Moonlight caught the faces of three beautiful girls with wide fierce eyes.

"I surrender," he whispered.

He awoke on the dirt floor of a shanty. His wallet was gone. His pants leg had been torn open and a stab wound in his thigh was bandaged with a dirty scarf. He was burning with fever. Blowflies had gathered. Maggots swarmed on the bloodsoaked cloth. It took all his concentration to untie the cloth and all his courage to shake the maggots into the yellow-black ooze of his leg.

Help me out here, fellas. He projected his thoughts to them, deliriously confident in their good will. *Clean it up for me. I might be here awhile.* Then he passed out.

Eventually people came for him. Lots of shouting. Pulling at him. Tying him down. Helicopters. A platinum-haired woman saying how much she loved him. Needles. Blackness.

Next time he made any sense of his surroundings, the room was white and sweet-smelling. Lana sat on the side of the bed, clutching his hand.

"My leg?"

"You were lucky. The wound was... clean when we found you." Tears filled the sky-blue of her eyes and were hastily brushed away. "But we're in hot water."

While Martin lay wasting in the shanty, the case had blown up. The hawkeyes rifled Martin's room, stole his notes, and made their own report to the Thai authorities, with Martin as the villain. Meanwhile, the Mae Sot hotel called Lana to complain that Martin had disappeared without paying his bill. By the time Lana arrived in Mae Sot, Taw Hla and his cousins had been arrested and warrants had been issued for Lana and Martin as co-conspirators in an illegal enterprise with foreign nationals. Lana turned herself in and enlisted the police to help her with a door-to-door search for Martin. They found him, airlifted him to Bangkok, and stuck a police guard outside his hospital door.

As soon as Martin could hoist himself up on crutches, the two were deported from Thailand in a splash of international publicity.

Jones-White had nothing but kudos for them. HAWC-I was thrilled. Having the information released through the vigilantes in Mae Sot had brought glory to the organization and had preserved Martin's cover. Lana had provided the additional information to permanently dismantle Taw Hla's organization. She was flying high.

Martin, on the other hand, had lost twenty pounds and could barely walk. Even though the deportation had been a sham and, Jones-White assured him, would be duly expunged, the publicity pushed his carefully tended reputation into the same league as criminal entrepreneurs. Even worse, however, was the betrayal of Taw Hla's friendship and the Karen cause.

"I'm quitting," he announced to Lana in their dining room, as he was trying to force down a curry that was making his stomach lurch. "Moving back to the States, maybe."

"Nonsense," she said. "This case turned out to be a major breakthrough for us. We're golden. Edwin says the CIA needs antiquities experts for an operation they're running out of Cambodia."

His laugh was wild, hysterical. "You're fucking insane." He pushed away from the table, grabbed the gin bottle, and limped into his study.

They sniped like that for days. A week later, Lana breezed in saying she'd accepted an assignment, nothing very hair-raising, a little snooping around is all, not even necessary to leave London.

Martin blew up. "I told you I was finished!"

"Then don't bother," Lana said, tossing her hair. "I'll do it myself."

"Oh, Christ," he growled. "Tell me what it is."

The British Museum was about to sink a fortune into a Khmer statue being offered by Jeremy Bellingham at New Cathay Galleries. It was nearly lifesized, carved in sandstone, and in fine condition. The price was right. It was not fake. The owner, Claude Leroux, appeared to have clear title. No theft reports were on file at Interpol or at the International Foundation for Art Research in New York.

Still, Reggie Gupta, the curator for South Asian acquisitions, was troubled. No one had ever seen the statue prior to this sale. Such monumental rarities usually found their way into exhibit catalogues, texts—something. What also had Gupta in a dither was the discovery that Leroux had amassed his wealth producing child pornography videos in Amsterdam. This news cast a deep shadow over his integrity.

So, as a final precaution, the British Central Bureau of Interpol referred Gupta to Jones-White Investigations. It was not a major case. Any shred of evidence that added to their suspicions would kill the deal. There had been a rash of such scandals in the art world—a museum buying a rare antiquity in good faith only to have someone emerge at the unveiling to lay claim to the precious acquisition. The British Museum wanted none of it.

Martin agreed to help if Lana did the legwork.

"What a doll," Lana remarked about Bellingham after their first meeting. "Young. Quite the charmer. And not an ethical bone in his body. I asked him to appraise our Tibetan bronzes and he scrawled his signature at the bottom of a sheet of Cathay letterhead. 'Type in whatever,' he said."

Martin gently tugged on a strand of her hair. "Perhaps the charmer is you, my dear."

She invited Bellingham home for dinner. He was clearly captivated by Lana, but it wasn't till he met Martin that he realized who they were.

"Moon and Tuthill! Why, of course, you're the two who got pinched in Thailand. Rotten bit of luck, eh? Just like the Thais to get in an uproar over some crummy pots, when the really good loot leaves right under their noses."

"No need for your sympathy," Martin snapped, already under the influence of his Bombay gin. "I made a fucking fortune there. Some of those 'crummy pots' were damn good and I shipped out a container-load before they caught up with us."

"Bravo, old man, bravo!"

As the evening progressed, Martin showed Bellingham his small but growing sculpture collection, bragging about how many things came from what were now considered world monument sites. Once Bellingham was persuaded of his bullshit, Martin pounced.

"So, Jeremy old man, I saw the statue you're selling the BM. I've had a hard-on for a find like that all my life. Any more where that came from?"

Jeremy winked. "If the price is right, you can have one just like it, sealed into a container of Thai silk, and shipped from Bangkok within the month. Complete with papers showing it's been in your family for a century."

Martin smiled.

For hours after Jeremy left, Lana and Martin argued. She thought Martin had been brilliant, but entirely too drunk. He thought he'd been brilliant, but not drunk enough. He considered the case closed, since they had enough information to advise the skittish museum staff not to buy. She claimed it was irresponsible to close the case without digging for more about the true source and nailing Bellingham. He thought Interpol should deal with it. She accused him of being a burned-out drunk. He agreed. She stormed off to bed. He passed out on the couch.

They barely spoke for days, although she bustled in and out, a bounce in her step, singing softly to herself. Martin decided to make up. It was early evening. She was dressing to go out.

Martin stood behind her, drew his hands across her shoulders and down her bare arms. Kissed her neck. "Stay home. Let's plan a vacation. Far away—Bermuda, Hawaii. I'll start eating, gain some weight, dry up. We need it, Lana, we need to have some fun. Just the two of us. No jobs."

She pulled away, concentrating on the clasp of a thin gold necklace that sparkled with tiny emeralds. "Sure, honey. As soon as I finish with the case."

"What? Lana, we are finished with the case. We finished it the other night. Didn't you call Edwin? Didn't you tell him the museum should call off the deal?"

She wiggled into a tight knit dress that exposed most of her legs. "There's much more to this case than meets the eye. If you weren't being such a drip, I'd tell you about it. Just another day or two and we'll have enough evidence for arrests."

"But the museum was going to close the sale today."

"Covered. I had lunch with Reggie Gupta the other day and told him to back out of the deal. The museum is in the clear, but—"

"Lana, for godsake, you blew your cover. How many years have you been doing this? We communicate with Jones-White, period. Little breeches in protocol can turn into great big trouble."

"You're really more paranoid by the day, Marty. I've known Reggie for centuries. He's a wonderful, honest man. I merely repeated what Bellingham told us at dinner and he was extremely grateful. Besides, Edwin's in Paris. I want to hand him the complete case when he gets back this weekend."

She slipped her feet into spiky heels and retrieved a short sable jacket from the back of the closet.

"Where the hell are you going?"

"Party at Jeremy's. I assumed you wouldn't be interested. Oh, the Spider's in the shop for a tune-up, so I'll take your car, if you don't mind."

"Where is this party?"

"His apartment, I think." She gave the address.

"Jesus, honey, that's Paddington. At least wear jeans and a sweater. You look like you're going to dinner with the Queen."

She spun around at him. "Don't tell me what I look like. You haven't noticed what I look like in weeks. You can grow roots on that couch for all I care. This two-bit case is turning out to be pretty darn interesting and I don't need Martin Moon telling me what to do or how to dress."

"All I'm saying is—"

"I can take care of myself." She marched out.

Martin shuffled to the bar in the living room and began to work his thumbnail around the seal on a fresh fifth of gin. Then he set it down, tired of being drunk, wishing Lana hadn't run off to Paddington alone.

He dozed, showered, dozed some more, then tried to read the newspaper, but he couldn't concentrate. Lana went to Paddington, to Bellingham, after she'd queered his deal with Gupta. Bellingham would know.

Martin put down the paper, dug out the phone book, and looked up Bellingham's address. Kensington. Not Paddington. What the hell was in Paddington and why was Bellingham luring her there? With all her damn schooling in animal behavior, Lana got cocky about reading people. She always assumed she'd have the upper hand in any situation, but sometimes she was wrong. Dead wrong.

He raced out of the house and hailed a cab.

The taxi driver found his old Jaguar on a dark block of warehouses. Then Martin found her keys on the sidewalk. He clutched them till they dug into his fingers as he stood, without breathing, scanning the windows around him for lights.

Screaming. Someone was screaming. *Lana!*

He began to dash from door to door, trying to home in on the location of the horrifying high-pitched keening. Now the cab driver joined him.

When he finally pushed a door open and heard Lana's screams coming from somewhere upstairs, he yelled at the driver. "Find a constable. Please!"

The building was a storage rental facility—a dimly lit labyrinth of makeshift lockers and padlocked doors and blocked stairways. A nightmare search of dead ends. He tried calling to her. "I'm here, Lana! Lana!" but he had no breath, no voice.

He followed her cries as far as the third floor. And then they stopped. The sudden silence paralyzed him. Without the beacon of her screams, he lost his bearings.

"Lana? Lana?" His voice was a whisper.

He reoriented himself to lights at the end of a long corridor. He ran toward them.

Martin found her. And she was dead. Not a heartbeat, not a flicker of an eyelash, not a sigh of farewell. He was barely aware of the taxi driver and a constable pulling him away. And yet he could still hear her screams, beating against the silence.

Rochester, NY

When Martin finished with his story, his face was damp with tears. He was surprised he still had any left to shed. Delia was clutching his hand. Her head rested on his shoulder.

"So you can see how I screwed everything up," he said softly. "Disaster piled on disaster… I couldn't do anything right. I just kept wading in deeper and deeper… till everything was gone. You can see how I can't possibly go back, I can't possibly help anyone, not anyone."

But as he spoke those words, he understood that he must.

TWO

When Delia awoke, sunlight from the window pressed in on her, made her snap her eyes shut, made her pull the down comforter over her head. She lay on Martin's couch, still in last night's clothes, a pillow under her head. The last thing she remembered was curling against him in a blur of exhaustion, listening to his heartbeat, worrying that his grief and his guilt ran too deep for him ever to leave his sanctuary.

She was tempted to hide out with him here, to have his body heat warm her frozen heart and heal her psychic wounds, but she had seen the upstairs. He slept on a monk's cot, next to a table piled with papers, and the rooms were filled with shipping boxes, some opened, the rest still sealed. His own wounds ran too deep. Healing would come with movement not with standing guard, not with hiding out.

The aroma of coffee filled the air. Peeking out from the cover, she saw Martin sitting on the floor, cross-legged, facing a blank spot on the wall. He was motionless. She covered her face again.

Next thing she knew, a hand pressed against her back. A voice whispered, "Morning, old love."

Delia exposed her face and squinted at him, crouched next to her. The sun brightened his face. The whites of his eyes were clear. His cheeks had color. His healthiness reassured her.

He smiled, touched her nose, then her bottom lip, and offered her his coffee. Propped on an elbow, she sipped.

"Did I see you meditating?" she asked.

41

"I try. Joined a Zen group in town to learn." He shrugged. "It helps."

He sat in the armchair. He was barefoot, wearing jeans and a sweatshirt. He grabbed reading glasses from the pile of books on the side table. He started to put them on but laid them back down.

"Tell me," he said, "do you know that Bellingham is in Thailand now? Is that why you're headed there?"

"The staff at New Cathay are very close-mouthed." Her voice rumbled heavy as she wrenched her mind back to her mission and the long road ahead. "Heard a rumor he's working out of Southeast Asia. Friend at the Thai consulate in New York did a little snooping and found he's been entering Thailand about once a month, possibly from Hong Kong. Haven't been able to pin down where he stays."

"What do you have on him so far?"

"For smuggling, practically nothing. What you told me last night confirmed what we already suspected, but it's no more than hearsay. His name's been connected with three other sales: in Tokyo, Singapore, and San Francisco. Too bad you don't know what Lana was onto—"

A flick of his eye made her hurry on.

"For murder, I have even less. Circumstantial association with at least two murders and my assault. René Malraux's death was written off as a local sex crime. And I told you I uncovered a rumor connecting Malraux and Bellingham. The Bangkok police report refers to Malraux's wife, but I haven't been able to locate her."

"Do you know just how Malraux and Bellingham were connected— doing business? If Malraux was a hawkeye, maybe he was harassing Bellingham."

"I have no idea." She set the empty mug on the floor and hugged her pillow.

Martin got up from his chair, picked up the mug, and sat on the edge of the couch. "So you're spinning your wheels."

She couldn't help but complain, "That's why I came here."

He exhaled. "And that's why I'm going with you."

Relief bloomed in her. From a forgotten place deep within her, it blossomed till her toes, her fingers, her lips, and her scalp tingled.

She squeezed his arm. "Thank you, thank you, thank you."

Setting the mug back on the floor, Martin touched her hair, drew a strand away from her eyes, then rested his hand on her back. It reminded her that she still hadn't told him about Tony.

She took a breath. "Martin, you remember Tony Savani?"

"Sure. Neat guy. Expensive taste in art. We spent some time with him in Bangkok. He's not connected with Bellingham, is he?"

"No. It's just that..." The moment had passed. Martin was rubbing her back through the comforter. She remembered other mornings long ago. "It's just that... he's been sending some business my way. I bought a few things at auction for him last month."

Martin scratched his head. "You don't say." He stood. "If Bellingham's trading in Bangkok, I bet Savani's done business with him."

"No. No, that's one base I covered. Says the name rings a bell. That's all." Delia had grilled Tony about Bellingham, but he deflected her questions and implied she was getting paranoid.

"Tony won't be a help," Delia reiterated, "so how else would you go about finding Bellingham?"

"Concentrate on the social angle, I guess," Martin said, squinting into the distance as he thought. "Who are his friends? Who does he meet with? Does he travel in diplomatic circles? Or does he pal around with Kuomintang Chinese and Corsicans—the kind of folks likely to be involved in large-scale smuggling? Say, are we out to put him in jail or simply put him out of business? I know you want to link him to your assault, but what's the client paying Jones-White for?"

"The idea is to discredit Bellingham and New Cathay Galleries—expose their illegal exports and put them out of business. If they're the ones."

Martin stood up and began opening windows. "It's monsoon season there now... Damn." He paused—a flashback maybe, but shook it off. "Tourists go home but there's a lot of partying among diplomats and business people. I have a tropical-weight tux packed away somewhere... Are you taking evening clothes?"

Delia conjured the image of Martin in a tuxedo—slouching against a wall, fondling a martini glass, dangling a cigarette—addicted more to the feel of it between his lips and fingers than to the nicotine. At a party, he was the flame who attracted the juiciest of moths. His beefy laugh and apt bits of gossip created the illusion of a big talker, when, in fact, his specialty was listening and gleaning information from the men and women who discovered him to be such delicious fun. This is how Delia always thought of Martin, not as the burned out wreck he described in last night's story.

Then Delia remembered the time she walked into a London cocktail party and saw him standing across the room with a stunning blonde. Lana. Who nearly spilled her drink laughing at something Martin said. Martin leaned over and kissed her neck...

"Oh, good grief, no," Delia said, as she chased off the memory and shed the comforter. She headed toward the kitchen and the coffee pot, trying to smooth out the wrinkles in her clothes. "I forgot how much work you did at dinner parties and gallery openings and charity balls. I suppose you'll expect me to loosen up Bellingham's friends by sleeping with them."

"What do you mean by that?"

Her remark had been half-joke, his question half-laughed. She pressed it, half-punishment for his quitting her backrub. Or for loving Lana best.

"Isn't that how she worked? That was the scuttlebutt—how she turned on to powerful, wicked men in spite of her devotion to that dear Martin Moon. At Jones-White, Giancarlo in Research liked to speculate whether it was Martin's deductions or Tuthill's seductions that made you such a successful duo."

He turned. His smile had vanished. "That's the most spiteful, the most unforgivable thing you've ever said to me."

A wave of nausea struck Delia. Her ears rang with the sudden embarrassment, the sudden likelihood that her barb was nothing more than vicious gossip. She had only ever known Lana by hearsay. The few times their paths crossed—at the occasional auction or party, Lana had been gracious and funny and smart.

Before Delia could mumble an apology, the doorbell rang and Jack let himself in.

"Hi, guys!"

Jack was following Delia's instructions to stop by early, but when he joined them in the kitchen, Martin looked surprised and Delia looked positively unnerved.

"Cinnamon rolls. Still warm," Jack said as he held out a paper bag to Martin.

The two recouped.

"Beautiful day out, isn't it?" Martin said as he put the rolls on a plate and poured Jack a cup of coffee.

Delia touched her tangled hair. "God, I must look like hell. I fell asleep in my clothes last night."

"No, you look fine," Jack said as he noted the smudged eye shadow and rumpled clothes.

"Remind me to play poker with you some day," she said.

"If you want to freshen up," Martin said to her, "make yourself at home upstairs."

"So, you two got our trip planned? I called Theresa this morning to tell her you invited me along to Thailand. She was really excited for me."

It didn't take a billboard for Jack to realize he'd blundered somehow. Delia blanched and darted her eyes toward Martin.

Martin's voice turned sharp. "You did what?"

Delia strained to smile. "Oh, I was going to talk it over with you, but it just escaped me. Yes, I asked Jack along. It'll be fun for him. Thailand is such a friendly place for tourists. He was game, ready for a vacation. I don't understand what the problem is."

Martin paced. "You were so damn sure I'd go, weren't you? After I told you *no*. After I told you *no*, you went right out and invited Jack to come with us."

Her voice was softer, tighter than his. "I knew... I knew that once you understood, once I had a chance to explain... I knew you'd help me... like you always have... like you always have."

His voice grew angrier. "Didn't you hear a word I said last night? Don't you have a clue how I'm dreading this whole *project*? I thought this was serious work. Deadly serious. And you're inviting people along for a *vacation*? Where's your judgment?"

A glob of chewed cinnamon roll wedged in Jack's throat.

"I did it for you. For *you*, okay? For moral support. I knew it would be hard on you, jumping back in the fray. I was trying to be sensitive. Thinking you might need a goddamn friend along the way. The kind of friend maybe I'm afraid I won't be. You'll see... and you'll be damn glad—" Delia blanched again and her hand flew to her belly. Her voice faded. "Damn glad when..." She spun away toward the living room and pounded up the stairs. They heard a door slam.

"Are you all right?" Jack called. Then to Martin: "Is she all right?"

They both stood, suspended, staring at her path, till they heard the shower running. The starch rinsed from Martin's body and he slumped against the kitchen counter.

"Damn her," Martin snarled, as he picked up a sponge and hurled it toward the doorway. It bounced limply off a chair. He pressed his thumb and fingertips against his reddening eyes. "She's so fucking impulsive. Since the day I met her she's been shooting off ahead of me, never giving me a chance to... And you can never get a straight answer out of her—"

Jack interrupted. "Look, I didn't know this would be such a big deal—I should have—maybe—let's just forget about me going with you guys."

Martin blew his nose on a paper towel and shook his head. "Maybe you'll keep me from killing her."

Delia put her jeans back on, with a fresh sweater. She was the world's biggest screwup. Her timing, way off. Bad omen.

She combed through her wet hair, forced her shoulders away from her ears, and massaged the furrow out of her brow. *Time to get back in the ring, kiddo.* So she stood tall, marched down the stairs, and headed toward the kitchen.

Martin glared at her and Jack gaped. Suddenly, she couldn't cross the threshold.

"Would one of you pitch me my handbag?"

With a nervous smile, Jack grabbed it by the long strap and tossed it. The side pocket was open and, as it landed, orange plastic prescription bottles tumbled onto the floor. She crouched to scoop them up, but Martin beat her to it.

"Now what the hell is this all about?" He snatched up a handful of bottles. "What are these? What in God's name are you on?" His dark eyes were full of anger. And fear.

"On?"

"On, damn it, *on.*" Crouching, he wrenched the side pocket all the way open and dumped its contents on the floor. More prescription bottles bounced out, along with a shower of multicolored pills in cellophane packets. His hands trembled as he pawed through the small mountain of pharmaceuticals. "What exactly are we dealing with here, Delia?"

She knelt next to him and tried to grab his hands. "Wait a minute. Wait. It's not what you think, for christsake."

LeHavre, France

A dozen years ago Martin had spent two weeks helping her break a pill addiction.

She had joined an Interpol investigation of national art treasures pouring out of East Germany. Her partner—and later her lover—was an Interpol agent, Dieter Waltheim. The work was grueling, involving frequent forty-eight-hour watches. He shared the secret behind his relentless energy—pep pills. In short order, she was hooked.

When the investigation got politically sensitive, Dieter was ordered back to Bonn. They'd been awake for days, following a truckload of merchandise across the continent. Dieter snapped. From their third-rate hotel room in LeHavre, France, he vanished into the night with all the pills. By morning she was strung out and desperate. She called Martin in London and by evening he was at her side.

The detox process was as brutal for him as it was for her. The smell of tobacco smoke made her vomit, so he quit his pack-a-day habit on the spot. For days he did nothing but hold her against his warm body in the chilly hotel room. He forced her to eat. After a few days, he dragged her on long walks through fog and freezing rain. They didn't say much. As she began to feel better, she tuned in to his long silences and heavy sighs. Full of shame, she packed up and went back to work.

Shortly after that, the long-overdue divorce papers arrived for her signature and the grapevine buzzed with news of Martin's engagement to the up-and-coming wildlife biologist Lana Tuthill, who was throwing it all away to join his business. She had no working-class, half-cubano, half-cracker, south-Florida background to overcome, but radiated the style bred from generations of elite scientists and physicians. And she'd never wind up in withdrawal, vomiting on Martin's shoes, because she was a champion teetotaler—nothing in her lungs, nothing up her nose, nothing in her veins, nothing past her lips but wholesome food and mineral water. Delia had been outclassed.

Martin and Delia crouched nose to nose on the floor. His eyes were stony. Jack hovered in the background.

"Start explaining," Martin growled.

"Half of these are empty." She threw a handful at the wastebasket but they bounced on the floor and Jack scooped them up. "Weren't *you* listening to *me* last night that I've spent months recovering from being nearly fucking killed?" Her voice quavered and tears streamed down her face.

"This one"—she picked up a bottle—"is penicillin, because of my—my spleen—my—they took out my spleen." She picked them up one by one and set them in a row. "Lomotil, in case of diarrhea. Compazine, in case of nausea. Chloral hydrate, if jetlag keeps me from sleeping. I *have* to sleep. Tylenol with codeine, for the pain from adhesions from all the surgery. I swear I've never taken any of them. And Valium for—but I'm switching to the Tofranil." She gathered the pill packets in a pile. "Vitamins and minerals. *Mightipaks* they're called. It's a system—different ones morning and night. Doctor I go to in London insisted it was a good idea."

"Sounds like a lot of crap," Martin muttered. "What's the Valium for?"

She was on her knees and curled over her belly. She covered her face with her hands and whispered, "Panic attacks."

"What?"

She uncurled herself and shouted, "Panic attacks, okay?"

Martin stood up and then Jack reached for her and helped her to her feet. He handed her a tissue for her tears and snot.

"The panic attacks—how often?" Martin demanded.

She squirmed away from the comfort of Jack's support. "Unpredictable."

"How often?"

"Once a week—every few days, I don't know."

"Coming more often or less often?"

"More," she whispered.

"Medication help?"

"Valium didn't. The Tofranil's new... but not so far, not noticeably... I don't know..."

"Special situations? Indoors, outdoors?"

Shaking her head, she closed her eyes. "Really, is all this interrogation necessary?"

"Don't you think it's only fair for Jack and me to know what we're getting into?"

"Okay, so you're traveling with a basket case."

She pitched away from him, but Martin caught her and pressed her to him. "Delia, damn it, I've known you too long. I can tell instantly when something's wrong. Ever since you showed up on my doorstep, I've had to work at peeling away the protective layers like a goddamn onion." His chest heaved slowly against hers as he stroked her damp hair. "It'll be all right now. One of us will be with you all the time, from now on. But no more secrets, no more unshared worries, okay?"

She cringed. The onion had lots of layers. But she had a job to do and a life to live. She had her entourage in place. Time to get back to work.

BANGKOK, THAILAND

Tony Savani picked up his extension. "Delia, where on God's earth are you?" He bit into his snack.

She laughed. "You'll never guess. Rochester, New York. What the heck are you chomping on?"

"Hm..." He tried to swallow. "It's sort of a candied pineapple, dipped in chocolate and coconut. Scrumptious... but it's... hmm... sticking to my teeth a bit." He heard her soft laugh. "Hmm... Anyway, you were supposed to be here days ago. I've been worried sick."

"Oh, gosh, didn't I say I'd be there sometime after June tenth? Today's the twelfth and I'm calling to tell you my plans. Is there a problem?"

"I'm sorry, darling. You think I'm pressuring you and I'm not." She'd reminded him more than once that she'd been prowling the world on her own for twenty years and hated the idea of having to check in constantly with someone. And yet Tony hated the idea of her disappearing like this for weeks on end. More and more he wanted her by his side always, but she was such a damned workaholic. Nothing slowed her down. If she were going to be his buying agent, she'd never be around. He'd have to think up something else to keep her near...

"It's just that—well, it's been a very frustrating day, Delia, and I could have used your advice. My buyer screwed up royally at the Hong Kong auction and lost the Baphuon Buddha—to the Heldt-Luther, no less."

"Who were you using?"

"No one I'll use again very soon." He hadn't told Delia about his relationship with Bellingham—no need. The authorities had cleared the young man of her assault but she still obsessed over him. Tony was trying to help her think about the future, not the painful past. "But the Buddha, Delia, how in the world will I spring it free from the Heldt-Luther? My Khmer collection will be ruined without that statue."

"Piece of cake. Unless the work's been on display in a major collection...?"

"No, not at all. It came from a private collection in Jakarta. No one in the business has seen it before. What's your idea?"

"Well, museums are getting more and more heat for buying items without enough research." Her voice was breezy, playful. "They wind up having to return the booty to the countries of origin at a huge loss, but it's really the bad press they can't stand. So, if I wanted this piece badly enough, I'd send in a stiff-backed HAWC-I type—quickly, before the acquisition is publicized—to inform Heldt-Luther that the statue was recently looted from Cambodia. Threatens to go public in a big way. Heldt-Luther gets nervous. *Your* representative then magically appears and offers to buy it on behalf of some national institution in Cambodia. They leap at the deal."

Jesus, it was brilliant. And Tony had the right connections to pull it off.

She was laughing. "I pulled off that caper myself once with a small museum, and the young curator was more than willing to sell off the offending piece before his board sniffed out the fake provenance I convinced him of. Gotta know all the angles in this business, right?"

They both laughed. Then there was a moment of hesitation on the other end of the line. "Tony, I ran into Martin Moon here in Rochester and he's going to go with me to Bangkok. He and a friend of his, Jack Scanlan. I'm expediting their visas through Betty Bhruksasri in New York, but we still won't get there till Friday. I booked rooms at the Tudor."

Tony felt a drop of sweat snake down his back. How do you *happen* to cross paths with your ex-husband in Rochester, New York? And how does that ex-husband wind up trailing after you to Thailand?

"What's the story?" he asked, trying to sound nonchalant.

"No story. He's had enough seclusion, wants to get back into the world,

50

find some new sculpture. Does it bother you? I mean, you're not jealous or anything—we've talked enough about Martin—you know we're just friends now—"

"Of course, it's fine, Delia. The man's always intrigued me. But I'm curious about how he's getting a visa. Maybe I'm wrong, but I thought he was deported from here for some sort of smuggling brouhaha. They can't look too kindly on his return."

"Oh that... no problem... Betty owes me one for that ivory button collection I found her. As long as he doesn't do anything to draw attention to himself, nobody'll even notice. If he wants to export something, I'll put the papers in my name."

"I see. How nice to have friends..."

BANGKOK, THAILAND

What struck Jack first about Bangkok was the heat—like walking into a giant clothes dryer, sucking air from his lungs and smelling both humid and baked at once. His jeans and polo shirt clung to his skin. His pulse raced as they worked their way through immigration officials, customs, and a throng of aggressive tour hawkers to the taxi stand.

When he was finally alone in his room at the Tudor Hotel, he cranked up the air conditioner and peeled off his clothes. He stood in front of the blower till he got gooseflesh.

Delia and Martin were satisfied with the meal they got during the Tokyo layover and were ready to sleep off their jetlag. Jack went along with the plan but, in fact, was wide awake and starved. No way could the candy bars and chips in the room's minibar satisfy him for the sixteen hours till breakfast.

Half an hour later, Jack was lost in the polyglot bustle of the hotel lobby, wondering what to do with U.S. dollars. He spotted the currency exchange counter.

"I need to change some dollars into—into—" In typical Scanlan fashion, what he remembered from his hasty research about Thailand was that addiction to opium was rampant, that the local malaria was resistant to traditional prophylaxis, and that four out of five cheap whores were HIV-positive. But the name of Thai currency escaped him.

The attendant smiled. "*Baht.*" In minutes, he walked away with a fistful of multicolored bills.

The hotel's Jasmine Palace restaurant was nearly empty except for a horde of waiters and a singer doing a passable imitation of James Taylor. *Come-a come-a come yeah yeah.* Something about the pacing, however, made it surreal, like a thirty-three RPM turntable moving at twenty-five.

A grinning waiter handed him a multi-page menu, a jumble of tiny print. The words were English but didn't make sense, and the references to fish's maw, serpent heads, wild boar, and sea leeches made him queasy. A half-dozen waiters hovered and smiled. Jack smiled back and tried to refocus on the menu.

A man with small chubby hands sat alone at the next table, gobbling a feast of several dishes. He caught his eye.

"Hi," Jack said. "What do you recommend?"

The pudgy young man took in the whole length of Jack's body. "Just arrived?" A British accent.

"Yeah. Must have a godawful case of jetlag. I'm looking at this menu, having a helluva time figuring out what it says. Looks like English, but I can't understand a word of it."

"Ah, welcome to Bangkok. Anything westernized you see is a thin veneer only. You Yanks are all taken in by the big sign outside the airport: *Pizza Hut welcomes you to Bangkok.* And all the billboards along the highway—Kodak, Xerox, Volkswagen, Sony—makes you think that the world's one great big shopping mall and that Bangkok is just another theme park. But, guess what, this ain't Disneyworld. Every day you're here something will happen to remind you of that. Don't you forget it."

Jack didn't need a lecture. "Well, I didn't expect Disneyworld, but until I get my bearings I wouldn't mind having a burger and a beer."

"Try Dick's All-American over on the next block." The stranger gave directions.

Jack stood. "Sounds great. Thanks." He poked out a hand. "Jack Scanlan. You staying at the Tudor?"

The man stared sullenly at Jack's massive hand.

Over the years, Delia had developed rituals for coping with jetlag. On their first night in Bangkok, having crossed thirteen time zones and reversed day and night, the rituals seemed particularly important. It wasn't simply the crankiness and fuzziness she feared, but the panics and the belly-aches they led to.

She unpacked her bag, glanced through the English *Bangkok Post*, pulled the drapes against the late afternoon sun, and did some easy stretches till she was sleepy. Then she popped her evening vitamin pak and soaked in a warm bath.

Sleep—a dreamless void—came quickly.

But then a soft *clickclick* was enough to set her swimming anxiously back to consciousness. The room was black. As she eased from her side onto her back, she heard the rattle of throat clearing.

"Martin? That you?" He was staying in the adjoining room.

Nothing.

Then, from inches away, a light struck her eyes and in its glare the blade of a knife flashed. Someone was standing next to the bed. He lowered the blade to her covers, to her chest, then touched the sharp tip on her sternum. Her mind blanked and her reflexes froze. She clutched the sheet as if that would protect her.

While the jacklight held her eyes, the knife traced a familiar line along her breastbone, its edge pressing into the sheet. Moving to softer flesh, it continued a course past Delia's waist to her scarred belly, then the flat side of the metal lay between her legs for a moment. Over the whirr of the air conditioner and the honking horns of distant traffic, no sound was made. Even her own breathing seemed suspended. Slowly, the flashlight backed away. A slit of yellow light appeared behind the figure, as it slipped through the doorway, and pulled the door shut.

Delia was paralyzed. Then a sudden stinging on her chest where the knife had been made her gulp air.

Vaulting out of bed, she slapped on the light, and threw herself at the door that connected her to Martin as she twisted the doorknob—his side was locked! How—? She began pounding on it.

"Martin!" She tried to control her voice, but then she screamed. "Martin!

Moon!" *Don't cry,* she kept telling herself, *you're alive, you're okay.* She tried to focus on the scratchy comfort of the carpet beneath her feet. "Moon!"

She pounded on the door. "Marty!" She tried to scream but there was no air in her lungs. Had he taken a sleeping pill? Or had the knife-wielding visitor already killed him? "Moon!"

The door opened and she flung herself at him. Martin, in a hotel bathrobe, caught her and held her till she could stop the awful mewling sound coming from her throat.

"Somebody—my room—broke in—knife, had a knife. Cut me. My chest, my stomach."

Martin pulled her into the light. "My God, where, where?" He touched her nightgown, looked at his fingers. Then she touched it. It was intact. She peeked down the neckline. No blood. No new marks.

"But I was sure—it stung—the knife—"

He hugged her again. "You're okay, babe. No one's going to hurt you now. You sure it wasn't a nightmare?"

"Not—not a dream—someone was there. Didn't say anything—just rubbed—rubbed the knife against me—knife like—like before." She gulped a sob.

"Jesus."

He walked her to the bed and sat her down. His face was a mask. His words were gentle but his voice was tight. He drew the bedspread around her shoulders, then pulled on his trousers.

What if he didn't believe her? What if he thought it was one of her crazy panic attacks? What if it was? What if it wasn't? Which was worse?

Dick's All-American Bar and Grill was a cool, dark lounge with sticky floors and smudged glassware. The place was nearly empty. The bartender—a big-boned black American gone to fat, with blurry tattoos and receding brown and gray hair—grunted toward a chalkboard when Jack asked about food. The choice was limited: hamburger, cheeseburger.

"Couple cheeseburgers and a beer. I just got here in Bangkok. Feeling a little disoriented. You Dick?"

The man squinted at him as he put a filmy glass on the bar, along with a large bottle of a beer called Singha. "Why'n't you go sit at a table so's I can concentrate," he said in a resonant baritone, as he turned to slap some meat on the grill.

Booths, lit by small sconces, lined the room. At one of them, a woman sat—or rather sprawled, her back against the wall and one foot up on the bench. She was shuffling through papers and typing into a laptop, while she smoked and sipped a ruddy brown liquid from a shot glass. With beer in hand, Jack sat at a table nearby.

"Good brand of sipping whiskey?" he asked, gesturing toward the bottle.

She glanced up, gave him an ice-blue stare, and went back to her work. Strangely, the look made him wish he'd gotten a regular short haircut instead of wearing the stupid ponytail that one of his sixth-graders had insisted was back in style.

The woman was gorgeous, in a strapping, athletic way: leggy, tan, buttery blonde hair twisted into a braid, wearing a white camp shirt, khaki shorts, and heavy walking shoes with short white socks.

When the bartender brought the burgers and another beer, Jack noticed that it was the woman's turn to sneak glances at him. The meat smelled gamey but Jack was too hungry to be fussy. As he took a big bite, the woman fixed her gaze on him, her mouth slightly open, pink tongue against snowy teeth—which might have set him a-tingle except that a stream of hot grease ran down his arm and the loathsome taste of the meat swamped his senses.

He gagged, grabbed a napkin to wipe his arm, and quickly debated whether to swallow the rancid mouthful or cough it into the napkin. In a split second he figured that the embarrassment of spitting it out wasn't half as bad as up-chucking.

The blonde smirked and he glared at her. "T'isn't beef," she said in clipped King's English. "Some sort of water buffalo, I suspect. And the grease is well-aged, no doubt. Dick's customers don't come in for the cuisine."

Jack might have smiled too if he weren't so damn hungry and if the smell wasn't still threatening to turn his stomach. "I only came here because a guy at the hotel recommended the food."

"Obviously a sadist." Her face got serious again. "Only reasons I come here are the air conditioning and the reliable current." Jack saw where the computer was plugged into the bottom of the sconce. She gestured toward the bar. "And Truman. Truman's a prince. And, well, I know the owner. Here, try this." She reached into a paper bag, pulled out an odd-looking green roll and handed it to him. "It's sticky rice in banana leaves. Simple, but fresh. Mind, you don't eat the leaves."

He unwrapped the packet and spooned some into his mouth. Delicious.

"Jack Scanlan," he said after another bite and a swallow of beer.

"Ingrid Lundquist. I'm working on my D.Phil.—archaeology."

While her husky voice and serious demeanor projected maturity, her face had the soft, unformed look of youth.

"Look pretty young for a doctoral student. Must be bright."

Ingrid shrugged. "Bright enough. I'm planning to make a name for myself in Southeast Asian archaeology and art history, concentrating on the Khmer Empire from the eleventh to the fourteenth centuries. I turned twenty-three this year and just got my second article published in the *Journal of Field Archaeology*. So I'm right on target."

Jack couldn't suppress a sigh. She sounded like his ex-wife, who bee-lined her way through med school into a prestigious Manhattan thoracic surgery practice. For Jack at that age, goals were what other people had. Football was his father's goal. Cornell was Monica's. Teaching hadn't been a goal. It just happened. Like Theresa. He did make ballet *her* goal, because he thought she was too pretty for basketball. The only real goal he ever had was the current one: get through each day without disaster to Theresa or to himself, in that order.

"What brings you to Thailand?" Ingrid asked.

"Oh, I came with two friends who are here on business. They're art dealers. I was ready for a vacation, so they invited me along. We're around the corner at the Tudor."

She straightened from her slouch. "What sort of art dealers?"

"Let's see, Delia Rivera, more of a broker, buys antique stuff for museums, whatever is on their list. Martin Moon, antiquities of one sort or another, statues and stuff. They're here looking for..." He was such a dunce. He'd heard them talk about what they were looking for, but he didn't remember. "For some really old stuff. Maybe what you said, Khmer. I dunno, I'm just along for the ride."

"Another set of bandits." Her voice was cold. "How can you bear to travel with such jackals?"

"Hey, they're the good guys. They wouldn't steal anything. They don't do black market."

"Ha!" A brittle laugh. "Southeast Asia is being strip-mined of its treasures by so-called honest dealers who close their eyes to the fact that the locals are plundering undocumented archeological sites and forging export licenses left and right. Don't you realize the loss to scholarship? We discover something new, only to find that the idol-runners have gotten there first, tramped all over everything, and stolen the best pieces. Your friends may think they're above all that, but it's their big bucks that encourage the looters."

Jack scratched his head. "Guess I never really thought about that kind of thing."

"Perhaps if your consciousness were raised a little, you'd be able to—to help your friends understand what we're fighting for. It's a matter of preserving a country's patrimony, don't you see?"

"Yeah." Jack really wasn't sure what she was talking about. He couldn't remember what the hell *patrimony* meant, if he ever knew.

Before she could go on, a man stalked into the bar and rushed toward them. "Ingrid. What in bloody hell are you still doing here? It's half past five and I'm bloody tired of waiting out in the sun." He was Australian by the sound of him, a lanky auburn man with a mustache, thinning hair, and no manners.

Ingrid unplugged and folded up her computer, stashed everything into her rucksack and, without giving Jack another look, stood up. As she turned to leave, slinging the bag over one shoulder, Jack noticed again how striking she was: square shoulders, straight back tapering to a narrow waist that flared to slim hips, atop long, perfect legs. And tall, maybe five-ten.

Dick's All-American was filling with patrons—mostly Asians—and over a cheap speaker an instrumental version of "Stormy Weather" muffled the voices. The Aussie muttered something to Ingrid and suddenly gave her a shove that made her lose her balance and fall backward.

In a single lunge from his chair, Jack caught her. "Hey, watch out," he yelled.

Jack had acted on instinct. His hands were still gripping Ingrid's shoulders, sensing whether she was stable on her feet, when he realized how boldly he'd stuck his king-sized body into someone else's business.

The Aussie apparently agreed. As Ingrid squirmed away, he closed the distance to Jack and jabbed him on the shoulder.

"Who the hell are you?" the Aussie shouted.

Jack moved his hands away from his body and stepped back. He was no brawler. "Somebody who doesn't like to see women punched around." Jack heard chair legs scraping on the floor, saw people standing, saw Truman lumbering from behind the bar. It suddenly struck him funny that everyone thought there was going to be a fight. He took another step back and grinned to the crowd.

A flash of fist smashed his face. Jack stumbled backward against a booth.

"Mind who you muck with around here, bucko," the Aussie said.

As the stars were clearing from Jack's eyes, Truman handed him a rag. "Tryin' a be a hero, get you killed, man. Take this here and go wash the blood off. Toilet's over there. Give you an icepack when you come out."

With bar patrons still staring, Jack squared his shoulders and tried to march with dignity toward the men's room. The cut wasn't much, a scratch really, but his eye watered and was beginning to swell. When he returned to the bar, Truman handed him a towel filled with ice and set a bottle of Singha in front of him. "Dick's sorry for the way Cal acted up. Drinks on the house till you feel okay to leave."

Jack followed the bartender's line of sight to a natty Asian man, dressed in a white suit, seated at a table with two others. The man nodded to Jack.

"That's All-American Dick?"

"Dick loves Americans, better believe it. Need any dope, Dickie'll fix you right up. Loves Americans. He's a great guy, I ain't lyin.'"

Jack stayed on. Between little clusters of customers, he talked to Truman Blue. In his slow, bassfiddle of a voice, Truman explained how he had deserted his unit in Vietnam in 1966 and had been in Bangkok ever since.

"My best buddies done got killed. I went a little crazy and killed a bunch of gooks. Called 'em gooks back then. When my head cleared, I seen they was all little girls and I was up for some fuckin' medal. Couldn't tell who was more fuckin' insane, me or the gooks or the army. Got the fuck out, fast. Practically walked the whole width of Cambodia to get to Thailand. You in Nam?"

"No. College deferment." The phrase felt prissy. "Then a bad shoulder 4F'd me."

"Lucky. Wisht I coulda gone to college. Too dumb. Got booted outta high school and got drafted practically the day I registered. Can't complain though, way things turned out. Got me a good job and a mighty sweet

58

woman. Only folks like Cal ruin it. He a nasty sumbitch. Tore after me once over a bar tab. Like to break my jaw."

It took Jack till closing time—hours of meandering conversation and a gallon of Singha—to get going back to his room at the Tudor. He had become comfortable at Dick's All-American Bar and Grill, with his new pal Truman. And he yearned for another glance at the long-legged Ingrid.

When Delia calmed and slumped against him, Martin helped her stretch out, tucked the sheet around her, then curled himself against her. He apologized for forgetting to unlock the connecting door. She slept. He stared into the darkness. The week in Rochester, waiting for their visas, had been peaceful. They'd been quiet together, dealing with their to-do lists, fixing meals, being as chaste as a couple of nuns. Her energy had wide swings but the panic attacks had been brief, manageable.

Now… Thailand. And the calm had shattered. How utterly ridiculous to be here again, in this country that had already once smashed his frail vessel.

He laid a hand on her hip. He wanted to whisk Delia away to safety. Then he wondered if he was ready to be in love again.

In the past couple months he saw women he was attracted to—one of the lawyers at the firm he was using and a nurse who worked out at the same gym. He had a lifetime of practice making small talk, but the idea of an evening or even a lunch full of light-hearted chatter—no.

He needed someone who shared a past with him. Like Delia. But damn, they'd been a bad pair. The good parts had been great. Wild. The rush to intimacy, frantic kisses, fervid embrace, feverish discarding of only enough clothing to… But then came the arguing, the endless haggling over constructing a life together.

But here she was, in his bed, in his arms but not in his arms. Had Delia changed? Had he? Of course, they'd each changed in a thousand ways over the years. And still, hadn't she always flitted just beyond his reach…?

Martin dreamed he was running alongside a creek, chasing after a trout.

The trout would drop deep, out of sight, then rise to nip at the mayflies on the surface. He knew this fish, longed to possess her, but the waters needed her. Suddenly, there were men ahead—men with grappling hooks and nets. Martin called out to warn her but the stream suddenly exploded. Blood everywhere. He screamed.

His eyes snapped open to the glare of a tropical morning. Delia was gone.

Jack battled with a shower head positioned for a race of people five-foot-five, shaved, and examined the greenish purple fistprint that threatened to close his eye. He was dressed and pondering the pile of yesterday's sweaty clothes, when he heard pounding on the door that connected to Martin's room.

He unlocked it. Martin barged in. "Have you seen—what the hell happened to your eye?"

"Uh, well, I got hungry last night and went out and some guy sucker-punched me when I interfered in a fight he was having with his girlfriend and—"

"Have you seen Delia this morning?"

"I just got up, haven't been—"

"Sonofabitch."

Martin turned back into his room. Jack followed.

"Did you check her room?"

"Oh, for christsake, of course I checked her room. But she spent the night in here because she said somebody broke into her room and threatened her with a knife. She was hysterical. I don't know whether it was a fucking dream or if some creep's been following her all along."

"Uh... maybe we should call the police?"

"Maybe we should find her and get the hell out of here. I knew this was a bad idea from the start. I knew this was going to be a disaster." He tapped his fist against the door jamb. "And you. How the hell did you manage to get in trouble the first few hours you're here? Didn't you ever learn how to dodge a right?"

Jack opened his mouth, but Martin veered back to Delia.

"She's gotta know that a stunt like this would make me crazy. What, am I supposed to sit here and wait? Sit here and worry that she's been lured away by some lunatic? This is so typical." He closed his eyes and took a deep breath. "Get a grip, get a grip, think... Savani. She was going to make contact with Tony Savani, a collector who lives here part of the year, maybe that's where she went."

Jack watched Martin as he cajoled the hotel operator into finding the number for Savani's Bangkok residence, then placed the call. But Savani was out and the person answering could not say where he'd gone.

While Martin spoke on the phone, he fumbled on his reading glasses and flipped through the flyers and pamphlets that came with each room. He picked out a booklet called *Thaiways: A Guide for Tourists & Businessmen*. When he hung up, he grabbed a pen and opened out the map on the inside cover.

"You don't mind helping me look for her, do you?"

"No, but..."

"Look." Martin made an X on the east bank of the sinuous Chao Phraya River. "There's a high-class shopping mall *here* catering to the rich tourists who stay at the Oriental or the Royal Orchid. Called River City. Third floor's all antique stores. Good place to touch base with a lot of dealers at once—she might have gone there—although I'll be damned if I know why she'd—" He shook it off. "If you find her, stay with her, okay? I'll check some of the more scattered shops, but first I'm going to do what I should have done days ago and that's call Jones-White to see what he knows and why he pushed Delia into this."

"Sure, but..." Jack stared helplessly at the map, his sore eye watering with the effort. "I managed to find my way around the corner to a bar, but how do I go about...?"

"Taxis. Did you change money?"

Jack nodded.

"There's a guy out front who arranges taxis. Everyone'll understand *River City Shopping*. Make sure you bargain with the driver. Once you get there, you'll find a lot of people speak passable English. And grab a card for the hotel so you can find your way back. Thanks, man."

Martin gave Jack a pat on the back that doubled as a shove out the door. "Let's meet back here at five."

"*Tuk-tuk? Tuk-tuk?*"

Before Jack had a chance to inquire about a taxi, a smiling boy with a missing tooth and long hair offered an alternative that looked like it might be fun.

It wasn't. *Tuk-tuks* were red and gold motorized versions of the three-wheel pedicab, sort of a wide motorcycle with a roof. While it maneuvered slightly better than automobiles along the jammed streets, it offered no protection from the heat or from the black exhaust fumes belched by the vehicles in front of it.

Jack tried to follow their route with the map, but the vibration made it impossible to focus on the small print. His eyes burned. The noise—of *tuk-tuks*, taxis, buses, and hordes of motorcycles—was deafening. No wonder there was little pedestrian traffic along this major boulevard. The pedestrians he saw—mostly people waiting for buses—held handkerchiefs over their mouths and noses.

By contrast, River City was the kind of glittering galleria that might have graced any upscale riverfront in the world. He expected to see Sharper Image, Abercrombie & Fitch, and Neiman-Marcus. But, as the man at the Jasmine Palace had said, the westernness was only superficial. An incomprehensible exhibition of Chinese booksellers monopolized the atrium. The first two floors, full of shops featuring silk goods, gemstones, and local handicrafts, were crowded with tourists and cliques of Thai teenagers.

The Thai women were uniformly beautiful, with their heavy black hair, delicate shapes, and large, liquid brown eyes. They excited him. But why? Why now? After years of self-imposed celibacy, why was he so agitated? In spite of the cooled air, he was sweating.

The third-floor shops were hushed and relatively deserted. After visiting three or four, Jack found them identical in their crowded displays of Buddhas—small, large, wooden, bronze, stone—frightening in their tranquility. Jack spent as little time as possible in each shop, backing out with a shy smile as soon as one of the solicitous clerks approached him.

Delia was nowhere. When he finally walked out into the melting afternoon, he didn't have to worry about hailing a cab. They were everywhere, eager for his business. He was definitely a long way from Rochester.

By late afternoon, his only purchase had been a red baseball cap against the sun, and now against the hard rain sweeping the streets. He found himself in front of Dick's All-American Bar and Grill.

His buddy Truman invited him to pull up a stool, but Jack spied the person he really wanted to see: Ingrid, in her booth, with her papers, her cigarette, and her bottle of whiskey. Beer in hand, an excited flutter in his stomach, he sauntered over to her, twisted a bentwood chair around backwards, and sat.

"Need a break?"

"No," she said, then looked up. Sighed. "Cal gave you quite a smack, didn't he?"

"What about you? He push you around like that very often?"

She tossed her head. "Cal—Caleb Clearwater—can be a bit melodramatic, but he's a wizard at getting fat grants... and he's my boss. Sorry you got socked, but perhaps you should mind your own business from now on." She went back to her papers, then, on second thought, pushed a plastic bag toward him. "Here, help yourself to some jackfruit. It's fresh. Truman's wife Eeju opened it up a minute ago."

The pulp of the jackfruit consisted of pale bite-sized pieces about the shape of small figs. The texture was smooth against his tongue, like an avocado, and the flavor was a rich burst of vanilla... and a little almond.

"Are you two—you and this Clearwater fellow—an item?"

She barked her brittle little laugh. "I told you: I'm their assistant—Cal and another fellow. Started about a month ago. They have a three-year grant from the Savani Foundation. We share a dumpy little apartment. It's cheaper than a hotel. We can stash our belongings there while we travel around. I'm trying to get this report done before we head up-country again on Tuesday. Don't have time for relationships."

He leaned forward, relaxing his forearms on the table. Ingrid eased away, pulling her foot up on the bench, her calloused knee a barrier between them.

"Where are your friends?" she asked. "Out arranging to ship a container of rare Buddhas back to the States?"

He wondered if her smiles were ever free of irony and changed the subject. "Why don't you tell me about your work."

She didn't need much encouragement.

"You do know what Angkor Wat is?"

Jack groped for an answer. "Sure. Some kind of temple in Cambodia... Khmer religion... uh..."

"Some kind of temple is right. The largest among twenty temples in Angkor. The largest religious edifice in the world. And it's Buddhist, Mahayana Buddhist. Khmer refers to the great Khmer Empire that spread into Thailand and reached its peak around the eleventh to thirteenth centuries."

Jack was noticing how blond her eyelashes were as he chewed more jackfruit.

"My only regret is not having any video gear with me. The fellows have a super system. Video keeps what you're seeing and what you're saying all nicely synchronized. Saves taking a heap of field notes."

When Truman came over to check Jack for a refill, Jack asked about Ingrid's drink.

"Mekhong whiskey. Cheap rice liquor. Regulars have their own bottles."

Jack bought a pint and let the rummy flavor warm his throat.

"My current project is really exciting," she continued. "Already we've discovered a brand new site from the old Khmer kingdom. Twelfth century, we think. It's been quite a surprise to find a site that far north. Actually, there's more than the fellows know, but I'm keeping a little information to myself, to qualify for a grant of my own. But listen, have you ever really looked at classic Khmer sculpture?"

"I visited River City this afternoon and saw carloads of Buddhas. Which ones have those little doodads on their heads?"

"Flames."

"What?"

"The *doodads* are flames. You're probably thinking of late Ayutthaya and Bangkok period pieces. Those aren't the ones I mean. I find them rather effete, don't you?"

Ingrid's leg finally came off the bench and her knee poked Jack's as she leaned forward and shaped the air with her hands. "Khmer idols are square, muscular, somewhat stiff. You must have seen reproductions at least..."

Her face was close. He murmured, "Big square forehead, wide mouth, full lips, and a shit-eatin' little grin?"

She laughed, no irony. "You do know them. Powerful, aren't they?"

"Quite."

"But what you see in museums and galleries can't compare with the natural context. Museums are like seeing a tiger in a taxidermy shop." Her voice became huskier. "Only in the jungle does the drama emerge. The stone is cool, ascetic, aloof." She laid a hand on her glass, caressing the rim. "And the jungle embraces the immobile rock with heated, thriving passion. The scene is quite erotic." She drank.

Quite.

"Doesn't your excavation cut the jungle back?" he asked. "Remove its... lovegrip?"

"That's the eternal struggle, isn't it? Classic forms against rampant romanticism. Discipline versus self-indulgence. Spirit struggling to overcome the flesh. When the sculptors of Angkor abandoned the classical forms for a more naturalistic style, giving in to the romance of the jungle around them, their work ground to a halt. The jungle closed in. It's the balance that's important. The tension."

Jack suddenly felt hot and studied his watch.

"What do you know, it's nearly five and my friends are expecting me. And we don't want to risk getting old Cal riled up again."

She gripped his arm. "One more thing. A favor. I have a favor to ask. This work of mine is important to Thailand. And to me. Please tell your dealer friends to give us a break. Please ask them not to demand better and better pieces till the idol-runners are forced deeper and deeper into pristine territories. The stuff that's already plundered should keep them satisfied for decades."

Jack laid his hand on hers but the electricity in the gesture made him draw it away. "Sure, Ingrid. But do me a favor too. Don't let Cal manhandle you, no matter how clever he is."

"I do what I need to do. But I'm in control, don't worry."

After Martin got Jack out the door, he dug into his wallet for his American Express card and the tattered list of his important numbers, neatly handwritten a lifetime ago. The card contained his numbers for Edwin Jones-White, his ex-employer. Or was he employed again? Delia had assured him she'd taken care of the paperwork.

Jones-White Investigations had two centers, one in London, and the other an apartment in St. Cloud, France, near the headquarters of its biggest client, Interpol. Edwin Jones-White, now in his seventies, had once been an Interpol agent, getting his start in the field of art-theft recovery after World War II, tracking down treasures hidden away by the Nazis.

Relieved that the AmEx card worked, Martin called St. Cloud, where it was 6 a.m.

"Jones-White," the voice answered, sounding as close as the next room.

"Edwin, it's Martin Moon."

"Martin, my boy. Can it really be you?" His voice quavered slightly. "Are you here? In France? London? Are you all right? Glory, it's good to hear your voice. I worry so... Listen to me, I'm babbling."

"I'm fine, Edwin, really fine. And I'm sorry I haven't been in touch." He'd only spoken to Edwin briefly, months ago, shortly after Lana's death and in an alcoholic haze. Since then, his lawyer had handled the dreary business of documenting his pay from Jones-White for the Tuthill people—a tricky business since Martin and Lana made that income appear on their books as *appraisals*, rather than *confidential informant* or *art recovery services*, a precaution against snooping by the wrong people.

"As long as you're okay, that's what counts. I take it the case with Emmaline Tuthill rages on. I received a subpoena for more information last week. Is that what you're calling about?"

"No, I arrived in Thailand yesterday. With Delia, of course."

Jones-White missed a beat. "Oh. Marguerite told me she'd heard Delia was headed in that direction. I'd rather hoped she'd decided against giving up everything for the bloke. But she deserves some happiness, after all she's been through, poor dear. But still... Funny that you should be with her... but then I never did make heads or tails of what went on between you two."

A little ache began to gnaw at the back of Martin's head. Why hadn't he called the old man from Rochester? Why had he let Delia handle everything? "Edwin, Delia came to me, to Rochester, and said you were eager to get me back to work."

"True enough. I have a pile of unsigned contracts you'd be perfect for."

"But she had a case, for the two of us."

"Nothing from this office."

"The case involves Khmer sculpture—Lopburi style—of suspicious provenance."

66

"I tore up that contract weeks ago. It was something the HAWC-I lads were hot and bothered about. They laid out all the facts but neglected to mention that they still had their amateur sleuths prying into the matter. We learned what a disaster that could be at Mae Sot, didn't we? Anyway, Delia discovered a *possible* connection to the murder of a French archaeologist there. You can't believe the state she came to me in, hysterical with fear and excitement, certain she'd latched onto the bugger who killed Lana and hurt Delia herself so badly. My heart broke for her. But I said, 'Enough!' and tore up the contract."

"You terminated the contract?" Martin sank back into the chair and massaged the nape of his neck. In his befuddlement, a small light went on. Jones-White knew his address in Rochester, but Delia didn't get it from him because she and Edwin hadn't actually talked about recruiting Martin. There was no contract. That's why she'd called on his father for his whereabouts. It was a sign of his rustiness that he hadn't immediately picked that up.

"Terminated it, indeed!" Edwin said. "Between the HAWC-I bullies and someone vicious enough to kill over smuggled art, I backed out. Delia's been through too much. I love her like a daughter. And I need to protect my people. With Lana gone and you run off, how could I dare put my darling Delia in the crosshairs? I'd be out of Asian antiquities altogether, not that I won't be anyway if she throws her lot in with what's-his-name."

"Which what's-his-name—?"

But Edwin was on a roll. "Did you know, Martin, that over the years Delia turned out to be my most productive agent? Always a steady stream of information, always rock solid, thoroughly checked out. And the amount of loot she recovered—a fantastic amount, merely by her steady chipping away, by her becoming the most discrete of all fences. None of the flamboyance of a Lana Tuthill, none of Lana's need for splash and glamour and danger. And, mind you, none of the angst of a Martin Moon. A real yeoman, that girl. And like a daughter to me. But now, must I really lose her to that—that—"

Martin's ears were ringing now and he leaned forward.

"Savani! Tony Savani, how could I forget. Not a bad chap, but not cut out for my operation either. Too bloody rich. Lana was rich too, but she had a different kind of—"

"Listen, Edwin, Delia hasn't confided in me about Savani. But she is on the HAWC-I project. She's paying for me and another fellow, friend of mine, as if it's out of her expense account. She's taking a purseful of pills for some kind of panic attacks and claims someone broke into her room last night. Scared the hell out of her. But then she ran off this morning before I woke up and I don't know where she is. Now you're telling me this isn't even an authorized case. I'm... out of my mind."

Jones-White asked calmly, "What do you want to do?"

"I want to find her and get us the hell out of here."

"Mmmm... you think that's smart? Delia has her own plans, you know."

"Why aren't the Thai authorities all over it? Why isn't this simply an Interpol issue?"

"Why not, indeed? I suspect the smuggling is back-burnered and no one in law enforcement is bothering to draw the map of mayhem. No one but Delia is connecting the dots."

Martin's mind raced. They'd come too far already. If he confronted Delia with her lie, she'd only dig in her heels. The project was more than a "job" and Delia had known that. If she was willing to risk her own safety for the truth and if he loved her, then his choice was clear, wasn't it?

But what about this thing with Tony Savani? Was she in love with someone else? Was she using him, abusing their friendship, to clear the decks for someone else? His face burned at the thought. No. Delia might launch herself into crazy projects but she wasn't a user. Anyway, maybe he had truths of his own that needed facing. He needed to be part of the world again.

"All right, Edwin. Here's the deal. We'll keep it simple," Martin said, trying to straddle the line between retreat and insanity. "We'll poke around for information, then pass it along to the authorities without getting our own hands dirty. S.O.P."

"Yes... trust the process. Makes sense. Why don't I chat up the St. Cloud fellows while I'm here. Maybe we can work something out. You'll be in a much better position with their blessing if things go awry like last time. Meanwhile, the firm will underwrite your expenses, don't worry."

"Nothing will go awry, trust me. But a little official backing wouldn't hurt." He gave the old man the hotel number and rang off.

Martin slumped back in the chair. Despite his decision, he wasn't at all happy. What the hell was wrong with Delia that she dragged him to Thailand on a pretense? *Don't you remember her scars, Marty? And the wild look of panic in her eyes? She needs you.* From his shirt pocket he took the Egyptian fish amulet that Delia had given him, that he'd carried for some reason ever since. He slipped it out of the silky bag and rubbed his thumb along the length of it. If this little fish had swum through two thousand years of history without breaking, maybe Martin would make it through today. And tomorrow.

If he was going to be angry at anybody, it should be himself, for screwing up so badly the last time he was here. Somehow that was the beginning of this whole nightmare—Lana's death, Delia's assault—and here he was again… to pay for his sins…

His father's harsh judgments sprang to mind. *Good Lord, Marty*, Winston Moon would say, *you've made a mess of things.*

Winston Moon was a gruff old economist whose single romantic blunder was to fall in love with the Basque émigré Kattalin Elizondo on a World Bank project in Paris after the War. The product of their union was Martin—a darkeyed, hyperactive, rebellious throwback to his Basque grandfather. And a lifelong pain in the butt to Winston.

It wasn't that Winston didn't love his son. It was just such an obvious strain to do so. In Winston's book, the men in Kat's family had been certifiably mad, no matter how heroically they died in Basque uprisings. His job was to save Marty from that madness and, by his own account, Winston had failed. Marty was Mr. Sociable in school, with mediocre grades. *Underachiever.* He majored in history. *Useless.* Instead of going to law school, he got a job at an antiquities emporium. *Irrelevant.* Instead of buying a house, he bought art. *Terrible investment.* And instead of settling near home, Marty moved to London. *Socialists!* Marriage—divorce—marriage. *Unstable.*

The last time he saw his parents was when they had dreamed up an excuse to pass through London after he and Lana arrived home from the Thai debacle. They found their son hobbled, drunk, and disgraced. The pain on their faces said it all. Yes, he felt the fierce love in his father's embrace, but Martin himself filled in the speech-bubble: *catastrophe.*

Martin tried to make it better by telling them about the undercover work, explaining that the deportation order would be expunged as soon as the dust settled on the case. His mother was thrilled. "An idealist, just like papa," she murmured. Winston merely shook his head.

When Lana died, Martin had resigned himself to his father's harshest judgment. But look at him now. He'd made a mess of his life, all right. But he survived. And he was starting over.

He looked at the phone. Maybe he'd call them. No, he needed to find Delia first.

THREE

As soon as Delia spied Tony Savani entering the coffee shop of the Siam Intercontinental Hotel, her pulse quickened. She made the appointment days ago, sitting in Martin's kitchen, where her strategy made perfect sense. But now it felt nutty. Trying to pursue a relationship with Tony on one level while she worked with Martin to find Bellingham on another was lunacy. A year ago she could have pulled it off. Now it was a longshot.

Already this morning she'd endured a sweaty panic, jerked awake by a sigh from a warm figure curled against her, no less disturbing for being only Martin.

Tony's face broke into a big grin when he saw her. "You," he said. She caught his hands and squeezed them before he sat down across from her. "You, you, you. My, God, Delia, we were apart too long. When I left you in London last month I had no idea how desperately I'd crave seeing you." He paused to study her face. His eyes were a haunting opal blue, made more dramatic by his olive skin, black hair, and gaunt face. "Are you all right?"

"Sure, but..." She took a breath. "But look, Tony, I think I'm being followed."

His smile faded. "What's this? Tell me."

A waiter set cups of coffee, glasses of papaya juice, and a plate of sliced pineapple between them. Before she could tell her story, Tony clucked. "You can't live on coffee and fruit." He sent the waiter for a portion of *jok*—rice porridge. "Now go on."

"Someone came into my room last night—with a knife—like the one that..." She stopped. Tony visibly stiffened, pushing back on his chair. He'd heard about her night terrors for months.

"Are you taking the medicines Dr. Courtland prescribed?"

"Yes," she said. "But last night, it wasn't a dream. I'm sure it wasn't."

He closed his hands around the juice glass and gazed into it. "I know," he said, "they seem so real." The pale eyes met hers again. "The trunk you sent from London arrived safely and your room is ready. A work space, too. You are planning to stay with me at the *khlong* house, aren't you? No phantom, real or otherwise, will ever threaten you again, I promise."

She missed her mouth and a drip of papaya juice splashed on her blouse. *Jesus.* Quickly, she dabbed it with a napkin. They were going to have to talk. For her own good, she couldn't live by riddle and innuendo much longer.

"Tony, what do you want from me? I mean, I'm having a hard time sorting out where this relationship is going. It's social but it's also business. We talked about my doing your traveling, your art buying for you. But then again, lately..." She felt her heart rate speed up. "You're sweeping me off my feet. This business about moving in with you—I can't tell if it's a job offer or a proposal... of a different nature..."

"Delia..." There was a long pause as he looked around the crowded café. "Are you sleeping with Martin Moon?"

Despite her nerves, years of conditioning in delicate negotiations made her shoulders drop instantly to a relaxed position. "Pardon me?"

Tony's face showed no particular emotion, except for a subtle arch of an eyebrow.

"The truth is *no*." Her voice was tender. "I explained to you about me and Moon. I fell for him when I was a kid. He was an 'older man'—dashing and romantic. The marriage was a flop. We kept rewriting the second act, but never made it to Broadway." Martin's favorite image. "We couldn't find the right plotline to get us to happily-ever-after, so we finally threw out the script. He met Lana. We managed to stay friends. It happens."

Tony poked a slice of pineapple with his fork and studied it. "Last night, near midnight—I couldn't wait to hear your voice—I called your room at the Tudor, but there was no answer."

"I told you, I was terrorized by some jerk with a knife. I was out of my mind with fright. Yes, I ran to Martin's room. Yes, I slept there." The lie came smoothly. "But we slept in separate beds, in our street clothes. There's nothing that attracts me to him anymore." *Except the hair on his chest, the dense muscles in his shoulders, the tender pressure of his hands, the touch of his lips against my hair...*

"... to Bangkok?"

"Sorry, what?"

"I still don't understand why he came with you to Bangkok."

"Okay, look. I was in New York for the Sotheby's auction, planning to fly from there directly to Bangkok. But... I started freaking out. The crowded auction rooms, the hotel, restaurants—and then the prospect of twenty-four hours in an airplane—I choked. Didn't know what the hell to do. Then I learned Martin was up the road a piece in Rochester. I caught a roomy old train and sort of threw myself at him."

She took Tony's hand and his eyes filled with sympathy. He was buying it. And, really, it was in his own best interest to let her finish the Bellingham business.

"It was so peaceful there, at Martin's," she continued, "that I got a grip on myself. When I told him I needed to get to Bangkok, he insisted on going along to make sure I was all right. What I told you about him wanting to begin traveling and buying art again was true. He's still too broken up about Lana to get involved with anyone. We're old friends, that's all. I needed a hand and he was there."

Tony took a deep breath and smiled. "Delia, I love you."

Delia smiled, too, and half-bought her own story.

"The fact that you can't tell whether I'm interested in business or romance isn't surprising, darling. My life doesn't fall out into separate categories very easily. My home is my office. My work is my play. I keep my hand in the family business when a particular product line appeals to me. I keep tabs on Foundation projects that interest me. And then there's my passion for antiquities. Whatever gives me pleasure, I do. Whatever I want, I get. I've never felt much attraction to traditional family life. I can't say that I've never been lonely, but I've never felt it so acutely till now. Till you, Delia."

She found herself nodding as he went on.

"You're a kindred spirit, sucking up energy from the cosmic hunt. But you haven't had my advantages. You're caught on a treadmill, having to grub all over the world for bits of stone and wood without keeping any of it for yourself. I want to give you more. I want to give you the wherewithal to be your own master, an income that will free you to deal only in the best

73

merchandise, the opportunity to build your own collection. A chance to get rid of the anxieties, the panic attacks, the nightmares. And I want to be the one you turn to when you're afraid."

She laughed, suppressing a stab of horror that he was about to propose marriage. "Sounds wonderful. How do you plan to pull off this miracle?"

"I've created a new foundation. It will support a museum specializing in jade, lapis lazuli and other worked stones. The geographic scope would initially be China and South Asia, but might eventually expand to include such works from the world over."

Delia's ears pricked. The project dealt with precisely the kind of treasures she loved. Her pulse quickened—not the thready precursor to panic, but genuine excitement. "Fantastic. What does it have to do with me?"

"I want you to be the director. To run the whole show. By my side."

A million questions sprang to mind, but what she sputtered first was: "I don't—I can't—I don't have any credentials to run a museum. A B.A. in Art History isn't worth a hill of beans anymore—"

"So we'll hire a curator with the right letters after his name. What you have is connections, an eye for quality, and a knack for getting what you want. That's the key to a great museum. The trust fund will generate half a million U.S. dollars a year, which, if carefully spent, will make our place one of the great specialty museums of the world. I've already acquired some important collections for it."

Our place. Delia grasped Savani's arm. "You know this is a dream come true, don't you? My own museum. Being able to keep what I buy. Organize it. Display it. Attract visitors from all over the world." Her mind was racing. She would proceed cautiously, do a lot of buying through agents, and get the core of the collection completed before they went public. Any gossip that a new museum had megabucks to invest in jade would send the market into overdrive. Their cash wouldn't go far in a hyped up market.

"Then I've won you over?"

"I'm yours. When do we go back to London?"

"London?" He looked blank.

"Oh. The museum is here? In Bangkok?"

"The museum, my darling, will be in Chiang Mai, up north. The house up there is the one I consider my real home. And Chiang Mai is the hub of my family's business." He leaned forward. His eyes were teasing and excited. "It's the Golden Triangle, Delia, notorious for the opium business, of course, but it's really a nexus for international trade of all sorts. You'll be fascinated, I'm sure of it."

"What's wrong with Bangkok?"

He leaned back. "What isn't wrong with Bangkok? The place is strangling on its own carbon monoxide. The rivers and canals are cesspools. I can hardly breathe but can't bear the thought of retrofitting a clunky air conditioning system to my lovely old house here. Besides, it's far too public. I can't keep my best collections here without attracting a lot of unwanted attention. The Chiang Mai house has my best treasures.

"I see." She'd never been to Chiang Mai, but doubted it was the kind of lively metropolis she loved.

"Anyway, I'd like to get started on the museum project as soon as possible. First thing is to get you settled out at the *khlong* house. There's plenty of room if Moon and the other fellow—what's his name?—want to stay with us. My car is outside..."

There was no reason on earth that Delia could not immediately dive into the museum project—except for her obsession with finding Jeremy Bellingham.

"Jack Scanlan. Look, I still have business commitments to close out, things up in the air with half a dozen dealers here."

"But you can do that from—"

"I know, I know. Once I get used to tooling around on those river taxis, your place on the canal—the *khlong*—will probably be as convenient as anywhere. But I'm so used to working out of hotels and the staff at the Tudor know me by now... I just think I could get my business out of the way that much quicker. Then I'll be able to devote all my energies to this incredible project."

Tony frowned, but only for a second. "Of course. Don't let me pressure you. You'll come when you're ready, I know that. Meanwhile, I insist the three of you join me for dinner tonight."

From the cool of the Tudor, Martin plunged into the inferno of the Bangkok afternoon. A yellow haze hung in the air. His Panama hat was only marginally effective in shielding his head and eyes from the acid sun. Walking down the side street toward Sukhumvit Road, he fended off the crowd of taxi and *tuk-tuk* drivers.

"Where you going? Where you going? Shopping?" each of them offered.

At a small stand on the corner a woman was weaving garlands of jasmine buds. On impulse, Martin bought one and returned to the front of the hotel, to the large spirit house located there.

Dollhouse-sized spirit houses were erected here and there in front of modern buildings to give a home to the local deities ousted from the land. These gods demanded daily offerings of flowers and incense. In return, they granted good luck.

Martin, who had denounced Christianity to his horrified parents at the wise old age of twelve, preferred to believe that each person, place, and thing had its own divinity, its own life-force, call it *qi* or *mana* or *pneuma*—its own *breath*. That's what made his hands tingle when he touched sculpture or when he caressed a woman. Draping the garland over the fence that surrounded the spirit house, he gazed for a moment at the wooden figurines inside, then headed back up the street.

By the time he reached the boulevard again, sweat was seeping through his shirt. But that was the challenge for men who wore pale linen suits in the tropics. It was one of the few challenges on this trip he knew he could deal with. His trick was simply not to resist it. Be hot, but look cool. Don't loosen the tie, don't tug at the underpants, and don't furiously mop the brow and back of the neck with a crumpled up handkerchief. Wear sweat like a Gucci accessory.

Martin started off down Sukhumvit Road. The first shop he came to was new. He was pleased to start with a place where he'd be unknown, which is why he deliberately sent Jack to the River City Shopping Centre. The core of old dealers in Bangkok knew him well enough to be aware of the problems he'd had the last time and may even know about Lana's murder and his subsequent retirement from the trade. He'd have to face them eventually, but it couldn't hurt to put it off till he had his lines right.

The shop had little of interest and the shopkeeper drew a blank at the mention of Jeremy Bellingham. The second shop was also new to him and specialized in Chinese antiques—porcelains and heavily carved rosewood furniture. He moved on.

Three shops later, Siam Treasures took him by surprise. He'd forgotten it was in this neighborhood. The shop had been run by Joe Kesmanee for decades and Martin had traded regularly with him. He took off his hat, squared his shoulders, and prepared to meet his past.

The shop was deserted and the shelves held little but mass-produced reproductions of Southeast Asian artifacts—a far cry from the upscale collectibles Joe had specialized in. A woman sat behind a desk, talking on the phone. Sara Kesmanee. Joe's daughter.

When she hung up, he spoke. "*Khun* Sara?" he asked, using the common polite address. Like all Thais, the family did not use their polysyllabic surnames except in formal situations. Like Thais who catered to tourists, they had adopted western nicknames to relieve *farangs*—western foreigners—the embarrassment of mispronunciation. Martin had not seen her since she was a giggly teenager, fascinated with Lana's platinum hair.

Her look was blank. Deep creases had dug into her young brow.

"My name is Martin Moon. I did business with your father over the years. We met once or twice."

He extended his hand. She hesitated, then grazed it with cool fingers. "Father is very old, very sick, lives in Pattaya with my aunt. I am running shop now." Then she nodded. "You have wife with blond hair, much joking."

"Yes. But she's gone now." He forced out the word: "Dead."

The furrow in her brow deepened. "My husband is dead too. What would you like to see, Mr. Moon?" She stepped out from behind the desk.

"Joe used to do a lot of business in Khmer items. I have a few bronzes from the thirteenth century—post-Bayon Brahman figures—and a strong Angkor-period sandstone. Now I'm intrigued by Lopburi-style pieces, from Thailand. Know of anything?"

Sara stiffened. "The Antiquities Department forbids the export of antique Buddhas. Only very small pieces will pass customs. I do not sell such items anymore. Neither do I sell treasures from Cambodia or Burma. In the spirit of the UNESCO Convention." Her voice had a reedy, tense quality.

"Sure. But on the other hand, well, some of that stuff has been on the market for decades, long removed from any meaningful context. And it teaches the *farangs* so much about Thai history, don't you think?"

Martin's bluster covered his surprise at Sara's pronouncement. Laws and treaties never stopped Joe Kesmanee from courting a sale. Thais in general were much more accommodating to people than to regulations.

Her cheeks colored, as her eyes dropped to the floor. "I am sorry. Maybe I will go out of business. Ancient artifacts should stay in their country of origin no matter what. My husband wanted it that way. He was a very good man. He loved Thailand." She leaned against a rosewood armoire and hugged herself with slender arms.

"Did he help run the shop? Was he a merchant, too?"

She shook her head. "Archaeologist. Very smart. Study at Oxford in England."

"Was he Thai or English?"

"Neither. He was French. René Malraux."

Martin scratched his ear. *René Malraux.* Delia's third possible victim of the beast who murdered Lana. Without thinking, he asked, "Were you dealing with Jeremy Bellingham at the time of René's murder?"

Sara muttered something in Thai and pulled herself along the cabinets and shelving, back to her chair behind the desk. "Who are you working with, Mr. Moon? Why are you here? Can't you see I'm doing my best to—"

"Please, Sara, I had no idea... I've simply been going from shop to shop... But I know the name *René Malraux.* I heard he'd been murdered. You see, my—well, it's just that Jeremy Bellingham—"

A customer walked into the shop. Sara stood and, with a small bow, told the woman she'd be with her shortly. She rubbed her eye with the heel of a hand. "I have nothing to say about Jeremy Bellingham. Nothing."

The customer cleared her throat. Sara said, "I must go," and started to turn away.

"Please, you have to tell me what you know about Bellingham."

Martin reached out for Sara's arm, but when he touched her she jumped back as if she'd been slapped. She bumped into the chair and it tipped over with a bang. She managed a pained smile toward the curious customer, but her eyes turned frantic.

"Did they send you here? Are you one of them now, testing me, making my business your business?"

"Honestly, if we could talk... Please."

"Go away," she snapped and hurried toward the customer.

Outside, after the dank atmosphere of the shop, the sun dizzied him. His questioning had been ham-handed, his listening faulty. A third Bellingham connection was confirmed, but was he actually the murderer?

Martin walked toward the corner past a line of food stands, through a cloud of charcoal smoke and the dense aroma of seared pork.

Why was Sara so spooked? The look in her eyes went beyond grief. It was the same look Delia had when she flew into his arms last night. Did some menace, real or imagined, stalk her too? The fear was contagious. Someone was watching him. He spun around.

Sooty slabs of ribs hung on hooks over a blackened grill. A row of equally sooty barbecued chickens hung by their feet nearby. A sooty man with one tooth smiled and gestured at the meat. Martin's stomach knotted.

He hurried away, toward a woman squatted on the sidewalk selling green mangoes. He asked for one and endured watching her slice it with deft snaps of a cleaver—*whack, whack, whack, whack.* Then he stood there on the shimmering pavement, leaning against a building, taking slices from the plastic bag, dipping them into another little pouch of salt, sugar and red pepper, and letting his mouth explode with the clash of tart-hot flavors. He was alive. He was alive in this fearsome place.

Vehicles creeping out of the side streets were honking their way onto the jammed boulevard. All the car windows were deeply tinted and the cyclists wore helmets with full, dark face plates.

A young man, a westerner, approached and looked pointedly at Martin. He wore a net t-shirt, shorts, running shoes, and baseball cap. A camera was slung by its strap over his shoulder. Martin held his breath. But the boy only smiled and ambled by.

At five o'clock, Jack stood in Martin's room facing a man distraught that Delia hadn't reappeared. Then the connecting door sprung open and Delia breezed in with a big smile.

"Oh, jeez, I'm late. Sorry. My appointment with Tony took longer than I expected and I had to make a couple other stops. I always forget how miserable the air is here—like living inside a tailpipe. You weren't waiting long, were you?"

Martin stared at her.

She frowned. "I told you yesterday about the appointment, didn't I? Yesterday? On the plane? And that we'd regroup at 5? Didn't I? Jesus, Martin, don't look at me like that. I'm sure I did." She put a hand over her eyes, but not before Jack caught the look of confusion.

Martin shook his head. "Maybe I forgot."

"You didn't worry, did you?" she asked.

"About you? Never."

"Well, look, Tony's invited us out to his house for dinner. He lives on one of the canals across the river. It's quite a way what with the traffic and all. He suggested we spend the night so pack your toothbrushes."

"Would you prefer it..." Martin asked, "I mean, would you feel safer if you moved out to Savani's for the rest of our stay here?"

"No," she said quickly, "it wouldn't work out at all." The fine lines around her eyes seemed to deepen.

At seven, Savani's driver picked them up in the longest Mercedes Jack had ever seen. The inside of the six-door monster was lousy with leather, walnut, and lamb's wool. It was the first backseat that ever allowed Jack to stretch out his legs.

"I guess I gotta say I'm impressed by your friends," he said.

Martin was fiddling with the window, even though the air conditioning was set to perfection. "I gotta say I am too. This is a 'reconditioned' model—a 500 SEL stretched out by three or four feet. They were becoming popular around Europe a few years back."

The house was as awesome as the ride in the stretch Mercedes. Perched on the bank of the Khlong Bangkok Noi—a wide, busy canal off the Chao Phraya River, it was teakwood dark and opulent, every surface adorned with a colorful clash of silk, every piece of furniture an obvious collector's item, even to Jack's untutored eye.

Tony Savani greeted them—a large-boned man, thin, but robust—like a marathon runner, someone with the metabolism of a blast furnace. His big colorless eyes devoured the three of them, but when Martin clapped a friendly hand on his shoulder, he stiffened and eased away, murmuring condolences over Lana's death.

Tony led them to his library, while a willowy young woman called Lucky followed with a tray of canapés. Her beauty had a frightening quality. The refined Asian features were marred by garish red betel stains on her lips and teeth and her eyes were an arresting pale blue against her caramel skin.

Tony poured drinks from crystal decanters, presuming to know what each of them liked. Jack was pleased to taste bourbon, with a splash of water. Tony proposed a toast to new beginnings.

Martin was suddenly quiet, then the blue crystal glass slipped from his hand, splashing his drink on Delia's skirt as it fell. He stared down at the cracked goblet.

Quickly, Lucky began to clean up the mess, while Savani escorted Delia out to get cleaned up. Jack had to prod Martin out of Lucky's way.

"Martin?"

Martin seemed to snap out of a trance. "Jesus. I thought it was wine. It was gin, Bombay." His eyes were a million miles away. "What a jolt—all those desperate, desolate old feelings. Jesus."

But, by the time Delia and Savani returned, Martin had shaken off the spooks. He declined a refill.

The incident left Jack edgy, suspicious that somehow the gin had been a cruel joke, even though the idea was ridiculous. Martin seemed fine. He was joking about jetlag and the Bangkok heat, then went on to rave about some little prints Savani was showing them. Jack found the pictures ugly and the conversation opaque.

Delia must have sensed his discomfort. She pulled him back into the circle by telling Tony about Theresa and her ballet—a subject Jack was always prepared for. He pulled out his wallet full of pictures and showed off his photogenic baby.

Later, as he folded the photo insert back into his wallet, Savani tilted his head near. Softly, without altering the lilt of his perfectly cultured voice, he said, "She's a stunning beauty that girl of yours. I have a *penchant* for young blondes. How about you?"

Jack stared at him, speechless, then looked toward Martin and Delia, but they'd been distracted by Lucky and her plate of hors d'oevres. Savani turned away to answer a question and, when he turned back, the jarring remark seemed forgotten, as if Jack had hallucinated.

After dinner, Tony led Martin and Delia to his galleries to see some nineteenth-century photos of Bangkok, but Jack wandered back into the library. It was full of well-organized art references. Jack found a shelf of books on Khmer sculpture. He was thinking of Ingrid. He glanced through a couple of books that showed pieces exhibition-style, against cool-gray museum backdrops. Then he came upon a book about an ancient site under excavation. It was full of the kind of scene Ingrid had rhapsodized over: stony gods succumbing to the embrace of vines and roots. Jack slowly paged through the book. His black eye watered.

After a while the three others joined him.

"Find something of interest?" Savani asked.

"Yeah. Yesterday I met an English archaeology student who's found some new sites up north—one she's working on with a team and another she's apparently keeping to herself. She was waxing poetic about seeing ancient statuary in its natural context. Says it's erotic."

"Gawd," Savani said. "No doubt a virginal little girl sent over from one of the women's colleges—they have an astounding capacity to see sex in everything around them—except men."

"If truth be told," Savani went on, "that ancient sculpture is better off out of the damn jungle. Mind you, I love what our archaeologists are doing to preserve some of the monuments *in situ*, but, really, unless they're diligently maintained, either the tree roots tear them apart or the pollution crumbles them to bits. And the kind of preventive maintenance they need gobbles up cash, take it from me. Oh, say, your girl wasn't Ingrid Lundquist, was it?"

Jack nodded.

"How on earth did you manage to meet her within hours of arriving?"

Jack mentioned Dick's All-American Bar and Grill.

"Hmmm... she's quite the darling of the young archaeology set. Talked me out of a grant to survey Angkor last winter. Did a super job—worthy of *National Geographic*. Keeping a new find to herself, eh? She'll use it, no doubt, to jockey for another fellowship. I find scholars extremely competitive. But I hate to hear she's been rapturing over the *erotic thrill* of the jungle. Any archaeologist worth her salt should be more committed to real preservation than to romantic visions." He guffawed again. *Haw-haw.*

They chatted a while longer and, finally, Delia mentioned needing sleep.

Savani caught her hand.

"Before we call it a night, my dear, I wonder if you told your friends our news." Ignoring her small sound of protest, Savani went on. "Within a week or so Delia will be moving in with me here, abandoning the rat race of the trade and assuming the directorship of a new jade museum in Chiang Mai. The Savani Museum."

Jack felt a sudden tilt in his universe. *Savani?* Delia had gone to such great lengths to get herself to Rochester, to give Martin the hard sell about joining her, but it turns out she's throwing her lot in with this jackass, with his Park Avenue affectations, and his *penchant* for young blondes?

He watched Delia's eyes seek out Martin.

"Isn't that exciting," Martin said, breaking out a generous smile. "I wish you both the best." He shook Savani's hand, then placed his hands lightly on Delia's shoulders and let his cheek graze hers.

The announcement made, his territory staked out, Savani showed them upstairs to their bedrooms.

"You're sure you don't want to take a dip in the pool before bed?" Savani asked them. "It lowers the body temperature, makes sleep come more easily."

They all declined and separated to their rooms. While Martin's and Delia's rooms were on the canal side of the house, Jack's overlooked a courtyard, a humid overgrowth of trees and plants that accommodated the wading pool.

The heavy canal air and a mild anxiety made Delia restless. Finally remembering her nightly dose of vitamins, she rose, swallowed the pills with a glass of water and stood gazing out her window. The canal was quiet now. Below, on the deck that ran along the water, she spotted a fellow insomniac. Martin. Maybe this would be a good time to clear up the whole Savani business with him.

Delia wrapped herself in a cotton robe from the trunk she'd sent ahead and found her way in the dark to Martin's side.

"Hot 'nough for you?" she murmured.

He grunted and crossed his arms.

"Are you mad at me?"

"Thought we weren't going to have secrets, that's all. Drives me crazy."

With the moon at his back, she barely saw the contours of his face, but his voice was tight.

"It really only transpired today. I mean, the friendship's been growing for some time now and he's been after me to move here, to be his agent, but the museum thing, that was a surprise, today. It's great though, isn't it, I mean, isn't it—?"

"Am I supposed to believe you can track down Bellingham with me and start up a museum with Tony at the same time? What does he know about—?"

"Nothing. Obviously, we'll finish the case first. But I can't turn my back on this offer. It's an opportunity of a lifetime."

"Is it?"

"I'm forty years old. I lost months of work this year and my savings disappeared. Tony got me on my feet again. With his help I tripled my income. His advice has been flawless and his contacts golden. But now I have to ask myself how long this can last. I've lived in hotels, out of suitcases for umpteen years and, until I got hurt, I thought I could wheel and deal till I dropped dead. But now... I'm scared. Some stability, a regular income might be good."

As she talked, he gradually relaxed his arms and tilted his head toward her.

"It's my head, Martin. These panic attacks... What if they're permanent? What if I get worse instead of better?"

Martin put his arm around her shoulders and pulled her close. "Delia, old love, PTSD is a known phenomenon and thousands of people are treated successfully for it every day. You just need to make sure you're getting the right care." His voice was confident, but she knew that he was afraid for her too.

He caressed her hair. "Look, Delia. I admit you're going through a hard time. But you have good instincts. You got your education. You zeroed in on a career that you had talent for and became a real success at it. You achieved everything you aimed for..."

Except you, she thought miserably. She twisted to press her face into the sweet dampness of his shirt and he wrapped his other arm around her.

"...now you've had this terrible trauma—both physical and emotional.

The head stuff—it will fade, it will fade..."

"When?" she asked, wondering if he believed a word he was saying.

"Well... maybe when we find Bellingham... maybe when we resolve the mysteries and you can rest easy again."

A fuzziness was coming over her. The night meds were kicking in. Suddenly, Delia was stabbed with her old passion for Martin Moon and awoke to all his familiar contours. She was intoxicated with him. She wanted his hand to slide from her hair to her ear to her neck and to slowly slip the cotton from her shoulders. She wanted to feel his lips against hers. Nothing else mattered. To hell with Tony. To hell with the museum...

But he was pulling away from her. "I'm glad we talked, babe. Get some sleep now."

They drifted apart and she turned away.

"Delia?"

Her heart leapt. "Yes?"

"I hope this museum thing works out for you."

"Oh. Yeah."

Jack dozed for a while but awoke in a sweat. The overhead fan, casting shadows in the moonlight, moved too slowly to stir the air. In the absolute quiet its *clickclickclunk* ground away at his nerves.

As a tonic, he allowed his mind's eye to linger on the image of Ingrid Lundquist. How the pale hair escaped from her braid and curled, barely visible, past her ear, onto her neck. How the squared-off shape of her camp shirt was sabotaged by the poking of small breasts. Did she wear a bra? As he toyed with the question, visualizing Ingrid from different angles, the heat became intolerable. *A penchant for young blondes.*

He sat up. His image in a long mirror at the foot of the bed mocked him. He dragged himself up and walked to the window. A lantern in the garden was still lit, as was the bottom of the green pool. Jack took off his pajama pants, wrapped himself in a towel and, in the corridor, found steps from a balcony to the floor of the courtyard.

Letting the towel drop, he stood at the edge of the pool. The water was still and clear enough to see the mottled green bottom. The air was acrid and smoky. As he gazed into the water, Ingrid invaded him again. *The penchant for young blondes.* She sat in her usual booth, one foot on the floor, the other on the seat and, with a tiny ironic smile, she unbuttoned her shirt. Then she reached for him.

As he squatted down to check how cold the water was, Jack let the fantasy run on.

A soft cough from the shadows made Jack turn. Another lantern clicked on. Tony Savani lay sprawled on a chaise, wrapped in a dark robe. Lucky was kneeling at his side, still dressed in the pale tunic she wore earlier.

Jack stood. *Where was his towel?*

"You really are quite wonderful to look at. A tribute to how gracefully the athletic male can mature. And the bruised face—it adds a certain new-male vulnerability."

Savani shifted slightly. "But you're lonely, I can tell. And tense. May I suggest Lucky accompany you back to your room. She's quite skilled in the art of Thai massage and I don't mind sharing her."

Tony licked his lips. Jack couldn't breathe. They stared into each other's eyes. Then Jack blinked and looked at the young woman. She was arranging items on a tray: a silver pipe, a spirit lamp, a saucer of dull black marbles. When she heard her name, she stopped and gazed up at Jack. Jack looked into her humid eyes. Then back to Savani's. Lucky. Savani. Deepset, hooded, pasty blue eyes. Both of them.

Jack backed away, mumbling nonsense, and finally stepped on his towel, which he swept up and around him. Savani laughed softly. Resisting the impulse to run, Jack walked back up the teakwood steps, across the balcony, and into the corridor, where he kept walking till he got to Delia's bedroom door. He opened it, without knocking, without thinking.

She lay curled on her side, the sheet snugged around her, silvery with moonlight. The ceiling fan above spun a smooth, cool current of air.

"Delia?" He didn't want to scare her, although he was sure his heartbeat drowned out his voice. "Delia?"

She stirred. He drew closer.

"Delia? It's Jack." Her bed was a fullsize futon on a low platform. He crouched next to it.

"Mmm."

He took her limp hand. "You can't live here with Savani, Delia. Please listen to me."

She groaned.

"He's not a nice man. He tried to pimp his daughter to me—Lucky, his daughter—and he smokes opium."

Her eyes fluttered, then closed again.

"Please listen." He laid his arms and head on the mattress and looked out the window at the moon.

At the sound of a boat putt-putting along the canal, Jack opened his eyes. The moon had disappeared. Delia was softly snoring. The odd posture had kinked his back and he had to maneuver around to his hands and knees before he could stand. Some paragon of manhood, he thought, as he shambled out of Delia's room and into his own.

Back in bed, he lay in a stupor. The clunking ceiling fan had stopped altogether. Sweat stung his eyes. Then, a willowy figure with a small lantern slipped into his room. At first he thought it was Delia. He prepared to smile, but his face froze when he saw the colorless eyes, the Asian features, the slender arms, the scarlet mouth.

Lucky placed the lantern behind his head and knelt next to his futon, narrower than Delia's.

She murmured something, thickly accented.

"Pardon me?"

"I am sorry for your discomfort, *Khun* Jack."

Did she mean the heat? Or his encounter with Savani? Or the fact that she was staring down the naked length of his body.

"I'm fine. Really."

But instead of going away, she continued to gaze at him, her eyes expectant. The garment slipped from her shoulders.

"I waited for you. I come to comfort you." She laid a hand on his chest. "You are like a god. Ivory and gold. You will like Thai massage."

He said nothing more. Did nothing to stop her hand from sliding along his torso. He had become a sandstone idol experiencing the encroachment of jungle vines and the roots of banyan trees—hot, moist, penetrating. He gripped the edges of the futon and closed his eyes. Lucky used only her hands and a tingling oil. The arid stone of his resistance crumbled away. When dawn threatened to light the room, she closed the shutters and touched him again.

Then she mopped him with a coarse, damp towel and disappeared. He curled around his pillow, all too aware of the sizzle of relaxation deep in every muscle. What *penchants* had Tony Savani really seen in him? What spell had been cast over him? Fathers and school teachers and protective companions were never supposed to reveal how weak they really were. He began to cry.

In the ash-pink dawn, Tony Savani turned from his computer screen to the window in his office. He held a bowl of spiced pecans in his lap. Despite the opium, he hadn't slept well. There was too much going on that disturbed him—an undercurrent among his three houseguests that he didn't get. He wanted to believe Delia's story about why Martin had come to Bangkok with her, and yet... the subtext eluded him.

One thing he didn't believe was that Delia had no romantic feelings left for Martin Moon. She hung on every word he spoke. No gesture escaped her. Even when her attentions were ostensibly somewhere else, she was aware of him. And he exuded such easy sensuality, such comfort with himself that it wouldn't take much to ignite the embers of their old love.

Tony had seen their embrace on the deck.

But he also knew that the one who disappeared for two hours into Delia's room was Jack. What a powder keg of desire that guy was.

Who was this Jack Scanlan, anyway? The sexual cross-currents were disturbing all right. But not knowing enough about Scanlan's real life, his real profession—that mystery hinted at deeper threats.

Tony turned back to the screen. The computer kept him in touch with Savani companies throughout the world. Lorna Craig, his confidential assistant based at P&S Worldwide in New York, had begun her research on their finances after Delia's first phone call from Rochester. The results were now in Tony's email. It was an easy place to start. P&S controlled Traders Bank International, through which Lorna had discovered his guests' banks and card companies. Within hours his document people had forged subpoenas for an electronic readout of their records.

Jack had a pittance in his checking account. The record showed it was replenished monthly with direct deposits from the Penfield School District, then a large portion was transferred immediately to an account owned by Monica Scanlan—child support, Tony guessed.

His VISA had not been used in nearly a year, except for a round-trip ticket to London—the daughter's ballet internship, no doubt.

So who was paying for Jack's trip to Bangkok? Martin Moon? Why would a man traveling with one of the most fascinating women in the world want to bring along a buddy? It didn't play. Besides—Tony brushed pecan glaze from his fingers and scrolled down the screen—Moon was broke too.

Moon, in fact, was worse off than Jack. He had two active accounts. One had received a sizable insurance payment, but large monthly chunks were paid out to a law firm. The other contained $835. Deposits were made sporadically, in odd amounts—so, he was selling, but nothing high-end. The VISA Gold had been maxed out at twenty-five thousand dollars. What had happened to all his assets? The inheritance? A clue: the business account of Moon & Tuthill Ltd. had been frozen. Hence the lawyers. How could he claim to be looking for Khmer sculpture when he was barely supporting himself? As he typed in a message for Craig to dig deeper, he couldn't help a satisfied smirk at Moon's misfortune.

So was Delia paying? Was she having a fling with one of them? Both of them? Whose room had she really slept in the other night? Jack was a perfect physical type for her—broad-shouldered, yet graceful, a little shy, rather endearing with all that hair—one of those gentle lovers.

The vision of Jack crawling into bed beside Delia made Tony twitch and the bowl slipped through his knees, scattering what was left of the pecans across the floor. *Damn.* He kicked the bowl. It was too outrageous. It would make a liar out of Delia and would ruin her for the partnership Tony so desperately wanted.

What possibilities remained but official ones? Was there an investigation going on? CIA? DEA? Interpol? Did Jack have an early career in law enforcement, semi-retired to a backwater teaching post? How and why had he latched onto Moon? Was someone paying for them both, using Delia to gain access to his secrets? He trusted no one. That was the Savani family tradition. That was how it had to be for him. As the chief strategist of the Savani family heroin empire, he knew that betrayal lurked everywhere.

At ten o'clock, Martin decided he better wake Jack. When Jack didn't respond to the knocks, Martin peeked in, then entered.

Jack's room was stifling and musky sweet. The ceiling fan was off, the louvers in the door's transom closed, and the shutters snapped shut against the morning breeze. In a tumbled mass of sheets, Jack stretched out, glistening with sweat and drugged with heat.

When Martin touched his shoulder, Jack woke with a start, cringing from the touch, eyes flashing across the room. "What? Are we leaving?"

"We just ate. We let you sleep, but I didn't know how godawful hot this room was. We'll leave as soon as you're ready. They saved breakfast."

"I'm ready now." He swung out of bed and started pulling clothes on, grunting impatiently as they stuck to his damp limbs.

"There's a shower down the hall, if..."

"I'm ready now," Jack snapped. "Just get me the hell out of here, okay?"

"What's wrong?"

Avoiding Martin's eyes, he mumbled something about the heat, then, "I'll meet you out by the car, okay?"

At the hotel Jack went immediately to his room and made a point of locking the connecting door. Martin thought nothing of it. Jetlag often combined with culture shock for quirky effects.

Delia had been subdued all morning, under the spell of fatigue that seemed to haunt her for hours after waking. It was a pattern that Martin found disturbing in a woman who'd once been a dogged, first-light jogger. But by the time they reached the hotel, she'd revived. It was noon. She wanted to get to work.

Leaving Jack to his own devices, Martin and Delia hurried off to visit the upscale antique dealers, broadcast their desire for Khmer-period sculpture, and nose around for information about Jeremy Bellingham.

They spent most of the afternoon at the River City Shopping Centre and the other shops surrounding the Oriental Hotel. Martin felt awkward at first, teamed up with Delia instead of Lana. Back in the day, back when they shared a tiny apartment in London, they had been more like rivals than partners, showing off to each other how much they knew, who they knew, and how skillfully they could cast their nets. They were kids and the antiquities world was their playground and their games were preparing them for adulthood. But when the first adult decision had to be made—whether to pool their profits for a house with a private viewing gallery or for an extended buying trip to Tokyo and Hong Kong—it stopped being fun. Suddenly, it no longer worked. And then she was gone.

How would it work now? Martin watched her. In contrast to her morning lethargy, she was highstrung and chatty, but her cheer was genuine, her energy focused. She charmed the dealers, dropped Bellingham's name, and introduced the topic of Lopburi-style sculpture with subtlety. Highly professional. No scent of emotional fragility. He relaxed.

At a shop that specialized in hill-tribe jewelry, he bought her an antique necklace from the Karen tribe—four strands of worn carnelian and rock crystal beads, separated by blue seed beads. Tiny bronze bells rustled as she walked. The gift was a risk. He had given her many necklaces over the years. Ancient beads had been her first love and he found them irresistibly seductive.

In the late afternoon, they stopped to eat. Martin was weary. The sensation was less physical than mental. While his mouth had run on amiably, his eyes and hands were absorbing the *qi* of Buddhist art. And his soul was absorbing the pain of seeing such devotional works turned into tourist commodities. As much as he himself ached to possess the finest bronze and sandstone statuary, something in him found sacrilege in the spectacle of River City, itself a glass and marble monument to materialism. Something in him agreed with the hawkeyes. All these monumental Buddhas and bodhisattvas belonged in the temples they were snatched from. It was the feeling that had kept him in the investigation business long after he'd stopped having fun as a dealer. He was particularly saddened to see how sacred Burmese antiques had flooded the Thai market, smuggled through the loosely guarded border by hungry insurgents and greedy middlemen. How many years would it be before Burma had no treasures left?

"What are you thinking, Marty?"

He looked up from a green papaya salad. "Just wondering how I can be so righteous about smuggling when I covet the damn stuff so much myself."

"The middle road is hard to find, isn't it?"

They talked philosophy, then Martin asked about the Chiang Mai museum. Delia spoke eagerly, her face lit with the possibilities. She

91

addressed the economics of a new museum with sophistication—downsides, upsides. But her excitement grew as she talked about the acquisitions—the precious carvings she'd be able to buy. Martin couldn't help but join in her enthusiasm.

The food and the conversation invigorated them both.

"Where to next?"

Martin still hadn't told Delia about his visit to Siam Treasures. Sara's fragility had made him worry over how to pursue an inquiry into René Malraux's murder. His impulse was to avoid involving Delia, to shield her from the woman whose nerves were as frayed as her own. But the day's work suggested that Delia might be less frayed than he. At least she was smoother, less rusty, and, after an afternoon of canvassing dealers, fresher.

He took her square, strong hand in his, studied it, and traced its curves while he spoke. "Delia, there's something I want you to consider..."

Jack threw himself on the bed. Why had he come to this godforsaken country? Why hadn't he been satisfied teaching remedial social studies to bored sixth-graders for the summer? Why did he let himself get talked into leaving his comfort zone? He felt angry at Delia: she had played to his needs, seduced him into this trip, and for what? To get him hot and bothered? To reignite sexual feelings that were going nowhere, that had no future?

In spite of being tired, Jack couldn't sleep, so he forced himself to shower and shave and dress, then went to the hotel coffee shop for lunch. It was bright and colorful, filled with rich aromas and travelers chatting in all languages. The waiters were cheerful and solicitous. Jack tried to use the prosaic gaiety of it all to talk himself out of his growing anxiety.

Jack was a serious person. He had been a monogamous husband. When Monica moved away, he still felt obliged to lead a chaste life, as a role model for Theresa and for his students. Friendships with a couple fellow teachers had threatened to turn sexual, but he backed off, avoiding the complications.

So why now?

Why *not* now? Wasn't it time he took some risks again? He was in Thailand, known since the Vietnam War as a friendly, recreational-sex playground. Shouldn't he... crack open a window in the boarded-up house of Scanlan?

Jack was on his third beer and the restaurant had become intolerable. The midday sun glinted in his eye, the other patrons were boisterous, and the waiters kept fussing over his table. He signed his room number to the check and was nearly out the front door before he spied the newsstand and sundry shop in the corner of the lobby.

In the shop, Jack shifted from one foot to the other and flipped magazine pages, while he scanned the shelves of candy bars and toothpaste and aspirin. *There they were.* Buying them would be an admission that he'd crossed a threshold. Whether it was for better or worse, whether he was taking a reasonable adult risk or had lost control, he didn't know. He didn't care. With the same embarrassment he felt the first time, twenty-five years ago, he bought a pack of condoms.

Outside the hotel, the blast of hot air took his breath away and the sunlight seared his eyes. He pulled on his baseball cap, ignored the calls of the taxi and *tuk-tuk* drivers and hurried around the block, plunging into the icy cave of Dick's All-American Bar and Grill. It was nearly empty except for Truman and, in her regular booth, Ingrid. Jack sat on a stool at the end of the bar where he could see the back of Ingrid's head and the smoke curling up from her cigarette.

"Hey, man," Truman greeted him. "Can o' brew?"

"You save my bottle of Mekhong?" Jack's gaze was fixed on Ingrid.

"Sure 'nuf. You look weirded out, Scanlan. Tense."

Jack barely grunted in response and Truman said no more as he dried glasses with a dirty towel.

When Jack finished two fingers of Mekhong, he asked, "Where does that door go?" He nodded toward a place just past Ingrid's booth. He'd seen people entering but seldom exiting throughout the first night he visited Dick's.

"Goes to the smoking room upstairs. Opium. Family business. Old regulars. Younger generation, they mostly buy number four—needle-pure heroin. They buy and scoot. But the old guys, lot of 'em spend the night. Guys who use the bunkroom, sort of a family." He paused. "Look, man, Eeju's brother has his own room up there. He won't be back in town till late tonight. If you need to crash or anything, go ahead and use it. It's to the left at the top of the stairs."

With a nod, Jack vacated the barstool and walked toward Ingrid. Or floated really since he could hardly feel his feet touch the floor. He slipped into the booth, next to her.

"Mind if I join you?" He tried to put some cheer into his voice, but it cracked, like a fourteen-year-old's.

She shot him one of her ironic smiles and pushed at her papers. "Heavens, if this is going to be a regular thing you might at least wait till tea. I really must get this report done."

"I was lonely... wanted to hear more about your work."

"Do tell. Well... look, did I show you these photos of Angkor Wat?"

She slid over a manila folder of eight-by-ten color enlargements. Then she twisted around, with her back against the wall, in order to face him. Once again, her knee stuck up between them, a shield. He leafed through the pictures.

"Most of them show irreparable damage wrought by years of neglect. But look, a few of these demonstrate what I was talking about yesterday—the dynamism between discipline and romance." She pulled out one in which the monumental form of a goddess was being ravished by the arm-like roots of a tree. "It has to be cut back, tamed, of course, or ultimately it will destroy."

"I hear Tony Savani financed this trip."

"How ever did you find that out?"

"He mentioned it. My friends and I had dinner at his house, spent the night."

"You lucky sod. All I get are short little business meetings. I've never been invited beyond his office. Isn't Mr. Savani absolutely fascinating?"

"I can't say as I liked him very much. Made me uncomfortable."

"Found your weak spot, did he? He's famous for that. I hadn't interviewed with him five minutes before he discovered I didn't know a damn thing about small bronzes. Hasn't let me forget it either."

"He said your work in Cambodia was worthy of *National Geographic*."

She beamed. "You talked about me? He actually said that? There, now, he can't be all bad, can he?"

"Must have some redeeming virtues. Looks like the woman I'm traveling with is going to move in with him. They're going to start some sort of little museum together. Jades."

A furrow appeared in her young brow. "But she's a dealer. You said she was an antiquities dealer. What did you say her name was?"

He told her.

She scribbled the name on a notebook page. "Can't think why he'd partner up with a dealer when he spends most of his time with archaeologists—who don't think too highly of profiteers."

Jack had suffered enough talk about Savani, but wondered about the validity of his other comment—about *virgins* being more likely to see eroticism in the jungle. The protective knee between them had relaxed as they talked, opened out a little to expose more of the paler skin of her inner thigh. Trying not to look obvious, he propped his elbow on the back of the booth and brushed a fingertip across her knee.

"Are you a virgin?" he asked in a low voice.

"What?" The knee dropped away from his finger, toward the tabletop. She made a small defiant motion with her chin. "I've been screwed plenty of times, if that's what you're asking."

Pushing the goddess picture toward her, Jack asked, "But never made love to? Never romanced?" As she stared at the photo, his hand slipped down along her thigh. "Your heart never warmed by jungle vines?" His fingernails teased the skin of her inner thigh.

"Don't be..." With a sharp intake of air, she closed her eyes. "...bloody ridiculous."

"Why not give it a try—see what happens."

Her eyes fluttered open and glanced between his hand and the photograph of the stone goddess. When she looked into his eyes, he saw her excitement was colored with mistrust.

"I promise," he said, "I promise I won't make you... crumble."

She touched his hand and nodded. Jack swept her papers into the rucksack, while she stowed the computer. Grabbing the pack strap and the necks of the liquor bottles in one hand, he drew her out of the booth with the other. She followed wordlessly.

The tiny room upstairs had a bare mattress on the floor and a forty-watt bulb dangling from a frayed cord. Clean sheets were stacked on a chair. Jack unfurled one over the mattress and crouched to tuck the edges under. When he turned back to Ingrid and held out his hands to her, her fingers met his, but not her eyes. She dropped to her knees and unzipped his fly. He caught her hands.

95

"Hey, wait," he whispered. "This is a romance, angel, remember?"

They stretched across the mattress, facing each other, fully clothed. He unbraided her hair and combed through it with his fingers till it hung loose and fine. He caressed her face, her arms, her back. With some shyness, she did the same to him. Gradually, he moved to more sensitive parts. At every hint of anxiety in her eyes, he retreated a bit. Giving a blow job had seemed less threatening to her than receiving a kiss. Slowly, she let herself respond.

She was still fully dressed when his touch brought on a climax. It was a long time before he slipped off her clothes, and longer still before he slipped off his own. By that time she was quivering, feverish, breathless, and yet the sight of how ready he was to penetrate turned her lips into a tense little line.

But he simply lay on his back, allowed her to take the lead, helped her with the condom, let her guide his hardness to the place that was more ready than he expected.

Oh, bliss, he thought.

They did not leave the little room till evening. Truman grinned. Then he told Ingrid that Caleb had been by for her.

"Took the liberty of tellin' him you left at the regular time. He kicked a chair or two and stomped off."

Jack was alarmed. Any man with two eyes could tell she'd been having sex all afternoon. Her eyes were muzzy, her cheeks whiskerburned, her lips swollen. He offered his hotel room to her, but she scoffed at the idea. She meant nothing to Cal. Anyway, she had a meeting first thing in the morning and she couldn't go in shorts.

Jack made her sit on a barstool and drink a glass of Coke while he brushed and rebraided her hair. Then he carried her rucksack and held her hand as they walked down the dark side street toward Sukhumvit Road. "I feel so good," he said. "Really good. Don't you?"

She squeezed his hand. When they reached the corner where he needed to turn toward the Tudor, he spoke again. "I like Thailand. I suddenly feel at home here." He surveyed the broad bright boulevard. "In fact, I'm even catching on to the language, yeah."

"What?"

"Sure. Look." He twisted her toward the avenue, put one hand around her waist and pointed with the other toward one of the innumerable neon signs filled with curlicue Thai script. "It's like reading those little numbers on the bottom of bank checks. Easy, once you get the hang of it. There, that one says *Alka-Seltzer*, and over there *sousaphone*, and there *suit and sandwich*."

They were struck with a case of the giggles. Suddenly, he had both arms around her and his lips at her ear. "Jesus, Ingrid, come back to my room with me. Let's forget about everything else for a while and have a fling."

"What? I'm not the type for flings."

"Neither am I. That's what's so wonderful, so crazy about it." He began to plot little kisses along her neck and slid his hand under her blouse. Before she could protest, he eased her behind a corrugated iron fence that guarded a construction site on the corner. She still faced away from him. She was breathless and responding to his fingertips. He unzipped her shorts.

"Oh, God," she moaned, then wrenched herself out of his arms.

"Wait," he gasped.

"It's gone... too far... already," she said, trembling, struggling to catch her breath, buttoning, tucking, zipping herself back together. "I can't... we can't... I don't want to be... your holiday fling... It's... too important... My work... Oh, God..." She grabbed her rucksack and jogged away.

He blew it. How stupid of him to unravel, in a single ham-handed gesture, the delicate bond they'd spent hours building. What a jerk.

As it began to rain, Jack ambled back to the Tudor, meandered through the lobby, bought a beer, walked out through the rear doorway, and stood gazing into the deep blue of the hotel swimming pool, not minding his damp clothes.

When the taxi stopped in front of Siam Treasures, Delia turned to Martin. "Go on back to the hotel. I'll be okay."

But he wouldn't hear of it. Although they decided that Delia would talk to Sara alone, Martin insisted on staying nearby. Across the street there was a noodle shop, an English-language bookstore, and a handicrafts shop. He would be in one or the other of those and would wait as long as she needed.

Delia was rattled that Martin had found Sara and she had not. For weeks she'd been carrying around the Bangkok police report that Jones-White got through Interpol. It said the wife was *Sara Malraux*. Delia assumed she was French and that she'd returned home. Sheer incompetence. She should have spoken to her weeks ago.

While a couple browsers took their time to leave the shop, Delia made small talk. Sara admired Delia's beads and provided some background on the Karen tribe that created necklaces with that design. She was pleasant, but edgy. Her eyes were bloodshot, devoid of any real interest in the topic of beads. They darted frequently to the window. Delia found herself doing the same—a spike of paranoia—and felt a drip of sweat trickle down her back.

When they were alone, Delia spoke more directly. "Madame Malraux—that is your name, isn't it?"

Sara nodded, the tension rising in her eyes.

"My name is Delia Rivera. I heard about the death of your husband, René. It was very tragic. Do you have any children?"

Sara only stared at her.

"Madame Malraux, I know about René's murder because I'm trying to locate the man who did it."

"You police?" she asked softly.

"No. I have my own story to tell, if you'll listen."

Sara let Delia speak, but she occupied herself by laying newly minted Thai amulets into precise rows and columns on a velvet-lined display tray. Delia watched Sara's hands as she told of her own assault and a search for justice that the law enforcement agencies of the world had turned their backs on. She went on to describe Lana's murder. By the time she finished, Sara had stopped fussing with the amulets and was finally looking at Delia's face.

"So, you see, Madame Malraux—"

"Please, call me Sara."

"You can see, *Khun* Sara, why I so desperately want to speak to you about the circumstances of René's death. I've been searching months for answers—answers that you may have."

With one more anxious glance toward the street, Sara agreed. "We'll have tea, okay?"

When Delia agreed, Sara locked the shop door and led Delia to a small kitchen in back. As twilight blanketed them, they sat with their tea on hard chairs at a Formica table.

Delia asked, "The day René was killed, was Jeremy Bellingham in town?"
Sara nodded.

It was, of course, a day Sara Kesmanee Malraux would never forget.

"The bronze is fantastic, Sara love." Jeremy Bellingham, smelling of tobacco and pungent aftershave, leaned across the counter, and spoke in a stage whisper. "Have it sent to London with the invoice."

"I heard that," René called from the kitchen. He limped into the shop with a bottle of chilled Chablis and two glasses, smiling broadly as he always did when Jeremy came to town. "You're totally incorrigible." His English was too fluent for his thick French accent: the words ran together in a slurry. "I cannot allow my wife to send a two-hundred-year-old Buddha out of the country for one of your customers to turn into a lamp. It's cultural thievery. Despicable. And Sara could be prosecuted."

Jeremy winked at her—eyes thick-lashed, golden, seductive. "You're so bloody pompous, René. Sara's been faking export papers ever since Joe taught her to write." He spoke to her again. "Sure you don't want any wine, love?"

She shook her head. "Too sour."

To her sadness, they turned away from her, back to the kitchen. She loved them both. But they loved each other better. Jeremy, with his high-class posture and tailored suits. René, always off-balance from childhood polio, threadbare clothes neatly patched. Strangest of friends.

She heard their argument begin.

"You can't be serious, René." Jeremy's voice had lost its playfulness. "Exporting a piece like that isn't going to rob Thailand of its bloody heritage. If you melted down all the Buddhas in Thailand you could fabricate a new fleet for the British Navy. It's simple commerce, old as mankind. Your Buddha for my pounds sterling keeps the roof over your head and the green grocer down the block alive for another month."

"I take none of the shop's profit. I live only off my Savani fellowship."

"Of course, of course. Pour me another glass."

"So where have you been?" René's voice softened and Sara found some merchandise to dust near the kitchen door so she could listen in. "I've missed you."

"Chiang Mai. That new Khmer site I told you about."

"Yes, yes, tell me more. How long are you going to keep it a secret? You promised to show me. If you're right, it could be the discovery of the century."

"Think you can tear yourself out of the bloody library for a couple weeks? Leave tomorrow?"

"A couple weeks? I don't know... it wouldn't be fair to Sara... to run off, you know, at the drop of a hat."

"Bloody hell. You're an archaeologist, you're supposed to get your hands dirty now and then. Far as I can tell, Sara runs the shop quite well by herself."

"It's just that..." René hesitated.

"Spit it out, for godsake."

"I'm worried... If you're up to something illegal, Jeremy, something unethical... I couldn't... It would tear me apart."

"*Unethical*, Christ." There was a long pause before Jeremy spoke again. "Pour me another."

The shop door banged and startled Sara from her eavesdropping. Two men, a rough-looking Australian and a pudgy Brit—archaeology friends of René's—stomped in. They filled the small shop with their sweeping gestures and their rancid sweat.

Cal reached out and tousled her hair—a gesture meant for a dog. "René around?"

Immediately Bruno imitated his action, except where Cal's eyes were cold, Bruno's leered and dropped to her blouse. She batted his hand away.

"In back," René called.

As they turned toward the kitchen, Sara hurried toward the counter to close the flaps on a cardboard box. But her haste caught Bruno's attention. The piece on top was free of its newspaper packing—a lovely little vase with a bowl bottom and long neck, made of red unglazed clay, inlaid with an intricate white design.

"Look at what we have here." Bruno picked up the vase, turned it over in his hands, then set it on the counter while he began to unpack the other items.

"Please," Sara protested, "they're none of your concern."

"The hell they aren't," Cal sniped as René and Jeremy emerged from the kitchen. He spoke to René. "Where'd you get these? They're fresh dug up, still covered with dirt."

René reddened. He hadn't seen them.

"I bought them this morning," Sara said. "A Karen merchant. He was at the end of his rope. Starving. The Burmese are attacking their villages again. They're desperate for cash."

Cal held the vase by its neck and shook it at René. "This is the sort of thing we're trying to stop, damn it. This is what HAWC-I is all about. We know so little about these cultures and faster than we can find the bloody sites they're selling it all off to the tourist trade."

Jeremy had eased himself behind the counter and was examining the pieces. "Cal, old buddy, careful with that Haripunchai water vessel. It looks like the only decent thing in the lot. The rest is *ordinaire*, poor man's pottery and pretty beat up at that."

"Whether it's *ordinaire* or not is beside the point," Cal said. "It's part of the world heritage and should have been properly excavated and catalogued."

"Tell that to the poor fellow who's going to feed his family for a week on what he made here," Jeremy retorted. "Ask him what the bloody hell he cares about world heritage. Ask him what the bloody hell you protectors of world heritage have done for his children lately."

Bruno snatched a chipped celadon bowl from Jeremy's hand. "Shouldn't be having children if they can't afford to feed them."

Jeremy yanked it back. "Don't fuck around with me, you self-righteous pig."

Bruno squared off, but Cal stepped between them. "You arrogant, hypocritical son of a bitch. Whose family do you say you're feeding when you haul giant sandstone Buddhas out of your secret treasure trove in Chiang Mai?"

Jeremy's head snapped toward René. Silence. Sara heard the clock tick five seconds. What had been a benign philosophical argument between the two friends Jeremy and René, suddenly plumed into a cosmic confrontation. Bruno and Cal faded away. Sara stopped breathing. Jeremy's face turned ruddy with anger as his eyes fixed on his pal. René was shaking his head, his mouth open to speak but no words came.

"You," Jeremy finally whispered. "You told them. You told them." Now his eyes began to redden. "René? My friend?"

René swiped the back of his hand against his sweating forehead. He seemed so small, so twisted in on himself. "I didn't mean for it to be..." He touched his lips.

"Didn't mean for it to be *what*? Didn't mean for it to be a *betrayal*?" Jeremy shouted. "Just *doing your duty*? Your duty to these pitiless ideologues, these heartless culturists who'd rather see a family starve than have their bloody digs disturbed?" He raised his fists and flung himself toward René, but Bruno and Cal caught his arms. "I thought you were a man. I thought you were loyal to—" His voice broke. "Let me go."

René stepped back, looking at the floor. "Let him go," he murmured.

When they released his arms, Jeremy stared at René for a moment longer, then turned and marched out the front door.

Slowly, one awkward step at a time, René moved toward the door. "He's right," he said to the floor. "I betrayed him."

"Bull," said Cal. "The bastard's nothing but a major league rip-off artist. Nothing but crocodile tears. Go on. Go beg his forgiveness. Get yourself back in his good graces. It's the only way we'll ever find the secret excavation."

"I will not betray him again. To hell with archaeology. To hell with HAWC-I. To hell with you."

The archaeologists scowled.

René turned to Sara. "I have to find him."

She nodded.

At noon the next day, Sara identified René's body. Whatever happened, she was too numb to imagine and didn't absorb a thing the police told her. Sara told them that René followed Jeremy out of the shop the night before. They would find Jeremy, the police assured her.

Her husband had followed Jeremy and then he was dead. She was alone.

The police dropped her at the *wat* so she could arrange the funeral ceremony and cremation—a Buddhist send-off for her dear René. She took a *tuk-tuk* home. Outside the shop, Bruno waited. She wished she could remember his last name, but both he and Cal had alphabet-soup names, like Thais.

As she opened the shop door, she blurted, "René is dead."

"I heard. Rotten luck. Came by for his papers." He followed her into the shop, close enough for her to feel his damp heat and smell the garlic on his breath.

She turned to him. "What papers?"

He caught her arms and squeezed her biceps. He stared into her eyes for a moment. "His research papers," he said with an air of hushed confidentiality. "His notes. We were both Savani fellows, so I have as much right to his papers as anyone. I can continue his work. Don't you agree?"

Sara tried to twist away but Bruno held on, pulling her a millimeter closer.

"Don't you agree?" he whispered.

"Yes, yes, all right."

In a daze she showed him the pantry René had converted to an office. Stacks of papers in manila folders surrounded the laptop computer on the desk. The shelves were filled with books, journals, reprints, and more manila folders of notes. Bruno sat down at the desk, turned on the lamp, and began disconnecting the laptop. Sara brought him a cardboard box.

To the sound of rustling papers and thick files being dropped into the box, Sara sat at her own desk in the shop and tried to reach Jeremy at the Majestic Hotel, but the operator said he'd checked out.

After she hung up the phone, she gazed out the window at the sun-washed traffic—everyone following their normal routines, cursing the congestion and the pollution, hurrying home to their families. But she was alone. Gradually, the air turned to lavender and the traffic thinned.

Hands on her shoulders startled her.

"There must be more notes somewhere," Bruno said. "Did he keep a diary?"

She wanted to pull away, but he held her too firmly and she felt weak, paralyzed. "I don't know. He was always writing in notebooks, but I can't read English well and French not at all."

The thick fingers of his right hand began to caress her neck. "Where else would he keep notebooks besides his office?"

"I—I don't know. Upstairs maybe. The bedroom."

His fingers groped around, touched her cheek, then rubbed her lips. "Are you hungry?" he murmured.

A horrified thrill brushed across her skin. She shook her head.

"Let's go upstairs and look." His hand moved away from her mouth, back to her neck, then down to the top of her blouse. "Then..." He flicked at the top button. "Then I think you'll need some nourishment."

"I'll go... bring whatever is there down here."

Bruno spun her chair around on its casters, grabbed her arms behind the elbows and lifted her to her feet. "We'll both go."

Sara trudged through the kitchen and up the stairs, feeling only despair. What did anything matter anymore?

In her bedroom she pointed to the folders and notebook on the night-stand and started to back out, but Bruno grabbed her arm. He held it as he opened each of the folders with his free hand and tossed them on the floor. Then he opened the notebook and flipped through the pages till the writing stopped. "Garbage," he muttered and dropped it on top of the folders.

"What are you looking for?"

"Directions to Bellingham's site up north. You know if René had them?"

She wanted him out of the bedroom. "Maybe I can find more notes downstairs."

"No," he said. "It's time for that nourishment I promised."

He pushed her onto the bed and unsnapped his pants.

The relief she felt when Bruno finally left turned to alarm the next afternoon when Cal showed up in his place. Where Bruno had stuck to her like a loathsome garden slug, Cal was nettlesome as a wasp. He swaggered around the shop.

"We're going to take care of this place for you, ducky. René was our mate and he wouldn't want us to abandon you. He'll look down from heaven and be right proud of his little Sara and his little shop that doesn't profit off Thai heritage."

"It was not his shop," she murmured. "It is my shop."

He didn't hear her as he began to pull merchandise off the shelves to determine which items should be "repatriated" to regional museums or, better yet, to archaeology projects.

"And listen up. Don't be telling the constables about the argument between Bellingham and René over that site up north. News of it'll get out and the place'll be run over with treasure hunters. Leave it'a me and Bruno to get to the bottom of it. In fact, don't even mention Jeremy. We want him to show up here again, but not with the coppers on his tail. You're going to tell us if you hear from him, aren't you, ducky?"

As he tore apart the shop, he demanded food and drink. For hours, she watched him reorganizing her merchandise, laying the groundwork for destroying the business that three generations of Kesmanees had toiled to build. Finally, she couldn't tolerate it any longer.

Stepping between him and the shelf he was emptying, she said, "Stop immediately and go away or I'll call the police and have you arrested for trespassing and vandalism."

Cal took a step back from her. He tilted his chin up and twisted his lips into an ugly line. Then his cupped hand boxed the side of her head so fast and so hard that a ringing bolt of pain shot through her ear as she fell to the floor. She cried out and clasped her hands over her head. He kicked her ribs. She cried out again, curling into a weeping ball.

Cal yanked her onto her back, pushed her legs apart, and tore her panties. Sweat dripped from his face. "Don't ever talk that way to me again," he huffed. "You're ours now, Bruno's and mine. This shop, René's research, your fine little body. Ours."

Delia figured Martin would be going crazy by now, wondering what the hell she was doing, but she knew she could rely on him to stay put while she took care of Sara. It didn't take much to persuade Sara to grab a few things and leave Bangkok for her family in Pattaya. They locked up the shop and exited by the back door onto a dark side street. Delia pressed some dollars into Sara's hand and put her in a taxi. Sara could get counsel from her family about the future of the Kesmanee shop and would be safe from her predators till Delia figured out what to do next.

It was 8 p.m. by the time Delia exited the side street onto Sukhumvit Road. The street glistened and steamed with the aftermath of a monsoon storm she hadn't been aware of. She spotted Martin in the window of the noodle shop. He jumped up and walked out to the curb as she threaded her way across the six lanes of evening traffic.

When she reached him, he was studying her face. "Everything okay?

You okay?"

Nothing was okay. Sara's story was horrifying, but there were now too many villains. Bellingham was there, angry and betrayed. But the two hawkeye-archaeologists rose to the level of depravity. How did the gentle Malraux get wound up with them? Right... they were all Savani fellows. So, did Tony know those creeps? She dare not mention them. He hated her *conspiracy theories*. But Martin was here. Martin would get it.

"I'm fine," she said. "Let's walk."

"Hungry? We can stop somewhere along here—"

"No."

They walked a block in silence.

"Funny," she said at last, "it's probably still in the eighties but I feel cold."

Martin took off his suit jacket and laid it across her shoulders. She slipped her hand into his. It was warm. They continued to stroll down the great congested avenue toward their hotel.

"She have new information?"

She tightened the grip on his hand. Where to begin?

"Delia?"

"You know I never actually met Jeremy Bellingham, only talked to him that once on the phone. You said Lana liked him. Did you?"

"Hell, I don't know. He seemed like the kind of engaging smooth-talker I might have been in my twenties. Eager to please."

"I went in there needing Sara to confirm that Jeremy Bellingham was around when Malraux was murdered and that he had some kind of motive for it..."

"And?"

"And I guess he did." They walked another half block. "Martin, if some-one's a true sociopath, he can come across as *engaging* and *eager to please* and still be a cold-hearted murderer, right? Like mobsters who are swell to their mothers? Like those sweet guys who show up to work on time every day and have chopped-up bodies in their refrigerators?"

"You having second thoughts about Bellingham? The business is full of charming rogues. Not always easy to sift out the psychopaths from the hucksters."

She stopped walking and put a trembling hand over her eyes. "I'm so confused," she said, hearing her voice clotted with tears. She didn't want Martin to think she couldn't handle the stress. She didn't want to be a

106

crybaby, but… here she was, weeping.

"Oh, babe." He pulled her into the doorway of a darkened shop and hugged her. "I shouldn't have let you go in there—not by yourself. I'm not being much help to you, am I?"

She snuffled. "I'm all right, really. But Sara's not. HAWC-I is still on the case. At least, a couple of hawkeyes have made Sara their personal mission. They're still out to find the illegal excavation, but they've also taken over her shop. When they're in town they supervise her merchandise and intimidate her customers—and, as the mood hits, they have sex—rape her."

Martin squeezed her closer but she pulled back enough to put her hands on his shoulders and look into his eyes. She swallowed her tears. "I had a single purpose, a mission to put Bellingham out of commission. But pulling the Bellingham thread just unraveled something bigger. I just caught a glimpse of a world much uglier than a single murderer. Something more deranged, more obscene, but beyond my reach, beyond my comprehension, beyond…" Her voice broke. "I'm so confused by this—and so damned angry."

She collapsed against him, letting all the misery of the world lose focus. She was so tired. And here was her dear old Martin, standing firm as a Greek pillar, holding her up. He understood. Martin always understood. She adored him.

Look, honey," Martin said, groping for words as he smoothed her hair with one hand and hugged her close with the other. He thought he should say something calming and sensible, about not getting over-involved, about not letting complications make her lose focus. About not risking her own recovery...

But he was suddenly overcome. Their carefully constructed *friendship pact* was crumbling. He was in love with her. He knew it last night at Savani's, but he'd been so peeved at her—her disappearance, the revelations from Edwin, and her new business alliance with Tony—that he refused to admit he was still vulnerable to her. Tonight was different. Tonight he had no doubts.

"Delia," he whispered and kissed her ear, her cheek, and when she moved her head, he found her lips. They were just little kisses, tender lip-tugging kisses.

They'd made love in a doorway once—he was remembering that too. They'd met by surprise at an auction in Madrid, months after a stormy breakup in Brussels. The auction went on past midnight. They both bought heavily and, across the hot, crowded, smoky room, made eyes. Their transactions complete, they met outside and, without a word, hurried toward her hotel. But they couldn't stop touching and, with frenzied giggles, slipped into a cavelike doorway on a darkened street.

But in Madrid they'd been celebrating, their spirits light enough to buoy Delia into his arms. Two acrobats floating on a trapeze of joy.

Tonight they would need a net. Tonight they would need to sink into the security of mattress, sheets, blankets, and pillows.

"I had her name. *Sara Malraux*," Delia said, her voice muffled as she pressed her face against his shirt. "I could have helped her weeks ago, if it weren't for my own damn—"

"Shh. Enough of that. You saw to her safety. She's okay now." He kissed her hair. "Let's hail a cab."

"You'll keep holding me?"

"Forever."

On the way back to the hotel, fantasies about his future with Delia caromed through Martin's imagination. He'd work doubly hard to settle with Emmaline Tuthill, so he'd have some capital. He'd move to Thailand, buy a house in Chiang Mai, and they'd live together while Delia did her museum work with Tony. She hadn't intimated any sexual relationship with Tony and Martin prayed it wasn't one more secret that would spill out at the wrong moment. No, he would have sensed it from her by now. If Tony had ideas—to hell with him.

It was nearly nine by the time they arrived back at the Tudor. The lobby buzzed with a group of agitated tourists who were demanding rooms after their plans to go south to the beaches were ruined by a domestic airline strike.

Grazing her back with his fingers, Martin suggested she move out of her room and into his—to free up a room for these poor tourists, of course.

And for safety's sake, of course, for her peace of mind. She nodded.

While Delia went to clear out her room, Martin dealt with the registration desk. There were several messages from a Mr. Cerniak at the American Embassy and, as he'd hoped, one from Jones-White. It was marked *urgent*, with a note to call at any hour. Before he turned away, the desk clerk said, "Oh, Mr. Moon, those gentlemen by tour desk, waiting for you, several hour."

The two Thai men, one dozing, the other reading a magazine, were some sort of officials. Martin could spot the boxy suits and ass-dragging demeanor in any country of the world.

Puzzled by the embassy message and the visitors, but deciding to talk to Edwin first, he headed for the public telephone. He could have called from the room, but didn't want to ruin the mood with Delia. It was the wrong moment to admit that he knew Edwin had cancelled the contract to track Bellingham's smuggling activities.

The call went through.

As soon as he recognized Martin's voice, Jones-White said, "I'm afraid there's been a bit of a dustup, old darling."

"What is it?"

"I'm really quite amazed that you were able to enter Thailand at all."

"What do you mean? Delia expedited the visas through a pal of hers at the New York consulate. What's up?"

"You recall that miserable business in Mae Sot—I never should have agreed to let them deport you, even though it seemed your best protection at the time. Contrary to the agreement I worked out with the Thais, your deportation record was never expunged. This morning I must have pulled one string too many at the Secretariat and suddenly everything came unraveled."

"Edwin, the point?"

"Your visa's been revoked. You're illegal. You must report to immigration officials or to the American Embassy at once. You'll be detained till the next flight out."

"You gotta be kidding me." Martin peeked around to the two waiting officials and pressed himself into the shadows. His mind was racing, even as it clung to the thought of romance with Delia. "How long do I have to duck immigration before you can get this straightened out?"

"Problem's not at this end. It's the Thais who are adamant about wanting you out of their country, who can't seem to recall the artifacts you rescued or the deal we negotiated. I suspect someone's yanking their chain. You don't have hawkeyes on your tail, do you?"

"That's all I need." He scanned the lobby. Were there hawkeyes stalking him as they had in Mae Sot? Amid the throng of annoyed tourists, he didn't see anyone particularly suspicious, but he did spot Jack out by the pool. He'd ask Jack to go get Delia and together they'd find a hotel off the radar.

"Look, old friend," Jones-White continued, "the upshot of all this is that you are *persona non grata* in Thailand. The Thais will not discuss the matter until you're out of there. They're not treating this as a bureaucratic snag but as a national affront. They've got the American Embassy in an uproar. I suggest you come straight here, to St. Cloud, where we can assemble all the right parties and clear it up once and for all."

"Like it got cleared up the last time? Forget it. I can't leave Delia. Not now." *Not now!* "We found René Malraux's wife and her story managed to heighten Delia's worst fears. She's upset and maybe even in danger. I can't walk out on her. I can't." They just needed a few days—he was sure of it—to sort through the Bellingham business. Maybe Tony Savani could provide them with a discreet shelter...

"Why not have her come with you, Martin?"

Martin pressed his forehead against the cold metal of the phone alcove. Savani. All her dreams of the museum. "It's not that simple," he told Edwin, feeling despair creeping into his voice. Whatever romantic illusions had led him to think he could begin life over again with Delia had to be measured against the real complexities of their lives. "It's like this, Edwin. If my troubles aren't easily solved, her name shouldn't be linked with mine. The whole point of my being here at all is to help her get her life back on track. She has plans. She has a future in this business, here in Thailand. I'm supposed to be a stepping stone, not a stumbling block."

"Your sentiments are noble, Martin, but I must warn you. If you don't act fast to end this misunderstanding, the international press will pick it up, I guarantee—*Deported American Smuggler Back in Thailand...*"

"Oh, God—Emmaline Tuthill. If she gets that news, all my pains to win her over will be shot to hell." Everything he ever worked for would be lost forever, surrendered to the Tuthill family.

"I don't understand that battle at all, Martin."

"The woman despises me—always has. Lana turned her back on staid upstate New York and a career in science, for the arts, for Europe, for me.

Me. A nobody."

"Martin, really—"

"And then the lovely daughter goes out one night in her sable coat to meet death in a Paddington warehouse—" Martin paused to swallow the lump in his throat. "If this hits the press, Emmaline will destroy me once and for all."

Edwin was silent.

For a moment, Martin saw his future, starting over in his late forties, hitting the road alone, desperate to turn each buy into a profitable sale, to parlay each sale into a savvy purchase. And if he were unwelcome in Thailand, Delia would be lost to him for good, settled into her new life in Chiang Mai.

The alternative? Hop on a plane to protect his fortune and his good name, but leave Delia in physical and emotional jeopardy, while her own dreams hung in the balance? Knowing Delia, she'd probably make out in the long run. But that's what he thought about Lana too. Strong, smart women always land on their feet… till they don't. He dropped the ball with Lana, let alcohol muddle his good sense and cloud his emotions. He became a weak partner and it pushed Lana into defiant risk-taking. But he was healthy now and damned if he was going to fumble this commitment to Delia.

Besides, he still felt her in his arms, pressed against his chest. His shirt was still stained with her tears.

"A couple days, Edwin, a couple days is all I need, then I'll turn myself in and dance to whatever tune they play. A couple days and Delia's nightmare will be behind her."

"There is no mercy in the air, Martin. The situation is beyond my control until—"

Martin hung up. He squared his back against the men he now knew to be immigration officers, and marched through the double doors to the pool area, deliberately bumping into Jack and pushing him out of the line of sight.

FOUR

BANGKOK, THAILAND

It took Jack a half second to break out of his Ingrid reverie.

"I'm in trouble," Martin said, drawing him into the shadows. "I need to get out of here, find a place to stay, somewhere they don't ask questions. My visa's been revoked. I'm illegal. Pair of cops are sitting in the lobby waiting for me. Delia's upstairs. Tell her to stay calm and I'll call as soon as I find a place. Stay close to her, okay?"

"But how are you going to find—"

Martin shook his head. "Taxi drivers usually know the places that don't ask for papers."

"Wait. I know somewhere." He handed Martin his baseball cap to hide his silver hair and they made a quick exit through a side door.

Within minutes they were at Dick's All-American, where Jack introduced Martin to Truman and inquired about the room where he and Ingrid had spent the afternoon. But Truman's brother-in-law was back in town, so his wife Eeju led the two men upstairs and offered Martin a cot in the opium den, which was half full of old men nodding off or puffing on pipes held by attendants. A few sipped tea. Jack's throat closed against the assault of heavy smoke.

"This will do fine," Martin said.

Martin must have seen the horrified look on Jack's face as he handed back the baseball cap. He squeezed Jack's arm in a gesture of thanks and farewell. "I'll be okay. Keep an eye on Delia, that's all."

Then Eeju drew him into the blue shadows.

Jack left his friend reluctantly. While Martin spoke with confidence and had given Jack clear instructions, his friend's eyes were bright with tension. As they parted, as Martin touched his arm, Jack had wanted to say, *wait*, had wanted to give Martin a bear hug of affection and support. But instead he merely stared after him.

Now to face the immigration cops. The thought disheartened him. His orders were to let himself be noticed in the lobby and to talk to them, to keep them from bothering Delia for now. Getting noticed wouldn't be hard. Jack stood out like a birch tree in a bonsai forest. But the instant he opened his mouth, they'd know he was lying.

Then he had a thought. Borrowing a knife from Truman, he cut the legs off his khaki pants mid-thigh, pulling at the torn edges to fray them. He gave Truman a few *baht* for the bandana around his neck and tied it under his hat to make a sweatband. Luckily, he had on his cross-trainers.

Off he ran, sprinting as fast as his long legs could be pushed. Around the block, once, twice, three times, he looked exactly as he meant to: a lunatic American jock who couldn't miss his daily run no matter what steamroom of a country he found himself in.

When Jack jogged into the hotel lobby, his face was strawberry red and dripping with sweat. As he picked up his room key, he continued to move around, loosening his shoulders, stretching his hamstrings.

He ventured a glance toward the cops. One of them nudged the other, they consulted a paper, then they both got up and strode toward him. They spoke too quickly.

"Say what?"

"I believe you must be Mr. John Francis Scanlan," said the one with the pencil thin moustache.

"Yeah?" Jack touched his toes.

"We are looking for Mr. Martin Elizondo Moon, your traveling companion. There is a slight irregularity with his papers and we must be asking him some question." They showed identification but the plastic-covered cards might have been gym memberships for all Jack absorbed.

"Haven't seen him since this morning," Jack puffed, thankful that his face was already as red as it could get and that the underarms of his shirt were already soaked, though now his sweat ran cold. Taking off his cap, he jogged in place lightly, counting on the breathlessness to camouflage the tension in his voice as he repeated what Martin told him to say. "But he did mention something about going to Patpong Street tonight. Told me not to expect him. Guy's a maniac for Thai massage." He pulled off the bandana to wipe his face and head. "Try again tomorrow morning—late morning." His attempt at a man-to-man chuckle aborted at the back of his throat.

As Jack backed into the elevator, the officials gave each other a weary glance.

In the room alone, *their* room now, Delia stood, hugging herself. Eyes closed. Smiling. Her brain was a muddle. Her legs ached. But Martin had stood by. Strong. Understanding. Knowing the right moment to pull her into his familiar arms...

The ringing phone jarred her. Jack's message was terse, his voice urgent. "Delia, I'm with Martin. Be there soon, but slight delay. Don't talk to *anyone* in the meantime, okay?"

Puzzled, but unwilling to let go of her silky mood, she agreed. She used the time to shower away the city grime. As she donned her nightgown and a hotel robe, she realized that for the first time in months, she was more aware of the swell of her breasts than of the scar that jagged between them. An annoying little thought nagged: that she was setting up an impossible situation, that she would have to choose—either Tony's exciting plans for their future, or Martin's addictive arms.

Think about it tomorrow, Scarlett. She danced around the room, rinsing out sweaty underwear, jotting notes, checking her cash. On impulse she placed a call to the Majestic Hotel, where Sara said Bellingham stayed.

"Who please?" asked the hotel operator, stymied by Delia's pronunciation.

Delia gave her Thai version. "Jedamy Belleenaham."

"Oh, Meestah Belleenaham. He not in room now. Leave message?"

"Can you tell me when he arrived?"

There was a pause at the other end while the operator consulted. "Arrive last week."

Delia hung up. He was here. And he was here the night someone broke into her room.

Pounding on the door startled her. It was Jack. He looked as if he just walked off a basketball court but there was no fun in his wide eyes. Gray streaks of sweat trickled down his cheeks.

While she tightened the belt of her robe, he pressed against the closed door and told her in a few breathless words about the trouble Martin was in, about the deportation order, and about the officials in the lobby.

"How did he find out? Who told him? Where is he now? What did you say to the immigration officers? Where *is* he? What's he going to do? Is he okay? *Where is he?*"

"He's safe for the night. The bar I discovered nearby has, uh, accommodations. I told the cops he went looking for girls on Patpong Street, but when they talk to you, hopefully not till tomorrow, you're supposed to say I was wrong. That Martin hired a guide and headed northeast, toward Phimai, to scope out a dealer."

Delia considered the story, then nodded. "You haven't told me how he found out. We were only separated for a few minutes before you called."

Jack sat in a chair near the window and, dropping his cap and the dirty bandana, stretched his shirt up to wipe his face. "Jones-White. Martin called him yesterday morning and then tonight, from the lobby. Yesterday, he told Martin that you were on your own. No contract. No job." He paused for a beat, letting her lie sink in. "It worried them, so Jones-White was trying to arrange some official sanction for your project, but somehow it backfired."

"Oh, boy." Delia looked away from the uncharacteristic hardness in Jack's eyes.

"Martin wants you to continue looking for Bellingham, if you don't mind me tagging along. He'll stay in the shadows, maybe find out more that way. He's afraid to leave you unprotected, but I think he's taking a helluva big risk not clearing this thing up right away." He stood. "I need a shower."

"You're acting like I'm the one who fucked him over."

"You could have told him the truth in the first place—that this was your own private vendetta."

"Now wait a minute. *Vendetta's* not fair—and I was planning to tell him. It just hadn't come up yet. I have enough money to cover our expenses, plus a fee for Martin. It was his own fault, not having enough trust in me, going behind my back and calling Edwin—if he hadn't called Edwin, the

116

hornets wouldn't be all stirred up. What gave him the idea—?"

"Remember, Martin woke up to find you missing yesterday morning."

"Missing? I told him on the flight what I planned to do first thing yesterday. I told him. I'm sure I told him. I can't be that flaky. Didn't you hear me tell him?"

Jack opened the connecting door.

"Please," she said. He looked back. "Leave it open?"

Her buoyant mood shattered, it didn't take more than two minutes alone for Delia to sweep up all her belongings and drag them into Jack's room, where there were two double beds. As he showered, she put Martin's papers, spare cash, Dopp kit, a shirt, and a change of underwear into a plastic shopping bag. Then she set about putting her own things in order. She was lining up pill bottles on the dresser and sorting vitamin packets when Jack stepped out of the bathroom, toweling his damp hair. She looked up. All he wore were lowslung, faded blue surgical scrubs.

"I'm afraid to be alone," she said.

He gave her a tired smile. Sitting on the chair near her, he watched her sort through the pills till she picked out a cellophane packet and tore it open.

"You really need that?"

"Think I'd lug around all this shit if it didn't do me any good?" She looked at him. There was something different, something she hadn't noticed before, something about his lips—a pinkness, a slight puffiness. He scratched his chest. "Don't you have a t-shirt or a robe or something?" she asked.

Ignoring the remark, he examined one of her vitamin packets. "Never saw some of these before."

"You an expert?"

"My kid's a competitive ballerina. Nuts are always pushing pills on her. I turn my head and she's got a new batch of 'supplements' I have to investigate. It's a racket."

The difference was in his voice, too—half a note deeper, a grade softer, a scale-point huskier.

"So what about mine?"

"It's just some of those capsules. You never see unmarked capsules in mass-produced packets. Must be made up special. Maybe they do it different in England." He tossed the packet back on the dresser, walked a step to the minibar, and stooped over to pull a beer from the fridge.

He stretched out on one of the beds, feet sticking over the edge, dewy bottle of Singha perched on his chest.

She held the eight pills in the palm of her hand. "I need them to sleep," she said. "I get all wired up during the day. I'm wired now. They help me sleep without having to take a sleeping pill."

"Then they're not vitamins. Tryptophan helps you relax a little, like a glass of warm milk. But when I went into your room last night, Delia, you weren't relaxed, you were zonked. And you are pretty hung-over in the morning—I noticed that."

Delia rolled the pills back onto the dresser. A seed of doubt had been planted. She'd experiment—go without.

"About last night, about your coming into my room... remind me what you said. Maybe I was zonked. You had some kind of nightmare, was that it?"

Jack frowned at her. "It was no dream. I went down to the wading pool. Savani and Lucky were there. He tried to pimp her to me."

Her jaw tightened. "Don't be ridiculous. Besides, Lucky's just a girl, no more than fourteen years old. Why would—?"

Jack sat up and sloshed the beer across his chest. "Fourteen?" he murmured, trying to dry himself with the bedspread. "What in God's name makes you think she's only fourteen?" He belted down the remaining beer, hurled the bottle into the trash, and continued to dry himself.

"Well, who knows—the women here have such delicate builds. But she's definitely a kid. Maybe he got her off the streets, maybe she's a massage girl."

Jack pulled on a t-shirt, then sat on the edge of the bed, his shoulders tensed. "Not just any massage girl." He refused to release Delia's eyes from his. "Didn't you see the resemblance? The coloring, the slinky body, the hooded white eyes? She's his daughter, I'd swear to it. And they smoke opium. I saw the pipe and the little opium globs and the lamp they use to heat it."

Delia rubbed at the pain knotting in her brow, back on the defensive. "First pills, now you're an opium expert?"

"It's Theresa. And I teach sixth grade. I do my research..."

She made an ugly grating sound in her throat to clear away the knot of frustration. "Look it," she whispered. "The only thing standing between me and the rest of my life is a madman who wouldn't mind ripping out the few guts I have left. That's what we ought to be worrying about. Just because you know how to use the internet doesn't make you any kind of expert. And I don't need a goddamn daddy to screen my friends and watch what pills I'm taking." She swept the batch of pills off the dresser into her hand, glanced around for the water pitcher, then changed her mind and flung them into the wastebasket.

Ingrid sat on the edge of the low concrete tub as she sponged the tepid water over herself. Every square inch of her skin still tingled. She ought to work for a couple more hours, but her concentration was blown. All she wanted was to crawl into bed, between clean sheets, and dream of Jack—the feel of his tongue on her lips, his mouth on her breast, his fingers between her legs...

She was patting herself dry when she heard footsteps on the stairs. Cal appeared at the doorway of the cramped bathroom-kitchenette.

"Where the hell were you?" he asked.

She continued to dry herself. "I had to look up something at the University library. Our report on the Li site has to go over to Mr. Savani tomorrow and I needed to verify my facts. I would have let you know but I never know where to reach you."

She pulled on a cotton wrapper. He brushed past her to get a bottle of beer from the small refrigerator, then followed her to her room, where he stretched out across the bed and watched her light a cigarette. The smoke helped blot out the smell of garlic and rancid spices that rose from the noodle shop downstairs.

Cal popped the snaps on his shirt. In the soft tone she dreaded he said, "So, Ingrid, love, you going to help me relax?"

"Look, Cal, I'm awfully tired and—"

"I know it's Bruno's night, but he won't be home for a couple hours yet. Good old Bruno never minds it if I take an extra turn now and then."

"No. You can't keep making me do this. I'm not a bloody whore."

"The hell you aren't." Cal set the bottle on the night stand, swung off the bed, and lunged at her.

She saw it coming but couldn't react fast enough. His fist caught her jaw and knocked her against the heavy desk. She bit her tongue.

"A bloody upper-crust high-toned whore."

"Don't," she cried. His second punch landed below her ribs and dropped her to her knees.

He yanked her to her feet and threw her on the bed, where he punched her again and again. She knew well enough not to scream. The last time she did he had broken the beer bottle and threatened to cut her face to ribbons.

"Stop," she whimpered. "I'll do whatever you want."

He shoved her down onto the foot of the bed and stood before her.

"Hurry it up," he said.

She unzipped his pants and sent her mind away to think about an article she'd write for *National Geographic*.

Two hours later, Ingrid huddled between the sheets. She comforted herself that the wheels were already in motion to get her out of there, even though she'd have to compromise her ethics to pull it off. Tomorrow's appointment had to go well. She'd make a smooth transition to a new project and her future in archaeology would no longer depend on the largesse of Bruno and Cal. And maybe, if things moved fast enough, she could schedule a few days with Jack.

Suddenly, her bedroom door opened. Light from the hall filled her small room as Bruno entered.

Jack rarely needed much sleep. At times it had been an advantage—during college and during Theresa's infancy, but in general it was a curse, leaving him far too much time to think.

Tonight, every noise in the hall was echoed by a thump in his chest. He worried over Ingrid. He worried over Martin. He worried over Lucky. He planned a phone call to Theresa, but, sticking to his promise not to call her more than once a week, it would have to wait a couple days.

He was also painfully aware that Delia lay awake in the other bed, squirming around and wrestling with covers. It wasn't till dawn that her tossing stilled and her breathing deepened.

Jack stared at her sprawled figure, tangled in sheets, robe and gown— the outstretched arms, the swells and curves of her torso, and the dense muscle of an exposed calf. Her beauty was darker, more voluptuous than Ingrid's...

Sleep must have finally overtaken him, because it was suddenly nine-thirty and someone was knocking on the door of what used to be Martin's room. With a sharp jab to Delia's shoulder, Jack lurched through the connecting doorway. The two immigration police stood there, long-faced, bedraggled, and surprised to see Jack.

"Ah... has Mr. Moon returned?"

Before Jack could muddle through an answer, Delia wiggled herself in front of him, retying her robe.

"Mr. Moon is no longer staying with us," she said, her voice husky with sleep. "He heard about a new dealer northeast of here and took off. We were supposed to be partners in this buying trip, but apparently he decided he works best alone." Then she gripped Jack's shoulder, as if to imply the break-up were more emotional than professional. Jack followed the cue, reached across her back, and pulled her a little closer. "I doubt he'll be back too soon. He took most of his clothes and asked me to put the rest of his things in hotel storage when we check out."

The officers seemed confused. "Mr. Scanlan told us Mr. Moon went out for Thai massage and would be back this morning." They were craning their necks to look around Jack into the room. Delia backed Jack out of the way and let them walk through the adjoining rooms.

"It was a misunderstanding. Mr. Moon was upset when he left, said some things that Jack misunderstood. You should have spoken with me," she said. Much to Jack's discomfort, she put her other hand on his chest and rested her head in the crook of his shoulder. Her voice softened. "If you don't have any more questions, gentlemen...?"

The officers were blushing as she swung the door shut.

"Jesus God," she muttered, pushing herself away from Jack. She held her hand against her forehead and closed her eyes. "Let's get cracking. We'll grab a bite, then I think I'll check Martin out of this room for good—keep our story consistent." She looked at Jack. "We'll manage with one room, okay?"

Dick's officially opened at 11 a.m. It was half-past the hour when Jack entered. Truman stood at his usual station talking with an unshaven man in a faded striped shirt and worn gray pants, a couple sizes too large. It was Martin.

Jack laid the shopping bag of Martin's belongings on the bar and clapped his shoulders. "Hey, man. How you doin'? Where'd you get the clothes?"

"Tru lent me these. And this." He picked up a battered straw hat. "They'll help me blend into the scenery a little better." He rubbed his silvery jaw. "Seedy look."

"And you slept okay here?"

"Slept like a baby, once I smoked the dope."

Jack's jaw dropped. Martin laughed.

"It's no big deal—opium's a good sedative, which is what I needed." He went on to explain his plan to watch them from a distance, to see if anyone was following Delia. Dick's would be his home base for a few days and Truman agreed to take messages for him. Truman grinned, happy to be part of the action.

Despite Martin's light-hearted tone of voice, every time the door behind Jack opened, his eyes darted over Jack's shoulder. And every time Martin's eyes darted, Jack stopped breathing for a second.

"Delia's okay? You told her to stay put, that you'd be right back?" Martin asked. Jack nodded. "I'm terrified something will happen and she'll be all alone."

"Martin, I swear I won't let you down."

Then Ingrid walked in. The change from her usual field clothes dazzled him. She wore a short skirt, dressy sandals instead of hiking boots, and a bright blouse with long sleeves and a high collar. Her flaxen hair was unbraided and brushed, one side pinned behind her ear and the other nearly covering the left side of her face. Only her worn rucksack spoiled the image.

"G'day," she called out to Truman. Then she saw Jack.

As Truman pulled her bottle of Mekhong off the shelf, he said, "You're lookin' mighty fine this morning."

But her eyes were locked on Jack's. "I told you I had an appointment."

And Jack's eyes followed her as she took her bottle and walked back to her booth. "That's Ingrid," he said to Martin, "the archaeologist I mentioned. I gotta say hi. Two minutes."

Martin donned his hat. "Talk to you later."

As Jack slid into the booth beside Ingrid, prepared to apologize for pressuring her the night before, the sparkle in her eyes told him it wasn't necessary. The mouth even threatened to smile. "I have all this work," she murmured, then his lips were on hers and, for a few short seconds, they devoured one another.

Jack reluctantly pulled away and explained that he couldn't stay anyway, that he needed to help out his friends with something, and that he wasn't quite sure when he'd be freed up.

The joy drained from her face and she turned to her papers. "Oh. Your scavenger friends."

To coax her into looking back at him, he pushed the strands of fine blonde hair away from the left side of her face. There was a dark welt on her cheek. With the light behind her, it was hard to see the skin clearly, but the bruise seemed to extend to her neck, under the tall collar.

"Sweetheart, look at me." When she didn't respond, he took her shoulders and pulled her around. She winced. "Cal hit you, didn't he?"

"Yes," she whispered.

He unbuttoned her collar, but still he couldn't see where the dark, swollen welts ended. He pressed his hand against her thigh and she flinched.

Words of outrage, words of comfort, words of warning surged through his mind, but they all felt inadequate. He checked his watch: already he'd been gone longer than Delia expected.

"Ingrid," he finally said, as he emptied his pockets of *baht*. "If I'm not back by five, take this and get yourself a hotel room. Tell Truman where you've gone, okay?"

She shook her head. "Look, right now I can only accomplish my goals by working with Cal and Bruno. An alternative is on the horizon, but I can't leave them till it comes through. If I start acting unreliable, no one else will ever hire me. I'll admit the two of them are quirky. They have this thing about..." She looked into Jack's eyes and changed what she was going to say. "These bruises are nothing. Nothing compared to the importance of the

123

project. We're going back up to Chiang Mai tomorrow afternoon. Unless I get a quick break on a new proposal I've made, best you should simply forget about me. I won't know anything till this evening at the earliest."

But her eyes held onto his and, even with the urgency of getting back to Delia, Jack couldn't walk out of Ingrid's life. He couldn't leave her so deluded. He couldn't believe she was such a hard case, couldn't believe that potsherds and crumbly old statues were more important than respect, than kindness, than love. He couldn't leave her to Cal.

"Why did he beat you?"

Her eyes skittered around the room. "I didn't want him..."

"Didn't want him what?"

"To... have sex with me. Not after... you. Not ever again, after you."

A brick dropped in his stomach. "Shit, I asked you before if there was something between you two. Why didn't you tell me then that—"

"It's not like there's *something between us,*" she barked. "It's... an arrangement is all. They were going to fire me because I wasn't companionable enough. Cal made it clear, what he and Bruno wanted. I'm out of money. If I can't work, I have to go home to England. And this project is more exciting and more important than I could have imagined—a career-maker. I agreed to whatever they wanted. The sex means nothing to me. I get nothing out of it."

"You have sex with both of them?"

"They take turns. Sometimes the other one—the odd man out watches. From the other room. It's a kink they've apparently had since their days together at boarding school. It was all very businesslike between us, till yesterday. Till you."

Tenderness battled anger and confusion as Jack pulled her into his arms. What the hell had she gotten herself into? What was wrong with her? Jack knew plenty of ambitious, hard-drive women—his ex-wife Monica, for one. None would ever think of debasing herself to get ahead. What the hell was Ingrid getting out of being raped that made her toss it off as the price of doing business? Why wasn't she angrier?

He had to return to Delia.

"Please," he said, as he stood to go, "please don't go back to them."

Delia wasn't at all pleased about being left behind while Jack met with Martin. So what if she hadn't slept all night and sizzled with irritation? Didn't mean Jack had to patronize her by insisting she rest. She eyed her lineup of pill bottles. If she took her morning regimen of pills, she'd be all right. But her conversation with Jack last night and the dramatic consequences of not taking her p.m. vitamins scared her. Not taking them was a risk. This was the wrong time to screw up her sleep cycle and invite more panic attacks. But she'd try it just for today, just for a few more hours.

She moved all Martin's belongings into Jack's room and called the desk clerk to check Martin out.

From her travel bag she pulled the two handguns she picked up the other day. After she'd met with Savani, she sought out an illegal gun dealer she'd met on a previous assignment. Since the assault, she'd read gun magazines, talked to experts, and spent many hours at a shooting range, but had stopped short of actually arming herself. It was time. No one would hurt her again. Before her was a .357 Magnum Auto Pistol that held a magazine of seven rounds and a pocket-sized Colt .45 that held six bullets. The Magnum felt large in her hands, but she could carry it in her purse, while Jack slipped the .45 into a pocket. Each was a man-stopper.

When she finished loading the two pistols, Delia called the Majestic Hotel. The operator again reported that Mr. Bellingham was out.

A hand touched her shoulder and Delia's eyes snapped open. A dream skittered away. Jack crouched next to her, his eyes dewy and strained.

"Martin? Is it Martin?" she asked, pulling herself up.

"Martin's okay."

"I must have fallen asleep." The time on her watch startled her. "You've been gone more than an hour. What's going on?"

"Nothing."

She hoisted herself out of bed, straightened her dress and ran her fingers through her hair. "God, I hate a bad liar." Nevermind, she needed to focus on the job. "Hey, you didn't bring a tie, did you?"

He changed into a short-sleeved oxford-cloth shirt, slightly rumpled, with a plain blue tie. He looked exactly like what he was: a school teacher on vacation.

She reached into her bag and pulled out the pocket pistol she expected him to carry.

"Take this."

He recoiled. "No thanks."

"*No thanks* is not an option. We're going to make contact with a murderer sooner or later and we need protection. I have another one in my purse."

"You should have given it to Martin, not me."

"Martin's not going to have a shoot-out with the immigration police. I'm the one going after a murderer and you're with me."

"Delia, I don't know how to use a gun. I haven't touched a gun since I gave up my Lone Ranger six-shooter in the second grade. Guns are obscene."

"Don't lecture me. We're talking about saving our hides here, not testifying before Congress. Look." She cornered him. "You unlock it, cock it, aim it, and shoot it. Use two hands and keep your elbows locked or you'll bloody your forehead. It holds six rounds." She took his hand and laid the pistol in it. His eyes pleaded with her. "Just put it in your pocket."

He mumbled something about shooting his balls off but did as he was told. She made him walk around the room till he stopped telegraphing his terror, then they set out for Chinatown.

The taxi dropped them off in the so-called Thieves' Market, a jumble of narrow streets, webbed with power lines strung between three-story buildings. Striped awnings, advertising signs, and laundry hung from balconies multiplied the chaos. At first glance, the district sold nothing but big electric motors, motorcycle parts, and household appliances. But scattered here and there were a good assortment of airless little antique shops. Like most shops along the narrow Bangkok side-streets, entire storefronts opened like rolltop desks, exposing the shops to dust and fumes yet attracting little breeze.

To Jack, Delia grumbled about the amount of junk she saw but, to the shopkeepers, she smiled, admired their goods, and figured out ways to bring up the name of Jeremy Bellingham. As much as possible, she forced herself to speak in her broken Chinese. At one shop, a display of eighteenth-century soapstone carvings absorbed her and made her mull over the possibility of selling the soft stone to clients who found themselves priced out of the jade market. Then she remembered that she had only one client now—Tony—and it was hard to imagine him priced out of any market.

For a while, Jack examined the merchandise, then complained that he was blinded by the sweat dripping into his eyes. He loosened his tie and the top button of his shirt. Although the traffic fumes along the narrow lanes were particularly noxious, he chose to stand outside on the sidewalk—pacing, checking his watch, and tapping at the pistol in his pocket. Delia wanted to tell him to fill his vacant eyes with some sharp observations, but she held her tongue. Better he look like an impatient boyfriend than a bodyguard. Just in case anyone watched.

By the time Delia and Jack got back to the hotel, at quarter of five, they were grimy with sweat, shop dust, and street pollution. But while Delia was buoyed up by the hours of poking around in the shops, Jack wore a slightly crazed look and thanked her for letting him have first crack at the shower.

Delia called the Majestic Hotel again. This time the operator patched her through and after a single ring the phone was picked up.

"Bellingham here."

The afternoon was a strain for Martin, as he followed Delia and Jack. Their pace was slow and methodical. Martin found it hard to look interested in motorcycle parts for as long as they spent in each shop. For a while, he thought he'd been wrong about someone tailing Delia, but there he was, the stalker, skillfully blending into the shop traffic. The man was thirtyish, a flabby Mediterranean type, in a plaid shirt.

When Delia and Jack hailed a cab to head back to the Tudor, the man lumbered to a motorcycle and took off after them. Martin hired a *tuk-tuk* back to Dick's All-American Bar and Grill.

"Hey, man," Truman said. "You look bushed. Have a seat, I'll bring you something. Brew?"

"Sounds wonderful." Truman pulled a quart-sized bottle out of the cooler. "Wait. I, uh, I think I better have a Coke." He dropped his bones

127

onto a stool and pushed his hat back. The sweat that soaked his clothes turned to ice in the frigid air. He rubbed his eyes.

"Have some pretzels, sir."

A well-dressed, middle-aged Chinese man sat down next to Martin and pushed a small bowl of snacks toward him.

"*Xiexie nin*," Martin said.

"*Nin shuo zhongguo hua bu shuo?*"

"*Wo shuo zhen bu hao.* Really, I can manage only a few polite phrases in Chinese."

"But your intonation is impeccable. And you knew I was Chinese, not Thai. Very few American tourists bother to sort out Asian faces. You don't mind if I join you?"

"Of course not, Mr.—"

"I am Dick Li. Your host, Mr. Moon."

Martin covered the surprise of losing his anonymity by gushing further amenities: what a friendly bar Mr. Li ran, how good his English was, etcetera, while Dick raised a hand to bring Truman scurrying over with a bottle of single malt Scotch and a shot glass. Dick poured himself a drink.

"You were going to tell me, Mr. Moon, how you came to be such a sophisticated traveler."

"I'm an art dealer. Done a lot of business in the East—Hong Kong, Japan, Korea, Philippines. Picked up a little Chinese when I spent a couple months in Taiwan trading in Paiwanese folk art. I've forgotten nearly all of it."

Dick drank his shot. "And you're looking for art deals here, in Bangkok?"

"This trip is for my own collection. Sculpture, especially early Khmer pieces. I haven't been buying for the trade in more than a year."

"And why is that?" Dick's small dark eyes were fastened on him.

"My partner... my wife..." *Spit it out.* "My wife died nearly a year ago. Took the wind out of my sails. This is my first trip abroad since then."

Dick clucked in sympathy. Then his eyes narrowed. "For a man who has been out of circulation so long, you certainly manage to find trouble. Abandoning the Tudor for a wooden plank in an opium den. Trading a bespoke suit for a workman's rags." He pushed a folded Thai newspaper toward Martin. "Your picture is in the afternoon edition. Says you're a smuggler."

Martin stared at the photo of a haggard man on crutches, his hand half-raised to block the camera flashes. A woman stood behind him, her eyes crinkled with laughter at something to her left. Lana. Their deportation at the Bangkok airport. The image had all the pop glamor of a mobster being led off to jail. If this picture were picked up by the wire services, Emmaline Tuthill would have a stroke. Or dance with joy that she could now be rid of him forever.

Martin winced. "This is an unfortunate misunderstanding. I'd like to explain, but—"

"Please, no need. I don't mind helping you," Dick Li said. "You are a likable fellow. But I am a family man. I must walk a fine line to protect them and to protect my business. Not that I don't take chances myself. Look at Truman there. A deserter from the U.S. Army. Muscles where his brains should be. Yet he is loving to Eeju and loyal to me. Works seven days a week, twelve hours or more a day, year in and year out. Truman took a liking to your friend Scanlan and has gone out on a limb for you—"

Martin started to apologize but Dick waved the words away. "Please, I am a busy man. I only want to see that we are all protected."

"Yes, of course. It's a giant mixup, really. The only way I can straighten it out is to leave Thailand, but, see, there's a woman with me who could be murdered if we can't locate the man who seems to have this thing against her—this vendetta or something—we're not even sure. And I can't bear to lose another... another..."

"Loved one." Dick was frowning.

"But look, Mr. Li, I'm not going to put you or your business at risk. I have a friend here in Bangkok, Tony Savani, and I can probably get some help from him."

"Savani, Savani." Dick reproduced the sound of Martin's Midwestern *a*, then his eyes widened. "You don't mean Antoine Savani?" He gave the name a French lilt: *sahvahNEE.* "Very wealthy. Owns a house on the *khlong* and properties in the north?"

"Antoine, eh? Sounds like him. You know each other?"

"What have you told him of your problem?"

"Nothing. It wasn't till yesterday, after we came back from his canal house, that I found out what hot water I'm in. I'd like to avoid involving him. Really, I've been hoping with a little vigilance things would sort themselves out."

"Things rarely get sorted out without someone to sort them. I'm sure you're a very brave and clever man, but Thailand is a complex country.

Much goes on beneath the surface. You must sleep well. Stay healthy."

"What—?"

"The only way a man can sleep on the hard wooden pallets here is to smoke. This is no time for you to dull your senses, Mr. Moon."

Martin nodded. "What I need is a cheap hotel that won't check my papers. And a place to make phone calls from."

"My wife is in the States with the twins looking at colleges. Only my son is home with me. You will stay with us."

The opulence of the Li home suggested that Dick's business extended far beyond the humble bar, grill, and opium den. The house was decorated in traditional Chinese style and the antique furnishings and art made Martin's pulse race with dealer's greed.

"My family was lucky. We were members of the Kuomintang. When Chiang Kai-shek and the KMT leadership fled to Taiwan after the communist takeover, my family left Swatow for Bangkok. We had the right connections to bring all the household furnishings and family treasures. Otherwise, they surely would have been destroyed."

Dick introduced his son Arthur, a thin youth who wore heavy glasses and sported a wry smile as he looked Martin over.

"Another Corsican gangster, pop?" he asked in perfect American English.

"Arthur! Mr. Moon is an American art dealer."

Dick explained that Arthur had graduated from Stanford in January and was planning to start business school at Columbia in September.

"Small world," Martin said. "My father taught economics at the business school there. He's *emeritus* now—retired—but still does some writing. Economic development, worked for the Reagan administration."

"My kind of guy."

Dick got Martin settled in a guest room and showed him the phone. He also asked the cook to prepare an evening meal for Martin, who shyly mentioned that he did not eat meat, so that rice and vegetables would be fine.

Once all the formalities of settling into someone else's home had been observed and Dick set back for the bar, Martin laid out his shrinking set of worldly possessions: Dopp kit, clean shirt and underwear, wallet, passport, and the precious amulet. Then he called Jones-White.

Edwin was relieved to hear from him. "Your disappearance is alarming the hell out of everyone. Everyone. The Thais are beginning to think they had good reason to deport someone so uncooperative. My protests that you have consistently been acting in the best interest of Thailand fall on deaf ears. Interpol is wondering whether you really do have something to hide. The American ambassador in Bangkok is apoplectic. And I'm sick with worry, old darling. You've never been so perilously on the wrong side of authority. Hiding out—it's all so, well, dramatic."

"What have you told them?"

"Only that I've lost contact."

"Any new information for me?"

"Well, who knows if it's relevant. I might not have pursued it at all, except that the record indicates René Malraux had a Savani Foundation fellowship and experience shows it's best to check out everything. Anyway, I discovered that our friend Tony Savani has a very colorful family history. Who would have guessed it, really? His speech is so classically upper-crust Manhattan. But, of course, it should have dawned on me that blue-bloods don't typically have surnames ending in vowels."

"What is it, Edwin?"

"Antoine Raoul Savani..."—now Jones-White gave it the French intonation—"is a naturalized American citizen, born in Marseilles, France. His father, François, was *un vrai Monsieur*, a respected boss in the Marseilles branch of the Corsican syndicate and enthusiastic Nazi collaborator."

"I'll be damned," murmured Martin.

"After the second war, his father made a fortune smuggling gold bullion and paper currency between Saigon and Marseilles. By the end of the First Indochina War—say '53, '54—he was running a large heroin refinery at his villa outside Marseilles. The morphine base was being imported largely from Turkey at that time, but the trickle from Indochina was growing.

"Tony's mother was Maria Pisani, whose brother Raoul was a captain with the French Expeditionary Corps in Indochina. He was crackerjack at organizing paramilitary units out of river pirates, Catholics, and hill tribes to fight the Viet Minh nationalists. He bought the loyalty of the hill tribes by buying their opium. To make a long story short, he also made a fortune by using local middlemen to sell the opium to his Corsican cousins in Saigon for shipment to Marseilles refineries."

"And Tony? Did he join the family business or simply inherit the profits?"

"Hard to say, hard to say. What I told you is easily accessible stuff—widely written about. When Tony was an infant, he was sent to live in New York City with an uncle. And it's fairly certain, though less well documented, that the New York Savanis were part of the action. But the heroin business has changed. Most of the opium is grown in Burma and Laos. It's shipped into northern Thailand and refined right there around Chiang Mai. Makes export a lot more compact, since a hundred pounds of opium can be reduced to a single pound of heroin. Gets shipped out in small packages, buried in big containers of legitimate Thai exports. There is a heavily guarded Savani family compound up north, near the Burma-Laos border. It is, I suspect, under fairly constant international scrutiny, but they're a very sophisticated lot."

"And Tony?"

"All we know is that Tony's made a second home in Thailand for some fifteen years and that he's rich as an oil magnate. A very generous magnate, to be sure. His Chiang Mai residence is far from the family compound and he has never been seen with any of his cousins. His security precautions are minimal. But the Corsican syndicates are, as I said, very sophisticated and the members have traditionally kept in touch across vast distances, rarely getting caught."

"Thanks, Edwin. A friend with his connections might come in handy, the fix I'm in. But I suppose it ought to make Delia think twice about linking her fate to his."

"Well, yes, but there is one more thing—purely circumstantial. You may need reminding that the Corsican syndicates have many specialties beyond the heroin trade. Art smuggling is one of them."

Delia hit the jackpot. Jeremy Bellingham was on the line. She jammed her knees against the dresser to steady them.

"Mr. Bellingham, this is Delia Rivera. We were working on a deal about a year ago, in London. Carved elephant tusks."

A pause. "What do you want from me?"

"I'm here in Bangkok and I heard from Sara Malraux that you stay at the Majestic when you're in town, so I thought I'd give you a call."

"Sara? You spoke with Sara?"

"She said you've been dealing in some fine Lopburi sculpture. I'm interested."

"What are you after, Miss Rivera?" He spoke sharply. "If it's information—information about who assaulted you back in London—you've come looking for the wrong person."

"Then, who is it I should be looking for? Tell me."

He shrieked, "How the bloody hell do I know? I'm as much a victim as you are. Everywhere I bloody go people are getting sliced to bits."

A pain shot through her belly, causing her to double over and sag into a chair. Jack was coming out of the bathroom and looked at her with alarm. Bellingham was still talking, his voice shrill.

"It's a bloody nightmare. I'm simply going about my business, then, suddenly, there's some kind of horrid assault and everyone's pointing the finger at me. It's turning me into a nervous wreck and, if I can't get a grip on myself, my career will go up in smoke."

"Are you saying that you don't know who hurt me? That you had nothing to do with it?"

"What bloody reason would I have? I'm an art dealer, not a psychopath. Those tusks were a five-thousand-pound sale, at twenty percent commission. Why the hell would I try to kill you?"

His explanation was venal enough to be credible. Jack handed her a glass of water. She drank.

"What about Lana? Lana Tuthill."

His groan caused Delia another jab of pain. "Tell me what you know," she demanded.

"I don't know anything, I swear. That Moon fellow told the police that she thought she was going to a party at my place. I didn't know what they were talking about. I hadn't spoken with her since the night I had dinner at their house." He began to sniffle. "Christ, I loved her. Such a vibrant woman. So proud. Everyone I knew worshipped her. I'm not a violent man, Delia, I swear."

"Calm down, okay?"

"But I need help!" he cried. "It's you, you who must have information, a description, a clue. Who is playing this grotesque game with me? Lana dazzled and flirted and swept me off my feet. You were a cash customer. And René... René and I were so close, such good friends, even if we argued endlessly about who should own the bloody artifacts. Such a gentle man..." He was crying again, a low keening that he wasn't even trying to choke back.

"Please," she said as the contagion of his tears made her throat tighten. "Please. We'll get together and think it out. Can you meet me? Now? Tonight?"

It took him a minute to calm down. "Not tonight." *Sniff.* "I have a meeting I can't put off."

"Then I'll meet you at your hotel tomorrow, first thing. Nine o'clock. Okay?"

"I suppose so. No. Make it ten."

Savani picked up the phone. "What is it, Jeremy?"

"I'm not sure, Mr. Savani. Suddenly, everyone's on my case—I don't know what I'm being set up for. Thought I'd better get your advice." His voice was thick, strained.

"Hold on." Tony pressed the handset to his chest. "Lucky, did the strawberries arrive from Japan yet?"

She smiled and nodded.

"Fetch us a bowl, will you, darling? With whipped cream. And another espresso, please." He returned the handset to his ear. "Go on."

"Well, first there's Ingrid Lundquist. She found the site up in Chiang Mai."

"The Li property, I know. I tried to discourage them."

"No. The ThaiCorp property—the site I've been working. She found it, then ferreted out the connection with New Cathay Galleries. Says her mates don't know she found it and she wants to cut a deal. I get permission for her to dig on the land and provide a letter of support for her to the Savani Foundation. In turn, once she gets the place surveyed, she closes her eyes to my continuing to sell off a few of the better pieces. If I don't cooperate, she goes directly to the Ministry of Antiquities with her notes and photos."

Tony rubbed his eyes. "What did you say to her?"

"I played ignorant, but she has too much information. Finally, I told her to give me a day to mull it over. But it smells like a set-up. She works with those hawkeyes, Clearwater and Andriotti. I called them up, spoke to Clearwater, told him not to be sending his girl over to pry into my business..."

"Oh, God," Tony muttered under his breath. Scanlan had mentioned Ingrid's "secret" Saturday night, and, stupidly, he hadn't connected it with the ThaiCorp site. Damn, this was bad.

Bellingham was still talking. "...You know, they were after me about the location of that site back when I was seeing a lot of René—"

"Back when you spilled the beans to René that you had access to a Khmer treasure trove. Back when you'd do anything to keep René in your pants." And here he was blabbing to Bruno and Cal. "Why the hell didn't you call me instead of them? Those two are lunatics."

"I, um..." Jeremy seemed to lose his voice. Tony heard a sharp intake of air. "I'm merely trying to..." He cleared his throat. "Merely trying to carry on..." More throat clearing. "Trying to take care of business... as you told me I must."

Few things were more moving than seeing Jeremy's princely face tear-streaked and desolate—as Tony had seen it only once, in Hong Kong, shortly after Malraux's death. He could see it now and a tiny burst of compassion took him by surprise.

Where was Lucky with the damn strawberries?

"Yes, yes, Jeremy, get on with your story. What advice is it you want at this stage of the game?"

Jeremy had composed himself. "Clearwater said he wanted to talk to me about it, so they're coming over to my hotel tonight. But that's only the half of it. I just got a call from Delia Rivera. You told me, you assured me her trip to Bangkok had nothing to do with me—"

"What did she want?" Tony sat upright.

"Same old business, about her bloody assault, Lana Tuthill's murder. And she's been talking to Sara Malraux. I told her this was as much a nightmare for me as for anyone, but she still thinks I know something. She wants to meet with me, to share information. I put her off till morning. She's coming here at ten. If truth be told, Mr. Savani, I'd like to take the first plane back to Hong Kong. I don't want to deal with any of them. Look, this may jeopardize my work with you, but it's probably best to tell you that I've been seeing a psychiatrist in Hong Kong. Since René—any undue stress—my behavior—I've become more compulsive… less in control of… I thought I could handle the hawkeyes, but having Rivera dredge up all the old business about—Tony, I need time. A few weeks with no pressure."

Jeremy's state of mind was worse than Tony had suspected. The man had unraveled.

"A few weeks it is, Jeremy," he said. "I had no idea how much René meant to you, no idea that you found such… fulfillment in his friendship." The words were vinegar on his tongue. "But you'll do me one last favor, won't you? I'll distract Delia from her appointment with you and get her interests moving in a new direction. But I'd appreciate it if you'd go ahead and meet with Bruno and Cal tonight, simply to find out what it is they know. If it really is Ingrid's ace in the hole, as I suspect it is, I can take care of her easily. If it's some sort of HAWC-I set-up—well, that makes it somewhat more complicated."

"Yes. Yes, all right."

As he hung up, Lucky rushed in with a tray containing a crystal bowl of scarlet berries, a mountain of whipped cream, and a small steaming cup.

"Good God, child, did you have to go all the way out to the airport?"

"We had to whip the cream."

He grabbed a strawberry by its dark green cap, glided it through the cream, and, closing his eyes, pressed his lips, teeth, and tongue against it. The explosion of sweetness did not erase the bitter aftertaste of his conversation with Jeremy. The man's stock had fallen to zero—a high-risk investment gone bust. Yet what Tony resented most was the cause of his collapse: *love*, the physical affection so exuberantly shared between Jeremy Bellingham and René Malraux. Damn them all.

In his cutoffs and running shoes, Jack trotted through the hotel lobby on his way to Dick's All-American Bar and Grill. His legs moved him along so fast through the blur of tourists that he was taken by surprise at suddenly being face-to-face with the man he'd met in the restaurant on the first night in Bangkok. The round-handed young man in the plaid shirt was equally surprised.

Jack greeted him with a smile of recognition, but before he could open his mouth the fellow evaded Jack's eyes and pushed past him through the entrance of the Jasmine Palace.

The first thing Jack did at Dick's All-American Bar and Grill was look toward Ingrid's booth even though it was past her usual quitting time. Four men sat there.

"Scanlan, what'll it be?"

"Martin. He around?"

"Left with Dick twenty minutes ago. Dick offered him a real bed for the night, but he told me to tell you that y'all are being followed, like you thought." Truman gave Martin's description of the watcher.

Jack's pulse picked up. It was the man he'd met in the restaurant, the man he just passed in the lobby. "He say anything else?"

"Said be real careful. Dick'll be back later if you want to leave a message."

Jack left word for Martin about Bellingham's call and the scheduled appointment. Delia wanted to talk it over with Martin beforehand. Truman suggested a little noodle shop with a back entrance that Martin could use.

"Truman, what time did Ingrid leave? Did she leave me any message?"

"Let's see, she scooted out about quarter o' five like usual. For some reason, she left her backpack with me and, yeah, she left this for you."

Truman rummaged around, then handed Jack a brown paper bag, the kind that Ingrid packed her lunch in. She had printed his name in big block letters—"Jack Scanlan"—then dawdled over it for a while, outlining the letters, creating shadows and 3D effects.

Jack unfolded the top and held the bag upside down over the bar. Out fluttered a dozen bills. The *baht* he'd given her for a hotel room. He shook it again and looked inside to see if there was a note, but the bag was empty. His cheeks burned.

"Owe you money?" Truman asked.

Jack stuffed the bills in his pocket and smoothed out the brown bag. "Did she say anything? About where she was going?"

Truman shook his head.

"She get here every day about 11:30?"

"Like clockwork."

Jack traced the letters of his name with his finger.

"She live nearby?"

"Nah, they got a place up in Chinatown. Don't know where exactly but

Eeju's been there. Took her home once when she had that bad belly, about a month, six weeks ago. Brought her some elixir, too."

Jack neatly folded the bag and slipped it into his pocket.

That night, despite belting down several shots, Jack couldn't sleep. Delia had stuck with her resolve not to take any more pills, so, in the other bed, she too battled with the blankets.

Jack's thoughts were full of Ingrid. Much to his surprise, the images were not sexual but domestic. He and Ingrid playing house. Cooking. Washing dishes. Doing laundry. Caring for the baby.

He had occasionally thought about having more children. Rearing Theresa had been the most successful thing he'd ever done, followed by his popularity with sixth-graders. He had a knack for kids.

They'd have a boy to start with. John Lundquist Scanlan. Or Thomas, after his father. He'd be a big son-of-a-gun but he wouldn't be browbeaten into football if he didn't want to play. Jack wouldn't mind having another girl, but wondered if he could ever prize her as much as he did Theresa.

It would work out well. The school district provided day care for teachers and Ingrid could join the faculty at the university.

His eyes opened. The sky was a dirty rose. The thoughts that had been coursing so logically through his mind were insane. Like he'd slipped into an alternate universe, where he was fifteen years younger and Ingrid gave a damn about playing house.

He got up, dressed, then stared out the window at traffic, trying to figure out how a winner like Ingrid managed to make such terrible choices.

At seven, Delia stirred, squinted at him, stumbled into the bathroom, and started the shower. The phone rang.

"Hello."

"Scanlan?"

"Yeah."

"The desk told me that both Martin and Delia have checked out. What's going on?" It was Tony Savani.

"Martin's off on his own a couple days. Phimai, something like that."

"Phimai? With all the trouble he's in? Story's in this morning's *Bangkok Post*—along with that dreadful photo. Wonder what he's after. Delia didn't go with him, did she?"

"She's here with me. She's in the shower at the moment." Dead air. "Leave a message?"

Savani's voice sharpened. "I don't understand who you are, Jack, or what you're doing with Delia. She's much too emotionally frail for a lot of complex entanglements. I would have gladly sent Lucky back with you if I'd known how hungry you are."

Jack yanked the phone as far from the bathroom door as possible and hissed, "You don't know what the fuck you're talking about. Delia's here because she's scared and because she trusts me. And as far as Lucky goes, she's your daughter, isn't she? And, Jesus, you lend her out like a good book?"

Savani laughed. "What's a good book for if you can't share it? You're very observant, Jack, to see we share the pale eyes that have haunted my mother's family for generations. She's incredibly skilled, wouldn't you say?"

"You're an insult to the animal kingdom."

Savani laughed again. "One mustn't get too righteous, my handsome friend, for the devil's in all of us. Even you." His voice softened. "Even you."

Jack didn't respond.

"Anyway, assuming Delia hasn't abandoned our project in favor of other—" Tony checked whatever he was about to say and cleared his throat. "Assuming Delia hasn't abandoned our project, tell her that she needs to join me for a drive up to Chiang Mai this morning. Museum business. My car will fetch her at nine-thirty, do you hear?"

"Do you think she's going to work with you once she knows your true colors?"

"Let me worry about Delia. And stop interfering. You'll only wind up hurting her and, and you'll also find yourself a sad man indeed. Consider that a threat."

Jack was watching traffic again when Delia came out of the bathroom. She wore a dusky green cotton dress and espadrilles. Her cheeks and the tip of her nose were rosy with a blush of sunburn and her eyes sparkled in spite of the tired shadows around them. The beads she'd worn constantly for two days rustled softly as she moved.

"Was that the phone?"

"Yeah. Wrong number." Jack didn't blush or stammer, because it didn't feel like a lie.

Ingrid slipped on the voile dress Mr. Savani seemed to like. She'd deliver the Li site report and the Cambodian slides by river taxi this evening, then finish packing for tomorrow's trip up north. Maybe she'd call Bellingham to see if he made any decision yet. Maybe she'd call Jack.

Suddenly, her bedroom door flew open.

"Damn it, Cal, can't I have any privacy?"

He closed the door behind him and leaned against it. "What have you been hiding from us, princess?"

"Cal, I have to take this report over to Mr. Savani. Can the games wait till later?"

"No." Cal snatched away the scarf that she'd hung over a hole in the wall—a peep-hole from the next room. A peephole perfect for a nosy camcorder. It was going to be one of those nights. Her mind geared down to a hopeless neutral. The reports would have to be sent by messenger in the morning. Her pretty dress would be ruined.

"What do you want me to do?" She heard the deadness in her voice.

"First, tell me where your notes are, your rucksack."

What? "None of your—"

He grabbed her shoulders and pulled her against him. "Wrong," he said softly. "You're being paid off our grant. Everything you learn belongs to us." He squeezed her bruised flanks. "Everything you are belongs to us. Now—the notes?"

"I left my pack at Dick's. After last night, my ribs, my back hurt too much to lug it all the way back here." Her pain was real enough, but she'd also had a premonition that her intellectual secrets were as vulnerable to violation as her body. She couldn't jeopardize her ticket out of this hell.

"Next. What kind of deal are you trying to pull off with Jeremy Bellingham?"

How could he know? The certainty that she could get herself out of this mess suddenly faltered. The numbness that she'd learned to turn on at Cal's touch suddenly burst into desperate pain.

"You're hurting me!"

"If you've found anything new, you high-toned bitch, it belongs to me. Me and Bruno."

As he groped for her breast, she lurched away, but he caught her and slammed her against the wall. He unbuckled his belt.

"And before we're finished, you'll tell me what Scanlan and his friends are really looking for here in Thailand and exactly—in detail—what kind of lover this Scanlan fellow is."

"No!" Over the weeks, Ingrid had become adept at stanching her impulse to cry, but now she lost control and the tears blinded her.

Martin woke early, taxied to within a block of the Tudor and found a lookout at the corner construction site, where he could watch the hotel's front entrance from between two poorly joined panels of corrugated iron. He stayed long enough to spy Delia's plaid-shirted stalker, to see Delia and Jack start down the block, and to see the stalker note their direction and move casually to the other side of the street.

Martin dashed through the construction site onto Sukhumvit Road and navigated through several narrow lanes till he reached the back entrance of the tiny eatery Truman had recommended. The air was heavy with spices and the eggy aroma of boiling noodles. For ten *baht* at the counter, Martin picked up a cup of instant coffee and a bowl of boiled rice. Settling into a back booth out of view from the front entrance, sorry for losing track of his reading glasses, he squinted at the morning edition of the *Bangkok Post*. The same grim photo that was featured in yesterday's Thai-language newspaper stared at him from page three. Small comfort: no one would ever identify him with the gaunt-gray man in the picture. The story was shrill and unbearably familiar—*American Art Smuggler At Large in Thailand*.

He hastily glanced at the other articles. All that caught his interest was a ten-line filler: The Heldt-Luther Museum in Texas sold a major piece of Khmer sculpture that had only recently been purchased in Hong Kong. Their spokesperson denied rumors about the statue's provenance and would only state that an opportunity came along to return the statue to a collection in Cambodia at no loss to the museum. *The beat goes on,* Martin thought.

With that, Delia and Jack arrived. Despite the puff of tiredness around her eyes, Delia was radiant—somewhere happily between the twitchy energy and heavy exhaustion he'd grown used to in the past week. It was Jack who looked tense. After they picked up their meals at the counter, they sat opposite him in the booth, and Delia slipped her hands across the table to him.

"You look like a bum," she whispered and Martin's heart danced.

"Or like a Corsican gangster, I'm told," he murmured, and squeezed her hands. "You were followed here."

She nodded. "I think we know who it is: a fucking hawkeye. Jack talked to him in the hotel restaurant our first night here and bumped into him again last night. He fits the description you left with Truman and the description of one of the hawkeyes who's been terrorizing Sara. You think I'm on their Most Wanted List or something? You think it's time we told HAWC-I we're on the same damn side? Their interference could really screw us up." She fidgeted with her beads and ignored the food on her plate.

"Let me handle it, babe." Martin hoped his voice disguised the anger that knotted in his chest—and the sudden rush of affection for the fire in Delia's eyes. "Tell me about Bellingham."

Delia described Bellingham's hysterical claims of innocence. "It was so unexpected. I'm at a loss about how to question him."

"You did a great job with Sara yesterday. Don't worry. But, please, keep Jack with you. Don't go to the guy's room alone."

"What do you want me to do?" Jack asked, wide-eyed.

"If Bellingham is telling the truth, be yourself—her traveling companion. But at the first whiff of a set-up, stick by her side and get the hell out, fast."

They strategized a little more and arranged to meet Martin afterward at the temple Wat Bovornivej, near the Majestic Hotel.

"I'll be waiting for you, whenever you get there," Martin said.

They had time to spare, so Martin decided to share the background information Jones-White had given him on Savani. Not wanting to make Delia think he'd drawn any unwarranted conclusions, he kept his voice light, his word choice factual.

"Say, Delia, did Tony ever mention...?" he began and finished before Delia said a word.

But the warmth of her eyes froze over. "I knew all that about his family. I'm not an idiot. I did my own research. I also know that Interpol doesn't have a shred of evidence about any connection to the Savani heroin

142

business. P&S Worldwide—the reformed branch of the family—exports handicrafts now: lacquer boxes, silk scarves, gift-shop crap. Not just from Thailand, but from all parts of the globe. That's it." She let Martin have the full force of her injured glare for another two seconds, then gave Jack a shove. "We gotta go."

Jack lurched out of the booth. Delia pushed past him. He glanced toward her, then spun around and leaned over the table.

"Savani's a demon, Martin," he whispered. "He smokes opium and pimps his daughter. Lucky, the Amerasian girl, is Savani's daughter. He as much as told me so."

"How do you—?"

Jack waved off the question.

"Does Delia—?"

"Doesn't want to hear it. Won't listen. She—"

Delia called from the doorway, "Scanlan, let's make tracks."

Jack spoke rapidly. "He called this morning, to arrange a trip to Chiang Mai. Today. Museum business, he said. I told him—"

"Jack!" she barked.

With one more pleading look, he hurried away.

Martin put on his hat and walked toward the front entrance, worrying over Delia's loyalty to Savani, envying it to tell the truth. And the hawkeyes, butting in... Suddenly, he was a porcupine of irritation. Look, there he was, across the street. The stalker. The hawkeye. The Bruno-or-Cal who routinely raped Sara Malraux. Staring in the direction Delia went.

Threading his way through the slow-moving cars on the narrow street, Martin approached the stalker from behind. Gave him a poke. "Hey, buddy."

Startled, the hawkeye turned.

"Who the hell are you and why won't you leave Delia alone?"

The hawkeye sneered. "Mr. Martin Moon. Incognito. Looking like a regular tough. I'm shakin' in me boots." He started to step away, but Martin gave him a shove into a shaded area between two buildings, a walkway toward the back edge of a public market.

"You better start talking to me, you bastard."

They stood nose to nose. The area was littered with scraps of wood and lengths of rusty pipe. It reeked of garbage, slow-cooked in the airless heat. A squadron of flies assaulted his face. He waved them away. Earlier, this lane had bustled with folks carting produce toward their market stalls, but it was empty now, oddly still against the background din of traffic.

"Talk or I swear to God you'll be sorry you were ever born."

Bruno's eyes darted over Martin's shoulder. Suddenly, there was a sharp jab in Martin's back. A hand clapped onto his shoulder and a voice behind him said, "Who's sorry now, bucko?"

Even after he saw all the vehicles with flashing lights parked outside, it took Jack a minute to realize that the crowd in the Majestic lobby was not the usual group of culture-shocked tourists. They were Thai, wore uniforms and suits, and moved with swiftness of purpose.

He and Delia skirted the bustle and asked at the desk if Mr. Bellingham could be summoned. The clerk stared dumbly at them.

"Belleena-ham. Je-lamee Belleena-ham," Delia tried.

"Ohhhh... Meestah Belleenna-ham, he die." Her eyes glowed with fascinated horror. "This morning maid find his body, maybe one hour ago."

Jack watched Delia's knuckles turn white as she clutched the marble reception desk.

"How?" she whispered.

But before the clerk could answer, the elevator door opened and someone began shouting orders. All eyes watched as men in white wheeled out a gurney. The body was in a black bag, but it was clear Jeremy hadn't died of natural causes. The men in white overalls wore rubber gloves and face masks, their clothes streaked with rusty stains. The men in suits carefully removed clear plastic ponchos and gloves and stuffed them into a large plastic bag that one of the medics held. Blood precautions.

"Murder," the clerk finally said. "Manager say he found naked. Many stabbings. Blood everywhere. Very bad for hotel. Many tourist move out. Very bad. You know Meestah Belleeena-ham? You friend?"

"No," said Delia. "Not at all. My husband here works for Xerox. We just got transferred to Bangkok from Singapore. A mutual friend told us to look up Jeremy if we had a chance. What a pity. Come on, Charlie, we're just in the way here."

She clutched Jack's arm and led him out a side door. They hurried down

144

the street. Jack's knees felt soft and he hovered on the edge of nausea. He put an arm around her shoulder. She put her hand on his. She was beginning to tremble, like a top losing its spin, talking, rattling on aimlessly about the absurdity of it all.

"It's crazy. I was sure he was the one—I figured him for a sociopath—one of those warped personalities—charmer by day, maniac by night. But Sara's description of him—he sounded so straightforward and pragmatic—it made me suspicious. And now here he is—butchered, just like—Jesus, why didn't I question him better yesterday? What the hell do we do now?"

Hanging on to each other, they hurried down Phra Sumen Road toward the temple.

Wat Bovornivej was an eye in the hurricane of Bangkok traffic. Monks in their saffron robes strolled the grounds in groups of two and three, while white-robed nuns scrubbed floors. Supplicants patted small squares of gold leaf onto statues of the Buddha, lit joss sticks, or draped garlands of flowers.

Martin had said he'd meet them at the *bot*, the main assembly hall, but the *bot* was locked. They meandered around, searching for him.

At a small stand, Delia bought a pair of finches in a tiny twig cage and, following custom, liberated them. They fluttered happily into the sunlight. But neither the freedom of the birds nor the serenity of the monks eased her growing anxiety. Martin was nowhere.

Back on the steps of the *bot*, Delia sat, sweat-streaked, her eyes wide and serious. "Something's happened."

"He probably didn't think we'd be here so soon. We'll wait..."

It was after noon when they gave up and taxied back to the Tudor. Delia ran ahead, while Jack checked for messages at the desk. There was one—from Savani. His car had been delayed but would be by shortly to pick up Delia for their trip north.

Jack shook his head. He was not a worldly man. He didn't see the pay-offs beyond the obstacle course of risks. He had the instincts of a protector and a sixth sense for evil. Delia saw Savani as a business partner, opening an exciting new chapter in her career. But he'd revealed himself to Jack as a man with dark secrets and a knack—a *penchant*—for manipulation. Jack shouldn't be interfering with Delia's plans, but why else did she bring him along? Why would anyone drag a sixth-grade teacher with them onto the path of murderers? She was recovering from assault and surgeries. She was a mess of nerves, and prone to panic. She needed his paranoid eyes.

He still had the note in his hand when he got off the elevator and heard Delia yelling from the room.

"This is insane. This is unacceptable!"

Their room had been ransacked. Their beds had been moved and torn apart, mattresses on the floor, bags emptied and drawers pulled out of the dresser. Delia was on the phone: "Doesn't this place have any semblance of security? Who the fuck are you handing out room keys to?"

She saw Jack and slammed the phone down.

"We need to get out of here." Her voice was making a clumsy transition from angry customer to terrified prey. Her eyes glowed with vulnerability. "We need to get somewhere safe." She gulped air. "Or we'll wind up like Bellingham."

Jack crumpled Savani's message and flung it into the wastebasket.

Caleb Clearwater took great pleasure in holding the knife against Martin Moon's ribs. Moon was just the type of maggot the world would be better off without. Besides, Cal was tired of watching him. Tired of watching rich men buy up the cultural heritage of the world's underclass. Tired of watching their generous tips, their fancy suits, their expensive haircuts. They told him archaeology was important and yet he was forced to live in shit-holes. It had been months since he'd had a real bath in a real porcelain tub with hot running water. He took a shower last night in Jeremy Bellingham's room after finishing his business—but the conditions were far from relaxing. Bellingham was also a patrician maggot.

He was tired of Martin Moon. Tired of traipsing around Bangkok after him, tired of trying to figure out what he was after, tired of puzzling over why someone of Mr. Savani's stature was so engaged with him and the other two Yanks.

Cal had called a contact at the Antiquities Ministry, alerting him about Moon's re-entry and reminding him about the deportation order. He thought Moon would be arrested by now. But no. Moon had eluded the coppers. Cal might have turned him in directly—he'd known Moon's exact location nearly every minute since the three returned from Mr. Savani's house, and yet, the fact that Moon was going to such effort to remain here had piqued his curiosity. He and Bruno decided to watch instead. But they had to leave Bangkok now. Jeremy Bellingham had shed light on certain mysteries that required immediate action. So Moon's time was up.

Jack moved quickly to sort the mess into the right suitcases. The road to a safe haven would not be traveled in Savani's fancy car, he was sure of that. They would head over to Dick's. Martin would be there, he was sure of that too.

The hotel manager showed up at the door and Delia ranted at him while she sorted out her own things. Then she chased him away.

Jack changed out his shirt and tie for cooler clothes… clothes for speed… clothes for safety. Delia did likewise. But still wore the Karen tribal beads Martin had given her.

"The gun," she said. "Make sure you have it." He made note of the fact that slipping a small pistol into his pocket did not feel as bizarre as it did day before yesterday.

They parked their bags in the hotel luggage room and checked out of the Tudor.

At Dick's All-American Bar and Grill, Truman was stacking glasses on metal shelves under the bar. No smoke rose from Ingrid's booth.

"Martin here?" Jack asked.

"Nah, but I gave Dick your message last night. Din he show up? I told Dick—"

"Yeah, he got the message okay, but we lost track of him this morning and I thought maybe you heard something."

"Not me. Dick don't come in till three or so. Maybe he knows…"

Jack glanced again at Ingrid's booth and felt a first flush of panic.

"If you're lookin' for Ingrid, she ain't showed up," Truman said. "There's a mystery for you. First time she ain't showed up ever. They was goin' up to Chiang Mai later, but she said she'd be in for most of the day anyway. Shoot, even that time she had the belly trouble, she showed up here and Eeju took her in a taxi back home and made her promise to take a couple days off. Strange way to live, if you ask me. Pretty young girl, rooming with two guys. Never did much care for neither Bruno ner Cal. Sure, Scanlan, you saw Cal's mean streak. And that Bruno is a lard-butt who'll do anything Cal says, I ain't lyin.'"

"Bruno and Cal? That's who she lives with—*Bruno* and *Cal*?" Delia asked. "The archaeologists?"

Truman nodded. "Caleb Clearwater, Bruno Andriotti. Cal got some fancy letters after his name. Don't know about Bruno."

Delia groaned. "Two archaeologists named Bruno and Cal were buddies of René Malraux, the archaeologist who got murdered. They've been coercing Sara Malraux into sex with them ever since the murder. Jesus, Scanlan, why didn't you tell me about these people you were making friends with?"

"Friends? I was *her* friend, not theirs." Jack touched his bruised eye with a knuckle. "I told you Cal was the one who socked me—well, I didn't know his name then. Ingrid mentioned the name of the second guy only yesterday—How could I know—? And who's Sara Malraux anyway?"

Delia was staring into the rows of liquor bottles behind the bar. "I have a bad feeling. A bad feeling… that they might be the ones who killed Bellingham… that they're the ones…" She touched her belly. "They're the ones."

Jack finally connected the dots.

"Oh my God," Jack said, trying to raise his voice above the clanging of the pulse in his ears. "I have more to tell. Night before last, Cal beat up Ingrid. Really bad. When I saw her yesterday, she sort of made light of it—like she was just fulfilling a contract—but from what she… intimated… the relationship—between the three of them—sounded incredibly… toxic. I gave her money to go to a hotel, but she left it behind, here with Truman. Now, well, you heard it, she hasn't shown up today…"

No one spoke for a moment.

"I'd like to go find her," Jack said. "How about you wait here for Martin and I'll make sure she's safe, bring her back here." He rubbed his head, struggling to comprehend the complexity of it all. "Unless they've already left for Chiang Mai."

"We'll go together." She took Jack's arm. "Truman, if, when Martin shows up, tie him down, ok?"

Truman nodded and fetched his wife. Using a small map Delia pulled from her purse, Eeju directed them to a street in Chinatown and gave them

148

a detailed description of the building's façade. "It small noodle shop. Must to go through shop to back stairs, up stairs."

"There's somethin' else," Truman reached under the bar and pulled out Ingrid's daypack. "I told you she left this here yesterday. Cal came in a while ago askin' about it."

"Did he say anything about Ingrid?"

"Nah, he was in a big huffy hurry. He just asked if I seen it, the rucksack or any of the papers. He ain't given to being polite with me. And I don't have no truck with him, not since he like to broke my jaw that time—I told you about that. Anyway, I said I ain't seen any of it. He asked if *you* might have taken it, 'that big Yank,' but I said I wouldn't know and he stormed out. Why'n't you take it now. If you find her, she'll be wanting it, I'm sure of that—her little computer's in there. If you don't... well, maybe it'll tell you something. Won't tell me nothing since I can't hardly read."

Jack thanked him and took the pack, wondering if it was the reason his hotel room had been torn up.

Outside, traffic was at a standstill. It took them half an hour to move a couple miles by *tuk-tuk*. Jack found himself slapping the frame of the vehicle with frustration. Delia finally grabbed his hand.

"Come on, we can go faster by foot."

With a smirk, Bruno stepped back from Martin's angry stare. Martin slowly moved his hands from his body and eased away from the knife point in his ribs. He turned. A lanky guy with the tanned, freckly hide of a cowboy, a fringe of thin auburn hair, and a thick mustache grinned at him. A front tooth was missing. The hand with the knife relaxed.

"Why have you been following Delia?" Martin insisted.

"My mate Bruno here has taken a fancy to her. He likes the dark ones with the lusty figures. Myself, I prefer blondes..."

"What do you want from her? Don't you know she's getting out of the business? Going to run a little museum up north with Tony Savani."

Cal ran his tongue across his teeth. "You think museum directors aren't as greedy as dealers? Most of them have the scruples of a termite colony.

As for Mr. Savani, we'll be setting things straight with him tomorrow up in Chiang Mai. As soon as we deal with you, Mr. Moon."

The familiarity of these two gnawed at Martin—their accents, their public school toughness, the pressure of the knife at his back.

Cal glanced at Bruno, Bruno shoved him against the wall, and, as his cheek grazed the brick, Martin remembered. Mae Sot. They were the gorillas who'd stabbed him in Mae Sot. But today, through Martin's sober and angry eyes, they were his own size, their faces, like his own, sagging and creased with age.

"Mae Sot. You're the ones—"

"That's not all, Mr. Grave Robber." Bruno had Martin's right arm twisted behind his back and pressed himself close. His knife was now drawn and threatened Martin's face.

"Bruno," Cal hissed. "Just stab him. We've got to get moving."

"Right here? In public?"

"The locals don't report anything between *farangs*. But it might be fun to tell Mr. Art Dealer here that he's being stabbed by the same knife that did in his rich bitch wife. Remember, Mr. Moon? Remember the Paddington warehouse?"

Martin pressed his cheek against the brick wall, as if it's scratchy texture would stop the shakes that attacked his knees, as if that would keep the ground from turning to foam. "You? You're the ones? You fucking hawkeyes murdered Lana?"

Cal's laughter rang off the buildings around them. "It's got to stop somewhere, Mr. Moon," he cried out. "You're all termites eating through the fabric of ancient civilizations. Termites is all you are. In the course of history, killing off a few of you to scare the rest away is morally correct. And it's beginning to look like we'll have to finish what we started with Miss Rivera—"

Something slithered through the dark rooms of Martin's mind, snapping through the delicate threads of his higher nature. For Lana, he could do nothing but grieve. But for Delia, his Delia...

He used his legs to spring back against Bruno, knocked him off balance, lunged at Cal's middle, and swung him into a wall, grazing Cal's head against the stone, causing him to crumple to the ground, and his knife to skitter along the broken pavement.

He spun around to Bruno. "You broke into Delia's room here to keep

150

her terrorized, didn't you? You thought you might be able to *manage* her like you do Sara Malraux, is that it?"

Bruno squared off, his knees bending to spring, knife still in hand. "She's one fearsome piece of tail—"

Martin's blow landed on Bruno's jaw. The punch was worthy of his childhood fights, but a stab of pain in his fist made him lose concentration long enough for Bruno to bounce off the wall and return a blow to Martin's belly that sent him sprawling. For the first time, he noticed heads peeking into the passageway from the market.

Cal's knife was two feet in front of him. As he reached out for it with both hands, Bruno smashed a length of metal pipe, once, twice across them.

The blows across his hands were so stunning, the world went white for a moment.

Before Martin's eyes refocused, he pulled back his arms, rolled away, and scrambled to his feet. Bruno was yanking Cal upright.

"I changed my mind. Killing him here is too easy," Cal was saying. He was in worse shape than Martin, gasping for breath. "Let's take him somewhere... back to the apartment—no—over to those abandoned shanties—where we took René. I want him naked, humiliated. I want him to die slow."

A frown of doubt replaced the fierce war mask on Bruno's face. "But the bus for Chiang Mai leaves in two hours and we've still got to find the notebook." He was breathing hard too.

"Don't care. We'll take a later bus."

"But if Rivera's on her way to Chiang Mai too, then—"

"Then we'll get her there." Cal swept his knife off the ground and lunged toward Martin.

Martin ducked away. He was pumped up enough to fight them all morning if he had to. But as he raised his fists to a boxer's pose, he saw that his hands no longer made fists, that his fingers refused to curl without stabbing pain. His only choice now was to run.

He loped off on his middle-aged legs into the market. The timid onlookers were shouting now, bringing more attention to the brawling *farangs*.

"Come on," Cal shrieked behind him.

"But the notebook, the bus..." Bruno protested.

Their arguing faded as Martin focused on the slapping of his shoes against the puddled cobblestones and on his own breathing. *Run!* He was in better shape than they were. *Run!* But when he turned his head to see if they were following, he slipped and crashed headlong into a basin of catfish. Immediately, sellers and customers were yanking him up out of the slithering mess, while an old woman screeched at him. Someone slapped his damp hat back on his head.

"I'm sorry," he gasped. "So sorry." Even as he regained his footing and panned the huge market for a glimpse of the hawkeyes, shooting pains made him clutch his hands to his chest. The loud old woman pointed to them, shaking her head, chattering at him, waving toward the street and a row of *tuk-tuks*.

He thought he heard Cal's voice, behind the fishmongers, yelling for him. If the hawkeyes followed him, that would keep them distracted from Delia and Chiang Mai. But the shooting pain in his arms reminded him how easily they could kill him. What good would that be?

He kept his head low and made a dash for the *tuk-tuks*.

FIVE

BANGKOK, THAILAND

Jack pushed his arms through the straps of the backpack, while Delia paid off the *tuk-tuk* driver. They set off at a trot. The steamy smog was as dense as the traffic. Their pace slowed as they gasped for breath in the oxygen-poor air. Sweat stung their eyes. Yet the running somehow felt good, burning off the accumulated muscle tension from the morning's disasters.

When they reached Ingrid's block, they easily found the noodle shop. As they walked through to the back, the cook asked their business.

"Ingrid Lundquist." Jack pointed. "Upstairs."

The noodle cook nodded. "Ee'rid. Very smart lady."

When Jack pounded on the door, the latch popped and it swung open. As hot as the shop was, the roiling heat of the apartment snatched his breath away. The air stank of pent-up restaurant smells—garlic, soy sauce, scorched spices and burned meat. No wonder she couldn't work here.

The long flight of stairs led to a gray square of daylight above.

"Ingrid?" he called, trying to sound neighborly as they stepped into the short hall. He reached into his pocket for Truman's bandana to wipe his face and the cool metal of his gun startled him and sharpened his voice. "Anybody home? Ingrid?"

Delia pushed the door closed behind them. The street noises were now muffled and the apartment was still.

He climbed halfway up, catching himself once as his foot nearly crashed through a broken tread. Ingrid's scrubbed looks had given Jack the impression that she came from money, that her daddy must be an

English gentleman. But, in the greasy light, as his head came even with the apartment floor and he saw the crumbling linoleum, the peeling wallpaper, and the chewed up woodwork, he wondered what father could let his child live in such squalor. The stale smells had turned to a stench, like backed up sewage.

"Jesus H. Christ," Delia whispered as her head came even with Jack's.

"Ingrid?" The only sound was a faint buzzing.

They completed the climb. At a glance, there were four rooms off a ten-by-ten landing, two with doors. At the far left, the living room was strewn with odd pieces of furniture. Next, a filthy kitchenette accommodated a squat toilet, a tiny fridge, a two-burner hotplate, and a square tub that looked like a janitor's slop sink.

Jack pushed at the first closed door. The bedroom looked vacated—empty closet, open empty drawers, balled up sheets on the twin beds. They apparently already left for the north—for good, from the looks of it.

The door to the right had a piece of lined notebook paper taped to it, with the handprinted message: *PRIVATE—Please Knock!* The buzzing came from inside.

"Ingrid?" He tapped the door and it swung open.

A swarm of blue-green flies congregated on a beefy red thing in the middle of the room. They busily flew in and out of an open window.

The sound of pounding surf filled Jack's ears, drowning out the buzz, till the bite of Delia's fingernails on his arm snapped him back.

Ingrid was dead. What remained was a bloody carcass with Ingrid's long legs, buttery blonde hair, and horrified face.

Jack sagged against the door jamb and pulled Delia tight to his chest. But neither of them could take their eyes away from the scene.

When the butchery had overloaded his senses, till all he saw were meaningless splotches of red, Jack looked at Ingrid's desk in the nearest corner. There was a small printer, an empty Mekhong bottle holding a long-stemmed yellow flower, and a clean ashtray. The drawers were pulled out of the desk, as were the dresser drawers in the far corner.

Delia shoved herself away from him and disappeared.

The floor between the door and the desk felt spongy as he walked over to look at what had been dumped on the floor. Other than blank computer paper and a worn map of Bangkok, the only thing of note was her passport. Ingrid Mae Lundquist, born Brighton, England, September 30, 1966—the year the Beatles were more popular than Jesus, the month Jack lost his virginity to Monica Galbraith, to the strains of Sonny and Cher. *I Got You, Babe*. The ocean started pouring back into his ears, but he shook it off, and, tossing the passport onto the desk, he left the room.

Delia was crouching over the toilet.

Jack looked into the other two rooms again. Ingrid's roommates had indeed vacated the place, their personal gear all gone.

Now Delia sat on the top step, hugging the newel post. Jack found a liter of water in the refrigerator, popped the cap, grabbed a towel, and sat next to her.

"Drink." It was the first word either of them had spoken and his voice sounded harsh and loud.

When they had finished all but a couple ounces, he poured the remainder on the towel and patted Delia's face. Her color was returning. He helped her to her feet and, as he walked her through the noodle shop, he snapped at the cook: "Call the police. Ingrid is dead."

M artin braced an elbow against the roof strut to pull himself into the *tuk-tuk*.

"Clinic? Fifty *baht*? Speak English! No question ask!" the driver yelled at him.

"Yes, yes, go."

The vehicle jerked into gear and headed into traffic. Martin turned to see the hawkeyes standing on the curb looking after him as the *tuk-tuk* swerved around the corner. Before long, Jack and Delia would be waiting for him at the *wat*, but he didn't want to risk the hawkeyes following him there. Whatever no-tell clinic the driver had in mind, Martin didn't trust it, so he redirected him to the Li house.

As Martin's adrenaline rush faded, white lightning began to pulse from both hands. He finally looked at them—swollen and distorted. Breakfast began to percolate in his stomach, but it wasn't due to the pain or the whipsawing of the *tuk-tuk* through traffic. He had finally seen the faces of Lana's murderers. Not the fair-haired smuggler Jeremy Bellingham, but hawkeyes. Scholars, archaeologists, wild-eyed, cruel men with white sweat-rings on their shirts, dandruff, and dirty fingernails. He squeezed his eyes shut to stop the tears.

At the Li home, with the *tuk-tuk* driver squawking for his fare, Martin used his thumb to ring the bell at the outside gate. Arthur opened the front door and trotted toward him.

"I'm hurt," Martin said, holding his swollen hands in front of him.

Arthur paid off the driver and escorted Martin to the kitchen table. "Your face is pretty scraped up, too. Awesome. You sure you're not a gang-ster? Sit here." Arthur spoke to the housekeeper in Chinese and she rushed out of the room. Then he set a pan in front of Martin, drew the hands into it, and dumped a tray of ice over them. Martin yelped and the room began to go black around the edges.

Arthur patted his face. "Don't pass out on me, man. *Amah* ran next door to get old Dr. Chin. You pick a fight in a fish market? Phew. Let me throw this hat away."

Dick Li, dressed in an off-white silk suit, newspaper in hand, entered the kitchen. "What's this I hear about injured hands?" He scowled. "Heav-ens, Arthur, get him a pick-me-up before he passes out."

Arthur dashed out for a bottle and shot glass. "Dr. Chin is coming up the walk. Here, have a swig of this. *Sanhuajiu.*" He poured and held the glass to Martin's mouth, the angle slightly too high. "Rice spirits." The liquid flowed freely till Martin had to turn his head and let a drop trickle down his chin. He squeezed his eyes shut. It was flowery and gruesome—a whore's slap in the face.

When he opened his eyes, Dr. Chin was lifting his hands from the ice. "Can you bend them?" Arthur translated. "Try to bend them." As Martin shook his head, Dr. Chin set one hand back on the ice and did something with the other that made Martin jump from his seat with a gasp. Arthur supplied him with another jolt of spirits.

After much consultation in Chinese among Dr. Chin, Arthur, Dick, and the *amah*, Dick spoke. "The metatarsals are broken. Arthur will go with you to the clinic. Don't worry, it's a very discreet place. A Chinese clinic."

Martin tried to protest. "I have to meet Delia and Jack at Wat Bovor-nivej—they're probably waiting for me by now."

The *amah* handed Arthur a sack with a change of clothes for Martin, then they helped him into Arthur's Mercedes.

156

His hands felt plugged into light sockets, snapping shock waves into every cell of his body. Still… "Can we please stop at the *wat* first? It wouldn't be fair to—"

"Clinic first," Arthur said, pulling into the sluggish traffic. "I'll check out the *wat* while you're getting fixed up."

"And the Tudor Hotel. If you miss them…"

"Tudor? That tourist dump? Thought you classy guys stayed at the Oriental."

"In another life, Arthur, another life."

At the clinic, a white-haired Chinese nurse gave him a shot of something that blunted the pain and turned the clinic into a soup of melting colors and muddled voices. He thought he heard the roar of helicopters. He thought he heard Lana's silvery voice. *It's all right, baby,* she was saying, *I'll take you home now.* She was grabbing his hands but he was falling away from her, falling, and the helicopters were louder, and he couldn't go home because Delia was in danger and Lana was dead and Delia was in danger and Lana was dead and Delia… Delia… Delia…

When his eyes refocused, he was lying in a different room, the dead things on the ends of his arms encased in damp white plaster halfway to his elbows. Purple fingertips, framed in cotton stockinet, poked uselessly from the casts. Arthur stood next to him.

"Those dudes smashed your hands up good. The doc says he got all the bones back in line, but—" Arthur looked around, then lowered his voice. "This isn't exactly Stanford Medical Center—the staff here dates back to Chiang Kai-shek. If you weren't a notorious outlaw, I would have taken you to the E.D. at the International Hospital." He shrugged. "Anyway, they want you to hang out here a couple hours till the casts are good and dry, then I'll take you back home."

"Delia?"

"No tall Americans at the *wat*. And the Tudor says they checked out.

Martin tried to get the logic flowing through his fuzzy brain.

With a stab of disappointment, Martin remembered Jack saying that Savani wanted her to go to Chiang Mai today. The hawkeyes mentioned it too. How did they know…? Would Delia really have gone without knowing where he was? And where was Jack? He asked Arthur to call Savani's place.

"Here's the scoop," said Arthur when he returned to Martin's side. "Savani's man Chen said his boss left for the north and that, as far he knew, Savani had arranged to pick up Delia at the Tudor.

Martin's sting of abandonment was suddenly replaced by fear.

"By the way, it's not a good day for you Buddha hunters. It's all over the news that an English dealer got stabbed to death overnight at the Majestic hotel—another second-class dive. Bellingham? You know him?"

Martin nodded. "Sort of." He felt cut adrift. Bellingham had been Delia's quest, the designated focus of all evil. The whole point of their mission together in Thailand. And now the poor man was just another tabloid-story knife victim, his young energy, his ambitions… drained away, like Lana's. His life, like hers, a sudden silence.

Delia had walked in on that spectacle this morning, hadn't she? And he hadn't been with her to soften the blow, to retrain their sights on the two merciless hawkeyes. So she had gone off with Tony. And Jack?

There were too many blank spaces in the day's story. Too much jeopardy still at large.

"Arthur, get me out of here now, hear? Help me hire a car. If Delia's gone to Chiang Mai, I've got to get to her. If she's gone with Savani, she's got to be warned. They both do. The guys who broke my hands are murderers. Probably Bellingham's murderers. They're on their way north, too, to get Savani, to get her."

Arthur's eyes widened. "Holy shit. I'll drive you myself."

Outside, the traffic was still as bad, the smog still as dense, but the heavy air smelled sweet. Delia clutched Jack's arm as they walked to Charoen Krung Road, the big avenue at the end of the block, where they spied a restaurant that looked like it catered to *farangs*. She wanted nothing more than to get back to Dick's and find Martin, but she was going to be sick if she didn't sit down and get a grip on herself.

The hostess pointedly avoided staring at their damp clothes, as she showed them to a booth with a curved banquette, which allowed Delia to continue holding onto Jack. He ordered whiskey, a pot of tea, and bowls of steamed rice.

They drank and ate mechanically. The bland grain, washed down with tea and whiskey, lay heavy on her stomach, but the chewing, the swallowing, the filling up was clearing her senses of their gory film. Yet none of it seemed very real. The coolness of the fork against her fingers seemed distant, as if the hand that fed her belonged to someone else. The tongue that pressed the grains of rice to the roof of her mouth seemed unfamiliar.

"Martin became a vegetarian." Jack stared at his rice.

"What?" she asked dully.

"After he saw... after he saw Lana like that—he can't look at meat, can't stomach it—the carnage—"

"Oh, Jesus, stop it. Stop."

They sat in silence.

When half the rice was eaten, she spoke again. She was less worried about the effect of carnage on her eating habits than on the answer to the riddle that had plagued her for months.

"Damn hawkeyes. They're taking justice into their own hands. Bellingham, the unethical dealer. Malraux, who chose Bellingham's friendship over the HAWC-I code. Maybe they meant to kill Bellingham along with Malraux, but he disappeared or they lost track of him till this week. And Lana... God, could they really have killed her too?" Delia caught herself tracing the line of her own scar and pulled her hand away. "Righteous bastards."

"Maybe it's not so much ideology as this Cal and Bruno got a screw loose between them."

"Nothing like a screw loose for a good cause. But why Ingrid? Wasn't she one of them, a hawkeye?"

Jack sighed. "Maybe for collaborating with the enemy. Like Bellingham's friend—Malraux."

He evaded Delia's eyes, pushed his plate aside, and unpacked Ingrid's rucksack. Along with the laptop, there were two fat notebooks—one marked *Kampuchea* and the other *Thai Sites*—and a stack of manila folders.

"She was working on two projects. Remember, Savani mentioned her foray into Cambodia. And her Thai project had something to do with a site north of here."

As Delia looked over his shoulder, Jack flipped through the Thai notebook. It was a chronological log with dated entries in a cramped hand, full of maps, drawings, and numbered photo references. He stopped at one page that held a particularly striking sketch of a mountain scene with a spired edifice labelled "*chedi*" in the foreground, and a modern satellite dish on a tower higher back on the hill.

"She was a good sketch artist," Delia said, "And conscientious about her notes."

He shuffled through a few more pages till he reached the most recent entries.

"Oh boy," he whispered.

On the last three or four pages the margins were decorated with little hearts and daisy vines—and his name. *Jack Scanlan, Jackie Scanlan, Jack Jack Jack, Mrs. John F. Scanlan, Ingrid Lundquist-Scanlan, Ingrid Scanlan, Mr. and Mrs. J. Scanlan, Dr. Ingrid Scanlan.* He slapped the notebook shut.

Delia watched her strong companion crumple over the pages. The tears came. He pressed the heels of his hands into his eyes and cried silently, his entire body trembling with grief. Delia rubbed his back.

Thailand had given the lonely school teacher a gift… then snatched it away.

The waitress brought another pot of tea.

As his tears subsided, with one hand still on his back, she paged through the *Kampuchea* notebook. He finally uncovered his eyes.

"Whirlwind romance?" she asked.

"Yeah. Stupid." He snuffled. "She was too young. Didn't use good sense. Yesterday morning, when I saw her at Dick's, when I found out she'd been beaten, she told me…" His voice began to quiver. "She told me how they were… using her." He rubbed a finger along worn edges of the notebook. "I begged her to leave them. She was afraid. And she was keeping secrets. I'm sure that's why she left her pack with Truman. I interfered with her delicate balancing act—pushed her—"

Delia forced her words past the lump in her throat. "Don't be too hard on yourself, Jack. This Cambodia notebook shows Ingrid was up to her eyeteeth in risky business."

With a shake of his head, he finished his whiskey. "Let's find Martin?"

Truman called out. "Scanlan, what the hell! We thought y'all went to Chiang Mai. Hey, Dick!"

A Chinese man spoke to the Thais at his table and, as they excused themselves, he beckoned to Delia and Jack. His face was grim.

"We're looking for Martin, Mr. Li," Delia said as they sat down.

He stared at her for an endless moment, his index finger and thumb kneading his lower lip. "Your friend was severely injured."

Her hand darted blindly toward Jack and landed on his arm. A jab of pain goose-stepped through her belly.

"He was assaulted by two men. *Hawkeyes* he called them."

"Oh..." was the only sound that would come from Delia's mouth and she could feel it turning to a moan.

"His hands are broken."

Jack exhaled audibly. "That's it? That's all? Just his hands?"

Delia's relief that Martin's torso hadn't been sliced open was marred by a wave of empathy for his fine sensuous hands—hands that delighted in the curves and angles of marble and wood and bronze. "Oh, Marty," she whispered as she cupped and rubbed her own hands, then looked at Dick. "They'll be okay, won't they?"

He shrugged. "My son insists that his treatment was inferior, but Mr. Moon refused any further attention. Instead, he has followed these hawkeyes to Chiang Mai in the hopes of keeping you, Miss Rivera, safe. He is somehow under the impression you are already headed north with Mr. Savani and that you and Savani are targeted to be the next victims. He simply refused to hear of any other option but to go after you himself."

"I don't understand. He must be delirious. I'm right here. And those hawkeyes are lunatics. Sadistic murderers. Martin's no match for them." Delia stood up. "I've got to get up there with him. What's the quickest way?"

Dick explained that his son was with Martin and that he'd be quite safe on the Li estate, but Delia wouldn't listen.

"If you insist... Let's see, with the airline strike, and at this time of day, your best bet is the night train. You'll have to race to catch the last train. But really, miss, if Mr. Moon is so afraid for you, wouldn't you be doing him the biggest favor by staying here, out of harm's way? I'll call my sister, tell her you're safe here, that he shouldn't worry."

She shook her head. "It's my job to see this through."

Reluctantly, Dick gave them instructions for getting the train and for reaching his son once they arrived in Chiang Mai. Delia pushed Jack ahead of her and hailed a cab outside the bar.

"The hotel? Our luggage?" Jack asked, still lugging Ingrid's rucksack.

"No time. We'll buy what we need. I have plenty of cash."

They bought their tickets with ten minutes to spare, relieved to find two second-class sleeping berths together.

"I better call Tony. I swore I wouldn't disappear on him. I wonder where Martin got the idea that—"

Jack looked stricken.

"What's the problem?"

He rubbed an eye. "He's not home. Savani. I mean, he's in Chiang Mai, or on his way at least. I'm pretty sure."

"What are you talking about?"

Rubbed the other eye. "That phone call this morning, when you were in the shower. It was him. He wanted you to drive to Chiang Mai with him today. Some kind of museum business, he said. I told Martin about it this morning. That's where—"

"And you didn't tell me?" She felt herself turning purple.

"Well, I thought we were supposed to meet Bellingham. Besides, the conversation took a nasty turn. He brought up Lucky—"

"I don't want to hear about it." She raced off ahead of him.

The train was crowded and airless.

"I thought I was protecting you," Jack complained as he sank into a seat clearly not contoured for someone his size. He wiped his face with a paper napkin he'd picked up somewhere.

Delia grunted in reply, fumbled with the window hardware in frustration till a porter came by, released the latches, and coaxed the window down into its storage bay. The air stirred. She sat opposite Jack, her arms and legs crossed.

A parade of bowing train staff began, pestering them to fill out supper orders, setting up the table between them, and peddling mai-tais and orange juice in glasses graced with orchids. Jack bought mai-tais.

Their silence didn't break till the train was lumbering past lively corrugated-iron shanty towns north of Bangkok. People squatted along the tracks cooking in woks and charcoal braziers, eating with their fingers, watching the night train pass.

"Jack." She interrupted his fixed gaze out the window. "I need to be straight with you about Tony and me. I've been trying to talk to Martin about it, but it's too awkward. One of you should understand."

"Yeah, okay."

She stared out at the passing scene.

"I ran into Tony after I got back from my China trip, after I'd heard about Lana's murder. I met him at a party. He's a legend in some circles for underwriting really offbeat archaeological projects, but he's also a legend among a much smaller circle of art collectors. If he takes a shine to something—say, Nepalese bronzes of Manjushri—he goes on the hunt to find the very best in the world. He buys—always through agents—he buys and buys, always trading up till he has the rarest, most perfect, most beautiful rendering, no matter what the price.

"Anyway, back to that party. I was tired, hadn't been eating right, and I got wasted. Tony amazed me. Here was this eccentric billionaire sitting with me all evening, gazing at me with those surrealistic eyes, listening to me cry in my cognac about Martin. I told him the whole fire and ice history, about my resentment toward Lana, and how bad I felt that she was dead, but how I also had this sort of guilty glee that—I don't know—that I'd outlived her, I guess. Things I'd hardly admitted, even to myself. It was pathetic. But he called the next day and asked me out.

"I have to admit I had a kernel of suspicion—about what I wasn't sure. He asked so many questions. But then again, I asked him a lot too. I checked him out and found out about his family history, but decided if he didn't mind mine, I didn't mind his.

"Then I was assaulted. I was barely conscious again when he was at my side. As soon as I could be moved, he rented a house for me outside London, hired nurses and rehab specialists. Found Dr. Courtland—the one who's been managing my panic attacks. Tony postponed his return to Thailand till I decided I needed to get back to work and, again, he helped me out.

"My point is that Tony hung in there with me, got me through the deepest trough of my life. And now he's giving me an opportunity of a lifetime, the chance to run a spectacular new museum. No one else in the world could do that for me, because, if you want to know the truth, I don't have the right credentials, haven't paid the right dues, yet he trusts I can do it. And I can. I feel very loyal to him right now."

Delia finally looked at Jack. His smile was tight-lipped, hardly what she'd call sympathetic.

"Okay," he murmured. "Okay." He drew a breath, as if to add something, but, with a shake of his head, he let it go.

"What? But what?" His gesture had exasperated her. "People can't do anything about their origins but spend their goddamn lives trying to live them down. I got the hell out of south fucking Florida because I was sick to death of Anglo assumptions about Cubans and Cuban assumptions about south Florida crackers, and everybody's ignorance about mixed race families— where I couldn't go a week without some knucklehead asking, 'What *are* you?'—oh, shit!" Her thoughts swerved from past to present. "My medicines. They're back in my luggage. Damn." She drummed her fingers on the table. "What if I—oh, to hell with it."

Jack laid his hand on hers. "Delia, what I was going say was that since you stopped taking your Dr. Courtland's medicines your moods have leveled off. You've had a couple restless nights, but your days aren't so frenzied. And look what we've gone through today. I haven't noticed any of your panic symptoms."

"Who needs panic when you have horror?" It was a flip response, but he was right.

With a sigh, Jack laid his head back against the seat and withdrew his hand.

Her tone had slapped him. His effort to be helpful drained away. She saw the tiredness in his eyes, still bloodshot from crying. His face was streaked with gray sweat-lines and speckles of napkin lint on top of his five-o'clock shadow. His hair was damp and breaking loose from its rubber band. And yet he still radiated angelic strength. No wonder Ingrid had fallen for him like a swooning tenth-grader, doodling her *Mrs. Ingrid Scanlan*s all over her notes. St. Jackie the Archangel.

Daylight was nearly gone. Delia turned to look out the window till there was nothing to see but a black landscape against a charcoal sky. The cool breeze and the gentle rumbling smoothed away her frustrations. She needed Jack to be on her side.

"I haven't had sex in more than two years," she said.

Jack shifted in his seat. "Nothing wrong with that."

"When Tony and I hit it off, I figured one thing would lead to another, like it happens, you know. But he was such a gentleman, a little shy about physical displays... Well, then I was assaulted. And raped. Too damaged to even consider sex. For months. I'm fine now. Probably... it will happen—right time, right place, right mood—everything will click into place." Something about *clicking into place* made her wince.

"Do you want it? I mean, do you get, uh, horny?"

164

"Yeah." She sighed, thinking how she'd been so ready to jump into bed with Martin just two nights ago—the night things started falling apart. No *clicking*, just *melting*.

Suddenly, she felt self-conscious and crossed her arms.

But Jack leaned forward. "You'll be okay, Delia," he whispered. "Listen to your heart."

Between Bangkok and Chiang Mai, Thailand

About three hours outside of Bangkok, Martin began to regret his decision to let Arthur Li escort him to the northern hills. The young man had been itching to haul ass in his father's new Mercedes sports car. With the top down, the afternoon sun warmed Martin's hands till it felt like a jazz drummer was practicing riffs on his bones. And he was still fighting off the woozy effect of the anesthetic. He asked Arthur to talk to him, but all the young business student could think about was the stock market, the future of leveraged buyouts, and bottom lines.

"You know, I think I read some articles by your father. Winston Moon, right? Economic development models, right? He was at your State Department when he worked for Reagan, right?"

"That's my old man."

"Didn't it break his heart when you became an art dealer? I mean, what kind of percentage is there in the art market? Unless you're cashing in on your family stash of Picassos and VanGoghs."

"Yeah, it broke what he calls his heart—thought I was an artsy fuck-off. But I worked hard—harder than any ivory-tower economist. Studied my ass off—the art, the markets, the people—and wound up making a decent living. Entrepreneurship and the American way. Made out fine." Till Emmaline Tuthill cut him off at the knees. "Now pull over so I can throw up."

Whether it was the lecture or the vomiting, Arthur treated Martin with a shade more respect, even to the point of closing the car roof and turning on the air conditioning.

"You want me to keep talking?" Arthur asked. "Looks to me like you better catch some shuteye."

"Your English is wonderful, Arthur, even though you're an irritating young Reaganite. Yes, keep talking."

Arthur grinned. "My parents have always spoken English. California and American TV did the rest. So... other than tangling with slimeballs, what brings you to Thailand?"

"It's a fishing expedition. I'm after sculpture. Specifically, Khmer sculpture. Know anything about it?"

"Sure. Mother made a habit of dragging me and the twins to all the famous sites. We got a couple really excellent pieces up at the house. I'll show you."

"Part of the old family collection?"

"No. Our engineer found them after a rain undermined a footing of the satellite tower. They're nice, not all weather-beaten like some I've seen. About two, two and a half feet tall. Buddhas. Probably worth a couple hundred bucks."

"If they were Khmer in the condition you describe, they'd be worth much more than that—five figures for sure."

"No kidding? Maybe there's something to this art racket after all."

"Then I hate to disappoint you. The Khmer empire did extend up to and beyond Chiang Mai, but their temple building was limited to the lowlands—Lopburi, Phimai. I heard the rumor too about a site up north, but it's awfully farfetched."

"Far be it from me to challenge the poohbahs of Southeast Asian art, but these little fellows are Khmer all right. They got muscles, broad faces, and fat lips—like nothing I've ever seen but Khmer. At first we thought there was just this cave. But once they started cleaning it out they found what's shaping up to be the stone foundation of a building. And if you don't believe me, there are some archaeologists going ape-shit over the stuff. They blocked off the area and started a survey. Twelfth century, they're saying." He swerved around a pothole and continued. "There's a rumor going around our staff that the property next to ours has an even bigger edifice—almost totally embedded now in the mountain—and they say it's filled with stone statues—great big ones. If they're as valuable as you say, I'm beginning to see what the excitement is all about."

"Think you can get me over to see them?"

Arthur gave him a sidelong glance. "Dunno, Martin. If you get carsick on a Mercedes suspension, you may not be ready to crawl around those hills. It's pretty rough terrain. Besides, you probably should check it out with Mr. Savani first."

"Tony Savani, his property adjoins yours?"

Arthur paused before he spoke again. "Well... you said he was a pal of yours, right? Don't tell him I told you, but only a very few insiders know it's Savani's land. The ninety-nine year lease is in the name of some multinational corporation owned by a rat's nest of other multinationals. ThaiCorp, something like that. Savani has his country house on the edge of the property, but no one realizes that the whole valley is his."

"He know about the rumors of a Khmer site on his property?"

Arthur shrugged.

"You're aware of his interest in archaeology?"

"I'm aware. Just about every archaeologist in Thailand has a grant from his foundation, including the ones who are poking around on our property. But, seeing as how you're such buddies with Mr. Savani, it would be no surprise to you that, around these parts, he's better known as the genius behind worldwide distribution of Thai Sparkle—heroin so pure you can snort it like cocaine." He stole a glance at Martin.

Martin nodded, absorbing the scrumptious bit of information without revealing a hint of surprise. "He's really amazing, isn't he?"

"I'll say. While the world keeps its hidden cameras trained on the infamous Savani family compound on the border, old Tony oversees the entire distribution network by computer. Totally cool. On the surface, he's got nothing to do with the heroin business, yet he rakes in millions. Pop's operation is strictly domestic. I'm trying to decide whether to move our business global or merely toward a more refined and profitable product domestically. I hope my studies at Columbia help me figure it out."

"Sure, maybe you could consult with my old man while you're there."

"Good idea, good idea. Hey, you're putting me on, aren't you?"

Martin laughed. "Hell no. I think the opium business would be just the kind of knotty economic development problem Winston would love to wrap his intellect around. And he adores young capitalists."

"I can't tell whether you're putting me on or not. It would be a great privilege to work with Winston Moon."

Martin laughed again, but his thoughts turned toward the many layers of Antoine Savani. To the world, a generous patron of the cultural community. To the art market insiders, an obsessive and secretive collector of the rarest antiquities. And now, to another group of insiders, a brilliant heroin distributor.

The hawkeyes may have discovered that their esteemed benefactor hoarded for himself the rarest of the very artifacts they sought to preserve on site. Or perhaps even that Tony was skimming treasures from his own property. But did Bruno and Cal know they were on their way to confront a heroin kingpin? His feeling about drugs aside, Martin prayed that Savani's genius would keep Delia and Jack safe.

"The archaeologists at work on your property—what are their names?"

"Clearwater and Andriotti."

The names meant nothing to Martin.

"But it was their assistant—an Oxford grad student—that I first mentioned the statues to. She hangs around my pop's bar—Ingrid Lundquist. Cool drink of water she is—a Norse goddess, nearly six feet tall, got this drop-dead stare—"

"Wait—their first names, are they Cal and Bruno?"

"Yeah. They're due back on the site tomorrow or the next day."

Between Bangkok and Chiang Mai, Thailand

The night train rolled northward. After a late dinner, Jack ran out of conversation, watched Delia fuss and fiddle with her bag, and gradually fell into a restless doze. A porter came through and roused them. With magical efficiency, he dismantled their table and converted their shallow cubby into upper and lower berths. The window was shut and a heavy steel shutter dropped over it.

Jack volunteered for the upper berth. Pulling the curtain shut and squirming out of his clothes, he soon discovered there was no air circulation. With the curtain open halfway, the oscillating ceiling fan gave him one second of breeze every ten seconds. He blinked the sweat from his eyes. Why the hell had the porter closed their window? Slowly, the rumble of the train lulled him into a fitful sleep.

Some time later, he awoke, wiggled back into his shorts, and swung down off the berth. Dull fluorescents lit the passage. He found the toilet at the end of the car.

All the passengers seemed settled behind their curtains, but as he made his way back, Delia popped out of her berth, dressed except for shoes. She was wild-eyed.

"I'm being baked alive. Did you see a porter? I have to get the window open or I'll die."

"Let me try."

He crawled into her berth. She'd managed to raise the metal shutter but couldn't work the window latches. He pushed and pulled and jimmied till he figured out how to release the window and drop it into its slot. Cool air billowed across him and chilled his sweat.

They sat crosslegged at either end of the mattress, watching the shadows speed by.

"This isn't the way things were supposed to turn out," she said. "Being on this sweaty fucking night train just proves what a mess I've made."

"What did you think, chasing down a murderer? How was it supposed to be?"

"Trying to recuperate in London, even with Tony's help—I couldn't get past the sense that my life had turned into a vast wasteland, barren and unproductive."

"The post-traumatic—"

"Whatever," she snapped. "I got bored to death thinking of myself as 'post-traumatic,' all full of new twitches and palpitations. That's not who I am. I'm the fisher, not some dumb-as-fuck flounder. I needed a process, like a ritual, you know? I needed to be born again." She ran her hand along the edge of the window. "No, wrong sacrament. I didn't need a new life so much as a reconciliation with my old one. Atonement—that's the right word, isn't it? *To atone: to become 'at one' with.* Are you falling asleep?"

"I'm wide awake," Jack said. And it was true. The chugging and jostling of the train focused the conversation like a campfire.

"I latched onto the idea of *ritual*—a rite of passage out of hell. And my thoughts jumped to Martin. My old flame. My friend. My fellow fisher on the sea of all that is sacred and time-worn and beautiful. Also suffering devastation. We would do this thing together—this ceremony, this reconciliation. We would assure that justice was done for our wounds and then

we would own our lives again. We would be *at one* with the universe again."
She turned from the dark landscape to face Jack, the train's fluorescents
lighting her eyes. "One person can't fight evil, you know. Evil is too powerful. It takes an alliance."

"Is that why you recruited me?"

"Yes. I may be broken, but my instincts are still—" She made a quiet
chuckle. "Christ. Nevermind. My *instincts* are totally fucked up. You had
no skin in this game and now look. You didn't need to be exposed to the
horrible way Ingrid died. How will you ever erase that?"

Jack stared out at the speeding shadows for a moment. "If I follow your
thinking, it's not about *erasure*, but about reconciliation. You recruited me
for your alliance and… now I've been initiated. I'm part of your mission
now, no turning back."

She laughed the kind of star-crossed laugh that sent tears streaming
down her face, glistening in the darkness. She wiped her eyes. "But it's a
mess, Jack. It was supposed to be 1-2-3 justice done, two plus two equals
old wounds healed, fresh starts, and harmony."

Jack wanted to reach over and pull her into his arms, but she had ele-
vated their dialogue to something spiritual and that demanded nobility
from her league of time-worn fishers. It demanded truth. "But, Delia, your
mission suffered a fatal flaw."

She went still, listening.

"You got Martin here on a pretense."

"What?"

"You told him this was a Jones-White job, that your job was work, not
a personal quest for cosmic atonement."

"Ohhhhh… yeah." A hand smoothed her hair back. "That. The fatal
flaw." Then she tipped her head back and closed her eyes. "I didn't count
on falling in love with him again either."

When Delia's head began to bob, Jack unfolded himself from the berth.
He nudged her to stretch out, then pulled the sheet over her. He climbed
back into the upper bunk.

After sleep that was a jumble of bright images and a mad concert of
sounds, Jack awoke to watch the sky turn from black to pale gray. The train
was climbing and they were surrounded by low misty hills, with mountains

in the distance. They were hurtling from the wickedness of Bangkok toward the mystery of Chiang Mai. He thought about their conversation in the dark—words exchanged between allies on a quest, words affirming their mission. He was no longer a hanger-on, but an initiate. A knight errant. He would serve.

Before long, passengers were stirring and the porters came through to convert their berths back to seats.

Over a greasy Western breakfast, there seemed to be a new intimacy between them, but one without need for words. Delia looked haggard, her crinkly hair puffed wildly out from her head.

When they pulled into Chiang Mai station, Jack stepped onto the platform first and reached up for Delia's hand. He had a crazy urge to hug her, but the impulse evaporated the instant Jack saw Tony Savani standing there. And his chivalrous spirit collapsed when Delia jogged away and wrapped Tony in her arms.

"Tony, what are you doing here?" she squealed.

"I came looking for you. I've been worried sick since you weren't at the hotel when I went by." He was smiling, but his eyes shot daggers at Jack. "I had to make a dozen phone calls last night, till I finally discovered you were in fact headed this way. I took a chance you'd be either on the Rapid that arrived at 6:20 or the Express. How did we get our signals crossed, Delia?"

"Pure craziness," she responded. "I'm sorry I caused so much confusion. It was a terrible, terrible day. You're terrific to find us, to be worried enough to meet us here." The cheer in her voice began to grind hoarse. "Terrible day. Left Bangkok... clothes on our backs. We need to—"

"Moon still off in Phimai?" Tony's cheer also vanished. "What does he think he's accomplishing by dodging the authorities? They won't simply deport him this time. They'll prosecute him for smuggling out all those ceramics. He'll go to prison."

"Phimai? Where did you hear...?" She glanced again at Jack and he opened his eyes wide so she could read his mind. "Actually, he wound up not going to Phimai, after all. I'll tell you the whole story when we get settled."

Taking Delia's arm, Savani turned away, then stopped, and faced Jack. "Where will you be staying?"

CHIANG MAI, THAILAND

Martin, in fact, did fade into a fractured sleep. When he awoke, it was dark. They were in the mountains and Arthur was driving like a maniac along a curvy dirt road. The top was down. The air was bracing. Martin's hands were throbbing.

"We're here," Arthur announced as they slammed to a halt.

The Li country house was modern, with all the conveniences, including air conditioning. Arthur had tried to explain the aunts and uncles who inhabited the place, but by the time they arrived all were asleep except for Auntie Mei Lin.

Now that he was standing, Martin slipped his arms into a double sling arrangement that felt like a strait jacket. His whole body ached. Mei Lin had anticipated how terrible he'd feel and immediately introduced him to an ancient, sinewy woman who reminded him of a leather doll—Manora, the family healer. She would tend to him while Arthur called Tony to make sure Jack and Delia were okay.

Manora undressed Martin carefully, bathed and shampooed him in deep hot fragrant water, dried him, and gently rubbed warmed oil into his skin. Then he lay down while she helped him sip one of her potions. Martin felt no shame at his nakedness as, slowly, all sensation—all the throbbing, the creakiness, the muscle tension—faded away. A tiny sadness nibbled at the edge of his drowsiness. Somewhere, since the time he sat in the noodle shop that morning, he had lost Delia's fish amulet. Bad omen...

The next time he opened his eyes, sun streamed into the room and the things at the end of his arms felt like hot, heavy boxing gloves. The cottony, sandpapery, silky world he loved was masked by pain without texture.

The Thai woman sat next to his bed puzzling over some needlework.

"Manora," he whispered.

She shaved him, then helped him dress in a stretchy cotton sweater and trousers with an elastic waistband, so that he wouldn't have to rely on others for zipper and snap aid.

A girl brought in breakfast. He drank tea and a fruity herb drink through a straw and managed the rice porridge—not very neatly—with a spoon stuck into his cast under his thumb.

When he finished, Manora sat across from him at the little table and massaged his swollen fingertips and the unplastered areas of his forearms. He asked if it would help the swelling and only then did he realize—so centered had he been on himself—that she spoke no English.

Arthur popped his head into the doorway. "Hey, you look almost human, man."

"Delia?"

"She's fine, but I got something for you to see." As he entered, he said something in Thai to Manora and she left with the tray of dishes. In his arms he cradled a hefty sandstone statue, which he stood on the breakfast table. "Tell me this isn't one of the finest Khmer-style statues you've ever seen."

Martin whistled. It was. The solid build of the little Buddha, the thin band at the forehead, the tiny flames of the diadem, the cone of the ushnisha all told him it was twelfth-century Khmer. And there was no question of its authenticity. Stylistically, it matched the larger statue Lana and he were investigating for the British Museum. His sorrow was that when he touched it, his fingertips were too painful to take pleasure in its surface or to sense the spirit within it.

Martin pulled his eyes away from the rare beauty. "Tell me about Delia."

"Sure. Turns out Jack and Delia didn't leave with Savani yesterday after all, but were looking high and low for you because you didn't show up at the *wat*."

"So where the heck are they now?"

"Pop called here last night to say that when he finally connected with them at the Bar and Grill, he told them you were coming up here, so they took the overnight express. Auntie Mei Lin forgot to mention it before Manora took you upstairs. Like Shakespeare, right? Comedy of errors?"

"Like Shakespeare." He shook his head. Where was his watch? "What time is it? Is it too late to get them at the station?"

"It's after noon, man. The train gets in before eight. But no sweat, I went there to pick them up and they got off the train all right— second-class sleeper—brutal. I saw them, just like you described yesterday: king-size all-American with ponytail, tall curly-hair beauty. They looked like hell."

Martin stood. "So where are they?"

Arthur shrugged. "Mr. Savani was there. They went with him."

Martin sank back into his chair. "Oh. Oh, dear, we've got to get word to Tony to be on the lookout for Bruno and Cal." Martin had explained to Arthur that his archaeologists and the murderous hawkeyes were one and the same.

"But listen," Arthur said. "I just got off the phone with Scanlan. I told him about the hawkeyes, but that poor guy was already totally freaked."

"Where's he going to stay?" Delia laughed. It was clear from Tony's voice that he hadn't meant the remark in jest, but Delia wasn't about to leave Jack behind. He could have gone to the Li house, of course—their original destination—but she wanted him near her. And she could see Tony's remark had struck Jack like a slap in the face. "With us, where else? Come on, Jack." She held out her hand toward him, as if to pull him along, and felt Tony's cold stare travel down the length of her arm.

Jack picked the rucksack off the ground and followed them to the car in silence.

Delia was surprised when it took over an hour to reach Tony's house. The city was left behind as they sped straight north on Highway 107 in Tony's Range Rover—the stretch Mercedes bunked in a Chiang Mai garage. The road traveled through farmland, dotted with villages, against a backdrop of lush rolling hills. Then they veered west and began to climb.

"Tony, I thought you lived in Chiang Mai."

"This is Chiang Mai. Chiang Mai Province. It's a stunningly beautiful place to live, don't you think, dear? The house is on the western edge near Mae Hong Son province. I adore it here."

She frowned and tried to imagine living in such horrendous isolation.

After the final leg of poorly maintained dirt roads, they arrived. The house itself was a grander version of his home along the canal. Tony explained it was actually several old Thai-style houses, transported board by board and joined together on the mountainside, much of it on stilts. The teak was heavily carved, with the curious Thai convention of making each

174

rectangle—walls, doors, windows—narrower at the top than the bottom.

They climbed the stairs to the front door, took off their shoes and stepped over the high threshold. The house was a dark forest of antiquities—intricate rosewood furniture, delicate porcelains, religious artifacts, ancient glazed terracottas, and fabulous silk tapestries. It was still, airless.

As she and Jack gawked, Lucky entered. Delia felt Jack's sudden prickle of tension a yard away.

"I'll show you around later," Tony said. "I know you're anxious to get cleaned up and perhaps take a nap. Second-class from Bangkok is an inhuman way to spend a night. Come, Delia, I'll show you your room. Lucky, tend to Mr. Scanlan."

Tony whisked her down the hall into a wing of bedrooms, to one designated for her.

"I can't believe you're finally with me again. Wait." He rushed out and returned in less than thirty seconds with a delicate silk robe. "You can use this to get out of those clothes. We can go shopping for more things in Chiang Mai. In fact, don't even send for your belongings in Bangkok. We'll make a totally fresh start. You are staying now, aren't you? For good?" When she failed to respond instantly, a shadow of sadness crossed his eyes, but he kept talking. "Now here, take this and freshen up. Through that door. Everything you need is there."

She showered for a long time, scrubbing off twenty-four hours of grime, and tied the gossamer silk around her. She hoped there was a modern washer and dryer hidden among the antiques. What she needed was a comfortable pair of shorts, a baggy t-shirt, and clean underwear.

She balled up the smelly clothes and stepped back into the bedroom. Tony was stretched out on the bed, propped against the pillows, sipping a pale frothy mixture from a goblet that dripped with condensation. He gestured toward another glass on the nightstand.

"I had her make one for you too—piña colada."

"Thanks." After the heavy breakfast on the train, she wasn't sure she was ready for seven-hundred rum-laden calories.

"Come here," he said, setting his drink on the tray.

After a microsecond of hesitation, she sat on the edge of the bed and twisted toward him. His eyes caressed her all-too-visible shape through the damp film of silk. Her breath stopped.

Oh, God, she thought, *I don't want this.* She suddenly realized that she didn't desire Tony. All along, she'd been pushing herself toward a life with him, concentrating on their common love of art and the art business, assuming that the physical part would develop as soon as she healed. But she was healed now. And hadn't she admitted the truth to Jack on the train? She'd fallen in love with Martin again. Now Tony's gaze felt more threatening than seductive.

The insight took only a fraction of a second. She pressed her legs together and folded her arms across her chest. "Tony, it's been a horrible twenty-four hours."

There was a slight shift in the line of his mouth.

She continued. "First of all, I found out that Jeremy Bellingham was murdered, in his Bangkok hotel room, night before last. He's been here, in and out of Bangkok for months, did you know that?"

"My, my."

"There's more. Remember we talked about Ingrid Lundquist the other night? She was murdered too."

Savani closed his eyes briefly, then sighed and eased himself to a sitting position next to Delia. "Ingrid, eh? Such intellect, such beauty—such a waste."

"I know who killed her."

Tony looked into her eyes. "What do you know about it, darling?"

"Jack got close to her. They'd been having this, this sort of a romance. He was worried about her." She was going to say more about Jack, but the set of Tony's jaw discouraged it.

"Anyway, this guy she lived with—Cal Clearwater—beat her up pretty badly a couple days ago and then she didn't show up at the bar where she does her work, so Jack got worried and we found out where she lived and went there and she was dead, lying there naked and sliced up, and Cal and the other roommate Andriotti had cleared out." Delia felt herself talking too fast, accumulating tension that was making her forget her own little romantic dilemma, forcing her to relive the larger horror that surrounded them all. "They did to her exactly what they tried to do to me and I think Bellingham was killed the same way. It's got to be them, Clearwater and the other one—Andriotti, who are the killers. *Hawkeyes*, for christsake, Tony. Wild-eyed lunatics who kill dealers they've decided are cultural criminals. It's insane, but it makes everything fit."

Savani stood. He straightened a line of Sawankhalok figurines on a shelf, then turned back to her.

"The injuries you suffered wounded you so deeply. But it was months ago, darling, halfway around the world. I don't want to be unkind, but you can't imagine that every stabbing death on earth is done by the same sadist who hurt you in London. In Thailand, every thug is adept with a knife. Besides, you said you were assaulted by one person, not two."

"But I was blindfolded, couldn't tell who was there."

"Anyway, Clearwater and Andriotti are Savani fellows—not brilliant, but certainly dogged explorers. True, they're HAWC-I activists, but—really! And why ever would they kill Ms. Lundquist? She was one of them, a tireless worker, and a hawkeye too."

"Jack thinks it's because of him, maybe because of his affair with her and some jealousies it may have sparked, but also—he didn't say it, but I know he thinks it—because of his association with me and Martin. Just like that archaeologist René Malraux was killed after he got friendly with Bellingham."

"How do you know that?"

"I met Sara Malraux. She told me. I talked to Bellingham himself the other day and he confirmed it. He sounded just as scared as I feel now, like the world was closing in on him."

Tony turned back to the blue-gray figurines. She was losing him, but babbled on, half-deliberately letting her emotions and his annoyance put distance between them.

"And Martin, Tony, they nearly killed Martin yesterday. The same two guys, I'm sure of it. The one, Andriotti, has been following me since we got to Bangkok and I'm sure now he's the one who broke into my hotel room the night we arrived. It was no nightmare." Tears welled up over the rims of her eyes and spilled down her cheeks. She could only whisper, "But Martin, they broke his hands, Tony. They broke his hands."

"Where is Moon now?"

She couldn't speak. He scowled at her.

"Where is he now, Delia? We need to make sure he's safe."

"Arthur Li. Arthur. Drove him. Up here. Last night. Should be safe at the Li house."

"What? Here? Jesus, what's wrong with him?" Tony muttered. "He could have avoided having the tar beat out of him if he'd only turned himself in at the embassy. What does he think he'll gain by hanging around here?"

She had no ready answer.

"You're falling apart again." His face was tense, worried. "Where are your pills? Did you bring them?"

She shook her head. It had been Savani who had invested so heavily in Dr. Courtland's remedies for her, who put so much confidence in the power of the right medications.

"Damn it, Delia, I can't have you coming unglued on me. Not now, not when we have so much to do. I want to take you up to meet an important jade trader." When her chin began to tremble again, his voice softened. "Collect yourself, darling. I'll be right back."

Savani returned with a tumbler of water and an unmarked bottle of pills. "Take two of these. You'll relax enough to nap. They're very mild."

She complied.

"I'm worried about you, darling. You're so overwrought, so full of fears."

Within minutes, the night train began to roar past her ears and Tony's words became more and more muffled. Her eyelids became hot wax, melting shut.

"You're safe now, darling," he cooed from a distance. "Safe..."

Not *mild*, Delia was thinking, not mild at all.

Jack couldn't hide his embarrassment at being alone with Lucky, whose eyes had not left the floor since she'd seen him.

"About the other night," he ventured, "it was, uh, a mistake for me to let you... uh, what I'm saying is—"

"No need," she interrupted. Her large eyes met his. "Come with me, please."

She led him down a statue-lined hallway. She gestured at a closed door. "Miss Rivera room." Then she showed him into a bedroom opposite a bath.

When he finished his shower and shave, he found clothes laid out on the bed for him. He assumed they were Savani's and knew instantly that they wouldn't fit, so he slipped on his cutoffs, then scooped his briefs, shirt, and socks off the floor, and loped down the hall to find Lucky.

"Got a washer and dryer here?"

She nodded and took the clothes.

"What about stores? Chiang Mai have any men's shops that sell large sizes?"

"Oh, yes. Many shops for *farangs*."

She scurried off, leaving Jack feeling naked amid the sumptuous trappings. He strolled outside and sat on the steps in the sun. The country air was hot, but not as suffocating as Bangkok. A breeze tousled his loose hair.

For a few minutes the emerald hills and cobalt sky turned down the volume on Jack's anxiety. Lucky rejoined him and sat quietly at the other end of the step, prim as a proper young lady next to a proper uncle. Neither spoke.

The screen door slammed behind them. Savani flung a ball of clothes at Lucky.

"Go take care of these."

She gathered up what looked like Delia's garments and ran into the house, eyes lowered.

"Whose bag is that?" Savani was eying the rucksack that hadn't been out of Jack's sight since he left Truman at the bar and that now held his two-pound pocket pistol.

"Mine," he said, at the same time spotting the initials *I.L.* etched in black marker on the canvas strap.

"Who are you, Scanlan? Where the hell are you from?" His voice was a tight growl.

Jack stood up, caught by surprise. "What?"

"Answer my question."

"What is it you want to know?"

"Who's paying your way?"

The question stopped Jack cold. He tried to keep his gaze steady. "Delia is."

"Why?"

"Took a liking to me, I guess. What business is it of yours anyway?"

"Are you fucking her?"

"None of your business if I am."

"Everything about her is my business." Tony's voice grew shrill. "Because she's mine."

"Maybe you better ask her about that—"

"Who is Edwin Jones-White?"

Jack spoke through a vacuum of stalled breath: "No idea."

"I'm having you checked out. If I find out that you've ever been associated with the CIA or the Drug Enforcement Administration or Interpol or—"

Jack nearly laughed. "You gotta be kidding."

Savani's colorless eyes bore down on him from the top of the stairs. "You are getting in my way, Scanlan, so make plans to leave. Soon."

"I'm not leaving without Delia."

"This is Delia's home now." Tony's voice cracked.

"She's going to have to tell me that herself." Jack felt his back, shoulders, and arms tense, anticipating an assault.

But Savani backed away an inch and inspected Jack's torso.

"No doubt you could knock me down and inflict a good deal of harm." He swiped at the moisture on his upper lip. "But let me tell you, I have more means to destroy you than you can imagine. No, I won't damage that hard body of yours, not until you force me to. But I can fix it so you won't be able to sleep an hour without nightmares, so you won't be able to look at yourself in a mirror, so you won't be able to find another moment's peace for the rest of your miserable life." He marched back into the house.

The man's words turned Jack to ice. A sourness erupted in the back of his throat. Grabbing Ingrid's pack, Jack aimed himself toward Delia.

When she didn't answer his knock, he barged into her room and found her sprawled on the big bed, legs bare, hair damp, face slack.

"Delia." He touched her arm. No response. He held her shoulders. "Delia, wake up, for godsake."

Her eyelids fluttered uselessly. Jack briefly laid his cheek against hers, then pulled a cover over her.

"Shit, shit, shit," he muttered, as he paced across the room.

There was a phone near one of the windows. Jack opened his wallet and pulled out a card that Dick Li had given him. As he waited for someone to answer, he focused on the tranquility of the view instead of the pounding in his chest.

"Hallo?"

"Uh...."

"Hallo?"

"Uh, I'd... uh, is Martin Moon there? Mr. Moon please?"

"American? Wait please."

A long minute passed, then: "This is Arthur Li. Who's calling?"

"This is Jack Scanlan, Martin's friend. Your father said we could find him with you."

"Oh, Jack Scanlan, yes." Arthur rattled on congenially about how he was expecting them and how he spotted them at the train station that morning. "But we're very close, just across the valley. You can see our house from there."

From the window, Jack did see the house, tucked into a distant hillside.

"I need to talk to Martin. Please."

"He's still asleep. You know he got his hands busted, right? Lotta pain. I'd hate to get him up unless it's an emergency."

Jack clutched the phone and propped himself against the window frame to keep from trembling. "No, no, it's no emergency. Don't wake him." He was losing control of his voice and tears were starting to seep from his eyes. He felt grotesquely tired. "I need his advice is all. I really need his advice. It's about—this advice I need."

"You okay, man? You sound a little ragged. Anything I can do? I'll jump in the Benz and bop on over for you and Ms. Rivera. I can be there in ten minutes."

Jack gazed at Delia. Out cold. And Savani's threats still rang in his ears. "No, that won't be necessary, not yet anyway. When he wakes up, tell him..." Tell him what? That Ingrid was dead, that Bellingham was dead, that Delia was lying in a drugged stupor, that Savani was going to rip his heart out? "Tell him I need his advice."

"Advice. Yeah, I think I can remember that. By the way, the guys who busted Martin's hands—he's convinced they're on their way to confront Mr. Savani and your friend Ms. Rivera. I doubt they'd get to Mr. Savani's house without being detected, but, still, be super careful, ok?"

"Careful, yes. Uh, look, don't have Martin call here. I'll call later this afternoon."

"Sure. Chill, man."

Martin asked Arthur what he meant by Jack being *freaked*.

"Well, all he really said was that he needed your *advice* and not to call, that he'd call later this afternoon. But he sounded wiped out, broken down. I offered to run over and get them, but he said no. I told him you were worried about those scumbags showing up, but I can't imagine anyone getting the drop on Mr. S."

Martin insisted he better talk directly to Savani, so Arthur brought in a cordless extension, punched in the number, and helped Martin cradle the phone between ear and shoulder. Tony greeted him warmly, expressed concern over his hands and puzzlement over why he landed at the Li house. Martin got to the point.

"Tony, the fellows who broke my hands are the archaeologists surveying the Li property here. They said they were on their way north to see you—*to set things straight,* they said—and to *finish what they started* with Delia. They're the ones who assaulted her in London. Their names are—"

"Yes, yes, Andriotti and Clearwater. Delia's telling me the same thing. But none of it makes any sense to me. I know them well. They may be a little nutty about this cultural property business, but—" There was a long pause. "Jesus, Martin, you don't think they found out about my collections, that they'd really do bodily harm to me after all I've done for them, do you? I'm their bread and butter—shouldn't they be loyal to their paycheck if not their paymaster?" His voice was bruised by the possibility.

"I think we'll be able to sort it out when the four of us get together and compare notes. For now, I want to make sure the three of you stay safe."

"No problem here. Listen, I'll send someone over to pick you up."

"Wait." Martin wanted to check out the Li dig and then sniff out what he could about the rumored site on the Savani property. He wouldn't be able to do that from Tony's. "It wouldn't be polite of me to run off so quickly. The Lis have gone out of their way to make me comfortable. The family healer has been caring for my hands and they're arranging a special dinner for me tonight." Arthur raised an eyebrow. "You wouldn't mind sending over someone for me tomorrow, would you? After lunch?"

"It's up to you. Give me a call whenever you're ready. But... we're all anxious to see you."

Arthur took the phone and gave Martin a quizzical look.

"I want to see where this Buddha came from before I leave here. And I'd like to hear more about the other site, the one on Savani's property."

"Aw, man, you don't want to go traipsing around these hills. It's too hot, too dirty. My motto is: if you can't get there in a sports car, it's not worth going." He chuckled, but saw Martin was serious. "Hey, don't you think you better take it easy? Another day at least?"

Martin stared at the casted hands that lay in front of him, his fingers thick and purple. "Believe it or not, I feel fine, except for this pair of training gloves." He looked up. "I was a Golden Gloves boxer in high school."

"No kidding? I did some boxing too. Thai style. Lotta kicking. Too sweaty. Kept breaking my glasses. I didn't think American kids whose fathers were economics professors went in for boxing."

"That's just the point. The public school I went to in Chicago was a mix of kids whose parents taught at the university and working-class Irish and Italians who loved their fistfights. I'd proudly show my scrapes and bruises to my mother and tell her what little kid I'd saved from what bully. She ate it up. Here was her scrappy son, the spittin' image of her dead father—all knotted muscles, defiant jaw, and righteous anger. Hellbent to stomp out bullies." He smiled at the old memory.

"Of course, my dad would lecture me that real men didn't settle their differences with their fists. But first chance I could, I signed up for boxing. Did pretty well at it, too."

"You box in college?"

"Nah. My boxing career was short-lived. I got knocked out and Dad yanked me off the team. Said he wasn't going to have a brain-damaged palooka for a son, period. By time I got to college... well, I was more interested in the arts."

"You meet Delia in college?"

Martin's gaze drifted out the window to the patchwork of hilly fields. "No, that was years later—met at a small auction house in Miami."

Delia was a kid from south Florida whose family all died young working in the fishing or boating industries. She saw nothing glamorous about running around half naked, doing manual labor. She wanted a career with clothing and make-up and people who appreciated her prodigious memory and organizational skills. She wound up on the staff of the auction house.

"It was a big pre-Columbian auction," Martin continued. "One of the last in the U.S. before buying and selling pre-Columbian became touchy. We hit it off, hung around together for a few days. But my business was just picking up steam in London, so I had to say goodbye. Next thing I know, she has a job at Sotheby's in London."

Her charm and her ambition had enchanted Martin. She made up some bullshit about having applications in at the London houses before she met him—his first insight into how she lived her life as a poker game—playing the odds, bluffing her way through. She was poker—plus boxing—bobbing and weaving and feinting her way into expedient friendships with elite dealers and grave-robbers alike. Even as she worked her day job, she began to line up small independent contracts. She could persuade anyone that they needed her help.

Arthur misunderstood her motives. "Gave up Miami for dreary old London? I see she was chasing her M.R.S. degree."

Martin laughed. "Hardly. She was chasing my business. Well, not *my* business, but how I managed to make it on my own. She wanted her own business but knew she had a lot to learn. And I thought she might be the kind of business partner I was looking for."

Martin and Delia fell in love over auction catalogs and estate sale notices, and in the back rooms of museums over dusty study collections. They were sponges for knowledge about the markets: the buyers, the sellers, and the artifacts. For fun they scanned obituaries, looking for known collectors, plotting how they might meet the bereaved family and get hired to broker the sale of dear old dad's boring coins or ugly idols. Or they would look up trouble spots on world maps and estimate the most likely paths of looters and refugees needing to exchange their valuable goods for hard currency. These were games they played on Sunday mornings and over late suppers. Between them, they developed a mental map of the antiquities trade across Asia and collection points in Europe and Great Britain. And they were making friends with the players, which in turn guided their trading. They called themselves *stone fishers* and lived their lives on the blue-water habitat of their precious ancient prey.

Amidst the fun, they got married.

But much to his alarm, their paths quickly diverged. He wanted to be "a London dealer," to move big-ticket items among a select few collectors and museums. She wanted to be a road warrior, a middleman, brokering deals between the source—or the nearest *entrepôt*—and the retailers.

It was Delia who introduced him to Jones-White.

"So then what happened, Martin?"

"Then?" Martin shook his head. "Then we drove each other crazy." How sad.

Jack figured that Savani would chase him out of Delia's room sooner or later, but he didn't want to leave her alone. Or, perhaps more honestly, he didn't want to be left alone.

So he sat at the phone table and stared out the window at the Li house. Slowly, the scene took on a familiar form. Was it a childhood memory of New York's Adirondacks with their ancient worn hills? Suddenly, he remembered.

Pulling out the *Thai Sites* notebook from Ingrid's pack, Jack flipped through till he found the sketch Delia had admired. Although drawn from a different angle, the landmarks were all there: the ribbon of highway meandering to the northwest, the Li house on the opposite hill's east face, the satellite dish atop a tower, the spire labeled *chedi*, and the rocky outcropping on the west side of the hill. The configuration of background mountains was identical.

Her notes dealt mainly with the Li site under the satellite dish, where she was trying to get a feel for the shape of the buried structure. Over the two-week period the field notes covered, she seemed to be doing most of the work herself, with occasional visits from Cal, whose pontifications she dutifully recorded, then contradicted with her own observations.

But in the pages near the sketch, her focus had shifted to another site, beyond the Li property line, on the southwestern slope of the same hill. With the help of Lahu tribesmen who worked for the Li family, she did some exploring on her own and discovered another cave-like temple opening, its interior populated with enormous Khmer-style statues. And she found the tracks where heavy equipment had already been hauling away some of the treasure. Her notes made it clear that this site would be the "Lundquist Discovery." No sharing with Cal or Bruno. It was her personal ticket to glory.

The rest of the notes formed a diary of her efforts to find the owner of the plundered site. Or the plunderers.

When Jack reached the pages where variations of his name were doodled all over, he didn't want to read any more. But his eyes were drawn to another sequence of doodles.

Who owns southwest site??

Who is ThaiCorp International??

ThaiCorp out of Zurich.

FLASH: ThaiCorp owns New Cathay Galleries—London!!

New Cathay rep—Jeremy Bellingham—works out of Majestic Hotel in Bangkok. Bellingham's name was underscored several times.

On Monday morning, the day Jack discovered her beating, a note said she'd gone to see Jeremy Bellingham. Apparently, her ambition—and perhaps her need to escape the grasp of the hawkeyes—had begun to outstrip her ideology. She wanted to strike a deal. He was noncommittal. Claimed to know nothing. But promised in a vague sort of way to check around and get back to her.

Monday night she was killed. And so was Bellingham.

A hand breezed across Jack's bare back. He jumped and slapped the notebook shut. It was Lucky.

"What do you want?" he snapped.

Her eyes dropped to the floor. "Your clothes are clean and dry. *Khun* Delia's too. I am laying them out on your bed. Also, we are having lunch if you are hungry."

"Oh. Thanks. You think it'd be too much trouble to bring a sandwich or something to my room? I don't feel too sociable."

"No trouble. But... *Khun* Tony is out for the afternoon. You would be having the dining room to yourself."

Jack dressed, tucked the rucksack out of sight, and went down to the dining room. The food was delicious and filling, but the room was oppressive. He had nothing against antiques, but the total effect here was dry and colorless. Worse, Lucky kept flitting around the periphery of his vision. Jack would catch her gazing at him, her eyes solemn and heavy-lidded, her lips full and parted to show a tracing of betel-red teeth. Then she would flee. It began to make Jack twitchy so, as soon as his belly was full, he retreated to his room, retrieved Ingrid's notebook, and tiptoed back to Delia's room.

Delia lay in exactly the same position he'd left her.

"Delia?" he murmured. No response. "I thought we were through with medicines, sweetheart. Did Tony make you take something?" Still nothing. He sat down at the phone and got through to Arthur, who helped Martin pick up an extension.

Martin greeted him heartily, sounding relaxed and comfortable and very close. "What a crazy mixup. Guess I assumed the two of you accepted Tony's invitation. Didn't know what else to think. They said she checked out of her room."

"Well, she did, but she actually just moved her stuff into my room. Things got... kind of nerve-wracking. Then we actually did check out."

"God, it's good to hear your voice, to know you're safe. Is Delia nearby?"

"Yeah. Look, Martin, those guys who attacked you—they're Caleb Clearwater and Bruno Andriotti, Ingrid's roommates and hawkeyes. Jeremy Bellingham is dead, probably by their hands. And Ingrid, she's dead too, almost definitely by them." He took a deep breath. "Delia and I found her body."

"Jesus. Delia okay?"

"Well..." Jack looked at her, so quiet, so vulnerable.

"Damn it, is she okay?"

"Yeah, yeah. But she must have taken something. She's in bed, out like a light."

"Sleeping pill. Good idea. How did you wind up at Savani's, after all?"

Jack ignored the question. "There's something else, too. Savani suddenly got real paranoid about me. Accused me of being CIA or some kind of narc. Was suspicious about why I'm with you two. Said I should stay out of his business or he'd figure out some way to destroy me. I wasn't included in his original invitation to Delia and he wants me out of here fast." The words were coming out okay, but his voice was all wrong, sort of high-pitched and raspy.

"Jack, I confirmed that Savani is a central player in his family's heroin business. He has good reason to be cautious of strangers. If you can tolerate the hostility a little longer, you and Delia are better off there. I want to look into something over here, then tomorrow I'll join you. Before long, I'll have to turn myself over to immigration, but I'd love to get some of this resolved first—at least expose Cal and Bruno somehow—get them behind bars before I have to leave. You'll manage there?"

"I guess so. Say, I'm not exactly sure who knows what but, out of the blue, Tony asked me who Edwin Jones-White is. I said I didn't know."

"Damn. He must be poking around, really nervous. I wonder where the hell he got Edwin's name. Well... anyway... you sound like you could use some sleep too. Maybe you could scrounge up some of what Delia took and log some sack time."

Something about Martin's cool-headedness rinsed away the gothic pall Jack was beginning to see everywhere. He'd gone too many days without a normal night's rest, even at his usual minimum. "I suppose you're right. But I need to tell you about one more thing..."

Jack gave Martin a detailed account of what he learned from Ingrid's notes. Martin devoured the information and had Jack draw a verbal picture of the exact whereabouts of the plundered cave.

"Her notes say the land is owned by ThaiCorp International out of Zurich, but she couldn't find out any more except that they also own a place called New Cathay Galleries. She had Jeremy Bellingham's name."

"This is fantastic," Martin said when Jack was finished. "You're fantastic, Jack. I know this trip's been rough on you, but we'd never be this far without your help."

Jack rubbed at the scratchiness in his eyes. "It's just that... I feel so damn far from home."

When Delia woke to the inky darkness, she lay quietly for a while, piecing together where she was and, then, where a light might be. She fumbled for the lamp next to her bed. It was 4 a.m. She was alone for the first time in days.

After slipping into her laundered clothes, she left her room. Hers was the first room in this wing of the house. She hadn't noticed before that the long hallway was full of small alcoves. She walked down the corridor. Each niche held an exquisite piece of Buddhist sculpture, lit with a single soft spotlight. She paused at one, looked carefully, then sighed.

A night breeze gave her gooseflesh.

She moved on to the half-open door of a lighted room. Inside, Jack lay sprawled across the bed. A bowl of prickly red lychees, a half-empty bottle of Mekhong, and a smudged glass sat on the nightstand.

She nudged him. With a groan, he opened his eyes, but had difficulty keeping them that way. He reached out his hand toward hers, but couldn't coordinate the connection. She took it.

"You okay?" he whispered.

"Tony gave me a sleeping pill that laid an elephant on my head, but otherwise I'm fine."

He squeezed her hand. "Talked to Martin... phone," he slurred.

She sat next to him on the bed. He smelled of booze and soap. "How is he?"

Jack squinted at her. "Talked to Arthur first. Said... lot of pain. But later... Martin... sounded okay... real good. Told him everything that happened. Shit, I'm drunk." His eyes closed for a few seconds and she thought he'd passed out. But he squinted at her again and groped under the pillow for one of Ingrid's notebooks.

"Read this, the end part. Khmer looting... out your window... down from the satellite dish... 'cross the valley..." He faded for good this time.

She was about to leave when she spied the pile of men's clothes on a chair. Must be Tony's and she didn't have to be a genius to know they wouldn't fit Jack, but they would suit her just fine. She also took the bowl of fruit.

Back in her room, she dressed in Tony's pants and shirt, rolling up legs and sleeves and using the belt from her shorts to cinch the waist. Then she brushed the tangles from her hair. Finally feeling comfortable, she settled down to study the notebook.

By sunrise, her belly full of lychees, Delia stood at her window comparing the scene in the sketch with what she saw. When she was finally convinced that the root of Ingrid's obsession was indeed the scene before her, she whispered, "Hot damn!"

Suddenly, she was full of energy. Determined to see the looters' cave immediately, she ran into Jack's room but he was dead to the world. Maybe she should talk to Tony before dashing out to explore, but the thought somehow made her edgy and she shucked it off.

As adventurous as Delia was, she was not outdoorsy. She couldn't think of anything to take on her hike other than the pistol she'd been lugging around in her purse. Who knew what wildlife stalked the forest? She tucked it into her waistband. It might help to have a compass, but she wasn't sure how to use one anyway. As an afterthought, she donned the Karen beads. They'd become an amulet—Martin's protective touch.

Her plan was simple. Walk down Savani's hill, keeping the rising sun to her right. If she reached the stream on the valley floor before she reached the old north-south road, she'd walk with the sun to her back till she reached the stone bridge that crossed the stream. The rest was a snap: stay on the road, past the *chedi* till she came to the rocky west face of the hill.

The first hint that it might not be so easy came when she confronted the underbrush that surrounded Savani's house. It looked impenetrable. Besides, from the ground, she could no longer see across the valley and lost all her landmarks. About all she had to go on was the position of the sun and the downhill slope of the mountain.

Finally, a few hundred feet behind the house, near some outbuildings, she found a path that seemed to go in the right direction. It was slow-going at first. The scree shot out from under her, causing her to grab for branches that snapped off in her hands. Thorns snatched at her clothes. Gradually, she caught the rhythm of the thing. The path began to level out and open up. The air was sticky warm. There was no apparent wildlife, except for the constant chirring of cicadas.

The narrow path joined the old road at the point where the stone bridge crossed the stream. From there the uphill climb began. Another half hour and she passed the *chedi*, which likely once housed relics of Buddhist disciples and was probably abandoned when a better road replaced the foot path as a thoroughfare. The satellite dish poked above the trees in the distance.

She looked for a path off to the right that might lead to the cave entrance Ingrid marked. A few hundred yards ahead loomed the rocky west face pictured in the sketch. About the height of a ten-story building, it was not vertical, but slanted at sixty degrees or so, the surface broken by scrubby trees, ledges, and outcroppings. At about the seventh story a deep ledge—maybe a cave—spanned the face. Hard to tell with the sun behind it.

She walked cautiously toward it, thinking she detected movement.

"Deliaaaaaaaah." A desperate voice, someone screaming at the top of his lungs. From up there. "Delia, run! Run!"

From that seventh-story hole, a body hurtled.

190

Martin rose with the first light. The thought of a trove of twelfth-century Khmer statues on the backside of this very hill had been nibbling at him ever since he talked to Jack. It was a major find and one that would have scholars puzzling for decades. He also knew it would be much less interesting if the important figures were sold off before it was even officially discovered.

Manora rose with him, shaved him, patted antiseptic on his abraded cheek, and helped him dress. Her massages and herbal remedies had done wonders for the swelling around the casts and for his general sense of well-being. He was itchy to get outdoors.

Yesterday, when Martin gave Arthur the news that the *cool drink of water*, Miss Lundquist, had died at the hands of her associates, the young man was shaken. What unnerved him even more was the jeopardy now posed to his family. The deranged archaeologists knew their way around the Li property too well, making it impossible to spot them coming near the house. The threat made Arthur dig in his heels against giving Martin a tour.

But Martin hated feeling helpless, hated sitting around waiting for something to happen, so he decided to go out on his own. Manora looked worried as she eased the double slings around his neck and opened the front door. The rest of the household was still asleep. The damp heat of morning roiled around him. With gestures, she offered to go with him, but he shook his head no.

Marching off in the direction of the satellite dish, Martin encountered a couple of Lahu workmen who bowed in greeting.

"*Sawatii krap*," Martin greeted in return, with a smile.

The dig near the satellite dish was surrounded by a high fence of sharpened bamboo poles, with a padlocked gate. Martin could only guess that the signs bore the Thai and Chinese equivalents of *Keep Out*. Peering through the cracks, he saw the piles of bricks that had once been an edifice. There was no way to tell whether the site had been visited during the past twenty-four hours. Down the slope, he could see the spire of the *chedi* that Jack had described and began to walk on a line aiming at a spot slightly uphill from it. There was no path that he could discern, but the undergrowth wasn't bad. Soon, however, the hill was too steep for Martin to keep his balance without removing his hands from the slings.

The view opened up to the hazy blue-green hills to the west. Beneath his feet now were the patterned ruts of a heavy, tracked vehicle. The tracks emerged from the valley below and continued to snake between piles of rubble to his right, toward what appeared to be a cave. He followed them.

As the path took him uphill, he saw that the "cave" was a partially excavated entrance to an ancient building, transformed by centuries of monsoons and mudslides into a hybrid work of man and nature. Perhaps the forest monks who once tended the *chedi* below had discovered this marvel and lived their hermits' lives within its sacred depths.

Inside the entrance, a crumbling brick staircase was faintly lit by natural light from a second level above. The wide steps were partly overlaid with a ramp of lashed bamboo—definitely not of ancient origin. He climbed up.

At the top of the stairs, Martin stepped into a spacious grotto that could have been a temple sanctuary. The far wall had fallen away to reveal a spectacular view of the hills. But it was not the scenery that commanded Martin's attention. Lying along the edge of the grotto, along with some crating lumber and straw packing material, were half a dozen stone figures of larger-than-life proportions.

"I'll be damned," he murmured as he walked closer and stooped to examine them. Four were slightly weather-worn, arms broken off. He knew the style. He felt a thrill—of delight, then of sickening horror. He knew the style—identical to the piece nearly purchased by the British Museum, before Lana tipped them off about suspicious provenance, the week she was murdered. The thought of Lana paralyzed him for a moment, but he forced himself to move on.

The other two statues were pristine, their outstretched arms intact. The early Khmer sculptors had misjudged the properties of stone and carved arms in graceful, unsupported positions. Their faulty engineering meant that, over time, the arms tended to break off. So Martin could conclude that the two were never mounted on display in a temple setting. However, a museum curator could brace those arms to preserve them forever. Or a savvy collector. Like himself.

He touched the stone, letting his swollen fingertips soak up the energy of the sculptor and the *qi* of the temple deities. *No*, the stone told him, no museum, no collector should have these. The site should be methodically excavated, its history researched, and the statues kept right here, in their sacred space. Martin hoped to God it wasn't Tony looting this temple, because only Tony and the Savani fortune could properly preserve its ancient splendor.

However, it was also clear to Martin that the looter was no common idol runner. Manpower and heavy equipment were needed to move these statues intact. The average plundering jackass would simply lop off the heads. Heads were portable. They sold more quickly and more profitably than the entire cumbersome figure. No, this looter was willing to commit a cultural felony, but not an atrocity.

Suddenly, Martin's fascination was interrupted by a hissing whisper, a falling stone. He froze. Footsteps beat up the stone staircase and Bruno and Cal burst into the grotto, knives drawn. Binoculars hung around their necks and their faces were scruffy with two-day beards.

Martin raised his heavy hands in surrender. His only weapon had already been neutralized.

"You were damn lucky to escape us the other day," Cal said. "But letting you go, we get the last laugh. Following you here, we can claim this new site and kill you at our leisure."

"I told you Scanlan had to have the notebook." Bruno's voice was breathy, seeking approval from Cal. "Wasn't I right this time? Moon would never have found this place without it. Unless, of course, our beloved benefactor, Mr. ThaiCorp himself, told him."

"What are you talking about?" Martin asked.

"Don't be stupid," Cal answered. "Jeremy told us the truth about Mr. Savani—the cautious and ever so discreet export of the less desirable pieces from this site. The less desirable ones—so that he could keep the best for himself, for his bloody secret collection. But we won't kill Mr. Savani, you can be sure. He's already guaranteed us a seat at the head-table of our profession. This 'new discovery' of ours will surely fatten our stipends."

Martin laughed. "You think a heroin magnate, a prince in the Corsican syndicate will let you blackmail him?"

The two exchanged a quick look that told Martin they hadn't known Tony's drug connection. Maybe Bellingham never knew.

"Shut up." Cal shoved Martin against the stone wall and landed a sharp punch to his solar plexus. While Martin gulped for air, they wrestled him to the ground, onto his back. Dumping his pack and binoculars, Cal sat astride him. Bruno yanked Martin's arms over his head and held them immobile, at an angle that made any motion painful. Martin's legs were free, but they kicked uselessly. He dully tried to figure out how they managed knives and fists simultaneously.

Cal grabbed Martin's t-shirt and, with a few deft snaps of his knife, ripped it open. Touching Martin's chest, he whispered, "Oh, yeah..."

The lecherous tone broke Martin out of his daze.

Cal leaned over and kissed Martin's nipple, then forced his tongue into Martin's mouth. Martin whipped his head to the side and spat, but Bruno did something to his fingers that sent a bolt of pain down his arm.

When Martin's eyes opened, Cal was unzipping his pants. "When was the last time you had Australian whiz for breakfast?" His penis was erect.

"You stick that thing in my mouth, I swear to God I'll have Australian prick for breakfast."

Cal roared with laughter. "Ain't we full of spit and vinegar? I love an angry man." He was stroking himself with his right hand, while his left held the knife tip to Martin's neck. "Or perhaps you're minding your health. We've been in a lot of naughty places lately. René Malraux was my first man, you know. And a pleasant surprise. Very hot." Cal's eyes were glazing over, his voice becoming breathy. "Then Bellingham... Bellingham... Bellingham..." Cal got up on his knees and leaned toward Martin's face. Martin bucked to one side, but Bruno repeated the horrible thing to his fingers. A wet glob struck his cheek. Martin whipped his head to the other side and rubbed his sullied cheek into the dirt. He had the most outrageous impulse to cry.

Sweat pouring off his face and drenching his shirt, Cal backed away and crouched across Martin's shins. He wasn't finished. Apparently confident that Bruno could keep Martin subdued, he slipped his knife into the leather sheath on his belt. Then, with a swift motion, he grabbed the elasticized waistbands of Martin's trousers and briefs and yanked them over his hips. The reflex of resistance was met with another jolt of pain up his arms.

"Please," Martin gasped.

"Please, indeed." Cal doubled over, making wet lapping noises, like a dog.

"Don't," Martin whispered, feeling no sensation but pain and a withering terror.

Cal moaned. His left hand snaked up to Martin's belly and ran his fingers through the thicket of hair. He moaned again and picked up the pace of his licking and gnawing.

"Please... don't."

Cal's right hand slid between Martin's legs and a finger began to work its way inside him.

"Don't," Martin whispered again, but didn't move because he couldn't bear the thought of Bruno hurting his hands again. As the second finger pushed into him, Martin's mind threatened to bail out, to flee to a blank, distant place, but he knew that would only guarantee his slow, painful death. *Alert, keep alert. Let them have your body but not your mind.*

The third finger.

"Cal, wait," Bruno said, releasing his hold on Martin's arms. "Someone's coming." He stood up and turned toward the wide high opening, staying in the shadows.

Cal raised his head. "Shit." He stood too, and zipped up.

It took a monumental effort for Martin to pull his arms from the strained position over his head and even greater effort to ignore the pain long enough to hook his thumbs beneath the waistband of his pants and guide them back up over his hips. He rolled to his side, again fighting the mad urge to cry.

"It's Rivera," Bruno said. "Should I go get her?"

Martin snapped out of his wallow.

Cal grunted. "I have a feeling she'll come straight up here. No need to be impatient."

Protect Delia! Get her away from here! Blinking sweat out of his eyes, Martin conjured up a plan.

"Look, fellas, let Delia alone." His voice was hoarse and shaky. "I'll make any kind of deal you want." He grunted as he labored to his elbows and knees, then planted a foot on the ground, hoping they didn't notice how he was bracing the toe of his other foot against the rough surface of the floor. "Tell me what you want. I'll weep if that turns you on. I'll fight if you want. But, please, let's hide till she goes away."

"Sorry, Mr. Moon," Bruno said, "I've been waiting too long to get into her knickers again, and to tell the truth, I'm not as turned on by your hairy torso as my mate is."

Now!

"Deliaaaaaaaah" he shrieked, as he launched himself at Bruno's knees. "Delia, run! Run!"

Martin watched Bruno go flying off the overhang. Heard him scream—till his head hit an outcropping with the wet *thunk* of a fallen melon.

"No!" Cal cried out. "No, Bruno!" He dropped to his knees just as Martin was scrambling up to his. They were head to head.

Tears brimmed in Cal's eyes. "What have you done? He was my mate, you cocksucker, since we were fourteen. Like a brother. I'm going to—"

"Shut up," Martin bellowed, as he braced his left cast against his right and swung at Cal's head. Cal's eyes rolled back. In slow motion, he toppled off the ledge and tumbled after his Bruno.

As Martin doubled himself around the pain that roared up his arms, he heard Delia.

She was shouting his name, coming closer and closer. Then her face appeared at the ledge. She hoisted herself up and scrambled toward him. "Oh, my God, tell me you're okay."

She dropped to her knees and started to embrace him, but he recoiled.

"Don't! Don't... touch me." He was beginning to tremble and couldn't seem to lock his eyes on hers.

"They hurt you," she whispered.

"No... not at all. I'm fine... really. I'm filthy is all.... And my hands... my... hands."

She sat on the ground, cross-legged. Martin, still crouched over on his knees, uncurled himself. The wave of pain was ebbing. As she saw the dirty smear on his cheek and the slashed t-shirt, she bit her lip. "We'll stay here a few minutes," she said, "catch our breath, then we'll walk up to the Li house."

He nodded. Her gaze shifted to the massive statues. For a minute they were quiet, the soft hum of cicadas in the background.

Then Delia spoke. "The statues... they're Tony's aren't they? I mean, he's the one exporting them, isn't he?"

"Yeah." Martin didn't want to talk, wanted to lie down and curl in around himself, but the sound of Delia's voice was so familiar, so strong, so comforting that he forced himself to go on. "Except for the best ones."

She nodded, her eyes still fixed on the statues. "I know. I think I've always known. Right from the start he was testing me. And I played my role too well. Delighted in my role. I pulled off insurance recoveries for Edwin, so proud to be able to do it in plain view, without anyone suspecting I was an agent. All Tony saw of me was a bent dealer. Who did I think he was falling in love with? He does love me—a kind of love." Her voice remained steady, her chin raised with bravado. "I couldn't admit he was bad. I wanted to be his passion, I wanted to be his partner, I wanted to run his museum. I wanted all the clues, all the evidence to go away. By sheer force of will, I wanted him to be good. Sin of pride."

"But you knew," Martin said, seeing for the first time that she was wearing the strands of beads he'd bought her. "That's why you asked me to come with you, Delia. Whether you realized it or not, you were after more than one truth."

She turned to look into his eyes, her face inches from his. Something, perhaps a twig, had scratched a thin line across her nose and cheek. "I'll be all right now."

A voice muttered from the steps: "Can't get rid of me so easy." Cal Clearwater shambled into the grotto, face and legs covered in blood, knife in hand. He glared at Martin. "I'll kill you if it's the last bloody thing I do."

Jack awoke to the crack of thunder. His watch read eleven o'clock. He hauled himself up, padded across the hall, and poked his head into Delia's room. Gone. So he sat on his bed, picked his socks off the floor, and studied the worn ribbing.

The night before was a blur. Shortly after he talked to Martin, he had asked Lucky if there was any Mekhong in the house. She fetched him a bottle. He sat on the front steps, threw back several shots, and retreated to his room. He napped. Picked at supper—a solo repeat of lunch. Back to his room. Lucky followed him with the bottle and a bowl of fruit, offering to stay with him. No. More sleep. Then Delia… words exchanged… and forgotten.

Now it was morning. And he nursed a headache.

Off his bedroom was a screened porch, furnished in wicker. The sky was dark and boiling and the air heavy as he stretched out on the chaise lounge. Sheets of rain swept in from the southwest. The air cooled and a fine mist dampened his skin.

"Good morning, *Khun* Jack." Lucky set a tea service and a plate of buttered toast and fresh pineapple on the low table next to him. "Slept well, I hope."

She wore long baggy pants and a t-shirt decorated with a map of the London subway system. The girlish effect was ruined by the fresh scarlet betel stains on her lips. She hung around.

The tea was heavily spiked. A hair of the dog, compliments of the house. Was this how Savani planned to deal with his unwelcome guest—immobilize him with alcohol?

Lucky stared at his bare legs. Was she part of the plan?

Jack balanced the saucer on his chest and sipped the warm brew, but the arrangement was less than perfect and the tea dribbled onto his neck. Lucky was there instantly, dabbing at him with a napkin. He flinched and grabbed her arm, sending the china crashing to the floor.

Her arm was so thin. A girl's arm.

"How old are you?" he demanded.

Her face was close enough for him to see a tiny enlarging of the pupil in her colorless eyes. "Twenty," she whispered.

"Do you smoke opium?" he whispered back.

"No."

"Do you have sex with Tony?"

"No."

"Is he your father?"

"No."

"Is there a Buddhist hell for girls who lie?"

She looked away. "Am not Buddhist. Am woman, not girl."

Jack relaxed his grip. "Look, I'll be leaving here soon and I want you to come with me to Bangkok."

Her face brightened. "Bangkok is no good. You stay here with me. Make babies. *Khun* Tony won't make babies." Her free hand moved to his belly. He grabbed it and sat up.

"No, no, no. You should live with a good family, go to school, be a regular kid."

She stared blankly at him.

"Where's Tony? I want to talk to him."

"In the other wing. In his office."

Savani was working at his desk. A printer hummed and clicked behind him while he studied a computer screen.

"What do you want?"

"When I leave, I'd like to take Lucky with me."

Savani gazed at him, head to toe. "I figured you'd begin to see her virtues. She's quite... skilled, for a girl."

Jack blushed and found himself protesting, stammering on about social services, foster homes, schools, normal child development, counseling services.

Savani roared with laughter. "Good God, Scanlan, this is Thailand. No one is interested in a little half-breed who's old enough to be married off by her own tribal standards. She's quick, she speaks English, and she gives good head. If you leave her in Bangkok, I guarantee she won't make her living as a tour guide."

"Then I'll see that she gets to the States."

With a sneer and a graceful wave of the hand, Savani said, "Have it your way. Take the girl and get the hell out of my life." His face sobered and the focus of his eyes sharpened. "But please understand, my righteous friend, you will pay a price."

Like hell you will," Delia said to the bloodied vision of Cal Clearwater scrambling back into the vast, secret Buddha space. Still crosslegged, full of serenely cold anger, she pulled the gun from her waistband in a smooth motion, gripped it with both hands, straightened her arms, aimed at Cal's middle, and, *bang*, killed him.

The crack of gunshot seemed to echo endlessly through the valley, till Delia realized the deep rumble was thunder. Lightning flashed in the distance.

They sat absolutely still for a full minute, staring at the wide-eyed corpse. She had defiled a Buddhist sanctuary—one thought. It was over—the other thought.

"Let's go," Martin said.

The next thought—she would never leave Martin's side. Their long ordeal had ended. And they were one.

Slowly, they got to their feet. They soaked in another long look at the powerful statues before descending the stone stairway.

The path toward the Li house was steep and, as rain began to pelt them, the earth turned to paste. Delia held onto Martin's upper arm for support, but he was slower than she, and inattentive to the path. Suddenly, he slipped and, in a reflex action to protect his hands, managed to topple them both, landing them in the mud.

They scrambled over to a broad-leafed banana tree, but it was a useless shelter against the blowing rain. They stared at each other's filthy faces, smiled, giggled, then giggled uncontrollably. Then her laughter convulsed into sobs and she threw her arms around him. Martin wept too.

Delia hugged him till the downpour diminished to a steamy drizzle and the cicadas resumed their droning. The greasy red earth caked up on the soles of their shoes as they climbed the rest of the way. They didn't say a word.

SIX

CHIANG MAI, THAILAND

The gringo mud monsters caused a commotion at the Li house. A small, muscular woman in black scowled at Delia as she took off Martin's shoes and whisked him away. Several Chinese women, babbling too fast for Delia to pick up the gist of their words, swept her along to a shower room, stripped off her clothes, gingerly set her gun on a counter, and pushed her under the hot spray.

She shampooed, scrubbed herself sore, and tried to swallow away the lump that was building again in the back of her throat. Not for the murder of Cal, but for the goddamned fool she'd been. Tony, his love for her, the museum—all an illusion. Her dream was over.

"No!" she cried and struck her fist against the shower wall. Dreams were for idiots, idealists. She'd taken on an assignment weeks ago and now she was going to finish it. She had given herself a quest. She had committed herself to a ritual of reconciliation and self-renewal. The process was uglier and harder than she'd ever imagined. But isn't that always the way?

When she finished rinsing away her illusions and buffing her armor of determination, Delia allowed a young maid to help her dress in a dark blue ikat-woven sarong, a loose satin blouse with cap sleeves, and man-sized flip-flops.

Her thoughts returned to Martin. What had they done to him in the cave? She'd make sure that he was safe, that his hands were taken care of, before she finished her business with Tony.

Dressed, her hair blown nearly dry, her beads and her gun in a paper bag, Delia was escorted to the living room. A young man in designer jeans, heavy glasses, and a Stanford sweatshirt greeted her and introduced himself as Arthur Li. He showed her to a luncheon buffet and she hungrily piled food onto her plate.

"Where's Martin? He okay?" she asked.

"He's on the phone. Be down shortly. Manora's been trying to patch up and dry out his casts. Whatever 'little stumble' he took out there played havoc with his hands. The med school hospital in Chiang Mai ought to be able to fix him up. He needs to go there, pronto."

"Yes, I'll see to it." She dug into her paper bag, pulled out the strands of Karen beads, and slid them over her head. They were damp.

Arthur handed her a key. "Pop needs me to go up to Chiang Rai today on some family business, but I offered to take Martin to Chiang Mai first. He refused. Said he wasn't going anywhere till you were safe and sound. Maybe if you take him..."

The pain in Martin's hands was so bad that he blacked out for a few seconds as he sat in the tub of hot water. He came to with Arthur holding his head above water and Manora holding one of her pungent herbs under his nose. Immediately, Arthur began to press him about going to Chiang Mai, but once Manora finished bathing him, gave him an elixir to sip, and began her gentle manipulations of his fingers and arms, he felt better. Good enough to notice the chafed discomfort in other parts of his anatomy. He shook off the memory of Cal's assault.

With his thumbs, he managed to pull on briefs and another pair of trousers with an elastic waistband, but he needed assistance with the t-shirt and with his hair. Manora improvised a couple of new slings out of black muslin.

Martin got the phone hooked between shoulder and ear and dialed with his thumb. He sat, then decided to stand. Jones-White answered.

Martin updated his old boss as thoroughly as possible: the Bellingham and Lundquist murders; the confessions of Bruno Andriotti and Caleb Clearwater; confirmation of Savani's involvement in the heroin trade; the discovery of the Khmer treasure cave, and the demise of Bruno and Cal.

202

Everything except his own injuries.

"Imagine that," Edwin mused. "Cultural vigilantes turned murderers. This may be the end of HAWC-I. But who's exporting the sculpture?"

"Tony is. The temple-cave is on land owned by Savani, under cover of ThaiCorp International, out of Zurich. And, according to Ingrid's notes, ThaiCorp owns New Cathay Galleries—Bellingham's lot. Before he died, Bellingham apparently confirmed Tony's hand in the whole business."

It took Edwin a moment to speak. "Bloody hell. I'd love for you to pursue it, but in good conscience I have to remind you to get out of there and report to the consulate in Chiang Mai. The press reports were very damaging. I took the liberty of contacting your lawyer, Martin, and Emmaline Tuthill has filed a petition with the court to accept this incident as *prima facie* evidence of your criminal career, that you've been a fraud all along."

So this was it. All he had left was... Delia.

"Martin? Did you hear me?"

"Loud and clear, Edwin. Loud and clear."

Before Martin joined Delia, he finished off Manora's potion. It was primarily rice spirits, which provided the immediate advantage of a sense of well-being and high color in his cheeks. His hands, however, still felt like buckets of loose bolts and hot nerves. He left a plate of food untouched.

Delia jumped out of her chair when he entered the dining room and he forced his face into the likeness of a grin.

"Hi, babe."

"Arthur lent me a truck." She held up the key. "I'll take you to Chiang Mai, get your hands properly taken care of."

The earnestness of her expression, the tension of her toes in the floppy thongs, made him long to hold her, to have her cling to him like she did in the rainstorm. He sculpted another smile. "Shortly, maybe as early as tonight, I'll turn myself over to Immigration and someone can look at the hands. But I want to talk with Tony first, get him to confirm the exports somehow, and—"

"I'll do that. I intended to do that. More than that. He's involved in more than looting off his own property. At least one of the statues at his place I saw in Beijing last year. I want to follow it through, figure out how he does it, get some evidence. I can do it all easier by myself."

"No. For godsakes, no. I'm here. We'll do it together."

She frowned. "Okay, but listen to me, if you do anything more to risk your hands, I'll never forgive you."

"All right, but if you have to run off somewhere, you'll take Jack."

"No promises. I've been working solo for twenty years—don't hamstring me."

Martin sighed. No use arguing with Delia when she dug in her heels.

The drive to Savani's was hair-raising. The road was narrow, steep, and deeply rutted. Although Delia seemed at ease with the right-side steering, she drove too fast, ground gears, cursed, and more than once nearly bounced Martin's head off the windshield. Without a seatbelt and without usable hands, Martin wound up bracing himself with one foot on the dashboard, the other against the transmission hump, and his left elbow out the window, clutched against the door.

When they pulled the Toyota up next to Savani's Range Rover, Delia said breathlessly, "I told you I could drive a truck." They laughed with relief, till they heard the hysteria creeping in again.

Martin touched her arm with the back of his plastered hand. "I love you, Delia. When this is over I want to make a home with you. Our home, however and wherever you like."

Her eyes met his. The laughter was draining from them, but she still smiled. "Haven't we been here before? Didn't we try to rewrite the second act a dozen times and failed? Didn't we decide we'd never make it to Broadway?"

His voice was soft. "Those weeks in France, after Dieter, remember? I thought it was a new beginning—I thought we began a whole new script. But suddenly you were gone, back to work."

She looked away, looked at her finger tracing a line on the steering wheel. "Baloney. We didn't even make love."

"We didn't have sex. But cradling you close to me through all those bad days, getting you to eat, watching you sleep, feeling your tears against my chest—I would have stayed with you there forever."

An edge sharpened her words. "Then how could you have let me go?"

"You were so definite about getting back to business, hitting the road. The prospect energized you and it began to make sense to me too—get you on your feet, get your spirit back. I thought I could wait a few weeks."

"A week after I got back to London the final divorce papers arrived.

How could you—?"

"I didn't have anything to do with it. The lawyer had been dawdling over those papers for years. They surprised me too."

"But then *she* came along."

"Then *she* came along," he whispered.

He watched her face as she studied the hills, steaming after the storm.

"I've had a good life," she finally said, her voice tight. "Wouldn't trade any of the million miles I traveled, or the languages I learned, or the cultures I plunged into." Her jaw began to quiver. "Or all the Dieters I fucked... or all the Savanis I conspired with... to get you out of my system."

Suddenly, Delia's door jerked open and Tony bellowed, "Delia, I've been worried sick. These hills aren't kind when the temperature breaks a hundred. But I see you rounded up Martin. Hey, someone gave you a good clobbering, didn't they, Moon."

Delia jumped out of the truck but looked back at Martin. The sight of Tony had changed his posture, from pained intensity, scrunched around his core, to something more open, more pseudo-casual. He put on his broadest smile as he looked squarely at Tony and made an inane joke about her driving. Tony laughed.

"Here, Martin, let me get that door for you." Tony started around the front of the truck.

"Got it." Martin managed the latch with his thumb and joined them on the path to the front steps.

Their shoes left outside, Tony ushered them toward a sitting room to the left of the entrance. "We have so much to talk about," Tony said.

"Mind if I freshen up first?" Delia thought she should find Jack.

"Go ahead. I need to check the fax."

Martin was left alone and Tony disappeared into the other wing. On her way to the bedroom wing, Delia looked into the dining room and saw Lucky unpacking tissue-wrapped items from a crate. A snatch of bright green made Delia stop.

Lucky looked more scrubbed than usual. Over short, baggy trousers, she wore a bright blue tunic, with red sleeves and multicolored trim around the neck and shoulders. Red leggings covered her thin calves.

"What a beautiful outfit, Lucky. It's from the Lisu tribe, isn't it?"

Lucky nodded. "I am a Lisu woman."

"Those jade pieces you have there?"

Pointing toward an empty glass case in the wall, Lucky said, "The carpenter finished this case last week. It will be filled with jade."

Before Delia had a chance to ask more, Tony called Lucky away. She lowered her eyes and scurried from the room.

Martin sank into a chair near the window and doubled over. "Sweet Jesus," he intoned under his breath. With his elbows propped on his knees, he tried to hold his throbbing hands above his head.

"Excuse please." Lucky startled him. She carried a tray. On it was a glass of ice with a straw. From a decorative bottle on a small bar, she poured out a clear liquid, then set the glass and bottle on a table, just the right height for him to lean over and sip.

He straightened up and thanked her, but she continued to stare at him till, out of politeness, he imbibed. The spicy savor of gin caused his pulse to kick.

Martin held it in his mouth and closed his eyes before he swallowed. Coriander from Morocco. Lemon peel from Spain. Juniper berries from Italy. Licorice, almond, orris root. Angelica. Cassia bark. How many hours had he spent during those first weeks without her, memorizing the list on the side of the bottle, the list of the famous Bombay Gin botanicals. The flavor held so many memories, yet so many memories had been sacrificed to its power.

But it was okay, he told himself with a cleansing breath. The sip he'd had at Tony's in Bangkok and the numerous elixirs he'd drunk with the Li family hadn't triggered the craving he once knew. Those days were over. He was okay. He took another drink. He was okay.

A slight discomfort made him shift in his seat and the experience in the cave flooded back. Cal's moaning, the slurping, sucking noises... *Don't be such a ninny*, Martin scolded himself. It was nothing. Meaningless brushes with fingers and lips. A ragged fingernail. Nothing to get freaky about. No harm done. No worse than a paper cut in an awkward place. But he began to tremble.

When Savani came in, Martin's glass was empty. He replenished it, then sat across from his guest at the window.

"So, Martin, bring me up to date."

"Delia and I found the cave across the valley, the one where the sandstone statues are coming from."

Savani glanced toward the closed door. "What a talented little ferret she is."

"We also ran into Bruno and Cal. They came after me. We fought… And I have to confess that we left them there—dead."

Savani barely raised an eyebrow. "Yes, one of the security staff heard the shot and found them. The world will not mourn. They were idiots."

"Yes, I imagine they would have given you a hard time about carting off those statues…"

"No doubt."

The room was stifling despite the soundless spin of the overhead fan. Martin shifted in his chair.

"Anyway," Martin continued, "getting rid of those two closes a grim chapter in our lives."

"So it does."

Outside, the alarm note of a large insect bore like a buzzsaw through the steady drone of cicadas.

Martin leaned forward. "So, Tony, any chance of me buying one of those statues, having you ship it to New York? Like I said, I've been after some important Khmer sculpture for years."

"Do tell."

"But those, those are better than important. I haven't seen any early Lopburi-style sandstone on the market for twenty years. Nothing of those proportions, in that condition. Not till recently."

Savani smiled. "Believe it. I've known about the site for years. Took me forever to pull enough strings to annex the land, but without private access I couldn't bring in the heavy equipment needed to move the statues intact. I've kept the best, of course, but it's been great fun leaking a few out into the market."

"I'd hardly use the term leaking. They must weigh half a ton. Can't exactly bury them in your luggage."

"Don't forget, my family runs an export business."

"Lana and I were looking into buying a Khmer statue—probably one of yours—from New Cathay, right before she died."

"Lana."

Tony snapped the name like a whip. The conversation stalled again.

"Lana."

His voice was softer this time and Martin strained forward in his chair to hear. He started to smile, but something in Savani's expression stopped him. Savani reached over and filled the gin glass again. The sun was low, harsh, draping the valley with a milky film and casting long shadows into the room. The ice in his glass had long melted.

"Did she ever tell you about us?" Tony asked.

Sweat glued Martin's shirt to his spine and trickled down his sides. Their eyes were locked together.

Tony went on. "About our affair?"

The teak paneling that surrounded them seemed to exhale hot air.

"It began that last trip of yours to Thailand, after you went off to tour the hilltop burial sites. You were so curious about the damn things. Most dealers are happy to know as little as possible..."

Martin lost track of Tony's words, heard Lana badgering him to go to the hills to gather firsthand evidence of the illegal digs. She'd been so firm, so insistent.

When Martin tuned in again, Savani's monologue was providing an account of his first encounters with her. "As soon as she packed you off with your Karen friends, she was at my door. Tired of missionary sex, wanted something a little more exotic. I'd been smoking opium and it unloosed my sexual imagination. She brought silk scarves..."

Martin couldn't bear to hear the details. He wanted to accuse Savani of being a liar, but the narrative rang true. Lana had loved games and gimmicks, costumes and competitions, action, whereas Martin preferred to lose himself in the endless sensations of the female body: the muscles curving into bone, the pressure of lips, the silkiness of hair, the pure chemistry of skin against skin. Oddly, with the passing of time, each was less able to compromise. With an alarming frequency, their lovemaking had begun to fail.

Or had it been the gin?

The landscape appeared to be melting, warm glaze oozing off the hillsides, but it was only sweat seeping into his eyes. He wiped each eye on the short sleeves of his t-shirt.

"Why are you telling me this now?" Martin whispered.

"Because those few weeks changed our lives forever—yours, mine, Delia's, Lana's. You see, I fell in love with your Lana. Almost instantly I knew I had to possess her. Those two cretins, Cal and Bruno, were hanging around Bangkok jonesing to expose some cultural crimes. When I told them you'd gone after Tak pottery, they flipped out. I suggested they catch up with you in Mae Sot and teach you a lesson."

"I nearly lost my leg on account of them."

"I wish you'd been killed."

Martin's glass was empty again. Savani poured.

"I tried to resign myself to losing her when you two left for London, but in less than forty-eight hours I was on a flight. We began to meet." Tony bit at one of his fingernails, then studied it. "But, unfortunately, she betrayed me, so..."

Martin's throat tightened.

"So I had her killed."

The afternoon haze seeped into the airless room and sucked the breath from Martin's lungs. New voices joined the insect chorus and struck a harmonic, with a jarring overtone that made Martin want to cover his ears. But he sat motionless.

"Cal and Bruno had trailed after me to London, making the usual nuisances of themselves—grubbing for money, griping about dealers. We struck a deal—you needn't know the details."

"You... paid them somehow... to kill Lana?"

"Somehow... yes."

"And Delia? Did you arrange her assault too?"

"God, Delia. Why am I attracted to such difficult women?"

"The assault?"

Tony's eyes averted to a shelf of delicate Chinese snuff jars. "My relationship with the men you killed, Martin, was not a simple one. They knew the kind of easygoing gray-market trade Delia did, so when they saw her with me, they became vehement in their attempts to warn me away from her. At the same time, I was frustrated. She was too independent, always running off, no commitments. I had a plan.

"I told the hawkeyes she was pressuring me—wanted to use my export organization to smuggle icons out of Russia, some such rot. The idea was to scare her. Just to scare her. They got carried away. Boys and their knives." He sighed. "But I loved nurturing her back to health, reshaping her business, redirecting her life—like taming a falcon." He nodded, then went on, his voice dreamy.

"The medicines helped, too. Dr. Courtland's 'vitamins' clipped her wings... convinced her she was crippled with PTSD... Just where I wanted her till I could bring her back to Thailand and help her make a home with me... me... Still... again... off she flew."

Savani shifted in his seat and looked again at Martin. The angle of the light washed the color completely from his eyes. Unreal. "I love Delia... in my way. But now—how ironic—I have found her to be as perfidious, as disloyal as Lana. I don't care much for murder—it is often necessary, but as a form of revenge it is particularly unsatisfying." His lip curled. His voice hardened. "I'm willing to give Delia another chance—but the moment she fails me, she'll wish she died at the hands of the hawkeyes."

Tony's whispered confessions were more potent than Martin's brutal encounters with Bruno and Cal. His mind could absorb no more and began to detach itself. It floated. It looked down on him. He had died, it told him, up in that temple-cave. There had been no reasonable way he could have escaped from two armed men, not with broken hands. He had died. And he had gone to hell.

Hell tasted like warm gin. And a pale-eyed Satan was showing him how something about the way he led his life, something about Martin's own brand of lust, greed, and intemperance had wound up destroying everyone he loved.

Martin laid his head against the back of the chair and thought of nothing but the stinging in his eyes. When he looked up again, the sky was a savage red and Savani was gone.

With a plate of cold chicken before him, Tony sat at his computer and scrolled through the new messages. He was fortunate that the family businesses gave him so much access to confidential records. The Savani family employed a retinue of investigators with phony police credentials, as well as document experts who could deliver fake subpoenas and court orders at a moment's notice. When all else failed, those schooled in the subtle arts of bribery and blackmail could be called upon.

He had also obtained a phone record from the Tudor and forwarded it to Lorna Craig,at P&S Worldwide.

There. The response from Lorna.

> Re: phone call from Tudor Hotel.
> St. Cloud, France: Edwin Jones-White. Law degree. Interpol, 1946-1961. Specialized in art theft recovery, mostly Nazi war loot. Left in 1961 for private practice—I was able to trace some contract work with insurance companies and police agencies, as well as with UNESCO and HAWC-I, apparently still tracking down loot. Uses a network of confidential informants from the art/antiquities trade to funnel information. Offices at St. Cloud and, in London, at Jones-White & Albemarle, Solicitors.
> Names of informants unavailable. All payments made to numbered accounts. But note: I checked recent phone records at Spanish Arms residential hotel, where Rivera stays in London. Numerous calls made to Jones-White & Albemarle number. The emergency instructions she left with the hotel staff list Heather Albemarle as her solicitor. Perhaps a coincidence.

Coincidence, my eye, Tony thought. He dipped a strip of cold chicken into spicy peanut sauce, dragged it through a dish of shredded coconut, and pressed the savory against his tongue.

Art theft recovery. Damn them all.

He swung around to the phone and punched in a London number.

Fucking Scanlan destroyed everything. Not only did he undermine Tony's partnership with Delia, but he also managed to spoil Ingrid. Tony had plans for that Creamsicle of a girl and her eye for spotting the best statuary among the most deteriorated ruins. She was the rose that bloomed from his thorny relationship with Bruno and Cal. Jack ruined it. Sent her running from Bruno and Cal, sent her careening toward Jeremy Bellingham, rushing him, throwing him into a tailspin.

Poor Jeremy. Perhaps it would have been kinder if he'd had Jeremy killed at the same time as his lover Malraux. Malraux had turned Jeremy into a blathering fool, running at the mouth about the Khmer temple discovery. It hadn't taken much to convince the hawkeyes to put Malraux's feet to the fire. The murder was supposed to bring Jeremy to his senses. But it didn't work. It only made Jeremy more desperately incompetent.

Together Ingrid and Jeremy would have blown the lid off his secret trove of Khmer treasures. Bruno and Cal had needed only a few broad hints to interpret things within their own warped worldview and to, once again, do the wet work. They'd grown to enjoy it so.

Now this Scanlan fellow. The root of the current fiasco. Handsome, seductive, sexual Scanlan.

Finally, the phone at the other end was picked up.

"Arnie, did you get the fax?"

"Yes, yes! I'm getting organized. I know just what to do. And the right moment will be very soon!"

Tony chuckled. "Good, I knew the job would appeal to you."

As they finished their chat, Lucky came in with his cup of espresso. How darling she looked in her Lisu tribal costume, even though she only wore it out of stubborn anger. She stood across the desk from him, glaring.

"*Scanlan*, yes," Tony continued with Arnie. "You still have the key to my apartment?"

"Sure, sure."

"Good. I wired the money directly to your account, as we agreed."

Lucky grabbed a small photograph from his desk and before he had a chance to snatch it away, she tucked it into her tunic pocket. He put his hand over the mouthpiece.

"What do you want with that?"

She spit a great scarlet glob of chewed betel onto the wooden floor.

"Lucky, you bitch, don't start going native on me now or I'll—"

"Go to Christian hell," she snapped and stomped out of the room.

Tony sighed. "Anyway, Arnie, I'll be away for a few days. Enjoy."

Now for Moon. If Scanlan had been a stab in the heart, Moon was a festering ulcer. The wound began with an insult shortly after their first meeting so many months ago in Bangkok. Tony had asked Moon if he'd attended a big Bangkok auction. Moon laughed.

"Incredible bunch of overrated garbage, wasn't it?" Moon had said. Lana was resting her head against his shoulder and he was combing his fingers through her loose hair. "The restorations stuck out like a sore thumb. That Pagan-period Buddha—the hands were clearly brand new. A total rip-off." He laughed again, a resonant, mocking laugh.

Unfortunately, Tony had purchased that restored Pagan Buddha through an agent. It was already on its way to Savani's Chiang Mai home. Worse, he discovered Moon had been right. Tony did not tolerate humiliation well—even in secret.

Tony's relationship with Lana had been complex and his resentment of Moon ran deep. How he relished Moon's misery.

Tony picked up the phone again and punched up the number of the provincial police. Speaking in Thai, he asked for Sam Boorisooni. After the pleasantries, Tony got to the point. "Sam, Immigration is after an American by the name of Martin Moon. Deported a year or so ago for illegal exports and conspiring with foreign nationals. Recently slipped back in. Thought you'd like to know he's here, at the house, with a confederate of his, John Francis Scanlan."

Sam was interested. No one made illegal exports in Sam's jurisdiction—not without Sam's getting part of the action. Besides, this Moon character was international news. Sam himself would oversee the arrest. He only needed a couple hours to assemble the necessary reinforcements.

"No need to tackle the roads tonight, Sam. He's good and drunk, likely to pass out before long, so I don't think he'll be running off. However, I'll be going up to one of the trading posts this evening, so—well, you know your way around. And Lucky will be here."

Tony hung up and reviewed the rest of his email. Night before last, the mail brought him news of Moon's dispute with Emmaline Tuthill. With glee, Tony made sure that the *New York Times* had picked up Moon's American-smuggler-at-large story—and that Lorna had sent a clipping to

Mrs. Tuthill.

Revenge was the sweetest of treats. Tonight he'd take Delia into the hills, where he would decide her fate. Too bad he couldn't also take Moon and Scanlan—the possible scenarios would be most amusing. But the idea was impractical... Delia he could still manipulate; the two men were hostile. Tony didn't mind watching violence or enjoying its fruits, but actually conducting it was what you paid other people to do. Forcibly getting someone all the way up to the trading post was no trivial task. It had to be organized in advance. Too bad...

Delia was humming to herself as she unpacked the jade pieces, examined them at a lamp, then set them on the dining room table. In the first packing case alone there were enough fine antiques to convince her that Tony's taste hadn't flagged when it came to jade. The carving was uniformly exquisite and the colors luminescent, ranging from the palest white to spinach green. One rhyton was a rare, rich lavender.

"Hi, babe."

"Martin, you can't believe what..."

As she spun around to the sound of his voice, her excited words died in her mouth. His shoulder was braced against the doorway. Except for the tar pits of his eyes, his face was pale gray, his smile forced, his breathing labored. Spotting the jades, he stepped over the threshold, walked toward her, pulled a chair away from the table with his foot, and sank into it.

She whispered, "You're not well. Let me—"

"No." His voice was clear, the word final. His eyes were still glued to the jades. "What's all this?"

"Well, these are apparently some of Tony's initial acquisitions for the 'museum.' Lucky was about to set them on display here. Some rocks, huh?"

He wiped his face on his sleeve, looked at the collection another few seconds, then raised his eyes to meet hers. "They look familiar."

"I'll say they do. They're from the cornerstone collection of the Burmese national museum. Been on the Jones-White hotsheet several months now. A group of Shan insurgents sacked the museum and stripped the best collections. These aren't merely illegal exports. They're blatantly stolen, with Interpol reports and all. I can't imagine any museum director in the world having the balls to display these."

"Delia, let's go home. Stick a couple of those in your bag, get Jack, and we'll take the truck down to Chiang Mai... Then we'll... we'll... have the evidence..." The slight slurring of words matched the whiff of gin she caught.

"Martin, are you drunk? How the hell did you—?"

"It's irrelevant. We gotta get outta here—no more fucking around with Tony. He's—"

"It isn't enough to send these jades back to Rangoon. It won't stop Tony. I want to know the whole story, see where the stuff is coming across the border. I want to see who does it and how they do it—get a feel for the volume of his business, get to know his middlemen—"

"Don't be ridiculous, Lana. You can't—"

"What? What did you say?"

"I said, don't be ridiculous—" He blinked. "Delia." With a slight shake of his head, he wiped his eyes against his sleeve and studied his fingers.

Delia was torn. The brutal day had caught up with him and he needed comfort, but the time wasn't right for tears. She was itchy to finish her business. Then... then, the comfort would be a joy.

Resting her hands on his shoulders, nudging a knot of muscle with her thumbs, she said, "Sit a minute, Marty. Let me see what they have to eat around here." She kissed his hair.

In the hallway, Delia met Lucky.

"Lucky, will there be a supper served tonight? Or could you bring something for Mr. Moon?" Her own stomach felt too jumpy for food.

"Staff night off. *Khun* Tony, *Khun* Jack having cold chicken."

Jack! She'd been on her way to find Jack when the jades had dazzled her. Better talk to Tony first, then she'd catch Jack up on the day's events.

"Yes, the chicken sounds perfect. Where's Tony?"

Lucky pointed out his office down the hall. By the time Delia walked the short distance, adrenaline had boosted her heart rate and dried her mouth.

Tony was standing behind his desk reading from a printer as it spewed out page after page of data. He looked up with a quick smile. "Be with you in a moment, darling. Some big shipments went out from Bangkok today—a product I'm particularly interested in." The fax machine began to chatter.

She closed the office door and joined him behind his desk.

"Be with you in a moment," he repeated, as he pulled the fax message out. He glanced at it, then dropped the page through the slit of the shredder. Confetti flew into a clear plastic sack.

"I looked at the jades Lucky was unpacking. They're from Rangoon, aren't they? The national museum."

With a smile, he turned. "Very astute of you, Ms. Rivera. You do know your jade. Did you pass Martin? He mention our conversation?"

She shook her head. "He's wiped out... not feeling well. I asked Lucky to take him some food. About the jades—will we have a problem putting that collection into the museum? I mean, you do have clear title? The Burmese aren't going to go ballistic on us when we open up, are they?"

He laughed as he powered down his computer. "Don't want an international incident marring your debut as a museum director? Don't give it another thought. My documentation is always impeccable. You can be sure I have a bill of sale for those beauties. The museum there is in disarray, the government has bigger things to worry about. Any sound of saber-rattling will quickly fade."

She feared as much, although she couldn't imagine how he'd reconcile them with the theft reports—unless a key official along the line were bribed to deny that these jades were the ones stolen from Burma. Or perhaps Tony would merely claim he'd been duped by an unscrupulous dealer and return the jades with impunity. Or most likely of all, the Savani jade museum would never be a public institution.

"Tony, I'm really impressed by how you managed to get that collection. I have so much to learn about the trade possibilities with Burma. Would you be willing to—"

"Teach you? That's what we've been leading up to, isn't it? This sort of partnership?" His smile broadened. "In fact," he said, turning and gathering up the papers on his desk, "your first lesson awaits. There's an important shipment coming by back road to my *entrepôt* in the western hills and I want to pick it up in person. Come with me. You'll find it fascinating."

"That's great!" Better than she'd hoped. "When do we leave?"

He glanced through the newly printed pages, stacked them on the other papers and dropped them into the shredder.

"Immediately." Savani grabbed her elbow and hurried her out of the office. "The Range Rover is gassed up and ready."

She balked. "You mean *immediately*?"

"Look, Delia, there's no need for you to go with me now if you prefer to rest a little. There'll be plenty of opportunities. Next month perhaps... No big deal. You seemed eager to learn is all and I really must go." He looked at his watch. "In fact, I've got to fly."

"But—but I can't go like this." She looked down at her sarong, although it wasn't her clothes she worried about. Mentally, she was unprepared. Tony was manipulating her and she was falling for it.

"You look like ninety percent of the women in Thailand. We're not visiting the king."

"Well—let me go to the bathroom at least. I'll meet you out by the car."

He frowned. "All right. Two minutes. If you're not outside in two minutes, I'll have to leave."

Delia raced down the corridor of the bedroom wing, looking for Jack. The entire wing was dark, except for the soft lights bathing the serene stone statues. Jack's room was empty. *Damn it, damn it, damn it.*

She dashed into her room to grab her shoulder bag. The gun! *Damn.* She left it at the Li house.

She flew back to where Martin sat, slumped over the dining room table, his arms stretched out in front of him. She touched his shoulder. Had the adrenaline turned her hand cold, or was he burning up? "Martin?" she whispered. A soft moan was the only response. *Damn it, damn it, damn it.*

She dug the truck key out of her bag and put it on the table. "Martin. The truck key. I'm leaving it with you. Listen, Martin. You get Jack to take you somewhere."

He twitched a response.

She had to go with Tony, but she couldn't simply run out. Racing back into Tony's office, she grabbed a blank sheet of paper from the bin of the laser printer and a black marker. This was insane, but was the only option she could think of. Her left-handed scrawl was nearly illegible and sweat smeared the ink as she wrote. *Edwin—Am at Savani n. of Chng Mai. Going w him to west. hills for pickup—M hurt + ill—send help—Delia.*

Seating the page on the fax machine, she punched Edwin's St. Cloud fax number. Was that where Martin said he was? The digital readout flashed *WAIT* for-fucking-ever. *Wait... wait... wait... wait... wait...*

The sound of a car engine starting made Delia jump. Finally, the machine began to chatter and the paper began to move.

"What are you doing?"

Delia jumped again. Lucky stood in the doorway. "Oh! Lucky, where's Jack?" Lucky stared. "Well, he's here, isn't he?" Lucky slowly nodded. "Do me a favor, sweetie. I'm going into the hills with Tony. Would you get Jack and tell him Martin's not feeling well and would he see to it that he's okay. The key to the pickup truck is on the dining room table if they want to go to Chiang Mai. Got that?"

Lucky merely frowned. The fax had finally finished transmitting and Delia dropped her message into the shredder. The horn honked. Delia dashed through the front door, stubbing her toe on the threshold, then scrambled to dig her flip-flops out of the pile of shoes on the landing.

Lucky pushed past her and barreled down the steps toward the car.

Tony honked again. Lucky gripped the open window of the driver's side of the car. She was speaking excitedly in Thai, not pausing when Delia opened the passenger door. Delia hesitated.

Tony snapped, "Get in, for godsake."

She obeyed.

Savani released the clutch and pushed the gear shift into reverse. Lucky screamed, "No!" and reached through the window and grabbed his shirt. It was clear that Lucky was begging for something and that Tony was refusing. Her pleas turned into a tantrum: big tears, gulping sobs, snarled lips, and very black looks at Delia. Tony's head-shaking and stern tone made Lucky all the more furious. The only word Delia picked up several times was *Scanlan*. Uneasiness pricked her.

Suddenly, Tony used both hands to shove Lucky away and jammed his foot on the gas pedal. Delia turned to see Lucky's silhouette crouched on the dusty road.

Jack witnessed the scene between Savani and Lucky from the screened porch adjoining his room, where he'd spent most of the day dozing in the dead heavy heat, trying not to dream of Ingrid, marking time till Delia returned from wherever, till Martin arrived, and till he could make plans to leave with Lucky. He hadn't said anything to Lucky yet, but tried to be pleasant to her throughout the afternoon as she waited on him. She kept his pitcher full of water and his plate full of delicacies. The occasional sip of Mekhong provided a sweet blur at the edge of his torpor. Twice he showered the sweat away.

Now it was evening. Lucky's screeching roused him. He was surprised to see that Delia had been back and was leaving already. But his sense of urgency was blunted. Only when he saw Lucky sprawled across the road did he think to act.

She was still lying there sobbing when he reached her. The night was suddenly bright with moon and stars. The rain had already evaporated from the soil. He knelt beside her.

"Lucky, what is it? Are you hurt? Sweetheart?" When he touched her shoulder, she spun around and lashed her arm against his face, a wild defensive gesture. He pulled away. "Hey, I already have one black eye."

She got up on her hands and knees. She spewed what could only be interpreted as curses. Jack started to get up, but she lunged at him, knocking him flat on his back and hurling herself on top of him, her hands pinning his shoulders.

"Look, sweetheart, I—"

She screeched out a long sentence that ended in the word *sweetheart*.

"Lucky—"

Another explosion of words, this time ending with *Lucky*.

"Speak to me in English, goddammit!"

She leaned her head over his face till her tears dropped onto his cheeks. "My name is not *Sweetheart* and not *Lucky*. My name is Ali-ya. I am a Lisu woman, from the hills. I don't want you to take me away."

Her burden relieved, she collapsed on Jack's chest and her angry sobs settled into soft weeping. Cautiously, he put one hand on her back, then the other, and then he was hugging her and smoothing her hair and looking into the stars. Soon, she was quiet.

Jack's thoughts were absorbed in the constellations overhead when he became aware of Lucky's breathing and the small, rhythmic movement of her knee in a very bad place.

"Don't do that, Lu—Alina."

"Ali-ya," she crooned. "Ali-ya. You go to the Lisu village with Ali-ya. Don't take Ali-ya to Bangkok."

"Please, Ali-ya, don't."

"You want it."

"No, I don't."

"You want it. I can feel you."

He jerked up and dumped her on the road. "If this is what you want, it should be with a Lisu man, your own age. I'm too old. Before… in Bangkok… that night… the massage… it was a mistake, very bad judgment on my part. Very bad."

With a scowl, she stood and marched away.

"Shit," he mumbled and lay back to study the stars.

When Jack walked into the house, all was quiet. Then he saw Martin at the dining table, his face hidden between his outstretched arms, apparently asleep. A plate of chicken and salad lay on the table, untouched. Jack knew that Martin wouldn't eat chicken any more than he would eat beef.

"Hey, man," Jack said as he patted Martin on the back. "Great to see you."

Martin was startled and pushed himself up against the back of the chair. His face was chalky except for the splotches of red where his cheek and forehead had rested against the table top. A humorless smile did nothing to dispel the pallor. "Jack… wondered where you were… good to see you, too." He stood, squared his shoulders, wobbled.

"You okay, buddy?"

"Super… hands a little achy… no big deal. Gotta find Delia. You pass her on your way in?" His words were slurred, without expression.

"Delia?" Jack glanced at the doorway. "She left with Savani, in his car, maybe half an hour ago."

Martin's face blanked. He walked into the hallway, then toward the sitting room. Jack followed. Martin turned to him and whispered, "You can't be serious. She went with him?"

Jack nodded.

"No. No. This isn't happening." He was turning toward the front door when his knees buckled.

Jack was fast. He managed to sweep his arms around Martin's waist as Martin staggered.

"I gotcha, I gotcha. Take a deep breath. Get your feet flat, push your knees back. Can you hook your arms over my shoulders? Yeah. Jesus, you're burning up."

Martin managed to steady himself, but still leaned against Jack. "She's all I have left. She's the rest of my life." Great gulping sobs swept over him.

Jack hugged his feverish friend, wondering if the whole household had gone mad.

"I don't know what's going on, man, but you got a helluva fever. We gotta get you cooled down, so I'm going to walk you over to the other wing and stick you in the shower, okay? Can you walk?"

Martin pulled away, his shoulder bouncing against the wall. "What the hell are you talking about? We've got to go after her, this instant. Tony's going to have her killed—like he did Lana."

"What?" Jack felt a rushing noise in his ears. "Oh, God." He looked around at the empty house. "Oh, God." As he wiped the sweat out of his eyes with the back of his hand, he saw that Martin was bone dry—even his eyes were free of tears. "Oh, God."

Martin tried to push past him, but Jack grabbed him. "How many pints of water you drink today, man?"

"'Bout a pint o' gin. Come on, we gotta go." More words came out but they were garbled.

"Oh, God. Look, you're dehydrated. We gotta get some liquid and some salt into you fast or you won't be good for anybody. You'll have a goddamn stroke and then I'll have to deal with this fucking mess and I don't have a clue about what's going on around here." Jack babbled on as he pushed the resistant Martin down the hall, into the bathroom. Sitting Martin on the toilet, wasting no motion, he turned on the shower, ripped down the shower curtains, tied them around Martin's forearms and got Martin to step into the tub, under the cold water, clothes and all. Martin seemed stunned, his eyes unfocused. Jack ran to the kitchen, rummaged around till he had a bowl of ice, two bottles of water, a salt shaker and a bag of salty corn chips.

Back in the bathroom, Jack found Martin crumpled into a seated position, water battering his head and splashing onto the floor. Jack stoppered the tub and dumped in the bowl of ice. Martin didn't react.

Then Jack started pouring water down Martin's throat and trying to get some salt into him. The salt in the shaker was mixed with dry rice and made Martin gag.

"Don't you dare throw up."

With the tub a quarter full, Jack turned the shower off. The dance of terror was returning to Martin's eyes. "We have to go after her." His words were slow, deliberate, less slurred than before. "I am not out of my mind."

"Sure, of course not. We just gotta take a minute, a minute to make sure you're okay. Then we'll do whatever you say. Now, talk to me, tell me what you ate and drank today."

"Told you—gin. And some kind of herbal elixir."

"You stupid sonofabitch. It's been something like a hundred and five degrees out there. And your body temperature is at least that hot. You're lucky you didn't start having seizures."

"My lucky day all right..." Martin closed his eyes.

"Don't fade out on me, man. Talk. Tell me what's been going on. But first, here, take another swig of this."

Martin opened his eyes and drank. "I killed a man today. Delia killed the other. Bruno and Cal."

Jack rocked back on his heels. "Jesus." A sudden wave of longing swept over him—Ingrid. "And the booze?"

"The booze was compliments of Antoine Savani, who allowed me to medicate myself while he told me that it was he who arranged Lana's murder and he who arranged Delia's stabbing. He who has now arranged Delia's final destiny. We need to go after her. Now."

A calmness settled over Jack. The same slowing of systems that struck him when he found Ingrid's body. Carefully, he dried his hand and laid it on Martin's forehead. "I think your fever's coming down. Let me help you out and we'll find some dry clothes while you tell me everything. Then we'll find Delia. And then we'll all go home."

Wrapped in a towel, Martin paced while Jack ransacked closets and drawers, looking for loose elasticized pants and a shirt large enough to span Martin's shoulders. Finally, they put together a lightweight ensemble and Jack got the damp slings back in place.

Lucky had appeared at the doorway, taking in the scene with sullen interest.

"I can't believe Delia went with him like that," Martin said. "We were supposed to finish this together. She really walked into it this time."

"We don't know anything for sure. They could be back any minute."

Martin turned to Lucky. "You know where they went, Lucky? How long they'll be gone?"

Lucky scowled.

"I believe she now prefers the name Ali-ya—her Lisu name."

"Okay, sure. Ali-ya, can you help?"

Ali-ya entered and sat primly in a straight-back chair. Her outfit was streaked with red dirt and her feet were dirty and calloused. But her face, framed in shining blue-black hair, glowed with a beauty made fierce by the fresh betel stains on her lips, tongue and teeth. She spit on the floor.

"Ali-ya, please," Jack pleaded.

"*Khun* Tony has business with the Shan people. Traders. He has a hut in an Akha village along the trading road. In the high hills. Very lovely. He always takes me with him but now he likes *farang* woman better than hill-tribe woman."

"How long will they be gone?" Martin asked, but she was glaring at Jack.

"*Khun* Tony sold me to *Khun* Jack to get *farang* woman."

"That's ridiculous," Jack said. "I didn't pay money for you. All I did was talk him into letting me take you somewhere where you wouldn't have to put up with his abuse—"

Lucky jumped up and, with her fists clenched, faced Jack. Her voice drowned him out. "*Khun* Tony sold me to you. But not for money. Doesn't need money. He traded me for *farang* woman. Said he is finished with me."

"What, you mean Delia?"

She spit again. "Don't be stupid. He likes *young* woman. *Khun* Tony has a friend in London. He faxed a picture." She pulled a crumpled wallet photo from her pocket and threw it on the floor. Martin recognized it as one of the photos Jack showed Savani on their visit to his *khlong* house. "Send friend to get yellow-haired woman Teesa-scana. Teesa. Scano-lan."

Martin watched Jack's face blanch to gray. "Theresa?" he whispered. In slow motion, he stood and gripped Lucky by the shoulders and yelled, "Theresa? My daughter Theresa?"

She nodded. "Tareesa. Yes."

He started shaking her. "You think I traded my *daughter* away to that animal for *you*?"

"Let me go," she screamed, as she tried to jerk herself out of his grip.

223

"You hurting me!"

Martin shouted, "Stop it, Jack, stop it. It's not her fault." But Jack was beyond hearing, till Martin kicked him hard enough in the back of the knee to make him buckle. Lucky twisted away. Jack scrambled to his feet and hurled himself at Martin, but Martin dodged him and Jack fell against the wall.

"You sonofabitch," he screamed. "If anything happens to Theresa... if anyone so much as scowls at her, I'll kill you for bringing me here. I'll kill everybody." He slid to the floor, scooped up the photograph, and clutched it to his chest. "How could this happen?"

SEVEN

CHIANG MAI, THAILAND

From somewhere within the nightmare exploding in his head, in his heart, in his soul, Jack realized that throwing a tantrum wasn't going to help his child. He covered his eyes for a moment, then hauled himself to his feet.

"I'm sorry," he mumbled as he pushed passed Martin. "You couldn't have known. I gotta get to London." He flew down the hallway, out the front door, yelling, "Lucky, where are the keys to that truck?" Then he reversed direction back into the house. "My passport."

Martin blocked him on the steps. "Wait. Jack, please. You can't leave."

"No choice, I have no choice." He put his hands on Martin's shoulders to skirt around him. "I have no choice, man."

Then it hit him—only one vehicle on the premises and Martin needed it to rescue Delia. "Oh, God. Don't do this to me, man. Don't make me choose between Delia and Theresa. Don't lay this on me. Don't make me choose." He couldn't help thinking that just days ago he'd made a choice between the beaten Ingrid and the endangered Delia. He honored his commitment to Delia and Ingrid was murdered. His jaw was quivering as he whispered again, "Don't make me choose." He marched into the house toward the bedroom wing.

"I'm not making you choose." Martin's voice was calm as he followed. "The truck is yours—do what you need to do—no pressure. I can figure out something. But take two minutes, okay? Listen to me?"

Jack stopped and turned to him.

"Running off like this isn't necessarily the quickest or best way to ensure Theresa's safety. Listen. The domestic airlines are on strike, so you'll have to drive the whole way to Bangkok. It'll take you all night. If you manage to get a plane tomorrow, it may be another twenty-four hours till you actually arrive. Before you do anything, let's make some phone calls, okay?"

Martin's words sank in. "I guess... you have a point."

As they headed for Savani's office, Martin asked Lucky to explain exactly what she knew about Savani's plan.

She glued her eyes to the floor. "*Khun* Tony told me to take the picture from Jack's wallet when he was in the shower. Made two phone calls to a man named Arnie in London. Told Arnie many details about the ballet school. Laughed, said dirty words—I did not understand everything." Her eyes brimmed with tears. "I saw him fax the picture. Then he said he traded me to *Khun* Jack for Tees Scanoran in London. Told me go to away with *Khun* Jack." She rubbed her eyes. "I hate Tony now. He fucked me over for the last time. I will return to be a proper Lisu woman. I will return to my Lisu name Ali-ya. I will go home."

Already seeing himself in a black suit, Jack could barely listen to Martin's patient questioning, but the upshot was that Lucky couldn't shed any additional light on Tony's plan.

Jack pulled a card full of typed numbers out of his wallet and placed his call to Theresa. The call turned to calls. Everyone he talked to—at the dorm, the rehearsal hall, and the school—assured him that she was about, that they'd seen her, that she was fine, but they couldn't spot her just that moment.

"I know this sounds stupid," he kept saying over and over, "but would you tell her that her dad called and that she shouldn't talk to any strangers. Thanks."

Jack managed to get hold of the London police but, in spite of the growing hysteria in his voice, the officer said the best they could do was go around and see that she was okay and warn her. They could not guard her.

"I'll call Jones-White," Martin said. "He'll send someone for her, take her to his own home if necessary, although, at the rate you've been leaving warning messages, she may not trust a soul." Jones-White's answering service in St. Cloud didn't have his current whereabouts, but promised to give him the message.

Leaving messages with strangers did not give either of them much comfort. On the other hand, now that the initial panic had subsided, Jack dreaded the idea of racing down the dark, strange roads of Thailand in a borrowed pick-up truck. He felt helpless.

Martin spoke to Lucky. "Is there some way I can catch up with Tony and Delia? Can you help me out?"

She nodded. "I can hike to the staff quarters—five kilometers—get a truck. I can drive."

Martin pondered the offer, then called the Li house to see if Arthur was available. He muddled along in Chinese enough to learn that Arthur had gone north to Chiang Rai. "Damn. If I could catch up with them fast enough I could beat the information about Arnie from Tony or get him back here to call off the scheme himself."

Jack sighed. In spite of being told that Martin had killed a man today, he found it hard to imagine his friend—so near collapse an hour ago—pumping it up again to be a threat to Savani. His face was still ashen, his eyes still gin-glazed.

"Look," Jack said, "if we find someone in this world we trust absolutely to get to Theresa, you can take the pick-up truck outside. I'll go with you. How fast could we catch up with them in that case, Ali-ya?"

"After the truck, you need horses. Tony has horses at Ban Hu Nam Mai. If we don't get horses, we can take the shortcut—steeper, no good for horses, but very fast. If the moon stays out and it doesn't rain, maybe we catch up by morning."

Morning? It sounded an eternity away. He looked at Martin.

"It's your decision," Martin said.

"One I hope to God doesn't haunt me for the rest of my life." He picked up the phone. He dreaded calling Monica, not because Theresa's danger would frighten her but because she was more likely to think Jack was overreacting. To convince her of the threat, he would have to paint a cruel picture that he'd prefer to keep repressing. He dialed her office at Columbia Presbyterian, but Monica Scanlan was in surgery for the next several hours. Jack let the phone clatter into its cradle. "Unbelievable," he muttered.

Martin thought. Once he had trusted friends in every city in Europe and Asia, but in a year the list had shrunk to nothing. Who was so death-and-taxes reliable that Jack wouldn't rush to start a lengthy, and very likely ineffective, odyssey to London?

"Oh, hell," he muttered as he maneuvered the phone to his ear and punched the Manhattan number with his thumb.

"Moon here."

"Father... Dad..."

"Marty, good God, that you?"

"Yes, I—"

"Son, where the hell are you and what kind of monkey business are you up to now? Your picture is in the *Times* and the State Department has been burning up my line demanding to know your whereabouts. I told them it'd be a miracle if I ever knew your damn whereabouts."

"I'm still in Thailand. Don't worry about the State Department—it's just a technicality. But I need your help."

"The State Department doesn't go around calling next of kin on technicalities. I still have connections there, you know. Are you drunk? You sound as if you've been drinking."

"Dad, if you're not interested in helping me, let me talk to mother."

"Don't you dare disturb your mother. She worries enough. I didn't show her the *Times* and I haven't told her about this State Department business. No need to, unless, well..." Winston's gruffness cranked down a notch. "What's this about needing help? What is it you need, Marty?"

The sudden softness in his father's voice caught Martin by surprise.

Emotion tightened Martin's voice as he explained the situation.

"I'm here with Delia and—"

"Delia! That charming girl is mixed up with—?"

"Dad, listen to me."

"Yes, yes, sorry, go on."

"I'm here with Delia and a friend from Rochester, Jack—full name *John Francis Scanlan*. We've learned that—" How was he going to put it, with Jack staring wide-eyed at him? "His daughter Theresa, *Theresa Scanlan*, is studying in London and we learned she is at risk of being kidnapped, okay? There are some very, very evil people involved in this… a conspiracy, a gang of thugs. We can't reach her to warn her and can't get in touch with her mother *Dr. Monica Scanlan* in Manhattan. Jack and I need to follow up from this end but we may find ourselves without access to a phone for a few hours."

"Yes, yes, all right. I'm getting this down. Better give me all the relevant numbers." His dad's voice turned calm and businesslike, all his bluster gone.

He gave his dad Edwin's numbers in St. Cloud and in London and all the numbers and addresses Jack had for Theresa and her mother. "There can't be any delay in getting her protection, Dad. The man we're dealing with on this end, *Antoine Savani,* is the one who had Lana killed." He heard his voice trembling as he spelled out the name. "Edwin has the resources and the know-how to help. Call when everything's set, okay?" He gave him numbers for Savani's Bangkok and Chiang Mai homes, and, as an afterthought, for Dick and Arthur Li.

"You can count on me. I won't leave the phone till I've arranged protection and talked with her myself. And the mother. And there must be someone at the consulate in London, too, who can pitch in. I'll take care of it, don't worry."

"Thank you."

"Delia, you say she's there with you? She okay?"

"No." Martin blurted it by mistake, but his father's confident support was irresistible. "No, she isn't okay. She's with Savani, up in the hills. Now that you're helping with Theresa, we can go after her and get Savani to call off this… kidnapping scheme."

"Good Lord, Marty. I know you won't let me talk sense into you, but I hope to hell you have help—the police, armed guards. You don't sound at all well. I'll call the embassy in Bangkok—get the ball rolling on—"

"Dad, no! I'm fine. Just a brush with heat exhaustion, but I'm okay now. I just need to be able to deal with one thing at a time. Do not, please, do not call the embassy here." His voice cracked hysterical, so he tried to reel it back in. *Be cool, man.* "And look, don't worry, I have a good team going with me." He looked at his purple fingers, at Jack's terrified eyes, and at Lucky, chewing a fresh glob of bright red betel as she raced around shuttering windows. "A great team. I'll give you a call as soon as I can."

"Marty…?"

"Yes?"

"You can count on me."

THE HILLS, THAILAND

Delia wondered whether she'd be pissing blood by the time the Range Rover quit bouncing over dirt trails. Tony drove like a madman, careening around hairpin curves, flying off the crests of hills without brakes.

"Wherever we're going, can't it wait till morning? This doesn't seem safe," she suggested. She had pictured them going into the hills on paved roads, not on goat paths.

He roared with laughter. "I know this road like the face of Buddha. Except, of course, when the rain washes out a piece. That keeps it exciting." He laughed again. "Only accident I ever had was when Lucky was driving. Rolled the old Land Rover right off the mountain. We got out before the thing exploded. Earned her name that night for sure."

"That makes me feel much better."

Delia didn't know which was worse. Her eyes open: anticipating sudden death around every corner. Or her eyes shut: obsessing about Martin, and whether Lucky, Jack, and Edwin would take care of him properly.

After two hours of driving, with little more speaking, Tony slammed on the brakes at the edge of a dark village. A young man scurried toward them.

"We'll rest here awhile." He took her elbow and escorted her up a steep rise toward the middle of the village. She tripped out of the flip-flops twice and cursed them. "Relax, darling, relax. This is a whole new world. Take the damn things off and relax."

They were greeted at the door of a hut by a woman who appeared to know Tony. Leaving their shoes outside, they entered into a bluish haze. The perimeter of the tamped earth floor was lined with woven bamboo mats and the only light came from small spirit lamps. Two men drank tea. Three others were curled on their sides, dozing.

Delia and Tony were shown to mats that lay perpendicular to each other in the corner. Tony stretched out, his head on a wooden headrest. Delia sat cross-legged on hers.

A young man squatted next to them with an opium pipe, a spirit lamp, and a saucer of small black beads.

The attendant began to heat the clay bowl of the pipe, scraped away some debris with a small wire, and placed a dab of the tarry opium near the small opening of the bowl. Tony watched intently and licked his lips before accepting the bamboo pipe stem into his mouth. The attendant rotated the pipe till the bead of opium caught the flame, bubbled, and vaporized. Tony inhaled deeply and sighed with pleasure. After a few puffs, the opium had dried to a crust and the attendant repeated the process, over and over, for about twenty minutes, till the first bead of opium was gone.

By that time, Delia's eyes and throat were burning with the acrid fumes. The attendant twisted toward her and began to scrape the pipe. Shaking her head, she said, "No, no, thank you." The attendant bowed and scooted away, returning shortly, with a glass of tea for each of them.

"I hope you're not going to be a... wet blanket about this," Tony drawled.

"It's not that I disapprove, but I haven't smoked a thing for a good fifteen years. I'd probably choke, then vomit. Wouldn't be a pretty sight. The side-stream smoke in this den is probably more than enough to, uh, help me relax."

"Lana tried it with me, you know. Made her a little queasy at first, but she was a sport about it. Became quite a turn-on for her."

"Lana? Martin's Lana?"

"I'd appreciate it if you didn't refer to her as *Martin's* Lana. She was once *my* Lana." He placed a hand over his eyes.

Delia had to ask: "You had an affair with Lana Tuthill? When?"

"Mmm... little over a year ago... shortly before she was killed... She inflamed... and infuriated me. I told Martin everything, you know, before we left this evening. He didn't take it very well. Not well at all."

The opium made Tony's mind tumble back to his first meeting with Lana at the Oriental Hotel. He didn't ordinarily stick around Bangkok when the rains came, but a shipment containing a hundred pounds of heroin had been tagged at the port for inspection. He was waiting to see who needed bribing. Meanwhile his house suffered water damage from the early monsoon and he was at loose ends. Lana recognized him in the elevator.

"You're Tony Savani, aren't you?"

"Why yes."

"This is fantastic. I was just telling my trust advisor about your fabulous fellowship program and how much it's done to develop young scholars."

"Thank you. It's really a gratifying way to invest in the future."

"I'm dying to start up something like it. What do you think of funding research in high-tech methods for detecting fake antiquities? My husband's idea but I think it's fabulous. Say, if you're not late for something, come have a drink."

Tony was charmed.

Lana took him to her suite, where Moon and another man sat cross-legged on the floor, in lively conversation, surrounded by empty boxes, crumpled tissue paper, and blue-gray Sawankhalok figurines. Books lay open on one table. Liquor bottles, glasses, and an ice bucket crowded another. Bowls of fresh fruit were everywhere. The room glowed with hospitality. A dry haven against the constant drumming of rain.

Moon looked up at him and smiled. A broad, welcoming smile. "Hi. Pull up a gin and join us."

Tony succumbed instantly to both of them. It would kill him not to be Moon's friend. It would kill him not to be Lana's passion. But his attraction to Lana won out and turned his anxious longing for Moon's friendship into envy and resentment—especially after Moon insulted his auction purchases.

That evening, after Moon went to bed and the other guests left, Tony stayed. He explained to Lana how the fellowship program worked, then they went on to discuss the local trade. Lana moved her chair close to his. After a while, she pulled off a long silk scarf that had bound back her shimmering hair.

"The thing is," she said, "Martin's become totally obsessed with Tak ceramics. They're delightful for sure, but this Taw Hla character he's taken up with... You know anything about him?"

"Oh, sure. A very clever fellow. He and his cousins have quite an organization."

She reached for his hand. He started to pull back but she caught it. "I won't hurt you," she murmured and tied one end of the scarf to his wrist. "I just don't want you to go till you've told me all about those mischievous Karens and their cunning little schemes." She had the other end of the scarf and made a game of reeling his hand toward the bamboo arm of her chair. She tied it there. "You weren't thinking of leaving quite yet, were you?"

CHIANG MAI, THAILAND

Outside, as Lucky turned off the house lights, the land was moonlit, the sky full of stars. Martin understood that, in the short run, it was more insane to chase Savani into the hills than it was to make a beeline for Bangkok, but he prayed that it would pay off faster.

He clambered into the passenger side of the truck, while Lucky and Jack argued over who would drive. It seemed ridiculous to put their lives in the hands of a kid, but, on the other hand, she claimed she had done it before and knew the road well. Sheer size and being the one who found the key on the dining room table made Jack the winner. Lucky spit and slid across the seat against Martin.

In the driver's seat, Jack grumbled about the right-side driving set-up, then twisted around. "Hey, no seatbelts."

"This is Thailand, remember?" said Martin.

"Shit." Jack gripped the top of the steering wheel and laid his head against his hands for a moment, then straightened up and started the engine.

They began to move. Lucky pointed to a break in the dark foliage and Jack, leaning tautly into the steering wheel, nosed the Toyota onto a narrow, rutted trail—a ridiculous excuse of a road.

It took Jack forever to get the truck out of first gear. Almost immediately, the truck bounced heavily into a pothole on the edge of the road and forced him to slam the steering wheel to the left to avoid crashing into the underbrush. "Jesus fucking Christ!"

"Better not go off the road," Lucky piped up. "Most dangerous. On the left, rocky wall behind small trees. On the right, very steep—truck could roll over. I can drive it better."

Jack grunted and the little bit of speed he'd picked up slackened. The pace became excruciating. Twice, trying to gentle it through deep gullies, the wheels spun and the engine stalled.

"Must go faster," Lucky scolded.

"How far is this fucking village we're headed for?" Jack growled.

"Two hours for *Khun* Tony or Ali-ya. Many days for chickenshit *farang*."

Two hours passed. The ascent was steep and rarely did Jack get the pickup out of first gear. When they came to a crest, where the dense foliage fell away and the road widened, Jack switched off the engine and got out. Martin and Lucky followed.

Leaning against the truck in the moonlight, looking at the stars, shining with sweat, kneading the muscles in his arms, Jack said, "This is harder than I thought it'd be."

Martin stood by uselessly, while Lucky passed a bottle of water.

"*Khun* Jack, next section is very easy. I will drive and let you rest. Then you drive again. I have driven many times, in the staff truck and in the Land Rover."

"That's hard to believe, sweet—Ali-ya. It seems to take all my arm and shoulder strength to hold the road. I don't see how someone your size—"

"It a matter of knowing how. Have to get up speed. I got the knack."

"What do you think, Martin?"

Martin had seen very young people speeding in trucks along mountain trails during his last visit to the hills. He had also seen squared wheels, busted tie rods, battered fenders, and crushed grills. Just because he hadn't seen one fly off a trail in a blaze of gasoline didn't mean it couldn't happen. But they were rapidly falling behind.

"Let's try her out."

The descent down the far side of the hill was not at all easy, but Lucky careered along with confidence. Martin's big mistake, however, was in graciously taking the middle seat, over the transmission hump, to give Jack room for his extra four inches of leg.

He realized this when, suddenly, the road disappeared in front of them and the steering wheel spun wildly out of Lucky's grasp and the front wheels began following a gully off the trail, off the hillside.

Reflexes made both he and Jack lunge for the wheel, but Jack couldn't reach around Martin and Martin's plastered hands only succeeded in bashing Lucky's fingers against the wheel.

Off the road, the truck pitched at an angle that made all three throw their arms up to protect them from the windshield. Lucky screamed. Briefly, it appeared that the thick vegetation would hold them, but they'd been going too fast and the lush growth was only a thin façade masking a barren field.

Martin was on top of Lucky, his arms entwined in the steering wheel and his right foot making a frantic stab at the brake pedal.

Too late.

The back wheels were off the ground and the truck began its tumble, once rear over front, then countless sidelong rolls. All three screamed.

THE HILLS, THAILAND

When they finished their tea, much to Delia's surprise, Tony stood up. "Time to go, love. The horses are waiting."

"You mean we're not sleeping? We're riding horses? After all that opium?"

"It wasn't all that much opium. I find it invigorates me, cleanses me of certain anxieties, clears my mind. Besides, the horses know the way."

After Tony spent another fifteen minutes conferring with the village headman, they mounted the horses and set off.

Delia expected the overnight ride to be a silent, lonely affair, crowded in by dark shadows, but the sky was moon-bright and the trail lively with traffic.

After the first mule caravan passed, going in the opposite direction, Delia trotted up next to Tony and asked who they were.

"PaO smugglers. A Burmese tribe. The border is about fifty kilometers from here. The deeper into Thailand they can get, the better their profits and the cheaper the goods they take home with them. Many prefer night travel when the moon is bright and the air cool."

"What—?"

"Opium, no doubt. A little late in the season, but perhaps they come far. Of course, they smuggle anything they can get their hands on. Tungsten, antimony, cattle, jade, whatever. Where the roads are better, teak logs. Going the other direction they take consumer goods—batteries, flashlights, radios—and medical supplies. Village we just left does a lot of trade, but not as much as the one we're headed for." Tony did seem more relaxed, his voice taking on a generous tone in the darkness.

They passed more smugglers with their heavily burdened mules. On foot came a raggedy group of refugees with a pair of horses, four head of cattle, and several dogs. The women had infants tied to their backs with lengths of cloth. The men carried older, sleeping children.

One of the women stopped, held out her hand, and spoke to Tony. He tossed her something and cantered away. She still had her hand extended when Delia passed, and Delia managed to find a coin in the bottom of her bag.

The shoulder bag she'd grabbed was essentially empty. Her handgun was at Li's. Her wallet and passport were locked in her suitcase. She had no makeup, no hairbrush, no toothbrush, no razor for the stubble on her legs. No pills to prevent malaria or to treat diarrhea. No underwear. Only a Chinese-style blouse that was too tight around the armpits and a sarong that she'd retied into bloomers so she could straddle the horse. And ridiculous shoes.

People often made the mistake of thinking that because she was from south Florida she must be comfortable outdoors, but, she had been a rebel. *Outdoors* was where her family did their sweaty work and it was full of things that cut, bruised, burned, and bit. She wanted to be indoors with her books and her maps of faraway places. Horseback riding had been a ghastly idea to her, till she lived in London, where a collector she was courting insisted she learn to ride so they could converse along the trails on his estate. Tonight she was glad for the skill.

As the inner muscles of her thighs began to strain, Delia wondered how long she'd have to survive out here and when she might have to face the things that cut, bruised, burned, and bit.

Dawn broke. Delia saw how the hillside sloped steeply down into blackened fields, where the second-growth forest had been slashed and burned—*swiddened*, Tony told her, the nutrients returned to the soil for future farming. Locals walked together along the road or across the fields with their hole-poking sticks and bags of seed grain. Some wore colorful traditional clothes; others wore stained t-shirts and trousers. All of them balanced flat-topped, broad-brimmed straw hats on their heads.

The sun grew merciless. By the time Delia and Tony arrived at the next village, her horse felt like a steam radiator.

The village was a random layout of bamboo huts, mostly on stilts. Several dogs started barking and one dashed toward them as they passed. Pigs rooted around in the dirt. Two cocks were squaring off against each other, while hens and chicks waddled along and pecked at unseen delicacies in the hard red earth.

Savani dismounted. "We'll rest here awhile, get something to eat, and pick up a rifle. Lucky usually packs the truck for these trips, but—well, you saw."

"Rifle?" Delia dismounted onto legs that felt like bowed rubber.

"This isn't a stroll through the Berkshires, my dear. These hills are thick with Burmese insurgents, Shans mostly. They're dead serious about their business—either making war on the Burmese government or managing opium fiefdoms or both. To the leaders, I'm a familiar face, of course, but there are lots of trigger-happy young buckaroos up here. Pays to be ready."

Tony turned away and Delia shambled after him.

When the truck finally bounced to a landing, Jack lay crushed against the door with Martin and Lucky piled on top of him. For a stunned moment, he listened to the chirring of cicadas and the clicking of hot metal... and the dripping of liquid beneath them.

Then Lucky screamed, "Get out! Get out!"

All three began squirming and flailing at once. Lucky cursed and grunted as she muscled the door above them open. She disappeared into the darkness, then the shadow of her head reappeared. She pulled at Martin.

"Out! Out! Hurry! Out!" Lucky commanded like a fearful midwife extracting infants from a tin can womb.

Martin got his feet up on Jack's hips and catapulted himself out of the cab. Then it was his turn to yell.

"Jack! Jack, you okay? Jack!"

Martin's shadow appeared next to Lucky's, the moonlight reflecting off the white cast outstretched to him.

"Hurry!" Lucky screamed.

A sharp pain shot down Jack's right leg and made his toes curl.

"Oh shit! I need a hand... back hurt."

"Fuck."

"Get him out," Lucky screamed.

Martin leaned in far enough to allow Jack to grab his arms above the elbow, but, in doing so, he lost his footing and his leverage.

"Lucky, brace your feet, throw your arms around my waist, and pull," Martin shouted.

They hauled Jack to his feet, got their arms under his armpits and yanked him out. They all fell into a heap, then Lucky and Martin popped up. Jack popped as far as his knees, gasped as a muscle spasm wrenched him crooked.

"Put your arms on our shoulders," Martin shouted.

As he obeyed, they yanked him to his feet and, as a unit, ran far enough and fast enough so that when the explosion came, it knocked the trio to the ground but left them intact. Panting, they lay on the side of the hill and watched the blaze.

Jack saw more than the truck going up in smoke. Their chance of catching up with Savani and canceling his order to kidnap Theresa had vanished.

"Nice driving, Lucky old *sweetheart*."

The barb hit its mark. With a whimper, she rolled to her feet and disappeared into the night. Martin exhaled audibly, but said nothing.

"Okay, so it's not her fault. I need my head examined for letting her drive at all."

The roar of the fire was fading and he could hear Lucky shuffling above them in the field. Soon the insects recovered from their shock and started up their buzzing, sawing, and trilling again.

"It's a miracle we weren't killed... that one of us didn't fly through the windshield." Jack allowed the moment to catch up with him. But then, *Theresa*.

"What about your back?"

"Fuck. It's fine." *I'm alive. Theresa.*

The flames died out and the stars reappeared. Jack turned to look at Martin's face, silvery in the moonlight, streaked with black, eyes closed. His arms were stretched out over his head.

"You okay, Martin?"

"Sure."

"I hope to hell your dad got through to Theresa and Jones-White."

"If there's anything I'm sure about in the world, it is the utter reliability of my old man."

It turned out that Lucky was gathering up supplies she'd packed in the bed of the truck, now strewn across the hill. In silence, she laid out sleeping bags for the men to lie on, leveled off a spot of earth, made a fire, set up a tripod and pot over it, poured in water from a plastic bottle, and threw in handfuls of food.

Out of one of the backpacks, she pulled a pint bottle and squatted next to Jack, offering it. "Not broken." It was Mekhong.

"All right, just what the doctor ordered." Jack peeled away the seal and unscrewed the cap. She was still squatting, with her eyes lowered. "Look, Ali-ya, the accident wasn't your fault. That was a nasty remark I made. I'm sorry. Thanks for trying to give me a rest. And thanks for helping me get away from there. Friends?"

She nodded.

"You drink?" He offered her the first swig and she accepted, although the puckering of her lips showed she wasn't a veteran. Then Jack turned to Martin, "Drink?"

"I better stick with water."

Lucky passed Jack the plastic water bottle and he dribbled some through Martin's lips. Jack took another slug of liquor. And another. Through the haze of rice spirits, the bland boiled rice and vegetables became a midnight feast.

While Lucky fed Martin, he teased her and she was full of giggles. Jack watched her exotic face—the refined Asian features contrasting with the colorless European eyes.

When she scurried off to clean up, Jack said, "I told Savani I was taking Lucky away to Bangkok. Maybe he was right—that she'd wind up a massage girl, or worse—a knockout in a gilded mini-dress and false eyelashes."

"Is that what made him angry? Angry enough to send someone after Theresa?"

Jack took another drink. His vision was beginning to blur.

"Dunno. Had something against me from the start. Suspicious." His words slurred. He remembered Tony's reaction to Delia's moving into his hotel room and to the sight of their getting off the train together at the Chiang Mai station. "Thought there was something going on 'tween Delia and me. And that business about me being some kind of narc—all sort of unhinged."

"Was there?"

"Was there what?"

"Something going on between you and Delia?"

"Shit."

"I got no claim on Delia, you know," Martin said, his voice rumbling with sadness. "We made our choices along the way... couldn't settle for one another... or the timing was wrong... or some damn thing. Good man like you, solid, strong, just what Delia needs. Salt of the earth. Just what my Delia needs. Anything left in that bottle?"

Jack dribbled some Mekhong through Martin's lips. "You don't un'er-stan'..." He swished his own mouth with liquor to clear the cotton away. "Nothing happened. No sex. I had sex with Ingrid and then she died. We discovered her. Me and Delia. That's what was going on between us, what we shared. The... carnage."

"The sudden silence."

"What?"

"That's what struck me when I found Lana like that."

The weight of the stars bore down on them, as Jack relived those few minutes in Ingrid's apartment.

Finally, he spoke. "Unreal, unexpected silence. All the chattering servo-mechanisms of a living being—like these noisy cicadas—suddenly switched off. Nothing." He felt tears spring from his eyes. "Except for the flies."

Martin awoke before dawn to a chorus of throbbing fingers over a heavy bass of sore muscles, stiff joints, and an off-key belly. The spoils of a mission gone mad. Scrambling along mountainsides, wrestling with Cal and Bruno, succumbing to the heat, surviving the truck crash. Not to mention all the booze. And the revelations. Theresa in peril. Delia in peril.

What the hell were they doing here, smack in the middle of nowhere? The stars were closer than the people who needed him. The only thing they had accomplished since yesterday was staying alive.

That was something.

He wriggled out of his sleeping bag and worked himself into a cross-legged semblance of a lotus position. How long had it been since he practiced *zazen*, the art of piercing the veil of misery to acknowledge the bliss that lay beyond? The only way he could get from here to where he needed to be was to become one with the stars. He breathed and began counting his exhales. As each disturbing thought and jab of pain floated into his awareness, a breath puffed it away.

Gradually, the stars disappeared into him and the rising sun illuminated the burnt-over world they inhabited—a field scorched black long before their truck accident, a field whose messy agricultural remains had been converted back to the simple carbonized nutrients needed for a new crop. The death before resurrection.

Lucky awoke and tended her cooking pot. Then Jack grunted and groaned his way out of his sleeping bag.

"How's the back?" Martin asked, his voice full of sandpaper.

Jack looked up. "Better. Okay, I guess. You?"

"Better too. We got any water left?"

They all moved gingerly. Large patches of Jack's left arm and leg had turned a greenish blue from being repeatedly thrown against the passenger door. His hair hung loose and uncombed, already damp with morning heat. Lucky's face bore crescent-shaped welts left by the steering wheel. They were filthy with field soot.

Martin's casts had been bashed during the tumble and twisted in the course of pulling Jack from the wreckage. He wondered how many times he could inflict new trauma without permanent damage—if the damage wasn't permanent already. Under the stopgap layer of adhesive tape that Manora applied yesterday afternoon, the plaster was sodden and crumbling. His fingers didn't lie in a flat row anymore. Clinging to his meditation, he tried to let go of the disturbing implications.

Among the supplies Lucky had thrown into the truck bed, then reclaimed in the field, were hats: Jack's red baseball cap and a straw one for Martin. She wrapped a towel around her own head for sun protection.

"So how far is the village where we get horses, Ali-ya?" Jack asked, as he checked his watch.

"I think maybe about thirty-five kilometers."

Jack's face fell. "Thirty-five kilometers is... is..."

"About twenty miles," Martin said. "Four or five hours at least, if we wind up walking the whole way. But let's be optimistic and plan on a truck coming by."

Jack started off impatiently, attacking the hills with long strides. Lucky and Martin put some energy into their step, but quickly fell behind. Their path was, on average, uphill. The landscape had no shadows: the red clay road, blackened fields, and stubby green shrubs were heat-lacquered to a high gloss against a flame-blue sky. Deep in the far-off valleys to their right, they spotted men and water buffalo at work in a patchwork of rice paddies.

As they walked, Lucky helped Martin drink water. Here and there, bamboo spouts tapping mountain springs allowed her to replenish their bottles. The advantage of the heat was that it baked away Martin's soreness and dried out the soggy casts. The mental magic of *zazen* eluded him now, so he struggled not to obsess about the state of his hands.

There were half a dozen things he tried not to think about, from the physical abuse he'd endured to the dangers looming ahead. He fumed about the affair between Savani and Lana. The damned humiliation of it. How thick-headed could he be? Had the rumors been correct? *Martin's deductions and Lana's seductions?* Sophisticated, man-of-the-world Martin Moon had never suspected.

Oh, there had been flirtations, of course. For both of them. Flirting and teasing were part of the calculus of the trade, although Martin had gotten peeved at her on more than one occasion for carrying on with greater zest than the objective needed. But he'd never really faced the possibility of an all-out, clothes-on-the-floor, rumpled-sheets kind of romance. Or whatever you call it when you use silk scarves.

In ten years with Lana, Martin had not slept with anyone else. Once or twice a year, Delia would boomerang into his life, but her needs were carefully framed as business troubles, something he could resolve with a loan or a few phone calls. He tried to be open, to share those visitations with Lana, but she wasn't interested.

Yet Delia's visits to him were not easy. While they didn't have sex, none of the old electricity had faded. When she was near, he behaved admirably. But once she'd gone, he'd drink too much, and inevitably get some sort of cold that would insinuate its achiness into every muscle and joint, till he took to his bed. With all his love for Lana, he still pined for Delia and anguished over the failure of their marriage. Rivera flu.

Was his response to Delia—a response so intense it made him physically ill—any less a betrayal than Lana's? Hell, there was no betrayal. It wasn't guilt that made him ill, it was his own damn virtue. Lana was the guilty one.

He hated her for it.

242

But he hated her more for dying. And she died because...

Why was it, exactly? Because of the British Museum case, sure. Because she'd discovered the connection between Bellingham and Savani—that's what she'd been so excited about—and the deal she blew was not only Bellingham's, but also Savani's. She warned Reggie Gupta and Gupta, ignorant of the connection, must have told Savani. Tony's lover was going around undermining his deals. No wonder his affection turned to bile. Lana had miscalculated the power of her charm.

It was too hot to hate, too late to cry. His thoughts drifted back to Delia. He should be furious with her for running off with Savani, but his immediate concern was simply reaching her.

In two hours, Lucky and Martin caught up with Jack. He was kneeling in front of a bamboo spout, hat off, head under the slow stream of water, letting it run over his hair and neck, then he turned around and settled on his butt.

"It's impossible to hurry, isn't it?"

The road stretched like curling ribbon toward the steep horizon. Jack put his hat back on.

Martin's optimism about hitching a ride went unrewarded. They dragged into the village at 3 p.m. after a grueling six-hour trek. While Lucky went to arrange horses, Jack and Martin found a grocery stand, chug-a-lugged bottles of warm orange Fanta, and munched on pastries sold in humid cellophane packages. Martin realized he'd left his wallet at Arthur Li's, so Jack paid.

The village was small, about fifteen bamboo cabins on stilts. Children raced around and stared at the newcomers, while the only adults they saw were a few young women—either pregnant or with nursing infants. The others must still be in the fields.

Lucky returned, her eyes downcast, her mouth a hard line, and announced that there were no horses to rent.

Jack cursed, while Martin squinted at the mountains ahead. His hamstrings were already tightening from the day's march, the soles of his feet burned, and his knees ached. The idea of tackling another long climb filled him with despair. But what choice did they have?

"You said there was a short cut, Ali-ya, a steep hiking path." Martin said. "We'll take that, okay?"

Hoof beats drew their attention to the road. Ten heavily armed men on mules, wearing a hodgepodge of olive drab and camouflage uniforms rode toward them. Responding to a word from the man at the lead, six of them jumped off and ran toward Jack, Martin, and Lucky with their rifles drawn. Instinctively, the two men eased their hands away from their bodies, while Lucky stepped behind Jack.

The leader spoke to them from astride his mule. "Americans?"

Jack and Martin nodded.

The leader scanned them head to toe. Martin knew they had the wrong look for tourists, wrong even for adventure travelers. They were too old, too bashed up, and, judging from Jack's eyes, too desperate-looking. They were also unshaven and filthy.

"Why you here?"

"I'm a writer, magazines," Martin said. "Ever hear of *National Geographic*? This here's my photographer. Scanlan. And the young woman is our guide. Our truck overturned about thirty-five kilometers back. Destroyed all our equipment. We decided to press on, get the story anyway."

The military man narrowed his eyes. "Very fortunate for you to have Lucky Savani as your guide."

"Yes," Martin improvised, "we're on our way to meet up with Mr. Savani himself."

The interrogator eyed their shoes. Jack wore light-weight cross-trainers and Martin, leather Rockports meant for city walking.

"Show me your papers."

Martin admitted he'd lost his, while Jack handed over his wallet. As the man flipped through Jack's credit cards, photos, and other wallet-sized rectangles, Martin asked, "Are you Burmese?"

"Shan. Shan United Army. I am Lieutenant Sayat. Very good friend Tony Savani." The man had a deep, deadpan voice.

"You speak excellent English."

Sayat held Jack's wallet by the photo insert, letting the wallet fall into the dust. "Scana-lan, you have many daughter."

"Just one. Those pictures... different ages..."

"But no press credential." He let the photos drop. Jack started for them, but one of the soldiers stuck a rifle barrel into his belly. Sayat turned to Martin. "What is name? What story looking for?"

Martin introduced himself and explained that they had heard about

244

antiques being smuggled from Burma and thought it might make an interesting story.

"Like ancient Buddha statue?"

"Sure. And jades. Tony Savani agreed to show us a trading post as long as we don't reveal the exact location—or his involvement."

"No write story on *Khun* Sa and opium trading?"

Martin said that everyone wrote about the famous opium warlord, but he was looking for a new slant on the Golden Triangle. When Sayat asked about his hands, he described a barroom brawl in Bangkok.

"I think you American Drug Enforcement agents. We must check out. You wait." Sayat spoke to his men and four of them began prodding Martin and Jack up the path with their gun barrels.

With a whimper, Lucky snagged her hand on the waistband of Jack's shorts, but Sayat barked an order and, with a whoop of laughter, the other two soldiers yanked Lucky away and pushed her in the opposite direction.

Jack shouted, "Hey, wait a minute. Leave her alone." He turned toward her, but the butt of a rifle slammed across his jaw and knocked him to the ground. A jab of a rifle barrel in Martin's back warned him not to try the same thing.

The blow had stunned Jack. By the time he struggled to his feet, Lucky had been dragged out of sight.

Prodded along till they reached the edge of the village, Martin and Jack were shoved toward what looked like a tiny log cabin on stilts, with log ceiling beams. It had a pitched roof made of thatch. The logs were small, no more than tree branches really, the spaces between them just enough for ventilation.

When the padlocked door was opened, the stench of urine and feces assaulted their nostrils.

Jack spun around. "What the hell is this?" The soldier behind him reared back. He stared up at the towering figure, then nudged him again. "Jesus, will you quit poking me?" he yelled. The soldier—a boy not much older than Lucky—backed up a pace.

Martin seized the advantage, braced his casted hands together and clocked the soldier at his side. As the boy fell, the second one swung toward him and Martin kicked him soundly in the balls.

Two down. But as he turned, a rifle barrel jammed into his belly. The terrified eyes of the soldier said he was ready to shoot. Martin raised his hands. Jack was doubled over, cursing, and the fourth soldier, the one Jack had surprised, held him in an arm lock.

They were shoved up the log ramp and into the fetid cabin.

Martin crouched on a dirty mat, curled around his throbbing hands. He was angry. He'd hurt his hands again for no gain. "I thought you were going to fight them, for christsake. They were small, scared. You had the advantage."

Massaging his jaw, Jack dropped to his knees and peered through the chinks. "Small, scared, and heavily armed."

"I had two of them down. The least you could have done—"

A cry pierced the air, female. Then a roar of laughter, male. Then another long scream. Lucky.

Martin hurled himself against the door.

While Savani prepared for the next leg of their journey, Delia discovered how adaptable a city-girl could be. The women of the Mien-tribe village were captivated by her ikat-woven sarong and the subtle patterns in her satin blouse. Using the international language of commerce—her fingers—she traded the Li clothes for a plain indigo cotton sarong, a straw hat, a long-sleeved indigo shirt, a length of cloth to use for a bra, a faded pair of calf-length, embroidered pants, canvas shoes, a straight razor, a bar of soap, and a comb. And she traded her leather shoulder bag for a light-weight woven one. They also wanted her beads, but she wouldn't part with them.

The woman who'd won the valued clothes by giving Delia the best deal, showed her to a shielded porch behind her large wood-plank hut and brought her a bucket of water. Delia bathed, shaved her underarms and legs with a minimum of nicks from the unwieldy razor, slipped on the pants and shoes, bound up her breasts in a makeshift bra, and donned the long-sleeved shirt as protection from the sun. She twisted her hair into a ponytail and stuffed it up under the broad-brimmed hat. Her new sarong and other supplies fit into her shoulder bag.

After a grand lunch with the headman's family, as Savani and Delia started up the trail on a fresh pair of horses, she felt oddly safe. Oddly relieved. Oddly invigorated.

She had no more uncertainties about her relationship with Tony. She would not have to figure out how to run a museum in the middle of nowhere. She had connected with friendly locals. She knew how to trade. She was simply on a job, one she'd done well for decades.

Although Tony now packed a rifle, the threat of attack by the roving buckaroos did not seem real. Rape and injury were part of her past. The men who did it were dead. Throughout the long night, she had occasionally been chilled by the stunned look on Cal's face as he stared down at his bullet wound. But even that vision was fading.

Her thoughts lingered on Martin, by now in Chiang Mai, perhaps on his way to London or New York. When would she see him again?

Delia's musings got her through the afternoon's ride in the brutal heat. With the sun low in the sky, she spied their destination from a high ridge. Forty or fifty Akha huts with enormous thatched roofs spilled from the peak at an impossible angle. She marveled that a rainy season mudslide hadn't washed them all away.

As they got nearer to the village, the two were joined on the trail by men and women walking home from the fields. They chatted with Tony, in a language neither Thai nor Burmese.

As in the other villages they'd passed through, the peasants were dressed in a combination of traditional indigo-dyed cottons and Western t-shirts. They bore wicker baskets on their backs and, as they walked, the women embroidered or spun thread from tufts of raw cotton at their waists. Many of the women had betel-stained teeth like Lucky's. Most striking were the elaborate silver headdresses of the Akha women, usually covered with a square of cloth to protect them from the sun.

The sky darkened and rumbled. A sudden breeze ruffled the leaves of the few squat trees along the path. A storm was closing in.

Finally, they arrived at the upper gate of the village. Really, it was a series of gates. Each consisted of two timber posts and a crossbar, which was decorated with small wooden guns, birds, helicopters, and airplanes. Tony called them *law kah*, gates that divided the world of the humans—signified by large wooden figures of crudely sexual men and women—from the world of evil forest spirits. A new gate and new sets of human figures were installed each year as the old ones deteriorated.

Adhering to custom, Tony and Delia dismounted before they walked through, in order to avoid touching any part of the sacred gates.

Delia looked back toward the narrow mountain trail as the first drops of rain pelted her. The scraggly forest hadn't seemed so evil. The sudden darkness, the whipping wind, and the hallowed gates felt far more ominous.

"Ohhhhhhhhh!" she cried out. "What the—" By looking back, she'd gotten herself tangled in some light bamboo chainwork that hung from the crossbeams like netting. A cluster of watching children turned and ran.

"Good God, Delia, can't you watch where you're walking! He grabbed the horse's reins from her hand. "You've desecrated the gates! There will be hell to pay. Stop where you are. Seriously, don't go any farther until—"

"What? Gimme a break. Am I supposed to sleep out there with the angry ghosts now?"

He didn't find any humor in her wisecrack and hurried ahead. The lightning was close and she counted seconds between thunder claps and sky-crackling lightening bolts.

A searing flash made her hair stand on end and choked her with ozone. The roof of a hut about a hundred feet away exploded into flames. The horses whinnied and broke away from Tony, crashing against the tunnel of gates as they ran back into the forest. Tony yelled at her, "Stay here! Don't move!" Then he ran off after the horses. A handful of boys trotted off with him.

There wasn't much the villagers could do about the fire. The hut was a tinder box. A woman ran out clutching an infant and a screaming toddler—all she saved before the flaming roof caved in.

The driving rain quickly turned the hut into a smoldering mess. Umbrellas sprouted as the villagers gathered to watch and to comfort their kinswoman. A boy tugged at a woman's sleeve and, when she turned, he pointed at Delia. The Akha woman stared at her. Her mouth was a gash of red betel stain and her eyes were vacant. Her skirt was slung low, exposing a slack belly. Her eyes raked over Delia, then widened at the sight of the damaged gates. Then she grabbed the boy's hand and scurried away.

Delia suddenly felt very tired.

The sheets of rain had subsided to big lazy drops by the time Tony walked through the gates with the horses. A small group of locals rushed toward him, talking excitedly. One of them led the horses away, as Tony returned to Delia's side.

He was thoroughly soaked and snappish. "You totally fucked this up."

"Me? What—?"

"You'll have to take up quarters down in the Chinese section for the time being. Tomorrow they'll sacrifice a pig to atone for your defiling the spirit gate. They think you caused Boo-se's hut to burn and the horses to spook."

Delia was flustered. "Well, if I have to, but can't you tell them—"

"Look, Delia, just shut up and do as you're told. It's fascinating to me that you provoked these people the very moment you arrived. They're sensitive to hostile forces, you know. I'll straighten it out, but it'll take time." A girl tugged at his arm. "I'm going to my cabin. Wait here for Yang Mi to show you the way. Whatever you do, don't touch any of the young women or girls—you'll defile them too."

"What kind of baloney is—?"

"They think you're a witch." His eyes burned into hers. "Because you have no womb."

Martin slammed his shoulder against the door again. The only effect was to make him notice how sunburned his skin had gotten beneath the gauzy shirt.

"Let me try," Jack said. The room was only six-foot square, not enough room for a running start. Jack hit the log door with a yelp. It didn't budge.

Brute force having failed, a systematic examination of the hut's construction also failed to reveal any weak points. They resorted to shouting for help, but only drew attention from clusters of small children, who would creep near, then run away.

Soon after night fell, despite sunburn, bruised muscles, aching joints, and growling bellies, they collapsed into exhausted sleep.

When they woke, they found their hosts had visited, leaving a ten-gallon earthenware jar of water, a big plastic ladle, and two tightly woven covered baskets full of greasy pork and rice.

As Martin clumsily used his fingertips to shovel clumps of rice into his mouth, he said, "The meat's all yours."

The rice was heavily spiced, bitter, and gluey, but welcome as ambrosia to his empty belly. Jack let him have it all as he gorged on pork.

Within an hour or so, Martin felt the day dissolve around him. Time stopped. Or had it speeded up? He couldn't decide as he stared at clouds of confetti through the chinks in his log prison. The air was white and suffocating, then gray and damp, then black and chilly. Roosters for miles around seemed to crow constantly, in a strangled *ruurraargh*. Thunder clapped and rumbled. He felt no more pain. He felt nothing. Blessed nothing.

Jack stared at his watch, the seconds slipping slowly by. The hut grew intolerable, a sauna gone berserk. The hot floor logs punched up at him through the sour straw mat. Sweat barely had a chance to seep, burning, into his eyes before it evaporated. Outside, hordes of insects roared like so many tiny jet engines. And a stubborn red ant liked the taste of his American flesh.

The pork breakfast was churning up his belly.

And something was wrong with Martin. For hours now, he lay dozing or staring blankly into space, unresponsive to Jack's questions. He didn't seem feverish, but who could tell in a room that must be a hundred and ten. Every so often, Jack would lift Martin's head and make him sip water, then he'd pour the rest of the ladle over Martin's chest and legs to cool him down. Then he'd empty a ladle over himself. The furnace-hot air baked them dry in no time, clothes and all.

Jack made a game of picking up ants and dropping them through the chinks in the floor. Red ants first.

When Martin's vision cleared, he saw that the sun was shining outside and that Jack was in distress—moaning, clutching his stomach with one hand and shifting around the floor mats with the other.

"What's the matter?"

"What do they call Montezuma's revenge in Thailand? Lucky for me—not so lucky for you—the gaps between the floor logs are gonna make a great toilet." He pulled off his shorts.

"Jesus." Martin rolled onto his side toward the wall. An excited snort from below made him pull up his mat and look down. In the foul crawl space, where the hillside dropped away, scavenger pigs gobbled up whatever dripped through the floor. He began to laugh.

"This isn't a damn bit funny," Jack grumbled.

Martin rolled onto his back, still laughing. "Just thinking of tomorrow's pork roast."

Jack sluiced water across the floor and poured water on one of the black muslin slings to use as a wash cloth. Then he held a ladle-full out for Martin. "Feeling better?"

Martin sat up to drink. "Better than what? Is that fresh food?"

"They must have come back while we were asleep, though, to tell you the truth, I can't remember sleeping."

Martin leaned over and picked at the lid on one of the baskets till it popped open. "Here. You have to eat the rice. These tarry bits—opium. Will make the diarrhea go away."

"You're kidding me."

"Let me be the mother for a change, damn it. If you don't eat the opium, the diarrhea will dehydrate you and you'll die and I'll be forced to sit here and watch the blowflies and the ants eat away your body till chunks of it start to fall through to the pigs."

"Some sweet mother you are." Jack picked up a clump of the bitter mixture and stuffed it into his mouth.

Martin planned to postpone eating his share of the rice till his mind cleared and he could think of an escape plan. But his mind didn't clear. Despair nibbled at him. The sweltering six-by-six-by-six-foot cube suffocated him. He began to wolf down the remaining opium-laced rice, but then had a better thought. He worked himself into a cross-legged posture, rested his hands in his lap, forced himself to focus on counting his exhales, and let the unseen stars cleanse his mind.

Soaked by the downpour, with mud up to her ankles, Delia was escorted to an empty hut on the lower edge of the village by a Chinese man. Although Yang Mi was *haw*—borne of migrants from Yunnan province in southwestern China, Delia found that her practical knowledge of Mandarin went a long way. He was a shopkeeper, a trader, and he made an immediate offer for the necklace Martin had given her. She refused. The rustle of its tiny bells made Martin feel close.

Delia was shown to a closet-sized Akha hut at the edge of the village, near the Chinese enclave. Like the other Akha houses, it was dark—made without windows, the eaves of the thatched roof sloping nearly to the ground. It reeked of cooking odors.

Yang Mi explained that the hut had been vacated that morning by a young couple forced to move to another village. Delia gathered that the woman had given birth to twins, a sign that she and her husband had somehow offended the great spirits. Immediately, the children had been smothered and removed far from the village for burial. The parents of the "reject children" had been banished to this lower edge of the village and, as soon as the woman could travel, they left to start a new life where their shame was unknown. The hut would need to be purified before another Akha would live in it, but apparently it was good enough for a *farang* witch.

Her host handed her a lantern and a book of matches, then went on his way.

Delia pushed the door shut from the inside and latched it with a loop of wire around a nail. Enough daylight streamed in from around the door to see without the lantern. She crawled onto a bamboo sleeping platform, grateful not to have to stretch out on the dirt floor, and slept.

Hours later, she stirred. Insect noises throbbed all around her. She touched herself, felt only skin and cloth, nothing crawling. A jagged fissure cutting across her abdomen from the bottom of her makeshift bra to the top of her pants reminded her of the Akha assumption that she had no womb. They'd been correct. It was a non-vital organ that got tossed in the garbage as the London surgeons pieced her back together after the assault.

Her overshirt was open. Had they seen the scar? Or had they seen it in her face? Something dried up, unproductive, unnatural?

Delia jerked her hands from the scar and pressed them against the firm, round muscles of her thighs and shoulders, the fullness of her bosom, the planes of her face. She was alive, damn it, and healthy. How dare they condemn her for what she lost, when they should rejoice over what she had. Modern medicine had given her a chance in a hundred to pull through and she'd snatched it.

The chorus of insects was gradually overpowered by the cock-crowing, dog-barking, pig-snorting songs of morning. And what sounded like jungle drumbeats, she later learned, were women pounding rice.

When Delia emerged from her hut, still trying to comb through the tangles in her hair, she gravitated toward the Chinese women. Flattered and amused at Delia's mangled Chinese, they fed her and pointed out the spring that supplied fresh water. Yang Mi's wife gave her a plastic bucket for carrying water from the spring to her cabin and, at Delia's request, a bottle of vinegar for rinsing the soap film from her hair. Quickly, she understood that the only smiling faces would come from the Chinese shopkeepers that lined the lower road of the village.

That afternoon, Tony made his appearance. His attitude was icy.

"They'll sacrifice another pig tomorrow morning to try to reverse the bad luck you've brought to the village. The place is in an uproar. A woman died during childbirth today—the worst kind of death. They'll be having ceremonies for days to rid the place of her ghost. They blame *you*, of course."

"What am I supposed to do about it?"

He glared at her. "You know, this trading post is critical to my work. If you screw yourself with the locals, you're worse than useless to me."

"But I get along fine with the Chinese. I'll just stay down here till we're ready to go."

He looked around, then squinted at her. "I'm waiting for a colleague to join me here. Meanwhile, an important shipment of jade will be delivered to Yang Mi. If you watch for that—and mind your own business—I'll deal with the Akha women."

Jack ate the bitter rice and slowly the cramping in his belly calmed. With the opium split between them, Martin didn't slip into a stupor, but now they were both half-stoned.

Martin sat cross-legged and stared through the walls, while Jack made a study of the village as seen in one-inch strips. The side of the cabin opposite the door faced downhill and at the foot of the hill was a wide slow stream that attracted women, children, and water buffalo throughout the day.

"Who are these people?" Jack asked as he watched a pregnant woman bathe herself. She was wrapped in a sarong from breasts to knees and surrounded by a gaggle of happy toddlers.

"Lahu," Martin said. "Migrated down from Yunnan through Burma. Came here in droves after the World War." He made a soft chuckle. "Experts in meeting the world demand for opium."

"What do they do?"

"What I said. Opium. No, I take that back." He unwound his lotus posture and rested his back against the wall. "I don't know what they do. They burn off shrubs, farm till the soil is depleted, then move their village down the road. They survive. Like the rest of us."

"They're so beautiful—graceful and delicate. And the babies don't cry. Have you noticed that? Dozens of kids here and in two and a half days I haven't heard one cry."

Martin mumbled something.

"What?"

He spoke louder. "I said they feel safe. Someone holds them constantly. If not the women, then the little girls. Their ears are always pressed against someone's heartbeat. Must be a fabulous sensation."

The sadness in Martin's voice made Jack turn toward him. He had his hands held up in front of his face, staring at his fingertips. When Jack looked back at the river, the Lahu woman had chased away the last of the naked babies. She stood, glanced around, and untied the sarong to dry herself.

"Look at this woman, Martin. She's gorgeous." She tied on a black skirt, taking a moment to tenderly smooth it over her belly, then pulled a yellow t-shirt over her swollen breasts. "God."

Martin heaved a sigh and twisted himself back into silence.

Darkness brought a breeze and some relief from the heat. Jack drifted off, but instead of dreaming of beautiful women and contented babies, his sleep was filled with black fluttering things, snapping, crunching, chewing things.

A scrabbling noise awoke him. Then Martin screamed. A low groan, pitching higher to a whine, then higher still to a terrified, tremulous shriek. Jack bolted upright in the pitch blackness. An animal. Must be an animal, tearing into Martin's flesh. Or—

Another shriek—louder, more terrified still.

"Nononononono..." Jack cried, as he rose to his knees and stretched out his hands.

Legs. Jack found his legs.

"Nononononono..." he continued to yell—a war cry against whatever had invaded their chamber and was devouring his friend, his brother, his soul, and he held one hand out to fend off the unseen beast, while the other fluttered frantically along the legs to the shorts, the belly, the chest. His outstretched hand caught a flailing cast. Martin fought. Jack fell across his chest and pinned both Martin's arms over his head. The quivering scream continued. Jack began to discern shapes in the gloom.

In the faint slivers of reflected starlight, there was no beast, no sadistic soldier.

"Martin. Wake up. Wake up. Martin."

With a sharp intake of breath, the wail stopped. Martin was gasping and Jack felt the pounding of both their hearts.

Jack lifted his head from Martin's chest. All he could see was the sharp outline of Martin's nose, the glint of silver hair, and black eyeholes.

Martin whispered something.

"What?"

"Please... don't."

The wounded tone of the appeal formed an icy film across Jack's skin.

"You're having a nightmare."

"Please... don't hurt me... again..."

"Wake up, Martin. You're giving me the creeps. Wake up."

There was a pause and the rhythm of Martin's breathing changed again. "Oh... Why are you pinning me down? You're hurting... my arms."

Jack released Martin's arms and shifted himself to the floor, leaving one arm across Martin's chest, gripping his shoulder. "I thought something, someone was hurting you. I was trying to... keep you safe."

A wince. "Too late for that."

In the blackness, a rooster crowed. Then he was answered by another. And another. Till each rooster in the village had his turn. The two men lay still, their breathing shallow, anxious.

"The hawkeyes assaulted me," Martin said.

"Your dream?"

"No. In the hills. The day we killed them." Martin laid his arm across his eyes. "Bruno held me down, while Cal..." His voice caught.

"Sweet Jesus," Jack whispered, pulling his arm from Martin's chest. "He raped you."

"No. Not really. It didn't amount to anything. Not when you come right down to it. Nothing really. Not like—" His voice began to quiver. "But it won't go away. They robbed me. They took away my hands, then they robbed me of the pleasure of... those other sensations. I have nothing left." He wept. "Lana's gone. Delia's gone. I'm gone. Gone."

"No." Jack laid a hand on Martin's forehead and smoothed back his damp hair. "No. You're not gone, Martin. Delia needs you. I need you."

After sharing a drink from the water scoop, Jack sat with his back against the wall, at Martin's head. Before long he heard the soft snore of sleep. But Jack was wide awake, gaping into the dappled darkness.

While Tony kept to himself in an area of the village where she wasn't welcome, Delia ingratiated herself with Yang Mi and the other *haw* shopkeepers by her eagerness to help with their chores, her diligence at improving her Chinese, and her ready smile. They generously answered all her questions about the trade routes and the traders.

It had been obvious to Delia from the start that there were too many shopkeepers for the size of the village, but gradually their role became clear. The village was a crossroads and the *haw* Chinese were expert middlemen, with smoothly operating supply lines of firearms, dry goods, and foodstuff hauled up from Chiang Mai. The Akha farmers bartered opium for supplies, often on credit against the next season's crop. The caravans of insurgents from Burma stocked up here for their skirmishes along the border. The hills were lively with travelers, those who hoisted their backpacks along the steep mountain footpaths and those, like Tony, who could afford pack animals.

The trading post was also well-known for the good prices it paid for Burmese antiquities. Even better prices were guaranteed for Chinese treasures. Tony sent traders up from Chiang Mai to collect the valuable merchandise and pay off the *haw* middlemen.

Yang Mi explained that Tony always looked over the merchandise personally, either here or at a warehouse in Chiang Mai. Unless it was a special order, like the jade shipment due any day, Tony tended to skim off maybe one artifact in a thousand for himself. The rest was trucked to his broker in Bangkok. Mi spoke of other border trading posts controlled by Savani. They attracted loot from Burma, Cambodia, Laos, and Malaysia. More enterprising traders brought artifacts from India, China, Indonesia, and the Himalayan nations. Tony's willingness to buy large quantities of high quality antiques from all parts of Asia ensured him first choice of many priceless treasures.

Delia was appalled. Easily accessible markets that guaranteed quick sales drove grave-robbers and thieves into a frenzy, encouraging them to take ever greater risks for merchandise, giving them incentives to raid ancient temple sites and important archaeological digs. Savani should be shot. How ironic that he was such a hero to archaeologists.

The expected shipment came at last. It was early afternoon when Mi pointed out the woven bamboo carry-basket. A caravan laden with guns and ordnance had just left, headed back for Burma.

"Tony's jades?"

He nodded.

"You'll let me see them? Now?" She brimmed with girlish eagerness.

"I suppose no harm."

Delia took the basket into his private quarters. Unlike the Akha houses, the Chinese houses had windows and the room was bright. They also had wooden floors.

Yang Soong, Mi's wife, worked at her loom, while Delia squatted over the basket and carefully pulled out the tissue-wrapped packets of jade.

"This is the shipment Savani *Xiansheng* has been waiting for."

"That very bad news," Soong murmured.

Delia thought she misunderstood the Chinese words and made Soong repeat them, then asked her why the news was bad.

"Lieutenant Sayat also arrive today. He from the Shan United Army—very cruel man. He is Savani *Xiansheng's* friend. Many rumor..."

"Yes, go on." Delia unwrapped the first jade and stared dumbly at it. Quickly, she unwrapped a second. Soong had been speaking, but Delia lost track of the words as the jades commanded her attention.

"You not listening," Soong said.

"I'm sorry. I simply can't believe my eyes." Delia continued to unwrap the jades and lay them out in front of her—staring at the distorted mirror of her dreams, the funhouse reflection of what she might have become if she'd thrown her lot in with Tony. "I'm sorry, Soong. I'm not following your Chinese. Again, please?"

"Savani waiting for Lieutenant Sayat. He giving you to Sayat—"

"What do you mean *giving*?" Her Chinese was so bad. Had Soong used the word she understood as *gift*?

Soong waved her arms in frustration. "Trade! One thing for other! Savani make promise to the Akha ... calm their fear of you. Savani take jades away, leave you to be Sayat's whore. Sayat take you. Take you with him. Make Akha happy."

"What's up, Madeleine?" Jack spoke through the widest space between the logs to a silent girl who came by every few hours all day long to look at him. She was eight or nine, with thick spikey hair and a broad nose. This morning, like other mornings, she towed a baby on her back, wrapped snuggly in a length of cloth. "Yankees win last night? I think they got a chance at the pennant this year, don't you?"

She smiled. It made her cheeks plump out. She'd said something once that sounded like *Madeleine* so that's what he called her. In some ways Madeleine, with her attentive and curious eyes, was better company than Martin, who clung to his opium dreams and his meditations as much as Jack resisted them. When Martin spoke, he spoke nostalgically. Not that

Jack didn't enjoy sharing his life history with Martin, but their conversation had the arthritic quality of two old men in rocking chairs: lives ended. At least Madeleine had a life.

It was Wednesday. Day six of their captivity in the log oven. Food and water were slid in through a movable panel at the bottom of the door, usually while they slept. Their minds never seemed clear enough to figure out how to take advantage of this knowledge. What water they didn't drink, they used to wash the salty film from their bodies and to rinse their waste through the floor down to the pigs. The opium-laced rice kept their bellies calm and their minds docile. Martin still avoided the shredded meat, which allowed Jack to feast on it.

Occasionally, Jack would suggest that they exercise—pushups and sit-ups, like hostages were supposed to do. Martin would agree. But they would continue to lie on their backs, staring at the ceiling beams. Broiled. Jack's most ambitious project involved fraying his mat to make tooth cleaners for the two of them.

Only Madeleine brought a spark of life to his day.

Day six. Madeleine smiling. Then, shouts came from the direction of the village. Madeleine waved her little fingers at Jack and trudged away.

More shouts. A man's voice. Then—Jack knew the angry foreign curses—Lucky.

Martin scrambled to his knees and joined Jack peering toward the noise. They had not eaten the morning's ration of rice, so they were at their most alert.

A woman in short black trousers and blue t-shirt appeared, walking toward the hut studying a ring of keys. Then a soldier came into view, pushing Lucky with one arm while trying to keep his rifle aimed at her with the other. She couldn't free herself, but was trying like hell. She stumbled. The soldier yanked her upright.

"They're going to put her in here with us," Jack said.

"Not unless they're extremely stupid." It was the most energetic statement Martin had made in a week. "If they try to open that door, they'll find out exactly what kind of *bushido* warriors they got locked up in here."

"What the hell are you talking about?"

The village woman was unlocking the padlock on their door.

"I know the secret of the samurai." He stood.

She slid something away and pulled the door open.

"Approach each battle," Martin continued, "as if you were already dead."

He wobbled, steadied himself with a hand on the wall, and stepped into the doorway. "Excuse me," he said to the villager and pushed past her.

"Martin," Jack cried out, but before he could lunge to stop him, Martin was down the short ramp, marching toward the soldier. "Martin," Jack screamed again, crouching in the doorway.

While Lucky continued to struggle, the soldier shouted an order and tried to keep the rifle aimed at Martin's middle. With a giant stride, Martin was in his face. In a single, smooth motion, he wrapped his right arm around the barrel of the rifle and clapped his clubbed left hand against the soldier's head. As the soldier began to crumple, Martin yanked the long-arm free and smacked the soldier's head again, this time with the rifle's stock.

Jack was one step out of the cabin and Lucky flew into his arms. She still wore the colorful blue Lisu tunic, short black pants, and red leggings, but they were in shreds and she was filthy, freshly bruised, and marred with what looked like cigarette burns. The red betel stains had faded from her mouth and she looked years younger. He held her tightly.

Martin turned back to them and manipulated the rifle around so that the stock was under his arm and the trigger area rested on his hand. He was a terrifying sight—silver hair spiked, a week-old, shimmering beard, and a burned-out, crazed look in his black eyes. The village woman spoke rapidly.

"What's she saying, Ali-ya?" Martin asked.

"She is very apologetic. Soldiers not welcome here."

"Where are the rest of the soldiers?"

"Gone for now, except this one."

Martin's face broke into a big white-toothed grin. "Let's get the hell out of here."

Jack gathered up the hats, shoes, socks, shirts, and slings from the hut and, on rubbery legs, headed toward the center of the village with Martin and Lucky. The air was unbelievably sweet.

"You're fucking crazy," Jack muttered to Martin. "You know that?"

"Sometimes it pays off. Especially when you got nothing to lose."

No one stopped them. No one looked at them straight on. They retrieved their backpacks from the corner of the grocery hut. They were intact. The old grocer woman, who kept her eyes downcast, had Jack's wallet and photo insert, also intact. Even his money was there. From the bottom of his pack, Jack dug out the pocket pistol, which had been out of reach the one time he might have used it. He stuck it in his pocket.

"Remind me to figure out how this thing works."

"We go now, okay?" Lucky asked.

"Sure." Jack surveyed the surrounding hills. "But where?"

"Ali-ya," Martin said, "do you know if Savani passed through here, on his way back home? Can you find out?"

She asked the grocer, then shook her head no.

"What do you want to do, Jack?"

Steaming mountains filled the horizons around them. The distance to anywhere was incalculable.

"How long to get to where Savani is?"

"Nearly a full day by horse. Winding road, goes through a Mien village. The foot trail takes only four or five hours. Very steep."

"He'll be there?" Jack asked. "He won't have gone on to somewhere else?"

She shook her head. "He does much business there."

Jack looked at Martin. "If he's only a few hours away, seems foolish to turn back now. We still ought to get him to call off the plan, even though Theresa's gotta be safe somewhere by now, right? And we need to get Delia, right?"

Squinting, Martin studied the ridge of mountains to their west, steeper than the ones they'd already traversed. His face was bleak. "Delia, yes..."

Soong's gossip about Delia being left behind for the pleasure of a Shan soldier was ridiculous. Anyway, Delia was too busy being stunned by the jades that lay before her. In all, there were twelve pieces of archaic jade, all from the Warring States period, about 400 to 200 B.C, worth six million easy in a slow market. The reason Delia knew the flawless pale nephrite so well was because it was the very same collection she had returned to Beijing last year. She had found the collection, which disappeared from the Imperial Palace during the 1947 Revolution, through dogged research and a final stroke of luck. For weeks, on a Jones-White contract, she negotiated for it in Taiwan with an aged Kuomintang general. When she finally succeeded, she secretly transported the treasure back to Beijing, to the national collection.

But obviously, as China grappled with a new wave of political "reform," the collection was spirited away once again, this time toward Savani's museum. Months of hard work shot to hell. And yet... From what she knew of the illegal marketplace in Beijing and what she'd learned from Yang Mi about Burmese smugglers, she could very nearly map out a Beijing-Chiang Mai antiquities network. With Antoine Savani at the receiving end. She didn't know whether to be angry or triumphant.

"This is simply incredible," she muttered in English.

"You okay, Delia?" Soong asked.

"Oh, yes, of course," she answered in Chinese as she began hastily rewrapping the jades. "I'll take these myself to Tony. Tell me which hut is his."

"But the Akha—Lieutenant Sayat—"

"Please. I need to talk to Tony. I'll be careful, really."

Yang Soong pointed her toward a double-sized Akha hut, the only one with a generator and a satellite dish. Along the way, Delia did not allow herself to be bothered by Akha children taunting her with pebbles or Akha women giving her wide berth, making a sign with their fingers, as if warding off the evil eye.

Delia marched uphill to his door, kicked off her shoes, and entered without knocking. The hut had ventilation louvers where the walls met the sloping roof. It had lamps, a ceiling fan, and a computer system. A young woman with embroidered leggings, a pleated indigo skirt, and a cap decorated with rows of silver cabochons, was clearing dishes from the table. She hissed at Delia and hurried out with her tray.

Muffled sounds came from behind a door at the back of the room. Delia set down the basket of jades, opened the door, and walked in. The room was heavy with smells of hot teak, cocoa, cinnamon, and dirty sheets. To her surprise, Tony was lying in bed—a futon on a bamboo platform—watching television.

She startled him. When her eyes adjusted to the darkness, she saw him sweeping a dark robe closed around him.

She stepped between him and the television. "Your jades arrived."

"Get out. Get out of here," he growled, as he fumbled for the remote and tried to turn off the TV. But she was in the way.

"I've had enough, Tony. I'm not welcome here. And the whole museum business is baloney, isn't it?"

"Get out of the way. I can't hear a thing you're saying."

The low-volume video soundtrack began to register. A woman was screaming.

She turned toward it. "What's this, a horror movie?"

"Delia! Wait, look at me."

A blindfolded woman in a torn mauve blouse and plum-colored skirt, pushed up around her hips, lay on a bed, her ankles and wrists bound. She sobbed and thrashed as a stocky man sat astride her.

"Oh..." Delia whispered, "that's me."

"Delia, please, let me—"

"You have a tape of me being raped." Her voice grew louder. She turned back to him. "Why are you lying here watching me being raped?" She trembled with rage.

Tony shrank from her. "Please, let me turn it off. Let me explain. Let me—no, don't watch any more."

But she turned around in time to see that the rapist had changed, that it was Caleb Clearwater on top of her now and that he had a knife in his hand and that he was drawing the knife along her breastbone...

She jammed her fist against the buttons till the tape stopped and the screen turned a solid blue. She punched again till the tape ejected. "How could you?" With both hands she banged the tape against the TV cabinet. "Where did you get this?" It didn't break. "How long have you known?" She began to pull the tape from the cassette. "Tell me," she screamed.

Tony was curled into the far corner of the platform, a striped blue sheet pulled against him. "I have an affliction, Delia. A curse." He looked up at Delia and she was surprised by the anguish in his eyes.

"What the hell are you talking about?"

"All my life, I have been so obsessively, explosively attracted to certain people. I fall in love. With beautiful, friendly, sensuous people. Like a moth to a fire cracker. They consume me. But I can't respond. Not directly. Lucky, Lana—even men—Martin... I can only watch... from afar."

A voyeur? The hairs rose on the back of her neck. Her hands were still tangled in video tape and she lifted it toward him. "This! This! Has nothing to do with..." Her voice was quivering. "...with beautiful, friendly, sensuous people. These men were murdering me, Tony. I thought you were my friend."

"I was desperate to be your friend. I loved you most of all. They weren't supposed to murder you. They weren't supposed to stab you—not like that."

The floor seemed to shift under her feet. She paused, expecting a shooting belly pain, expecting the breath to be crushed out of her chest. But all she felt was the hot breeze of the ceiling fan and a dryness in her mouth. "Why do you have this tape?"

He looked at her hands. "I asked them to make it. The tapes never betray. People betray. People betray the ones who love them most. The tapes never betray. The tapes are my truth."

She dropped the mess onto the floor and turned around. Spotting a storage cabinet, she yanked open the door. Tony was up on his knees, scrambling toward her.

"Get out of here, Delia. There's no need for you to—"

"Oh, God."

In a neat row, the neatly labeled video tapes lined up. She pulled them out one at a time, slowly, at first, *Lucky and... Lucky and... Lucky and...* Then faster, *Ingrid & Cal, Ingrid & Bruno, Ingrid... Ingrid...* When she came to *Sara Malraux*, she threw the tape at Tony.

"You sick bastard."

Tony ducked. *Jeremy & René.* She pitched it and the corner glanced off his head.

"Ow, stop it." Tony cried out and lunged for her. She swung out of the way as she grabbed another tape—*Lana at Paddington.*

Tony stood between her and the door, rubbing his head, his pale eyes awash in tears. "Give me that fucking tape."

She backed up a step and hugged it to her chest.

"Are there more?"

He held out his hand. "Just give it to me, Delia."

"Are there more, you depraved sonofabitch?"

His eyes hardened. "Of course there are more. Including one of Lucky and Jack that was air-expressed to London for Theresa to see what her father's capable of doing with other men's daughters."

She tried to push past him, but he slammed the door and leaned against it. "I can't let you leave with that tape."

"How will you stop me?"

"I'll strangle you, Delia, with my bare hands." He blinked.

She put her face near his. "It'll be one helluva struggle, Tony, and during the course of it I'll gouge out your filthy evil eyes and you'll never have a fucking moment of pleasure for the rest of your maggot-infested life."

Tony blinked again. Slowly, he stepped away from the door. "You won't get far."

"Just watch me."

In the outer room, Delia grabbed the basket of jades, stowed the tape under the lid, and ran. Outside in the balmy bright air, she stopped for a single deep breath, then pounded down the path toward her hut, nearly running into a muscular man in military camouflage.

EIGHT

THE HILLS, THAILAND

Tony slumped onto the bed, his knees shaking, tears streaming from his eyes. Reaching into a drawer, he pulled out a foil pouch of smoked almonds. Unable to tear it open with his trembling hands, he threw it at the video screen.

"Damn. Damn it."

The front door slammed.

"Tony! My friend, you here?"

Tony quickly swiped his eyes on the sleeve of his robe and made sure it was pulled shut. "In here, Bo."

Lieutenant Sayat walked to the back room, not bothering with the formality of removing his boots. He surveyed the mess without a word.

"Damn you, it's about time you showed up. The woman who just left here. Did you see her?"

"Greetings to you also. She was headed for the Chinese quarter."

"Kill her."

"What, just like that? No games? No Sony camcorder?"

Tony stood and began to gather up the tapes, so that Bo Sayat wouldn't see the angry tears that still seeped from his eyes. "I don't care what the hell you do with her."

"I have other news for you," said Sayat. "Part of the reason for my delay."

"Out with it."

"Down in the Lahu village we ran into Lucky and two Americans looking for you. We found them very suspicious."

Tony froze. "Their names?"

"Scana-lan and Moon."

"That little cunt," Tony muttered. "What did you do with them?"

"We lock up Americans. I want to move on, but my men they need rest. We just kill some Burmese soldiers who ambush us near border. So we camp at opium den, had Lucky for entertainment—didn't think you would mind. Unfortunately, she not seem to enjoy herself like old days."

Tony felt a sudden shiver, a sudden weakness that made him whisper, "Did you tape it?"

"We could have used the money," Bo said. "But the system you gave Lahu headman—it cursed by dead battery."

"They're all still locked up?"

"Yes."

"Kill them too."

"What, even Lucky?"

"I said kill them, damn it. Kill them. I'm sick to death of games."

"But Lucky, she your daughter—family—how can you—?"

Tony pitched one of the tapes at the wall. "She's not my fucking daughter." The heat of tears stung his eyes again.

"But you say—and the eyes..."

"Her grandfather was a fucking German missionary. I have no fucking daughter." His secrets were tumbling from the darkness. He hated how the light made him seem abnormal and perverse. He pitched another tape. "Get out. Get out. Take care of business, damn it."

Sayat left and Tony collapsed into his bed. *Shame* and *guilt* were emotions felt by idiots. He was a powerful man. He made the rules. Anyone who questioned that wasn't long for this world. Tony grabbed a handful of Delia's tangled mess of tape and curled himself around it.

*T*ime to move. Time to get away. Go. Pushing her cabin door shut, Delia kicked off her flip-flops and put on her canvas shoes. As she threw the rest of her possessions into the shoulder bag, the door creaked open. It was the Shan soldier she passed on the path.

"Miss Rivera, I been looking forward to meet you."

"Who are you?"

"I am Tony's friend, Lieutenant Sayat. May I call you *Delia*?"

"Sure, whatever." She took a good look at him. He was a short guy who reeked of tobacco smoke. He leered at her.

"We can talk? I never made good conversation with American woman. You come to my hut?"

"Later, if you don't mind. I have to bring this basket back to Yang Mi, but I need to find something in my purse first."

"Perhaps we have conversation here instead?"

Delia froze, her back still toward him. In her hand was the straight razor she traded for at the Mien village.

He came near.

She opened the razor.

"You have wonderful round buttocks," he said.

A hand cupped her ass.

She spun around and clapped her right hand on his shoulder. She had a momentary advantage of surprise. Before he could knock her away, she parked her left fist against his cheek so that the razor was in front of his eye. She had his attention.

"Don't touch me," she hissed, staring into his wide eyes, about an inch below hers. "Don't ever touch me, unless you want me to cut more than your face." With icy steadiness, she drew the razor down his cheek, praying her insanity would show him who was boss—or at least knock him off his game long enough for her to disappear.

The pain took a second to register. He gasped and patted the blood streaming from his face. He swung at her, cursing, but she had grabbed the bag and basket and dashed out the door.

As she ran down the path away from the village into the forest, he was screaming in Chinese, demanding someone get him a doctor.

Slowly, Tony dressed, munched on stale, sweet banana chips, and switched on the computer to check the day's business in New York, London, Bangkok, and Hong Kong. All was well. Most importantly, according to his London email, the Baphuon-style Buddha that Jeremy had lost to the Heldt-Luther had arrived by air freight in Bangkok. Delia's plan had worked. The Heldt-Luther curator had been aghast that there might be any Cambodian claims against the statue—a rumor planted with HAWC-I. New Cathay Galleries had stepped in. They purported to represent a private party in Phnom Penh who was willing to pay twenty-five percent over their purchase price to bring the statue back to Cambodia. The Heldt-Luther directors bit. They salvaged both their reputation and their investment. Now the prize was Tony's.

Tony couldn't wait to tell Delia that he rescued the piece, that she was a genius, but... The impulse saddened him.

Someone was at his door—Yang Mi.

"Sir... I thought you'd want the jades locked up. Soong said Delia brought them up here."

Tony's skin grew cold. "What? Delia was here but—where is she now?"

"No one has seen her for quite some time." Yang Mi's voice lowered. "You don't think—?"

"Where is Lieutenant Sayat?"

"He had some sort of accident—a deep gash in his face. Pu-Tse is stitching it."

"Get him the hell up here. Is there a horse gone?"

"Not that I know of."

"Radio Ban Hu Nam Mai and tell the headman to detain her if she passes through."

Mi scratched his head. "The Akha say that evil spirits have possessed the radio again. The spirit priest has been sent for."

"For godsake, Mi, I can communicate with the major cities of the world from here. Why is it we can never seem to contact the next village?"

Mi shrugged and looked at the floor.

"I'll take care of it. Get out of here. Get out." Tony spun around and pressed the heels of his hands to his eyes. More fucking tears. "Damn you,

Delia," he cried, as he wiped his face and headed for the gun case. "I loved you best of all."

Until she hit the trailhead, Delia expected someone to chase her down or call her back. No one did. Just like that, she was free. Walking away with the clothes on her back, a razor folded into the palm of her hand, and a treasure in jade. And a video tape that would resolve Lana's murder.

Going home. She felt so light, so strong, so full of energy that she'd walk all the way to Bangkok if necessary. Her week at the Akha village gave her invaluable information on Burmese smuggling routes and between these jades and the Rangoon jades back at his house, she might be able to put Tony out of the antiquities smuggling business. In time she might be able to dismantle the whole network. It would require her to come back to the wild mountain and forest communities of Asia. The prospect would have terrified her only days ago, but now it energized her.

Dense foliage crowded the path, which quickly became steep and often required that she sit and slide or scramble on all fours. Not having had time to change into her trousers was a nuisance. She wound up retying her sarong into bloomers.

After a couple of hours, a noise up ahead made her stop. Voices. She peeked around the bend. The trail below flattened out a bit and the scrubby woods gave way to steep cultivated fields, waiting for the rains to begin in earnest.

The big, scruffy men looked like pale giants. They were with a bedraggled Lisu woman wearing a straw hat. The taller man with a red cap was climbing out of the field, zipping his pants.

Delia opened the razor and squinted at them.

The silver-haired man rested a white arm on the girl's shoulder and her arm circled his waist. It wasn't clear who was supporting whom. The red-cap man pulled the pack off his back, took out a bottle of water and offered it to the girl. She drank, then the red-cap man touched the silver man's shoulder and held the bottle to his lips. His friend drank and a flash of white teeth brightened his face.

271

Delia savored the warm flush of recognition. *I'm hallucinating.* No. She found them: Martin, the wellspring of everything good she'd ever done with her life. Jack, the truth seer, the protector. But how could they be here? Martin was supposed to be in Chiang Mai, getting his hands fixed, getting his legal problems straightened out. But—she was engulfed with joy.

Stowing the razor in her bag, she struggled to keep her balance as she scuffled and slid down the hill toward them.

"Martin! Jack! It's me. Delia." It was all she could think to cry out, not wanting to frighten them if she had become as unrecognizable as they. "What are you doing here?"

Jack caught her first and kissed her hair, her cheeks, her ears, her eyes. "Sweet Jesus, sweet Jesus," he crooned. He was sticky and smelly and shaky and welcome as roses.

She twisted around to Martin and all she could see were his stained and cracked casts and his discolored fingers. "Marty…" She held out her arms.

"You're alive," he murmured and a grin softened the deep shadows under his eyes. They embraced. She pressed her lips to his. Then her tongue. Suddenly, she had to brace one knee against the other to keep them from buckling. His kiss was the same honey surprise it was some twenty years ago.

When she finally pulled away, his eyes were beaming through the tears.

"Let's go home," she whispered.

Martin couldn't take his eyes off her. They'd both been in the hills for a week, but while he felt like a withered hothouse plant, Delia had taken root and thrived. Her muscles were visibly taut with energy. The sunlight that sapped him lit up the copper highlights in her wild hair and the subtle greens in her golden-brown eyes. Her skin was bronzed, her face lustrous with roses and pinks. He wondered if he'd ever seen her so beautiful.

The three spoke quickly about where they'd been.

"I managed to make enemies of an entire village, except for the Chinese traders. Wait till I tell you…"

"We were jailed by Shan soldiers till this morning—stoned on opium for a week..."

Lucky drifted off and sat under a half-dead tree.

"What's with her?"

"One of Savani's cronies," Martin said, "a Lieutenant Sayat, made Ali-ya—that's her Lisu name—made her entertain his patrol for the week. She's exhausted and hurting."

"Jesus," Delia said and glanced back up the hill.

Martin wrapped his aching arms around her again, kissed her hair and sensed her curves against him. "I'm afraid we can't go home yet, babe. We have to go up there and get Tony." He explained the threat to Theresa Scanlan.

"That's why I have to get to Savani," Jack said. "Find out what he really ordered. Get him to call off this Arnie character. My baby is in danger." He glanced toward Lucky. "Unthinkable danger. You'll show us the way? Now?"

"It's not that easy." She still clung to Martin, her fingers massaging the muscles in his back. "If I have to go back for Theresa's sake, I will. But believe me, we can't just walk into that village without a plan. Those people are Tony's friends. Even the Chinese, who were very good to me, must owe their first loyalty to Tony. And Sayat is there. You can take my word for it, he'll show me no mercy. It'll be dark soon. We need to rest and plan." She scanned the hillside. "There."

Like most of the fields they'd passed, this one boasted a hut for resting during the height of the day's heat. It was a simple structure, bamboo poles connecting a floor to a thatched roof. This shelter had the deluxe feature of coarse bamboo shades that unrolled to form crude walls on all four sides. Frayed mats covered the floor.

Jack had not allowed Martin or Lucky to carry a pack on the steep climb, so they'd brought only a single sleeping bag, a flashlight, and a minimum of food. He opened up the sleeping bag and spread it across the floor and unpacked the bag of fresh lychees and rolls of sticky rice that the Lahu villagers had given them.

Martin sat with his back against a post. Despite his blurry, achy exhaustion, looking at Delia made him certain that everything would be okay now. Beautiful Delia.

She accepted a roll of rice from Jack, unwrapped it from the banana leaf, and launched into a long-winded story about the jades in her carrybasket and their journey from Taiwan to Beijing to the Burmese smuggling route.

Lucky sat close to Jack and nibbled the fruit. Jack borrowed Delia's comb and gently began to work out the knots and tangles in Lucky's hair as they talked about ways to reach Savani. Delia suggested they wait till dawn to tackle the difficult trail. While the two men hid, she would return the jades to Tony, ostensibly throwing herself on his mercy. She'd try to get weapons. She'd draw him to the edge of the village and they'd drag him off. It was a ridiculous plan, full of desperate bravado.

Martin stretched out on the floor, gazing at her as the color rose in her face. She wore a homespun sarong that exposed much of her legs as she sat. She'd taken off her shoes and long-sleeved shirt, leaving a swath of indigo cloth twisted and cinched around her bosom, mashing her breasts too severely, allowing only a hint of soft, damp flesh over the top edge, and revealing the deep scar along her midriff. He watched her breathe. And he became aware of his own breath.

They fell silent.

With a glance at Martin, Jack scooted around to his knees. "Come on, Ali-ya, let's walk down the hill a ways and see if there's a stream. A bath will do us good." She frowned at him. "Come on, sweetheart." He helped Lucky off the platform and peeked back around the crooked shade. "We'll be gone an hour or so."

When Jack and Lucky disappeared, Delia crawled close to Martin. She looked at the crumbling casts and touched the purple, misaligned fingers. She caught his eyes.

"You're in pain."

"Maybe... maybe..." He lightly ran his fingers across her skin—up her arm, across her shoulder to her neck. "It's more like listening to a concert on AM radio. In a thunderstorm. Not pain so much as static." He outlined her lips. "And deprivation."

Then he hooked her hand with his thumb and pulled it to his mouth. With his eyes closed, he kissed and nibbled each salty finger. A symphony of sensation rose above the static and a sigh of pleasure escaped his lips.

She drew her hand away, unbuttoned his shirt and slid her fingers across his chest and belly. "And you've lost weight," she murmured. Leaning over, she kissed his neck, his chest, the soft place below his ribs. He floated in the thrill of her touch.

When she looked into his face again, her lips were moist and rosy. "Why didn't you get someone else to go after Tony? Why did you risk your hands, your life, to follow me?"

Using his thumbs again, he unhitched the cloth that cinched her breasts, pulled her toward him and kissed her lips. For a long minute they writhed together, delighting in the old familiarities. A dozen years had not diminished her sensual purity—the uncluttered connection between her body and soul. And a dozen years had not diminished his joy in sensing it. Cal's slavering assault had not destroyed him after all. Delia and the bliss they found in one another was all that mattered anymore and if she stayed close enough to him, all the evil in the world would disappear.

She lay on her back. He spoke. "Why..." He kissed one breast, sucked at the nipple till it hardened. "Why..." He kissed the other till she groaned. "Why..." He scooted up and rubbed his nose against hers. "Why do you keep running away from me?"

Her fingers dragged across his chest, to his waistband, intensifying the silky sensation between his legs. She was pushing away his pants, touching him, taking his breath away.

"Why..." she said, "do you keep letting me go? Letting me think... that I need to go?"

Their legs became tangled and her sarong pulled loose. His knee found a place between her thighs and nuzzled it till she began to tremble.

They shifted around. "I was a damn fool... for ever, ever letting you go." And then they were one.

They lay still. The late afternoon heat had melted his skin into hers. As the shivers of climax wore off, they stirred, clinging, searching, tasting, rediscovering. They finally unglued themselves only because Jack and Lucky would be returning soon. Martin wished that he could call a time-out on this unending adventure, that the bad guys, the good guys, the weather, his hungry belly, his busted hands would give him twenty-four hours—even twelve, even two—to spend with Delia, to ring in the new beginning.

But instead, Martin pulled on his pants while Delia tied the sarong around her hips and the scarf around her bosom. She lay next to him, on her back. He propped himself on an elbow, laid a heavy hand across her midriff and caressed her with his thumb.

"What now, old love?" he murmured.

"I want time to stop. I want this hut to be the universe. I love you."

He kissed her again, also wanting the moment to last forever.

But the sound of a dog barking in the distance started time rolling again.

"Truth is, Delia, I'm afraid. A place called *home* is impossibly far away. I'm a wreck. I'm illegal. You're carrying a zillion dollars worth of stolen property. Theresa Scanlan's going to wind up in Lucky's shoes if we don't figure out an effective plan. Tony Savani is a wicked man, babe. Have you found out yet that he...?"

Yes," she said, laying a finger on his lips. "But I know something else too. It's only a tiny comfort amid a great big horror, but you should know that Tony did not have an affair with Lana. I'll tell you..."

Martin lay back. "It isn't important. It's all my fault anyway. I stopped being very attentive, I think, too wrapped up in myself to notice—"

"No, listen. When Tony told me about their affair, he said how turned on she was by opium."

"That's ridiculous. She didn't ingest anything stronger than ginger ale—ever."

"I know, but I was too rattled by the news to see it was all pure fabrication. When Lana came along, he was obviously infatuated. Something may have occurred between them, but it was not an affair. He's a voyeur—can't get it off unless he's watching someone else do it." She looked down at the spot she was touching on his chest. "The more violent and sadistic, the better."

Martin closed his eyes. Tony must have sensed Lana's love of sex games. He had used that insight skillfully in making his story credible to Martin. But not in a million years would Lana have submitted to anyone's brutality while Savani jerked off. Her games required energy and props and elaborate fantasy, but never cruelty. Seductions in a thousand tiresome formats, but no make-believe rapes.

And yet... the drama played through Martin's head. He and Lana danced on a razor's edge. During the last two or three years, they'd begun to improvise quarrels with one another to tease secrets from their informants. But their scenes were coming too easily and he feared they sprang from a deep store of impatience with one another, the frustrations of a relationship going sour.

She'd probably been pumping Savani for what he knew about the Tak burial treasures. With their shared background of wealth, their shared

276

passion for grand art, and their shared talent for operating beneath the surface of things, how easy it would have been for her to feign irritation with Martin while intimating her fantasies. What unspoken promises were made? What promises broken?

Delia caressed his cheek, then touched her fingers to his lips.

"I love you," was all he could think to say, to thank her for trying to give Lana back to him and for being here in his wretched arms.

She drew her fingers down to the hairs on his chest. "There's one more thing. No, two."

"Hmm?"

"About Theresa. It would fit the pattern if the person Savani sent after her were the actual, well, abuser—rather than Tony himself. Theresa's, uh, end of innocence may start the moment she's picked up, may have already started. They won't need to bring her to Thailand or keep her till Tony returns to London."

"Shit—but, wait a minute, if Savani's a voyeur, if that's his pleasure, then wouldn't he want to be there? Wouldn't he—?"

"That's the other thing. Tony uses video tape. Whatever is done to Theresa will be taped, for Tony—and maybe for Jack—to see. There's also a tape of an... encounter... between Jack and Lucky that night at the *khlong* house. It was expressed to his pal in London, to show Theresa."

Martin felt dizzy. It was all too much for him to absorb.

"But that's not the end of it, Martin. Tony struck some kind of deal with the hawkeyes—"

"The killings, I know."

"More than that. Bruno and Cal supplied Tony with video tapes of their sexual adventures, including their *victories* against cultural criminals, including..." She gulped air and her nails dug into Martin's skin. "Including the murders. I took the tape of Lana's murder. It's in the basket."

Only Delia's grip on his flesh convinced Martin that this wasn't a nightmare. He knew that if he ever slipped under Tony's thrall, that sooner or later he'd be shown those tapes. He'd crack apart. And Jack. Jack wouldn't be able to bear the thought of a sex tape being shown to Theresa, much less—

Suddenly, one of the bamboo shades was ripped from its makeshift fitting. A slender silhouette stood against the oyster shell sky. Tony!

Tony Savani raised his rifle waist-high and waved it at Martin, then Delia. His face was horror-struck.

277

Tony was aghast at the sight of Delia lying in Moon's arms. Her tracks had led him to believe she'd be alone. And Moon was supposed to be locked up in Ban Hu Nam Mai. But here they were, his traitor Delia clinging to his nemesis Martin Moon, her hand on his hairy chest. The hut was redolent with sexual smells. Tony felt the twinge of arousal.

But the impulse to be a party to their passion exploded into hatred.

"You whore, you thief," he screamed and pulled the trigger. The bullet went high and ripped through the bamboo shade behind her.

She yelped and scrambled to her knees. Moon sprang to a crouch in front of her, clearly ready to lunge at Tony's knees. But Moon would be dead if he tried.

Tony cocked the rifle again and was taking aim at Moon when a hand clapped his shoulder and a hard thing jammed against his back.

"Put down the gun, Tony," Jack shouted, too loud, too tremulously. "Or I'll put a hole in your spine. Now."

Tony's pulse quickened and he let the rifle barrel dip to the floor.

Delia sprang up and pulled the rifle from his hand. Raising his hands, Tony turned slowly toward Jack. Wild eyes. Sweat dripping from his scruffy beard. Stubby pistol in his hands. Arms rigid. Legs braced. No doubt he would shoot.

"I didn't think you were the violent type," Tony murmured.

"I'm not violent. I'm fucking crazy. Just crazy enough to figure out how to do a whole hell of a lot of damage to you without having mercy enough to let you die."

Savani surveyed the empty field over Jack's shoulder. "Is Lucky with you?"

"You pimped her for the last time, you cocksucker."

A cry came from beyond the hut and Lucky was pushed into view by his friend Lieutenant Sayat, who had joined Tony in his search for Delia. Sayat held Lucky's arms twisted behind her and pointed his long-barreled .45 at her midsection.

"I suggest you drop toy gun, Scana-lan."

Thank goodness. Tony sagged against a bamboo post, suddenly famished.

J ack saw Delia lower the rifle barrel and saw Martin raise his hands. He turned his head and saw the soldier with the handgun poking at Lucky.

What bullshit was this now?

"No," he shouted and spun around to point the gun at the soldier, who was ten or twelve feet away. His foe was a short, square man—the same man who had interrogated them in the Lahu village a week ago, now with half his face bandaged. He was the man who derailed their mission to find Savani and to protect Theresa. Jack screamed at him: "I'm going to blow your head off."

"Jack," Delia said in a stage whisper. "Put the damn gun down. It's no match for his."

Jack refused to believe her. "You said this was a .45—a man-stopper, you said." He couldn't talk any lower than a shout.

"Not at this range, for godsake. You're not even holding it steady."

"Put gun down, Scana-lan, or I kill Lucky."

"Killing means nothing to him. Better do what he says," Tony advised softly.

Lucky was crying now. "*Khun* Tony," she begged, dropping to a crouch. "Make Lieuten' Sayat go away. Please."

Sayat let go of her wrists and pulled her up by her hair till she screamed, then put the gun barrel against her head.

Tony looked away.

"Jack," Martin said, "put the gun down. Think of Theresa. We've got to get out of here in one piece. He's going to kill Lucky, then he'll kill you."

"I'm tired of these cocksuckers thinking they can get away with any kind of rotten abuse just because they're rich, just because they carry a big motherfucking gun." He wanted to wipe the sweat out of his eyes, but his hands were frozen to the pistol.

Lucky's eyes met his. "*Khun* Jack, help me."

He stiffened his arms, trying to focus on the sight. His eyes locked with Sayat's. Sayat let go of Lucky to put both hands on his weapon, to take aim at Jack. But an odd thing happened: a black circle appeared over Sayat's eyebrow. Only then did Jack register the explosion and the spray of red mist against the white sky. Sayat crumpled to the ground.

Jack stared at the gun in his hand. Had he shot it? Weren't you supposed to feel it if a gun went off in your hand?

Dumbfounded, he turned to the others. Delia was still aiming the rifle at the spot where Sayat had stood. Slowly, she lowered it and the world began to move again. Tony covered his face with his hands. Martin scrambled to his feet. Lucky threw her arms around Jack, sobbing.

Delia. Delia killed the soldier.

Delia shifted her gaze from Sayat's fallen body to Jack. Her eyes were hard, but she managed a sour smile. He put the safety back on his unused weapon and slipped it into his pocket. Then he patted Lucky's back to quiet her sobs. To Delia, he whispered, "Thank you."

NINE

The Hills, Thailand

Night fell. The trail was treacherous but the waning moon was bright. Martin followed Delia's sure-footed lead down the steep mountain trail. Armed with Sayat's .45 and burdened with her jades, she had taken the lead in the solemn procession, using the flashlight only to light up the sections that required ladder-like descents. Martin felt no weariness. Delia had restored his life to him.

Savani walked behind him, with Jack aiming the rifle at his spine, nudging him with it now and then to remind him of his jeopardy.

They'd said goodbye to Lucky. She wanted to go home. Over the hill was a Lisu settlement. She would hike there and tend to the disposal of Sayat's body before the Shans discovered it. Shyly, she hugged Delia and Martin. Jack held her close, kissed her forehead, and couldn't speak. She and Tony made no eye contact, had nothing to say.

On the trail, Tony began to fret about his tape collection up in the Akha village. The isolation of the village and the loyalty of the villagers had made it the safest of places for his secret pleasure. But Delia had breeched it. She destroyed one: *Delia at Hampstead*. And stole another: *Lana at Paddington*.

His need for tapes had been the final blow to his infatuation with Lana.

The day after she'd teased him with the silk scarf, Moon left for Tak. She seemed anxious and irritated with Moon and wanted to know all Tony could tell her about what Moon had gotten himself into. Tony invited her to his room and offered to arrange a therapeutic massage with Lucky. She accepted. The bedroom door was left open a crack and Tony watched.

The next day, he asked if he could video her massage. The idea titillated her. She arrived in a white one-piece bathing suit. While Lucky, in a demure white tunic, kneaded her muscles, Lana joked and flirted with the camera. It was during this session that Tony decided he could never let her return to Moon, that she would be happiest with him. He sent the hawkeyes after Moon.

But suddenly Lana was gone. The news of her dramatic rescue of Moon in the Mae Sot shanty crushed and angered him.

He followed them to London and contrived a chance meeting with her at his New Cathay Galleries. She seemed thrilled to see him and went immediately with him for tea, where he introduced her to his friend Claude Leroux, the ostensible owner of the statue Cathay was selling to the British Museum.

Tony could hardly believe how she sparkled with affection for him. Yet he was no longer satisfied with the innocent massage tape that helped him sleep at night.

Apart from his role as a tool in Tony's art deals, Claude Leroux was a pornographic filmmaker, specializing in "candid" real life videos. He arranged for Claude to get a video of Lana more in keeping with his erotic taste.

Then, the deal with the British Museum fell through. Tony was beside himself. The curator Reggie Gupta had been his ally, snapping up good buys, no questions asked, so what the hell had happened? Tony arranged to meet with him.

On the very day of his meeting, he had invited Lana to lunch at a flat leased by New Cathay. A hidden camera had been set up to record the planned event—luncheon to seduction to dish-smashing fornication.

Leroux greeted her, told her Tony had been called away, and escorted her to the dining room, where a video camera had been set up behind the one-way mirror. They lunched and they flirted. She asked him about the Khmer statue he was trying to sell and he laughed, saying he knew little about it, that it was New Cathay's deal, merely a tax write-off for himself.

As Claude got up to fill her water glass and pour himself some brandy, he shifted the subject to his production company.

"You are a most stunning beauty, Lana. I'd love to put you in one of my films."

She peered into the mirror in front of her and chuckled. "I might have been an actress once, but I'm too old. My skin is no good." She traced the web of fine lines around her smile.

He stood behind her. "Skin is the easiest of all problems to deal with on film." Drawing his hands through her long hair, he said, "It is the lack of radiance which is impossible to fix."

Her eyes fluttered slightly and her lips parted. She continued to look at herself—at the camera, as he pulled her head back against his stomach and ran a finger across her face.

"You have marvelous cheekbones," he said, "and a delicate nose. Expressive lips and a flawless chin."

She seemed hypnotized as his hand slipped into her blouse. The motion snapped her out of her reverie.

"Whoa! Stop it," she said, but he held on and pulled the small buttons from their holes to expose the top of her lacy slip. "Stop, this instant."

He paused, his hands drawing back to gently massage her shoulders. "Calm down," he said. "I thought you loved Tony, that you would do this for Tony."

She pulled away and stood up, buttoning her blouse. "What are you talking about?"

"Tony wants a film of you. Of us. Making love with the fiery passion you have shown me you're capable of. He will watch the film night after night. It will give him the kind of climax that he longs for, that he deserves."

He tried to grab her, but she slapped him. "I should have guessed that skinny self-important jackass couldn't get it off in the normal way. Him and his tapes. Jesus!" The implications suddenly sunk in. "Unbelievable. He's jerking off to that tape he made of me in Bangkok? And he wants something hotter? Well, you tell him that he better get his disgusting little thrills elsewhere. You tell that impotent little creep that any hint of passion he found in those tapes was strictly compliments of the man I love—Martin Moon, hear? A man who knows how to do more with his hands than jerk himself off." She emphasized each angry word. "Tell him that any longing he saw in my eyes was my undying love for Martin Moon. Is that clear?"

Leroux had backed away as Lana ranted. Her rage finally spent, she composed herself. "Look, I'm sorry," she said breathlessly, sweeping her hand across her forehead. "You don't need to tell Tony any of this. I don't mean to hurt him. It's just that I'm not... I'm not who he thinks I am."

Tony arrived in time to see Lana storming out of the building and got to the tape before Claude had a chance to erase it. He was already furious with Gupta's intimation that it was Lana Tuthill who had warned him away from the smuggled statue. The tape shattered him.

And it destroyed her.

It was midnight when Delia led the group into the Lahu village. She located Savani's Range Rover among the darkened huts, parked under a thatched roof. The ignition key was under the floor mat.

Delia drove. Totally focused on their mission, she felt like she had been driving these hills all her life. Martin sat next to her, with the rifle between his legs. And Jack sat in the back with Savani, aiming the handgun at his ribs.

They reached the Savani estate well before dawn. The air was heavy and filled with the steady sawing of cicadas. There were no other signs of life.

After Savani unlocked the front door, Jack prodded him directly to his office and, after yanking drawers onto the floor to make sure there were no hidden weapons, sat him down at the desk. Martin slumped into a chair behind Tony. Delia stood behind Martin, massaging his shoulders.

"What the hell do you want from me?" Tony demanded.

"Pick up the phone," Jack said, "and call whoever you sent to snatch my daughter and tell him if I don't hear she's absolutely safe pretty damn quick I'm going to start inflicting some serious bodily harm."

"What are you talking about?"

"Lucky told me, so don't act dumb. And you better start dialing because I'm getting itchy."

"Going to have Delia do your dirty work again?"

"You sonofabitch." Jack picked up a Tibetan bronze from the desk, dropped it to the floor, then stepped on it. An arm cracked off.

Martin gasped.

Savani tried to jump up from his chair, scolding, "Jesus, Scanlan, that's eight hundred years old."

But Jack shoved him back.

"All it is to me is a corroded hunk of metal. Dial."

Savani punched in the number.

"Midge, Savani here. Arnie in?... I know it's late but... What?... Not in a week?... I asked him to do something for me, a week ten days ago. You don't know if—what?... Yes, sorry about that. If you hear from him, give me a call, or tell him to get in touch. It's urgent." He hung up. His big colorless eyes gazed at Jack. "Well, you heard. Hasn't been home in a week. He isn't terribly reliable, I'm afraid. But I called on him," Savani said, "because he likes to ball young blondes. Preferably virgins, preferably virgins who aren't in the mood. If you hang around long enough perhaps you'll even get to see—"

Martin jumped from his chair and gave Tony a sharp poke in the nose with his right cast. Tony yelped.

"Stop your bullshit, Tony." With two hands he scooped up a pad of paper and a pen and dropped them in front of Tony. "Write down this Arnie's full name, address, and phone number or I'll pop you again."

With irritating slowness, Tony wrote. When he put the pen down, Delia snatched the pad away.

Tony sneered at Martin as he dabbed the drop of blood from his upper lip. "It's too late, you know. I promised Scanlan he'd never sleep another night if he didn't stay out of my affairs. But he didn't listen."

Jack was turning gray, the gun wobbling in his hand.

"Sit down, Jack. Call London. Delia, get the rifle."

CHIANG MAI, THAILAND

Jack grabbed a side chair, banged it up against the desk, sat heavily, and called Theresa's dorm. His legs had turned to boiled pasta. After endless ringing, a sleep-thick voice answered.

"I'm trying to reach Theresa Scanlan. This is her father."

A pause. "Oh, *Tess* you mean?" A singsong voice.

"Yeah."

"Hang on—oh, Mr. Scanlan?"

"Yeah?"

"I forgot, she's gone away."

The seed of relief died sproutless. "What do you mean? Who is this?"

"M'name's Lizzie Wentworth. She went off about, oh I'd say, a week ago—chap was a friend of yours. Told me as she packed up some things. Said he was going to take her to a posh hotel, like. We're on break now so the timing was perfect. Somethin' amiss, Mr. Scanlan?"

What use was it to grill this girl about why Theresa had not gotten or not heeded all the messages he'd left about talking to strangers. In fact, it appeared she'd ignored the major motif of his entire protective fatherhood. Why? She'd never been a willful brat like other children. Why did she pick this moment to defy him?

"Did you see him? Did she say his name? Jones-White? Dugan?"

"Can't say as I recall. Didn't see 'im either, but 'e sounded like a gent."

"Thanks, Lizzie." As he hung up, Jack looked up at Martin. "She's gone."

Martin began calling the numbers for Jones-White. The service at St. Cloud would only say he'd left France and suggested calling London. A night clerk at the London office said only that he would forward their urgent message as soon as he could find out where Mr. Jones-White was. An answering machine picked up the call at Edwin's London home.

"Edwin. Martin here. At Savani's in Chiang Mai." He read off the phone number.

There was no answer at the Moon apartment in Manhattan. He talked to the machine: "Dad, it's Martin. Call me." He read off Savani's number again.

"We're really batting a thousand," Martin muttered.

Jack sighed deeply, picked up the phone again, and dialed Monica's private line. He calculated the time of day in New York and figured she'd be in her office, dictating surgery notes. "Boy, I hate to have to do this."

"Thoracic Center. Dr. Scanlan's office." Not Monica.

"Hello, this is Jack Scanlan, Dr. Scanlan's ex. I need to reach her immediately."

"I'm sorry. Dr. Scanlan is on vacation. Perhaps you can try her at home."

Vacation?

He heard voices conferring on the other end of the line. Then someone else got on. "Mr. Scanlan?" A hesitation. "Are you okay? We heard you went missing. In Taiwan?"

"Thailand. What?" It sank in that he'd been off the grid for more than a week. "I'm fine, fine. Need to get in touch with Monica and Theresa. Please, if you know anything... Did Monica go to London?" Maybe Winston Moon had done his job and all was well.

More conferring on the other end. "Where can you be reached, Mr. Scanlan?" The voice had gone stiffer, colder. "If Monica calls, we'll tell her to get in touch."

Or maybe disaster had struck. Maybe the authorities in London had notified her that—

"Sweet Jesus, is Monica's regular assistant there? Emily? She knows my voice. I'm not some kind of weirdo."

"I'm sorry, sir. All we can do is pass along your information."

Jack gave her Savani's number. Then he dialed Monica's apartment. Nothing. He hung up and slumped back.

They all stared at each other in silence. An impasse.

Finally, Jack stood and unlatched a set of window shutters. A breeze rushed in and the sky was pearly with first light. In the distance, he heard engines, like trucks, coming closer. Then he saw the billows of dust coming up from the road below the house.

He turned and saw Savani's ears were pricked. When he looked back, four modified pickup trucks were pulling into the driveway. Lights were flashing on the cabs. Suits and uniforms jumped out and headed for the front door.

"I'll get it," Jack said.

As he opened the door, all weapons were drawn. One of the uniforms caught Jack by surprise and pushed him against the wall while another one frisked him and took away the pocket pistol and the .45.

As they marched into the office, Savani broke into a big smile.

The suit who seemed to be the leader also smiled. "How's my old friend, *Khun* Tony?"

Delia wasn't sure what to do with the rifle she had trained on Tony, but one of the policemen resolved the dilemma as he yanked it from her hands.

Tony stood. "My friends, I'd like you to meet Sam Boorisuni, chief of the Chiang Mai provincial police. And a dear friend of mine."

Khun Sam pulled some papers from his breast pocket and consulted them. "Is there a Mr. Martin Elizondo Moon present?"

Martin stepped from behind the desk. "That's me."

"Please put your hands on top of your head."

"Well, you can see, they're broken. I can't do much—"

A policeman jabbed him in the ribs. Martin responded quickly and was frisked.

"Mr. Moon." Sam read from his papers. "I have a warrant here for your arrest as an illegal alien. Your visa is invalid as there is an outstanding order of deportation against you. The Royal Police will be taking you now to Bangkok for further proceedings."

Martin sagged, wordless, and was escorted to the entrance hallway. Tony smirked.

"Now." Sam consulted his papers again. "Miss Delia Maria Rivera and Mr. John Francis Scanlan, please step forward."

They complied, but Jack started huffing as if he were going to spout something about being an American citizen.

"Stay cool," Delia hissed at him.

Khun Sam went on, using his crib sheets to get the wording correct. "I must inform the two of you that you are being charged with aiding and abetting a known fugitive. You are now in police custody."

Jack exploded: "What kind of fucking setup is this? Martin's no criminal, but you better look into your pal Savani here—"

The butt of a rifle was slammed into Jack's stomach and, as he doubled over, the cop shoved him back against the wall.

"I must remind you, Mr. Scanlan, this is not America. Resisting arrest is an admission of guilt and reason to shoot you."

"*Khun* Sam," Delia spoke up, doing her best to look demure and vulnerable. "If you're taking us away now, may we please bring our things along?

There are clothes and other belongings in my room—and my passport. And in Mr. Scanlan's room, his luggage and rucksack. And over there in the corner, my carrybasket."

Savani snapped to attention. "The basket is not hers, it's mine, for godsake."

"No, it isn't." She let her chest heave as if she were about to break into tears. "I had to look all over for souvenirs that good. I have receipts and everything."

"You little liar," Tony growled.

Sam sent someone for their belongings. After a quick glance at the contents of the basket, Sam handed it to her. He was obviously not a connoisseur of jades and didn't dig deep enough to uncover the video. "We will check it out, *Khun* Tony."

Escorted to the hallway, surrounded by cops, Delia and Jack joined Martin on a bench. Then she saw the scene shift in Savani's office.

The three remaining cops turned their guns at Tony and Sam stiffened his posture. He rustled through his papers, then cleared his throat.

"*Khun* Tony. Mr. Antoine Raoul Savani. This is very difficult for me, but I am obliged to inform you that you are under arrest for the illegal export of ancient Thai Buddha statues."

Tony made a startled laugh. "You're kidding."

"This is very hard. Not a joke. I am only a humble provincial official. This is a warrant issued by national police. Please walk out from behind the desk with your hands on your head."

By the time Tony was searched, he was fuming. "Don't I pay you enough?"

"My hands are tied." Sam consulted his papers again. "I must also inform you that the British government has requested your extradition, let me see, as the owner of New Cathay Galleries, for importation of antiquities without making the correct declarations. But Bangkok has decided they must pursue their own charges first, then reach an agreement with London."

"This is crazy. The Minister of Antiquities knows me—is my friend—he knows what good I do here." Delia began to hear panic in his voice. "And the British—they can't possibly connect me to New Cathay—" With a flash in his eye, he glanced up at Delia. She was tempted to grin, but maintained her poker face.

"Anyway, those are nuisance charges. People don't get extradited for not filling out the right forms. What is this about, Sam?"

"I am only the messenger, dear friend."

"Then you'll let me sit at my desk and contact my lawyers."

Khun Sam acquiesced.

"I need to call my cook to get over here, to get me some food. We haven't eaten in twenty-four hours."

Delia saw that Tony was delaying them, keeping the group on his premises. It made her anxious. She wanted to get away, to get beyond the realm of evil-doing.

Martin was thrilled with the turn of events, relieved that Savani might get his comeuppance. And Martin himself could ride the wave of bureaucratic legalities that faced him, no problem now. Delia was here. Her energy would buoy him up through any rough seas. But he was uneasy too. There was still no word about Theresa. And as his adrenaline ebbed, the full force of his aches and pains rolled back in.

Outside, a truck door slammed and a minute later the front door opened. He couldn't believe his eyes.

It was Edwin Jones-White.

He and Delia jumped up to hug him.

"Edwin!"

Once the flurry of hugs and exclamations died down, Jones-White sat with them on the foyer bench—one eye on the proceedings in Savani's office—and told his story.

"When I got your call, Martin, what ten days ago now, I knew this was big trouble. I was on my way to raise a ruckus at the Thai Embassy in Paris when Delia's fax came through."

Martin turned to her. "You faxed Edwin? When?"

"Before I left for the hills with Tony. I thought you needed help." She shrugged. "Silly me."

"I got the U.S. Consulate in Chiang Mai to ask the local constabulary to help, but you were gone," Edwin continued. "And no sign of you in Chiang Mai hospitals or clinics. I couldn't budge them to do more. Interpol was dithering about getting involved, so I went straight from the Thai embassy to Orly and hopped a plane headed in this direction. Figured I'd better see this one through myself. Too many people in this country are on Savani's payroll. Missing foreigners might embarrass the Thai government PR-wise, but on the other hand, the Royal Police don't want to start rousting hill tribe villages, much less heroin supply chains, not on my say-so—very complicated politics here, as you know."

"You're amazing. Thank you so much, Edwin," Martin said.

"Well, I spent the week doing a sort of shuttle diplomacy among all the parties. The other day I came this way to negotiate a private search party with the provincial police. I was lodging nearby when they got word the lights had gone on here. They kindly invited me to join them."

"So what now?" Martin asked.

"Bangkok. We'll get your status straightened out in no time. And the charges against Delia and Jack will be dismissed. It was a mechanism to extract them from whatever sticky situation we might find them in. Savani will go to court—with an army of lawyers no doubt. He is indeed well-connected, but the King is apoplectic that Savani has desecrated an historical site and exported sacred Buddhist statuary. Meanwhile, the American DEA chaps and Interpol are furiously working on putting evidence together about the heroin connection—of much greater interest to them than Buddhas—but I seriously doubt it'll amount to much. I wager that his papers are shredded to dust and that his computers are only empty boxes linked up by passwords to computers in parts unknown."

"You don't know the half of it yet..." Delia said.

"Excuse me, sir." Jack interrupted and leaned over to address Edwin. "From your story, it sounds like you didn't pass through London."

"Haven't been home in weeks," Edwin said with a sigh. "Giancarlo's been handling our other cases. Barely had time to leave messages for my wife this week."

Jack stared at the carpet. "Mr. Jones-White, do you know where my daughter is?"

As Martin feared, Edwin looked confused. "Daughter? I, uh, don't believe I know what you're referring to."

Martin jumped in. "You didn't get a call from my father, about Theresa Scanlan? Savani sent someone to kidnap her in London. We wanted to make sure she was taken somewhere safe. That's what this whole week-long fiasco has been about." He felt himself growing weary, sagging with despair. "When we called this morning... her friend said..." He let his voice trail off. Edwin was shaking his head no.

Jack covered his eyes. "Oh my God," he whispered over and over. "Oh my God."

Jack was helpless against the nightmare unfolding in his imagination. Where would they find her? How would he endure? How would he break the news to Monica? Did she already know? Is that why she wasn't in her office? Why the staff there were all hushed and uncommunicative? How would he ever claw his way free from this bizarre foreign world? How would he ever face a classroom of sixth-graders again? *Where are you, my baby girl?*

The movie of Theresa's life started unreeling in his mind—her baby jumps and squeals of delight, transforming week by week into long-limbed grace. He could hear her voice...*Oh, Daddy!*

He could hear her voice.

"Daddeeeeeeeeeeee!"

He could hear her voice. Shouting. "Where's my father? Where is he? Daddeeeeeee!"

The voice was real. Everyone was reacting, jumping up. Jack got on his feet.

When one of the guards opened the front door, a young woman was racing up the steps.

"Daddeeeee!"

Theresa leaped into his arms, throwing her legs around his waist, nearly knocking him over. "You're alive. Oh, Daddy, I was afraid they killed you!"

As he held onto her, he took measure of her condition. She was clean. She was wearing cotton trousers and a t-shirt he had bought for her back in Rochester. She smelled of nothing but sweet childhood.

Right behind her was Monica, a stout old man in a gray suit, and a Chinese youth.

"Dad?" Martin blinked his eyes at the sight of Winston Moon stepping over the high threshold in the company of Arthur Li.

The old man's intense blue eyes met his. "Good God, Marty, you look like something the cat dragged in." Then they were in each other's arms, hugging, and Martin began to cry.

When he got a grip on himself, he spoke: "Dad, tell me what—"

"Hell, I couldn't get hold of your Jones-White fellow. But I got hold of Monica, who got hold of Theresa. Monica had a big surgery scheduled, so I told her I'd go get Tess to a safe place and she could follow. I found my passport and hailed a cab to JFK." He was grinning over his man-of-action moment.

One of the guards dragged in chairs for the four newcomers then stepped outside with his comrades.

"Tess was on break so I got her to a quiet hotel and Monica joined us the next day. But then you guys were nowhere to be found. I finally got hold of young Arthur here and he said the truck he lent you was found crashed and burned in the hills. You, Jack, Delia, all vanished into thin air. Well, sorry, that's when I called the State Department and booked a flight. The memory of what happened to you last time here—I'll be damned if I let that happen again. Monica insisted on coming with me to find Jack and Tess wouldn't hear of being left behind."

Arthur piped in. "They've been camping out at our place the last couple nights. I knew I'd like your pops, Martin."

"I wouldn't call it *camping*," Monica interjected. "More like *keeping vigil*. There were terrible rumors coming this way through the Li family network in the hills and no one with any authority seemed able to lift a finger."

Her somber words made Martin take note of how exhausted everyone looked behind their smiles and tales of derring-do. His gaze moved to Savani seated behind his desk, staring at the new arrivals, his face the mask of evil. They needed to get out of here.

Martin stood up. He would ask the police chief to let them leave for Bangkok while his men waited for Savani to line up his squadron of lawyers.

Tony stood up too.

Tony Savani was annoyed by all the commotion occurring in his very private home. Who was the old Brit hugging Delia? And where was that damn cook? His staff were never this slow to show up after one of his trips to the hills. And what a nuisance this police business was. Thai officialdom did not mess with the Savani family.

His phone rang. It was his principal business attorney in Bangkok finally getting back to him. "You kicked the wrong cat this time, Tony. The King himself is in an uproar. Takes his Buddhas very seriously. You can expect visitations shortly from the Antiquities Ministry at your Chiang Mai estate. The government has impounded all your Thai Handicraft containers at the port and notified port authorities around the world to inspect all the containers that they can intercept. And you know what they'll find in addition to national treasures."

"How fast can you make it all go away?" Tony asked.

"You're looking at an ordeal. The *Bangkok Post* already has a reporter on the story. And the phones at your Foundation office have been ringing off the hook with calls from archaeology groups, including HAWC-I. The Royal Police will be bringing you to Bangkok, Tony. No way around it."

Tony's face burned as he slammed the phone down. What was wrong with everybody? Why had they all turned against him, conspiring to expose and humiliate him after all his generosity, after all his support of Thai culture? He would not be made a mockery of in court.

He would need to execute his back-up plan. He had people in place who could quickly move him north through Laos into China, then to his secret haven in the Philippines. One phone call away. Then a trapdoor in the bathroom only ten feet from his desk. A tunnel. A friendly face at the other end. Gone forever to his own private paradise.

More commotion outside—another truck, shouting. He looked out. The girl! With Arthur? What fresh outrage was this? Tony sat alone and stony behind his desk as he watched the delirious reunions in the other room.

The girl. He had been eager to receive Arnie Dugan's tape of her "awakening." How did Dugan screw up? The scene unfolding before his eyes was unbearable—a slap in the face, an affront to his power. He might disappear to his tropical haven but it pained him to know that these grinning fools would simply close ranks behind him… that Antoine Raoul Savani would be quickly forgotten. No, he could not escape before someone paid a price.

How much mayhem could he cause and still be allowed to visit his bathroom before they carted him away? The police guards had relaxed. They weren't interested in all the *farangs* hugging and kissing. They stood out on the steps smoking. *Khun* Sam had also left his chair and strolled out to see what was going on. Now he too was outdoors lighting up with his men.

Tony reached under his chair, into a customized pocket that hid a loaded 9-mm.

Martin stared at Tony, then was stunned by the sight of a gun in Tony's hand. Where were the police? He could feel the hairs on his arms and neck prickling.

He took a step away from the group—from his father, from his lover, from his dear friends. They had traveled so far from home, full of love, full of courage. Back in Rochester, he had been content to live the life of an isolated, sorrowful soul, wrapped in legal paperwork. But Jack had befriended him. And Delia sought him out and demanded his engagement. His father had dropped everything. Jones-White had dropped everything. For him.

And what had he given them in return? Delia had done the heavy lifting—exposed the secrets, secured the evidence, and twice saved his life. Martin only wound up bruised and broken. His only achievement was to keep one foot ahead of the other, treading the long road.

Now, one more step.

Savani began striding toward the group, his eyes crazed, both hands on the pistol. Raising his arms.

Martin bolted toward him, lunging, throwing himself at Savani and the weapon, yelling, "Noooooooooo."

The gun fired. Heat blasted through Martin's middle as they fell together.

"No more," Martin cried and rammed his cast against Savani's throat.

He heard a scream. Two screams. Then, the world stopped turning, the sun switched off, and all was cold. Martin took note of the sudden silence.

TEN

BANGKOK, THAILAND

The police car parked in the lot at the Interpol office. Delia and Edwin got out. The two Royal Thai police, who had met the medevac plane and who had been at her side ever since, held umbrellas over them and walked them through the glass doorway.

Night had fallen on this endless day. Delia was still clutching the carry-basket of stolen jades, plus the video tape. She was still in the blouse and sarong she'd donned a thousand years ago. Now her clothes were rain-dampened and streaked with Martin's blood.

In a small waiting room, the two were joined by members of the British, U.S., and Chinese embassy staffs, then escorted to a conference room, where a stenographer was setting up her equipment.

Delia was numb. The last time she slept had been in the Akha village. But she was following protocol, protecting her precious cargo's chain of custody, vowing that justice would be done.

When all parties were seated, she told her stories and signed affidavits for hours. She explained how she knew about the Chinese Warring State jades, that she had already recovered them once and returned them to Beijing. She went on to describe the jades stolen from the Burmese national collection, as well as other antiquities she had seen on Savani's Chiang Mai premises.

After the Chinese representatives left, she described the video tape *Lana at Paddington* and specified the location of others like it in the Akha village.

She followed with sworn statements about Savani's confession of his involvement in her own assault in London, about his conspiring with a London predator named Dugan, and about his murderous pistol assault yesterday in Chiang Mai. Edwin gave his own statement of yesterday's assault.

Tony Savani was alive, with a fractured larynx, in a heavily guarded hospital room in Chiang Mai. She needed to make sure he never saw another day of freedom in his miserable life.

It was the pandemonium that brought Martin around—a din of gunshots and screams with a disturbing undertone of sighs and slurping. He had to get away. They were hurting him, tugging at him. Something wet struck his cheek.

With a gasp, he awoke. He stared into a set of startled blue eyes. A gnarled hand was dabbing his cheek with a white cloth. Rain pelted the windows and thunder cracked in the distance. The room was lit with a single lamp on the table next to him. He was strapped down and hooked up to myriad tubes and blinking-beeping monitors.

"Okay. Marty. Okay, now, you're okay." Winston Moon set the washcloth on the sidetable. "You were sweating... I thought..." He patted Martin's shoulder and turned back to the items on the table. "Let's see here. Nurse said you'd be thirsty. Are you thirsty?"

Martin's mouth and throat were glue. He managed a grunt and a nod.

"Let's see. I'm supposed to drip a little from this sponge between your lips. And ice chips, we can get some ice chips, too."

Martin lapped it up.

"Now she said you'd be nauseated and that I could ring for something if you couldn't cope."

"Tell me how I am," Martin croaked. He could wiggle his toes, but that seemed to be all he could manage. "How bad?"

Winston sat back, looking a shade more relaxed to hear his son speak. "You're fine. Bullet took out some muscle and nicked the whatchamacallit, the iliac crest on your pelvis. They did some surgery. Put you on IV painkiller. Catheter."

"Where are we?"

"Bangkok. The Chiang Mai medics stopped the bleeding and decided you were stable enough to be medevacked to the international hospital in Bangkok. Young Arthur made everything happen very fast."

Martin closed his eyes. He floated. Whose body was he in? His arms felt like feathers. Had he grown wings? He flew back to his hospital room. "My hands?"

"Once they patched your side, the ortho team came in and reset your metacarpals."

Martin had been sure that his hands had crumbled into leather sacks of bone meal, but Winston reassured him that the clean fractures identified at the clinic in Bangkok were still only that. But the repeated trauma to the casts had knocked the bones out of alignment, caused pressure on the nerves, and broke some blood vessels. The orthopod straightened it all out.

His father unhitched a restraint so that Martin could raise his hands to see. The plaster casts were gone, replaced by lightweight plastic braces that liberated his swollen fingers.

"The braces will give you better mobility, but, they told me to warn you,"—his father's face was serious—"not to use them as weapons."

"Oh. Oh, God. Savani?"

"Fractured his larynx. Still in Chiang Mai, under guard of course."

Martin suffered a momentary pang of disappointment. He wanted Tony to be dead, done with. But the stern gaze of his father's eyes reminded him that fist fights were for boys.

"Anyone else? Hurt?"

Winston laid a hand on Martin's arm. "No. You saw to that." Winston scratched his head. "Apparently you have a talent for this business."

Martin sighed. "I always thought my talents were intellectual—observation, memory, right questions at the right time. On this trip, what got me through was animal cunning—and my fists. Plus a little crazy. Scares me." *Scares me a lot.*

With a slight nod, Winston squeezed his son's arm.

Martin looked around. Private room, door closed. Window draped against the night. He wanted to ask about Delia, but was scared of that too—scared of her being gone.

"Thanks for taking care of Theresa. I never expected you to—"

"To be a man of action?" His eyes sparkled.

"Dad..."

"By the way," Winston said as he reached into his jacket pocket, "Arthur gave me this for you. Said he found it under the front seat of his car. Put it in an amulet case, on a cord, so you won't lose it again."

It was the ancient Egyptian fish amulet that Delia had given him in Rochester. It made him smile.

"Present from Delia."

"A lovely thing it is indeed," Winston said and laid the treasure in Martin's open hand.

Martin coaxed his fingers around it, then glanced toward the door again. "What time is it?"

Winston leaned over to dribble a few drops through Martin's lips. "About 1 a.m. Delia was here till they assured her you would be okay, then she and Edwin went to the Interpol office."

"I've really been no help to her at all. I couldn't keep up. Wound up injured, captive... drunk. You've been right about me all along, Dad. *World's greatest underachiever.*"

"Good gracious, Marty, what on earth are you talking about? You excelled at everything you ever put your mind to!"

Martin couldn't help rolling his eyes and shifting his gaze away from his old man. But Winston laid a hand on his forearm.

"Look at me. You tell me you feel a rift between what you thought were your intellectual gifts and what turned out to be some kind of animal cunning. Your gift has always been your pursuit of beauty and rightness— maybe an inborn love of symmetry, balance. And you pursued them always with such an eyes-open sense of enchantment, following wherever the path led, even when it led through hell. I'm an anxious old professor, Marty, and I can't always turn off my lecturing voice, but your life, Marty, has been such a gift to me."

Martin felt himself floating again, wondering if the intravenous pain-killer was making him hallucinate a version of his father. But, no, this Winston Moon was real and he was squeezing Martin's arm in a hospital bed in Bangkok.

"Marty?"

Martin's eyes fluttered open and refocused. "Where's Delia?"

"She's at Interpol with Edwin. She'll be here in the morning."

"She's amazing," Martin said. "Figured everything out. Didn't need me at all. Could have done this by herself—"

"Nonsense," his father interrupted. "Arthur couldn't stop talking about—and Delia—on our way down here—told me everything. You had to face down your demons to come back to Thailand—you carried on when—"

"I should be there with her, at the Interpol office, filing reports, standing next to her like a true partner."

"Is that what you think partnership is, Marty? I hope it's the morphine talking, letting you droop into self-pity like this. A partner isn't your twin, your doppelgänger. A partner is your foil, the person who goads you into doing your best. Don't you think risking everything to accompany Delia on her quest gave her the energy to see it through? Her wounds, what you worried were her frailties, made *you* step back into the world. Don't you think *your* wounds, *your* flaws, your own vulnerabilities made *her* stronger, made *her* step up to the challenges?"

Martin considered this wisdom. "Maybe."

Winston stood up, took the amulet from Martin's hand, and looped the cord around his neck. Then he leaned over and kissed Martin's forehead.

"You gave Delia her life back."

"M r. Moon is awake," the nurse told Jack. "You can see him now."
Jack roused himself from a doze and followed her to Martin's room. He had spent time with Theresa and Monica, but when they went to bed, he headed back to the hospital.

The minute he saw Martin and Winston, he choked up. "Thank you both for everything," he croaked. "I don't know how I'll ever repay you."

Winston beamed at him. But Martin shook his head. "I should be apologizing to *you* for dragging you through this mess, for exposing you to so much—"

"Of the world and its amazing complexity?"

"And its profound evils."

"But evils that might be beaten back with intelligence and energy."

The thought hung silently among them for a moment, then Jack spoke again.

"Delia got a call through to me a while ago. She just finished at Interpol and was finally at the hotel. She was going to clean up, catch forty winks, then head over here. She gave me news. The Interpol guys got word from London that Arnold Dugan had been picked up at Savani's flat... with a blond teenager." He shook his head, not wishing to remember the state she was found in. "I'm so thankful, Winston, for your help, for saving my family from that ordeal. And to you, Martin, for knowing your father would come through."

Martin sighed. "So much craziness..."

"Anyway, you're looking good, Martin. I hate to admit I'm anxious as hell to get out of Bangkok, but Monica and I are hoping we can get a flight out of here tomorrow, uh, today for the three of us. Back to Manhattan. I thought I'd hang out with them for a while till Theresa's classes start again in London. And till I have to start getting ready for a new batch of sixth-graders in the fall." He chuckled. "My whole perspective on the world has changed, but there I'll be again—*Mr. Scanlan*, in his khakis, his blue oxford-cloth shirt, and his striped tie." He touched his tangled hair. "Haircut in order too."

"Sometime you stop knowing what *normal* means any more," Martin said. "What about you, Dad? Why don't you head back with the Scanlans. It's a terribly long couple of flights. Good if you were traveling with friends."

"I don't want to leave you quite yet, Marty." He reached out to grip Martin's shoulder. "I want to see you up and about first."

"But Delia's here with me. And Mom must be lonely..."

Winston agreed. "Can you include me in your plans, Jack?"

Jack nodded and turned to Martin. "So I'll see you back at the ranch... sometime?"

Martin smiled and made a mock salute with his braced hand. "Till *sometime*."

Shortly after dawn, Delia crept into Martin's hospital room. She was rolling Martin's suitcase, which, along with her own and Jack's, had been retrieved from the storeroom at the Tudor.

Both of them, father and son, slept. Winston, with his head slumped on his chest, a *London Economist* in hand, glasses on his lap. Martin, laid out like a corpse. A prickly sensation swept across her.

She walked around to the back of Winston's chair and put her hands on his shoulders. He started.

"Kat dear?"

"Me, Delia," she whispered. "Why don't you lie down in the lounge? I'll sit with him."

"Oh." He rubbed his eyes, checked his watch, and gathered himself to his feet. "He woke up about one. We talked and Jack came in. Woke again around three and around five. He was asking about you."

"You'll get some rest now?"

"If you're okay, dear, I think I'll taxi over to the hotel and wash up. Jack got me a noon flight with his family back to New York. Marty was adamant he'd be okay without me."

"That's good, yes. I'm fine, a little groggy is all."

They hugged their goodbyes. Winston planted another kiss on his son's forehead, but it didn't wake him.

When she was alone with Martin, she spent a long time standing at the bedside, staring at him. He looked spooky: gaunt, with a week's silver beard on his bloodless skin.

She had done that to him.

When she found him he had been so robust, so contented. She'd faulted him for that, goaded him into sharing the hunt for her assailants, while all along she nursed an infatuation with Tony, his collections, his connections, and then his glorious phantom museum. What a dope.

Jack and Martin had saved her. They'd rescued her from Savani's temptations and restored her health. But at a cost. Jack took his first emotional risks in years and wound up seeing Ingrid butchered and Lucky tortured and Sayat killed and his daughter nearly lost. And here Martin lay, his body and his tranquility broken.

His eyes fluttered open and caught hers. A big sleepy grin warmed his features.

"I was afraid you'd be gone," he whispered.

"I'm so sorry."

"For what?"

She glanced at his midsection and hands. "For all this."

"Come closer."

She pulled the chair as close as possible and sat.

"All I lost was some weight, some blood, and some illusions about how contented I thought I was. And I found you again."

He reached out and with his index finger touched her cheek, the bridge of her nose, and her lip. She stroked the hair on his chest and was about to lean over to kiss him when a nurse walked in.

"Pardon me, Madame."

Reluctantly, Delia pulled away.

"I will be disconnecting Mr. Moon from all these devices. Then I will get him up on his feet. Please excuse?"

"Up?" Delia asked stupidly.

"Mr. Moon doing fine. He can probably go to a hotel this evening."

The news brought smiles to both their faces.

"Delia, I've been hearing rain outside..."

"Yes, heavy monsoon. They say it'll last the week."

"How soon can we get out of Thailand? How soon can we go home?"

Outside Martin's room, Delia became aware of an anxious heartbeat. *Home.* It sounded like an ending and she wanted a beginning. Through the turmoil of the past forty, fifty, sixty hours, she'd kept having visions of adventures to come. The two of them together, tracing the China-to-Thailand smuggling routes, plugging in the Burma connection. Together, helping the authorities sort through Savani's possessions to repatriate his illicit antiquities. Together, exposing the violent radicals who threatened to ruin the laudable goals of HAWC-I.

She felt a new energy building inside her that would make a suburban townhouse on the northern edge of New York State only a temporary stopover on her way to the next assignment. But she refused to lose Martin again.

What was she going to do? What were they going to do?

Shortly after Delia left to find them some accommodations, Edwin Jones-White popped in. After Martin gave him a quick account of his medical condition, Edwin reported.

"As you know, Delia and I spent into the wee hours of the morning at Interpol, giving our statements, transferring the jades to the Chinese consulate, and setting the stage for Antoine Savani's prosecution. Staff from the Antiquities Ministry here have officially impounded the contents of his Chiang Mai home and sent a team of experts to assess the archaeological ruins on his property. And I just got word that New Cathay Galleries has already been raided."

"But what about murder?" Martin asked. "He confessed to me, I swear it, that he ordered the hawkeyes to kill Lana. And Delia's assault—"

Edwin held up his hand. "After Delia left, I stayed at Interpol. The chief prosecutor, members of the British embassy staff, and I watched the tape that Delia took from Savani, the tape of Lana's murder. It's been passed along to experts now to make sure it isn't some sort of pastiche, that it will stand up in court. But if I were Antoine Savani, I'd get a good lawyer and plea bargain like hell."

"It implicates him?"

"Clearly. I won't say any more than that."

Martin closed his eyes. "So it's really over then."

Edwin sighed. "His days of peaceful wealth and power among the elites of London and Bangkok—those days are over for sure. But the man has vast resources and deep connections. I wouldn't be at all surprised if he disappears."

Edwin shifted in his chair to reach the handkerchief in his pocket and blew his nose. "You'll also be interested to know that, at Interpol's insistence, the Mexican authorities have begun an investigation at HAWC-I headquarters."

"It's about time."

The two men sat quietly, making a study of the sound of Bangkok rain.

"So what's next for Martin Moon?" Edwin asked. "A return to the Rochester legal battlefield?"

"Oh my God, no." He said this without thinking and, in fact, couldn't remember the last time Emmaline Tuthill crossed his mind. "It's gone, Edwin. I don't give a rat's ass about any of it anymore. All I want is Delia, to start over again with her." But a wave of panic struck him. "Edwin, I don't know what the hell I'm doing. I'm crazy in love with Delia, like it was in our twenties. But Rochester would be a painful exile for her. I don't know what to do."

"Do you want to be a London art dealer again? Private showroom? Elite clientele?"

Martin thought for a moment. "No. I let that go too. I think I let it go before Lana died, but couldn't find a way out."

Edwin nodded. "Sometimes love is not enough."

Martin felt the kick of his pulse again. "What are you saying?"

"You and Delia loved each other when you were pups. But you wanted different things. And you were each bull-headed about pursuing your own path."

"So you're telling me it can't work?"

"Is that what I'm saying? Is that what you think?"

"You're saying that I can't be bull-headed. That Delia has made more… invigorating choices. That I should give up everything and follow Delia. Isn't that what I've done?" Martin held up his braced hands with a wry smile. "I surrender. All that remains is—"

"Your gifts."

"What?"

"You completed your dark journey of the soul. You survived, with a few scars. 'Happily ever after' is not in your cards. Your decisions with Delia will not revolve around which townhouse to rent or which color to paint the picket fence. Whatever degree of wisdom or enlightenment you've achieved, now you must return to the world and share it."

Martin ran his fingers through his hair as he thought. He'd been thinking of his recent life as a string of failures: being a drunk, letting himself get stabbed in Mae Sot, letting Lana die, letting himself be assaulted again—and again—by the hawkeyes, dragging Jack through the mess, jeopardizing Jack's daughter, getting captured in the hills… one disaster after another.

"Do you see my point?" Edwin asked.

Where would Martin be without all the people who rescued him along the way? From Lana in Mae Sot to the Li family in Bangkok. And Delia, who not only pulled him out of his funk, but saved him from the predations of Cal and Bruno, and then from the vicious Shan officer in the hills. And Jack—how would he ever repay Jack? Then his father. And Edwin.

And how many strangers had pointed the way to safety?

Martin shook his head. "All I can say is that a lot of people put themselves out for me. I'd be dead three times over, if not in body then in spirit, without their hands outstretched to me." He paused. "Those are my gifts."

Edwin smiled.

Delia suddenly appeared at the door, beaming. "I made some plans! Your friend Arthur Li is giving us the use of their family beach house down south in Krabi, as soon as you can travel."

Oh, yes! But his elation vanished as quickly as it came. "Aren't they going to boot me out of the country?"

Edwin spoke. "I have an appointment tomorrow morning with someone who owes me one. This time, I'll personally see to it that the old deportation order is expunged and the smuggling charges dropped. And I'll make sure you have official documents to that effect."

"And I hope you don't mind," Delia continued, "but when we've had enough of a beach hideaway in monsoon season, I'd like to go to Singapore. Since we're in the neighborhood, so to speak, one of my traders there has been after me for months to check out the merch he's collecting from Indonesia. He thinks it's perfect for the European market. Then, Sydney, okay? There's a small museum I was buying for and I really need to reconnect with the director."

Her eyes were on fire with a crazy mixture of determination and anxious hope. Martin knew what she was thinking. Would he douse her enthusiasm by insisting on a return to the white-sock coziness of Rochester? Or would he join her expedition, explore the eternal trade routes once again, and reconnect with the world?

He nodded his head. "You take the lead, babe. I'm ready for anything."

Delia knelt next to his chair and threw her arms around him.

THE END

If you enjoyed this book, please share it with a friend and consider writing a review for your favorite book-lovers website.

About the Author

Susan Barrett Price is author of the thriller *Passion and Peril on the Silk Road* and the illustrated novella *Tribe of the Breakaway Beads*. She works from her studio in upstate New York.

Learn more at *www.MadInPursuit.com*

Made in the USA
Middletown, DE
21 October 2015